To Vicky

Table of Contents

About the Book

Barefoot on a Frosty Morn is a literary and genealogical tapestry of several families over three centuries. The genealogical threads stretch back to England and France and unfold in step with America's continental expansion. The families crisscross north, south, and west as the tapestry grows in richness and complexity. A final episode sheds light on the earliest roots of the story. The reader has a perspective only partially available to the personalities immersed in the stories. Episodes are woven around some American milestones: the Revolution, the Civil War and WWII. These resonate and enrich but do not hinder the genealogical flow of the novel. In its conception and execution *Barefoot on a Frosty Morn* is unlike any writing before it. It surpasses the limits of history and narrates the essence of the American vision of life.

BAREFOOT
ON A
FROSTY MORN

An American Genealogical Novel

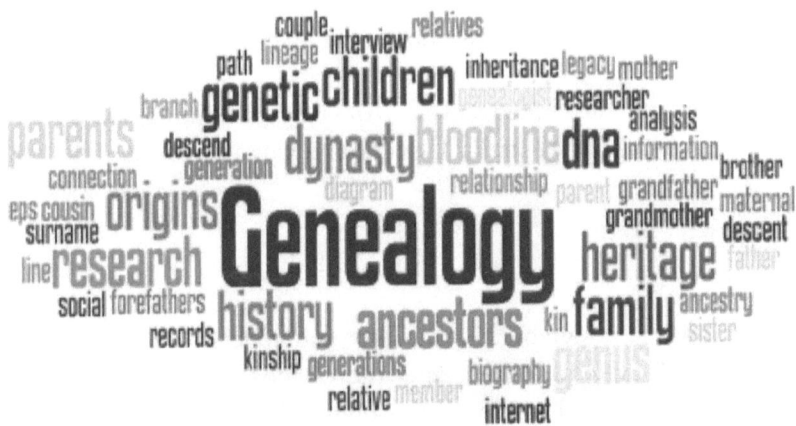

HAROLD RALEY

TotalRecall Publications, Inc.
1103 Middlecreek
Friendswood, TX 77546
281-992-3131 TEL
www.totalrecallpress.com

Copyright © 2017 by: Harold Raley

ISBN: 978-1-59095-342-6
UPC: 6-43977-43428-9

Library of Congress Control Number: 2016956843

Printed in the United States of America with simultaneous printings in Australia, Canada, and United Kingdom.

FIRST EDITION
1 2 3 4 5 6 7 8 9 10

Chapter 1:
Milady's Trunk

Forefathers.com
[*Early Virginians*, Vol I, Entry 67, pp. 68-69: Sir Henry Beaufort-DuCordier, 1599-1673, was born on the Beaufort-Pickford Manor in Yorkshire, England of a distinguished Anglo-Norman family traceable to Count Guilbert de Beaufort, 1040-1089, confidant of William the Conqueror. The son of Sir Thomas Beaufort-Montague and his second wife Lady Thérèse DuCordier, he and his sons John and Pickford fought against the Cromwell insurgents in the English Civil War. The Beaufort sons perished and Sir Henry was gravely wounded in the final Royalist defeat. During two years of imprisonment and convalescence in the Tower of London he may have been attracted for a time to the pacifist theology of George Fox. This alleged dalliance with Quaker theology scandalized royalists, including his half-brother Sir William Beaufort-Essex, whose machinations after the Stuart Restoration led to a royal assize against Sir Henry in 1663. The Crown expropriated his estates and gave him a choice of execution or exile. With his wife and daughters Madelaine-Marie and Katherine Elizabeth, he survived on the meager charity of his DuCordier relatives in Rouen, France until 1670 when Lady Mary died. Sir Henry then received royal permission to resettle in Hampton in the Virginia Colony, where he died in 1673. Sir Henry and Baron DuCordier, distant cousin and husband to Madelaine-Marie, had many disagreements which soured the family relationships. Katherine wrote several times to sister Madelaine, but her letters went unanswered. There is, however considerable documentation of Katherine and her descendants in America.]

In its usual careless way, fate decreed that in May of 1671 Sir Henry Beaufort-DuCordier, 72, should arrive widowed, exhausted, and all but penniless in Hampton of the Virginia Colony with blonde, beautiful daughter Katherine Elizabeth, 18, and his only remaining servant Matthew Stokesbury, 23, as Richard Blackwell, 31, was consolidating a fortune from land, lumber, cattle, and shipping enterprises.

With a purse much weightier than his pedigree, Blackwell dismissed Old World class differences with New World brashness, and with his characteristic boldness wasted no time in asking Sir Henry for Katherine's hand in marriage.

The prospect of his daughter marrying below her class duly troubled Sir Henry, but aware of his approaching mortality he desired above all else to leave Katherine materially well situated. The possibilities of doing so were few. An old Yorkshire friend and comrade in arms, himself newly established in Hampton, had promised Sir Henry help but died shortly before his arrival. The man's family, fearful of offending the colonial authorities and dreading unwelcome requests for aid from the impoverished old aristocrat, shunned him as though he were a biblical leper. In these straitened circumstances Sir Henry reasoned that a union with commoner Blackwell not only would assure Katherine's future but also might restore in his last days some of the comforts the family enjoyed before the Cromwell debacle. He had entertained similar hopes when his older daughter Madelaine-Marie married her distant cousin Baron Roger-Antoine DuCordier. But this hope was quickly dashed. The Baron was extraordinarily fractious in his emotions and pathologically miserly with his purse. Sir Henry grieved over the fate of Madelaine-Marie but was powerless to remedy the state into which she was now sunk. Thus beset with misgivings and praying that circumstances would not repeat themselves in the case of his younger daughter, he gave his consent and ordered Katherine to prepare herself to become Richard's bride.

But unbeknownst to Sir Henry, Katherine had other hopes. With even more swiftness than Blackwell, Phillip Sterling, 25, adventurer, soldier, singer, and favorite with the plantation gentry, had won her heart with his seductive songs, erotic good looks, and eloquent pleas of true and eternal love. Possessing nothing, he was free to promise her everything.

A war of wills commenced between father and daughter and battle lines were drawn. Sir Henry claimed the traditional paternal right to marry his daughter to a man of his choosing, even to a commoner. Katherine protested that she loved another—Phillip, if he had to know, yes, Phillip Sterling—and that no father in these modern times had the right to overrule a woman's heart with antiquated Old World customs.

"Heart! Heart! 'Od's blood! What hath heart to do with the matter at hand?" Sir Henry thundered in his antique speech. "Will thy strutting jack-a-dandy provide thee roof and warmth with his magical song and verse? Will his poetical fauncies and capering daunces feed thee when thou hungerest? Or clothe thee decently according to thy estate? Tis commonly bandied in this towne that Sterling is an idle runabout who giveth no thought to the morrow and maketh no provision for leaner days. Sweet Katherine, well do I know his kind; heedless of life's common demaunds, in a trice would hee traipse away to new adventures, leaving thee shivering barefoot on a frosty morn. No, I say, by the Saviour's Blood, no! Darling Katherine, thou canst take to husband no such man! Thou, the apple of mine eye, the light of my old age, by God's grace must have a better provision. My days of mortal life are but in few numbered and it were a double wound of death to pass from this life without leaving thee conveniently wedded to a provident husband. Though thou mayest forget all else I tell thee, sweet Katherine, remember well these words: long after the springtime of young love hath passed and the poetry and song are but fading echoes, the harsh demaunds of this cruel world will abide to trample underfoot the rootless fauncies that beguile thy reason. No, No, dear Katherine, I say a thousand times no, I cannot give thee in marriage to a man who lacketh the manly will and material wherewithal to provide thee a pleasant living. Think with thy head, sweet Katherine, rein in thy riotous heart, and thou wilt see the wisdom and fatherly affection that govern my intentions for thee."

Eventually, after many tears and screams of protest Katherine grudgingly realized that her aged father was right. The ruination of her family in the Royalist cause and their privations amongst miserly relatives in France and indifferent acquaintances in the Virginia Colony were painful lessons she had not forgotten. And despite her feigned aristocratic aloofness in material matters, she had inherited determination and foresight, ancestral traits that in earlier ages had won the Beauforts, DuCordiers, Montagues, and Montgomerys lands and noble titles in England, France, and Wales. Thus, despite her strong-willed character, in the end Katherine could not bring herself to trample her father's will. She loved Sir Henry dearly and her respect for him had grown all the greater as she watched him stand unbowed as his fortunes crumbled, his wife and sons died, and feckless friends turned their back on him. He lived by the chivalric code of olden times, a man whose word was sacred and dishonor worse than death. Sir Henry was magnanimous in victory and undaunted in defeat. When all was said and done Katherine could not bring herself to add further burdens to Sir Henry's misfortunes. She made her decision: her heart ached for Phillip but her head ruled otherwise. She would marry Richard but only under two conditions: first, that he provide Sir Henry a decent residence and, second, that although she would live under his roof, until she might decide otherwise, their union was to be a formal bond without physical consummation. Richard generously complied with the first but objected energetically to the second.

"It shall be as I have said, or it shall not be at all," she stated in an unmistakable tone of finality. "I remind you, sir, that it is you, not I, who seek this marriage."

"Very well, Miss Beaufort, but I shall nourish the hope that in time our marriage will grow into a deeper union."

"I promise nothing, sir, beyond what I have said."

She kept her word and married Blackwell in January of 1672, sending most of her remaining possessions to his mansion in a great trunk inherited from her French *grand-mère*, Marie-Angélique DuCordier, and to which she alone had a key.

Looking to provide for his faithful servant Matthew Stokesbury, Sir Henry requested, and Richard granted, that upon the old aristocrat's decease the Welshman would serve in their household, even though Katherine had never really warmed to Stokesbury, who, she feared, knew too many of her secrets to be trusted.

But just as Sir Henry invoked Old World paternal authority

to marry her to Richard, so Katherine, reflecting formative years spent among her DuCordier relatives in France, privately claimed the unwritten French right of a woman in a loveless *mariage de convenance* to compensatory liberties, including, should she so choose, an occasional discreet indiscretion. Her loyalty to Sir Henry was unbreakable, but her fidelity to Richard, beyond her stated conditions, was unsworn and untested. Her head would rule and she would wed Blackwell, but her unbridled heart would reserve its right to private subversions.

If Katherine was secretive in her movements and sentiments, Richard was perceptive in his. He had not become one of the richest and most powerful men in the Virginia Colony by allowing others—men and women—to outwit him. He trusted no man fully and women not at all, for he proclaimed as an unarguable fact that by nature the fair sex was susceptible to beguilement and seduction.

Thus began a cat and mouse game between them. Richard was angrily aware that his young bride did not love him and for that reason was all the more determined that at least she would not dupe him. For her part, Katherine was equally committed to guarding her womanly prerogatives and keeping at arm's length a man who to her was more a stranger than a spouse. From the first, mutual distrust and suspicion distanced them and prevented any sort of intimacy. William removed into the east wing of his mansion from which he ran his enterprises and orchestrated espionage of his wife, leaving the more finely appointed west wing to Katherine, her maids, and her intrigues.

Soon after their wedding and almost coincident with Sir Henry's demise, rumors began reaching Richard's ears that servants had seen Phillip Sterling prowling about the estate.

Alarmed and angry, Richard ordered increased vigil over the grounds, but despite these precautions, Matthew Stokesbury, now elevated to majordomo of the household with the passing of Sir Henry, claimed to have seen Sterling, or someone resembling him, running from the west wing of the mansion early on a December morning. Richard readily believed what he quickly suspected and flew into a jealous rage, swearing openly to kill his rival should he discover him trespassing on his property. Weeks passed during which Matthew reported more rumors of Sterling's nocturnal prowling. But try as he might, Richard and his men could discover neither hard proof nor circumstantial evidence of his wife's infidelity. And because he lacked firm evidence, he could make no credible accusation against her. But the less he knew the more he imagined. Their relationship, confined to meals, church, and social events, was tense but formally correct.

One morning Matthew hurried to Master Blackwell with the disturbing news that an hour before daybreak guards had seen a man leap from a window above the rose garden. But before servants could detain him, the intruder disappeared, as best they could tell in the foggy gloom, perhaps into the west wing of the mansion itself. They searched but found nobody.

"You have searched everywhere?" asked the angry Richard.

"Yes, sir, everywhere except . . ." responded Matthew, hanging his head.

"Except where? Regard me, man, when I am speaking to you!"

"Sir, everywhere except Milady's room. Naturally we dared not go into her chamber but summoned her maids instead to enter therein."

"And what did they find?"

"Sir, they reported no trace of an intruder but instead found Milady staring silently at her locked trunk. She was not her usual talkative self, so they said, and responded not a word to their inquiries. They described her as fully dressed for the day but with eyes red from weeping."

Richard muttered an oath under his breath. Then, his mind in turmoil with inflammatory images, he ran to her bedroom, taking only enough time to arm himself with a pistol and saber.

"Madam," he asked as calmly as he could manage, "what is the matter here?"

"Nothing is the matter here, Mr. Blackwell, though from the voices and noise I hear, there appears to be commotion outside. See to it, sir, and leave me in peace. I am not ready to receive anyone."

"Mayhap you have already received a person, Madam," he said, glancing at closets and bed coverings. Seeing nothing untoward, he approached the trunk with drawn pistol and rapped it with the handle.

"Your actions and insinuations belittle you and offend me. Sir, explain yourself."

"I believe it is you, Madam, who owe me an explanation. Tell me, what is in this trunk?"

"What the trunk contains is my affair. But if you must know, as surely you do, it holds my personal belongings."

"Then you will not object to opening it in my presence?"

"Indeed I object, sir, and most strongly, for your words cast doubt on my honesty."

"By opening it and verifying the truth of your words, madam, you could easily allay any doubts I might have."

"Your doubts would be laid to rest only for the moment. Matthew would soon poison your mind anew and manipulate your thoughts and actions with more gossip. Allow me to point out clearly what is at stake here for you, Mr. Blackwell. If I open the trunk and it reveals only my belongings, as I have truthfully declared, then you, sir, will be exposed for the fool you are hard bent on becoming. Regardless of any orders we might give them to keep silent about the matter, servants would gossip, as servants always do, word would spread, and you, sir, would be the laughingstock of Hampton. On the other hand, should you discover, as you seem to suspect, that it conceals a lover, it would prove to the whole world that you are a miserable cuckold, deceived in your own house and under your very nose. Everyone in Hampton would then scorn and mock you. No, Mr. Blackwell, out of respect for you and this household I will not open the trunk. You may open it yourself, if you choose to do so, but be prepared for the belittling consequences of your act. And if you wish to speak to me further of this or any other matter, sir, hereafter I shall be at the residence my father left me."

With that she summoned Rose, her African maid, to pack her personal items in a silk satchel, removed a heavy brass key from an *étui* and tossed it contemptuously on the floor, and, head high and young Rose in matching posture, marched haughtily from the room.

Richard bent to retrieve the heavy key and moved to open the trunk. But then he stopped and thought for several minutes, tapping the key in the palm of his hand. Suddenly he pocketed it and stepped outside the room to call Matthew.

"Yes, sir?"

"Hie you to the dock and fetch Captain Bradford. And tell him to bring four stout men with him."

"Yes, sir, at once."

Captain Bradford appeared within the hour.

"Captain, I know that many matters claim your attention before you sail the *Bristol Maid* for Jamaica tomorrow. But the order I shall give you now stands above all others. Have your sailors rope this trunk tightly and carry it aboard the vessel. On pain of flogging—hear me well—on pain of flogging, if not death itself, for any man who would dare disobey my orders, now become yours, do not open it under any circumstances, regardless of any sounds issuing from it during the transport. Should the sailors query you about the trunk and its contents, tell them only that you act under my direct orders and bid them in the strongest voice to stay a distance from it. Keep it under your personal vigilance until you are well out to sea beyond sight of land. Then order the ship's carpenter to weight it heavily for sinking and heave it overboard. And never speak to me again of this trunk. Is that clearly understood, Captain?"

"Perfectly, sir, it shall be done as you order. But as Captain, may I be privy to its offending contents?"

"The contents are not your concern, Captain, but mine alone. Kindly follow my orders and query me no further."

"Of course, sir, they shall be carried out to the letter."

"Then see to it. That is all. Good day to you, Captain."

Captain Bradford's men staggered under inordinate weight of the trunk. Blackwell made no comment, but inwardly he was convinced that Sterling—a strapping muscular man—must indeed be locked in the trunk. Excellent, excellent, he thought to himself, reasoning that if Sterling drowned in the trunk and the body should by happenstance be discovered, then, if queried, he would say that his wife told him it contained only personal items and that he ordered it to be disposed of at sea consequent to disputes it had occasioned in their marriage. In which case, the guilt would shift to her. And if she should confess that Sterling was indeed sealed inside, then her lie and the fact that only she could unlock the trunk from the outside would both destroy her reputation and absolve Richard of all but the mildest degree of culpability. Such was the jealous ire her behavior had aroused in him.

When Katherine learned from the servants what Richard had done with her trunk and how he had dealt with his dilemma she shook her head and sighed. Tears came to her eyes as she realized fully for the first time the dangerous game she had been playing. "Oh God, why did I let the matter play out to this gruesome end? But there was no other way except to do as Phillip instructed me. To do otherwise would have been to risk having him discovered in my room to the ruination of my reputation and his probable death. Had Richard discovered him, he would have killed him without ado with a pistol ball to the head. There was no other way, no other way," she whispered to herself several times. "Now that my sweet Phillip is gone. Oh, *mon Dieu*, my God, how shall I live without him? How, how, dear God? But I have only myself to blame. I chose my lot and must forever silence the truth of it. Now my life must be with Richard and all other feelings must be set aside. But oh, dear God, to think that I shall never see sweet Phillip again! Never! Never again! But my loveless life must go on, bleak and bitter as it is."

Despite her despondency, she was stunned by the astuteness

with which Richard resolved the seemingly irresolvable dilemma of the trunk, thus placing the onus squarely on her. He is more cunning than I thought, she whispered to herself. I underestimated him. No wonder he has amassed power and fortune. Her grudging admiration of Richard weakened her loathing of him but without replacing it with warmer feelings. Nevertheless, it was a prelude to a rapprochement of sorts, and she admitted to herself that prudence, if not love, must oblige her to suffer the dreaded consummation of their marriage.

Within the week she took the first step toward ending her estrangement by returning to Richard's house. But her return was not peaceful; the first two nights, loud, angry disputes and accusations of the most intimate matters issued from her bedroom to the scandalous entertainment and gossip of the eavesdropping maids. Then, abruptly, on the third eve, the quarrels subsided and the next morning the maids discovered that Master Richard and Lady Katherine had slept in the same bed.

Soon thereafter Richard sternly rebuked Matthew Stokesbury for what he described as the "bootless accusations" that had so agitated Madam Blackwell. Nevertheless, despite increasingly severe tongue lashings he kept Stokesbury in his service and position until 1679, when in a violent rage he ordered him flogged and expelled from his estate.

Thinking the matter of the trunk resolved in this draconian manner, Katherine and Richard did not speak of it again and unable to foresee a better life, reconciled themselves to a marriage rooted more in truce than troth.

But the resolution was soon reopened to questions. Three days after Captain Bradford sailed for Jamaica, a powerful storm, plowing its way up the American coast, battered Hampton, tearing roofs from houses, flooding the lowlands, uprooting trees, and raising Richard's fears that it had swamped the Bristol Maid. Indeed later evidence confirmed that the vessel was lost and likely all aboard perished in the storm. Seamen arriving from Charles Towne[1] some weeks later reported seeing a broken mast, torn sails, cables, spars, casks, and a portion of the Bristol Maid hull washed up on the outer Carolina banks. The remains of two corpses among the wreckage provided gruesome evidence of the disaster when a sailor identified one of the corpses as Captain Bradford.

The loss of the Bristol Maid aroused only abstract feelings of regret in Katherine. She barely knew Captain Bradford and the crewmen, for Richard chose to tell her little about his commercial affairs.

Blackwell soon recouped the loss of his vessel and cargo, but an unidentified assassin murdered him in 1679, leaving Katherine with two infants, Henry, 5, and Mary, 4. She assumed personal supervision of her husband's complicated affairs and with considerable skill and determination kept the enterprises solvent. Other, more personal matters, however, took an unexpected and less fortunate turn, as related in the following accounts.

---

1 Founded in 1670, Charles Towne was named in honor of King Charles II. In 1680 the city was relocated to Oyster Point, its present site. In 1783 at the conclusion of the American Revolution its name was changed to Charleston.

Forefathers.com

Can anyone help me? I'm trying to trace an ancestor on my father's side, a woman named Katherine Beaufort of Hampton, Virginia or Charleston, South Carolina. According to family accounts, she first married a Blackwell and then my xxxx-grandfather Stafford, although some documents list his surname as Sterling, unless Sterling was another husband. My Grandmother always said she was our ancestor and told stories of her struggle to provide for her family after her husband abandoned her. I think she was born in France around 1649 or 1650, and according to my Grandmother she belonged to the nobility. Any help will be appreciated.

--Cindy Stafford Brown, Atlanta, Georgia.

. . .

Cindy, I think the Katherine Beaufort you are talking about was also an ancestor of mine, which must make us cousins of some kind. So hi there, Cuz! But my Grandpa told me that Katherine Beaufort was born in England, not France, and migrated to the Virginia Colony with her father and maybe one or two brothers in the 1670s. She came from a noble family, the daughter of a baron or earl or something like that. She married a Blackwell in Hampton, Virginia and had two children by him, a boy and a girl, before he left her for a West Indies woman. Grandpa spent years researching our family history so I think the information is reliable.

--Beth Hawkins, Des Moines, Iowa.

. . .

With due respect to your Grandfather's research, Beth, I believe the information you gave Cindy is wrong. According to my family genealogy, Katherine Beaufort was born in England of noble lineage. Against her father's wishes she married a commoner named Phillip Blackwell. They migrated to Virginia in the 1670s and she moved on to Charleston, South Carolina a few years later. She had three children by her husband before leaving him for a Jamaican man named Stafford. I lost track of her after that. But she may have moved to Boston or, possibly, returned to England after many years in America. Not sure, but hope this helps clarify the matter.

--Will Blackwell, Indianapolis, Indiana.

...

Chapter 2.
Barefoot on a Frosty Morn

Forefathers.Com

[_Early Carolina Settlers_, Vol. III, p. 42: Phillip Stafford, aka Phillip Sterling, 1646-1710(?), a native of Stafford, England, was one of twin sons born to Daniel Stafford (1618-1670) and Sally Woolsey Stafford (1619-1672), and brother to younger siblings Garth and Martha. A mason by craft, Daniel Stafford probably trained his sons to follow him in his trade. David Woolsey Stafford was a dutiful son who later migrated with Garth and Martha to Boston in the Massachusetts Colony. But the younger twin Phillip, said to have a "devious and insubordinate nature," fled England accused of serial thefts and scandals, several of which rose to the level of punishable offenses against public order. He surfaced in France where he fought in the royal armies of King Louis XIV. French records show he was arrested and sentenced to death for killing a French nobleman. But while awaiting execution, he escaped from prison by an ingenious ruse and later boasted that no prison could hold him and no lock deter him. He may have returned clandestinely to England, but there is no verification of it. A 1670 passenger list names a "Phillip Sterling" who disembarked in Hampton in May of that year. Supposedly, Stafford perished under strange circumstances around 1672, but apparently he survived for many more years. After a brief stay in Charles Towne of the Carolina Colony, he apparently settled in Barbados and later in Martinique. His son Daniel Stafford states that his father, now a slaver, sailed for the slave coast of Africa in 1710 and was heard from no more.]

...

With the benevolent wisdom that Providence often grants loving parents, Sir Henry Beaufort had warned his daughter Katherine about Phillip Sterling. Her father's unflattering portrait failed to persuade her, yet moved by powerful filial affection, Katherine overruled her passion for Phillip and forced herself to wed Richard Blackwell instead. But she could not deny herself love a second time after Richard was murdered in 1679, a crime that remained unsolved in the colonial archives, and Phillip, believed dead, reappeared months later in a manner soon to be told. At first Katherine had the troubling thought that Phillip had to do with Richard's murder, but when she asked him about it, he responded that even if he had decided to kill his rival he would have been within his rights.

"Was it not Blackwell's wish, indeed his intention, to take my life? Would I, then, have no right to defend myself against him?" he asked rhetorically and with a wave of his hand dismissed other questions.

Katherine convinced herself that even if his moral reasoning was flawed, Phillip could not be an accomplice to murder, much less guilty of it himself. With self-serving logic she concluded that her feelings alone exonerated him of wrongdoing. Her heart would not mislead her into loving an assassin and thus no further proof of his innocence was needed.

If in practical matters Katherine was resourceful and levelheaded, in sentiment she inclined, as did her mother, to dreaminess, a consequence, according to Sir Henry, of shunning devotional books and reading instead frivolous stories of chivalric romance and other unedifying tales. Since girlhood she had been enchanted by the idealistic philosophy of French thinker Blaise Pascal and embraced wholeheartedly his premise that the heart has its reasons the head cannot understand. Had she not experienced the conflict in her own case in deciding whom to wed? In any case, she reasoned, when played out to its last consequences, love conquers all, and with equally invincible benevolence, forgives all. As it was told in her favorite stories, so it must needs happen in life.

The practical, stolid Hampton townspeople were a world removed from her overblown philosophic idealism and fanciful daydreams of idylls and chivalric romances. They still had misgivings about Sir Henry and his daughter, but these were mild compared to the gossip that swirled through Hampton when instead of withdrawing into genteel retirement, as widowhood and custom dictated and the townspeople expected, Katherine took personal control of Richard's enterprises. Thus it was an annoyance though no surprise to her that several vestrymen from St. John Parish and prominent townsmen should pay her a visit. After polite and practiced expressions of sympathy for the family tragedy, they reached the point of their visit.

"Madam," said Church Senior Warden William Glover, "if, at the behest of these gentlemen, I may speak to you in terms as respectful in intention as they are forthright in meaning, it does not seem meet to church and town folk of Hampton, in whose representation we come, that as a highborn lady you should engage yourself in ordinary commerce. Our chief concern, madam, touches on the questionable moral integrity of the commercial community and the proper decorum regarding your ladyship. We fear both may be offended if you, a Christian of the nobility, should be exposed to the uncouth language and tawdry sentiments that commonly attend the worldly commerce of the ruder sort of men."

"I thank you for your concern, Warden Glover, gentlemen," Katherine responded, nodding to one and all but with a crimson blush of annoyance on her cheeks. "But in this matter I had no other recourse except direct involvement in my late husband's commercial affairs."

"Madam Blackwell," asked land broker and planter George Bradmore, "did you consider offering his enterprises for purchase and entering into retirement as befits a gentlewoman of your station?"

"Indeed I did so consider, Master Bradmore, but the offers I received were so meager as to seem closer to robbery—you will pardon my blunt words, gentlemen—than to legitimate purchase of my properties."

Almost to a man the delegation registered in their facial grimaces their disapproval of her strong language. The exception was stout Bradmore whose florid face turned a cherry red. For had he not secretly orchestrated a scheme to take advantage of her supposed naïveté in matters of business and acquire her lucrative shipping interests and choicest lands for prices far below their fair market value?

"Why may I ask then, Madam Blackwell," Glover asked, "did you not seek the aid and counsel of knowledgeable and estimable men versed in these matters and who could have guided you along a proper course of action?"

"Warden Glover, during those trying days no one save a few kindhearted women of the community offered sympathy in my grief, and of course none could give me reliable business counsel. As you know, our family standing in this community was unsettled during my father's lifetime and remained no less strained after his passing. You, sir, well know that the Church withheld its permission for his remains to be buried in St. John's cemetery. It was Rector Palmer's decision to deny him not only the accustomed Church rites of burial but also the merest Christian blessing at his funeral. The decision was to an extreme distressing to me, and my father's mortal remains yet lie unblessed yonder in a small family plot set aside for that doleful purpose. Thankfully, there were no such misgivings about my late husband's religious standing, yet old grievances still existed that made the circumstances of his death doubly hard for me to bear."

"Madam, I was not invested with the office of Senior Warden of the Church when Sir Henry passed away," Glover said hurriedly. "Had I been so, be assured that I should have acted as forcefully and correctly as Christian charity urges on your family's behalf. But you must needs understand, as surely you do, that the Church could not give its blessing to the questionable religious doctrines Sir Henry was said to profess."

"Had anyone bothered to inquire, sir, it would have been clear to all that my father had long since ceased to entertain doctrines, if indeed ever he inclined to them, at odds with the teachings of our Mother Church. The mistaken judgment about his religion was a supposition founded, so I believe, on his old-fashioned manner of speaking and not on any degree of sympathy for the variant Quaker beliefs of which he was accused. His antiquated speech had a simpler origin. It still lingered in his youth amongst the nobility and higher gentry of Yorkshire where he was born. Nor indeed had it completely died away in my early girlhood there, for I well recall hearing elderly folk so speak. To sum the matter plainly, gentlemen, it had naught to do with my father's religious beliefs before or at the time of his death."

"I should be the last person to question the truth of what you say and the first to believe it, madam," Glover responded in a calmer voice. "And I do hope you will recall my actions on behalf of your family in the case of the late Mr. Blackwell's tragic passing, actions which I believe were in complete conformity with our Christian faith."

"Indeed, I do so recall them, and am grateful, sir, and shall continue to be so, for all you did."

"Madam, gentlemen, we busy ourselves with matters that though touching do skirt our main concern," magistrate Benjamin Thompson reminded them, visibly annoyed and impatient to get back to his pressing affairs. "More to the point, madam, are we to understand that it is your intention to continue oversight of the commercial affairs of your lamented late husband?"

"Only for a time, master Thompson, only for a time. Gentlemen, given the concerns you have raised touching on the singularity of my situation, no doubt you will be interested and mayhap relieved to know that I shall close out my affairs in Hampton and remove my family from the Virginia Colony altogether. This provided I receive a fair remuneration for the holdings and enterprises left me by my late husband."

The surprised men looked at one another. "We are taken aback to hear you are considering departure from Hampton, madam," Glover replied, trying but failing to mask his jubilance with a look of Christian compunction. "We had hoped you would remain amongst us, perhaps in a retired state as befitting one of your genteel—"

Spurred to alertness by the good news, Bradmore leaned forward in his creaking chair and interrupted him, "Madam, most assuredly a favorable arrangement can be made for the equitable sale of your properties. I, for one, unselfishly offer you my help and advice if departure from Hampton is your decision. Though, of course, we shall all be saddened by your leaving."

The dignified delegation left shortly thereafter, happily congratulating one another and eager to report the successful outcome of their mission. Bradmore chatted but little, silently calculating how he was to acquire the Blackwell properties for himself.

None knew that Phillip Sterling—yes, Phillip Sterling in the flesh—had persuaded Katherine to make this decision. With the same cunning he had used to outwit servants on the eve of Katherine's wedding day, gaining entry to her room and in a passionate embrace in which, if one dare surmise correctly such sensitive matters, relieved her of maidenly virtue, so now he reappeared, materializing as silently as a ghost in the early morning hours of a chilly March night. Katherine awoke to find a hand over her mouth to stifle her screams. At first she feared violation or robbery, but as she began to make out the man's features in the gloom the greater terror of confronting a ghost paralyzed her. But then he spoke in the seductive baritone voice of the man she had loved so deeply.

"Gentle, sweet Katherine, gentle now, my love," Phillip said softly. Then bending next to her ear, he whispered in French, a language they had often spoken to each other, "*C'est moi, chérie. Je suis revenu, vivant, pas un revenant*" (It is I, darling, I have returned, a living person, not a ghost).

Katherine commenced to tremble uncontrollably in wonder and resurgent emotions. Could it really be Philip? It was impossible, but his deep baritone voice convinced her; it was Phillip, unmistakably Phillip, whom she thought to have lost forever, who now took his hand from her mouth and gathered her in his arms. Again she felt the urge to cry out, not in terror but in orgiastic, resurrected love long stifled and thought forever buried. He smothered her words and questions with kisses both to silence and to arouse her, and she responded with a matching passion that quickly transported them altogether beyond the need of sensible words.

Their lovemaking lasted for hours.

And in the morning light long after he had vanished as silently as he came, she remembered his kisses and relived his embrace, wondering if it was all a dream.

It was not; his return was real and repeated in several visits in the dead of night. Yet the rekindling of their love and his return to Hampton, even the practical matters of where he had taken residence and how he slipped in and out of the town unseen and without the barking of dogs were secrets he said should remain so for the moment at least. He promised to explain to her the mystery of the trunk and to clarify other puzzling matters. "Mere trifles," he said provisionally, but he gave no further thought to keeping his word once given. For him his deeds spoke for themselves without any need of explanatory details. He acted as it pleased him, which alone was reason and justification enough. He felt no urge to please others, much less to inform them of his methods.

Not that Katherine objected; silence and secrecy suited her at least as well. Only six months had passed since Richard's death and she knew better than to stir ugly gossip by curtailing her mourning and having her name publicly linked to her former suitor whose reputation was both celebrated and sullied by the infamous episode of the trunk. Now and then yielding to curiosity and temptation, Katherine asked him how he had escaped the sealed and locked trunk. But he laughed and repeated only his claim that no lock could deter him. At times she all but believed he possessed magical powers of the dark arts.

During respites in their passionate trysts it took but little effort on Phillip's part to persuade Katherine to leave Hampton for Charles Towne in the Carolina Colony. His descriptions of its balmy climate, abundant commercial opportunities, and lax official oversight in England's southernmost mainland colony alone would have been enough to sway her. But to these attractions he added others. There, he told her, they could live in unmolested happiness as man and wife and no doubt easily enrich themselves in thriving Charles Towne through trade with a deeper south. For Katherine there was another reason she kept to herself: she longed to put a healing distance between her and Richard's death, for which she felt a lingering, sordid guilt. She wondered also how Phillip knew so much about the Carolina colony, but of this curious matter she said nothing at the moment. There were many chapters in the life of this strange, fascinating man that she was content to ignore, at least for the moment, provided she be allowed to keep her own secrets. Her inner life was vast and wondrously turbulent in its fancies, but she suspected that his was even more complex in real deeds and adventures. She loved him with an unquenchable passion, and the more she adored him, the more her effervescent imagination found reasons to love him even more.

Within days, Bradmore presented an offer to purchase her town properties and outlying plantations. This time he eschewed intermediaries and acted under his own name, offering a price much elevated over the first. Hat in hand, he explained his situation to her.

"Madam, I shall not withhold from you that at the moment it is far from convenient for me to tender an offer for these properties. My monies, a right modest sum to begin with, I assure you, are in the greater portion invested co-jointly in London and cannot singly be withdrawn. This circumstance reduces my disposable funds to a precarious level. Yet I took to heart our recent discussion of your intentions and am willing because of it to risk extending myself in order to aid you in disencumbering yourself of your holdings."

Discounting George Bradmore's customary lies and duplicitous affairs, of which she and everyone in Hampton were well aware, Katherine perceived that in this case there was a solid kernel of truth in his declaration. The offer, though not as high as she wished, was substantial enough to entertain. Bradmore was miserly but not moronic; he knew that others also desired the prime plantations and holdings and would push past him if he dallied or tried to place an inferior bid before her. And foremost in his favor, he could pay in genuine Spanish dollars, not in the colonial paper scrip, which in lieu of English coin frequently circulated in the Colonies, but not always honored at face value and was not acceptable in all places. On Phillip's advice and with minor upward adjustments in her favor and upon receipt of a substantial earnest, she accepted Bradmore's offer.

Katherine demurred only when it came to her ship, the *Kingston Elizabeth*, which Richard had purchased in replacement of the star-crossed *Bristol Maid*. She would have need of it, she explained to Bradmore, to remove her family and household belongings to her new home in Charles Towne.

He assured her that there were passable wagon roads to the Carolina Colony, but Katherine rejoined that she refused to endure the hardships and dangers of a land passage, especially the infestations of mosquitoes in the marshes, beasts in the forests, and natives along the route who were only sporadically peaceful. "No, Master Bradmore," she said with finality, "my vessel will not be a part of the transaction."

The transfer of funds and deeds duly completed, servants dismissed, scant farewells exchanged, her furniture and other belongings secured on the lower decks of the vessel, it remained only for Phillip to make his public appearance in Hampton to climax the events. Astonishment, disbelief, and lurid insinuations on the part of the townspeople attended his return. Everyone asked questions but no one had reliable information about where he had been and what had happened to him. And he offered only the most insubstantial answers. The man was a deep enigma, and for many of the townspeople he provoked in equal portions admiration and distrust. As for Katherine, she could not wait to fly away with her knight errant, as the old idylls described. For a time all her dreams returned with the imaginary extravagances of her girlhood.

They sailed from Hampton on a June morning to fair weather and a calm sea. Katherine, who was superstitious about signs and omens, took it as a propitious beginning of their life together. Phillip was busy conferring with the captain about the ship and the winds and absentmindedly dismissed her romantic fantasies with a quick kiss on the cheek.

Henry and Mary were wildly excited by the voyage and Katherine was soon busy supervising them and answering their childish questions about swooping seagulls and playful dolphins that cavorted alongside the ship. Phillip was still a mere stranger to them, which caused them to cling all the more to their mother. Katherine hoped he would soon win their trust and affection, but in the short time since he first appeared publicly in Katherine's company, he had paid the children only scant attention. For her part, Mary was inexplicably afraid of Phillip and her mother could not persuade her to sit on his knee.

On the other hand, in an oblique way Phillip was protective of Katherine herself. In the brief time of his return to Hampton most of the townspeople had turned openly against Katherine, reviving and enlarging suspicions about her earlier relationship with Phillip and speculating about Richard's unsolved murder. Malicious gossips whispered that Phillip could have had something to do with Richard's death and that Katherine might have been an active or passive accomplice to the crime. And in the eternal way of gossip, what began as unfounded whisper quickly spread abroad as fact.

Phillip quickly put them off track by offering a reasonable but false account of his whereabouts at the time of Richard's murder and his reappearance in Hampton. Dispirited in the months following Katherine's marriage to Richard, he explained to them, he had sailed for England, arriving just in time to bury his aged mother and settle her small estate. Although only distant kin remained in Stafford—his father had died two years earlier—he decided to settle himself anew in his ancestral town and blot from memory his troubles in France and sentimental disappointments in America. As for exaggerated reports of youthful misdeeds in Stafford, time had so erased these calumnies from collective memory that even should they have had substance, it would have occurred to no one to activate legal proceedings against him. By chance he happened upon a sailor recently on shore leave in the Virginia Colony who told him of Richard Blackwell's murder. He saw a chance to resurrect his unrequited love for Katherine returned to Hampton for that singular purpose. He described himself as the happiest and most fortunate man on earth. For rare is the man, he said gaily, who gets a second chance at the love of his life. He laughed uproariously when reminded of the episode of Katherine's trunk.

"In all likelihood I was either boarding a ship in Chesapeake Bay for Plymouth or already at sea when Blackwell—with due respect for the deceased—had his comical bout of lunacy with her trunk. I concede that he was an able man in commercial matters, but he understood women not a whit, being as unable to distinguish between a highborn lady and a serving girl, as a boorish plowman would see no degree of difference between an Arabian stallion and a decrepit nag. Know, also, that in my fighting days in France I learned secrets that allow me to slip about undetected when I wish, though I fear no man living in singular combat if such an encounter should befall, as indeed it has many times, ever to the mortal disadvantage of my adversaries. Be assured that I would never put a lady's good name at risk or cast doubts on my valor by such an unworthy ruse as Blackwell imagined. He failed by such childish follies to be a proper husband to Katherine. I intend to see that she has a happier life at my side."

In this way, he deflected criticism from himself and softened some of the suspicions about Katherine. Nevertheless, if the good folk of Hampton could tolerate Phillip's love for beautiful Katherine, they remained scandalized by her haste to suspend mourning for Richard and fly to the company and—if the gossips were right—the arms of her former suitor. In any case, the margins of forgiveness for the sexes were, as always, unequal: laxly cast for Phillip and his extravagant transgressions, narrowly drawn for Katherine and her lesser trespasses.

As if Katherine's improper behavior were not provocation enough, the outraged town folk lacked but little to froth at the mouth when word spread in Hampton that she intended to sail unwed in Phillip's shipboard company. Former Senior Warden William Glover and other Church worthies urged an appeal to colonial authorities in Williamsburg to thwart this immoral atrocity, but the majority of the pragmatic townspeople were content to let them depart, thus happily ridding Hampton of further scandal.

No one asked Katherine herself, but had they queried her about this crowning impropriety, she would have reminded them that no civil magistrate or ecclesiastical authority would be willing to marry them in Hampton or Williamsburg. Besides, she was anxious to depart and avert further disapproval. She counted her years in Virginia as wasted and unhappy, much unlike her former sentimental expectations for her life in Colony, and were brightened only by Phillip's advent and the births of precious little Henry and Mary.

Winds and skies held fair for most of the voyage, but high winds made it necessary for the ship to stand off shore for two days before the sea was calm enough for safe docking in Charles Towne harbor. Phillip hired drivers and high-wheeled oxen-drawn wains to transport Katherine's furniture and belongings to spacious lodgings in the better part of the growing town. She and the children gaily squabbled over their living arrangements.

She was anxious to bring into conformity to common decency her irregular relationship with Phillip as quickly and discreetly as it should be possible. In the meantime to forestall gossip and repeat the unpleasantness suffered in Hampton, she asked Phillip to take lodging elsewhere.

"You understand my reasons, do you not, my darling?" she asked apologetically. "I am thinking of us as a family and should like to make a happier beginning in this town than I did in Hampton. There would be lingering gossip about us were we to live here unwed as man and wife. I must think of the children and our future happiness."

"Of course, of course, my dear. I understand perfectly. I shall take lodging at the inn only a few doors removed from here."

"But let us wed at the earliest possible moment, my love," she pleaded. "Time apart from you is torture for me. You know how much I adore you, do you not, my precious darling?"

"Indeed, yet no more than I love and adore you, dearest Katherine. But now that we are alone and the children are abed, I must explain a few things to you, my dear, being foremost among them that I cannot marry you under the name Phillip Sterling."

"What are you saying? I don't understand."

"The matter will seem bizarre to you, my dear, but in

essence it is simple. Sterling is not my surname. I took the name when I came to America, and on this wise: I fled France unjustly pursued as a fugitive by the King's officers. It seemed prudent to begin life in America as Phillip Sterling, a new name for a new life, in the unlikely but possible event that French authorities should extend their pursuit of me to the English Colonies."

"Then, pray, what is your real surname?"

"Phillip Stafford is my birth name, taken in olden times no doubt from the name of my ancestral village in England. It is an honorable surname, though not of high lineage as is your family. I am the descended from sturdy yeoman stock who have risen to middling means and standing, my dear, and it is the name under which I propose to marry you so that our union may have an honest and upright beginning. Mayhap I could live here unmolested as Phillip Sterling. Yet the son of a Duke I was forced to dispatch to the next world defending myself in a duel was the much beloved young nephew of the Queen's bastard brother. He deemed it murder and swore he would not rest until he had exacted vengeance. His family is the northern branch of the Trémont aristocracy. You will pardon my saying so, mindful of your excellent ancestry, my dear, but it is always murder when by accident or reason a commoner kills a nobleman. That, in sum, my dear, is why as an expedient precaution I took the name Phillip Sterling."

"Do the Duke's agents pursue you still and are there risks that yet imperil you so far from France?"

"I learned from friends in England that the Queen's brother has died and his nephew was banished to Quebec for crimes that would have merited execution for one of lesser birth. For the first time in many years I breathe easier, thankful to the Almighty that a nightmarish chapter of my life is at an end. Now at last I can be myself again and live my life under my birth name. Europe's old ways, which aggrieved us both, seem less forceful in this New World. And there is a simpler reason: I prefer my own name."

Katherine stared at Phillip for a moment before responding. Then taking both his hands in hers, she leaned close to him and said: "Then, Master Phillip Stafford, I shall love you as devotedly under this name as I have heartily loved you heretofore as Phillip Sterling. But I hope most earnestly that you have no more surprises to unnerve me further, as so many events have done in growing measure since Richard's death."

"None, my dear," he laughed. "Now you know all my secrets, as you are in full possession of all my love."

"Not all your secrets, my darling," she smiled. "There yet remains the mystery of your uncanny escape from the trunk and the way you came and went without detection in Hampton. At times I wonder if you are versed in devilish arts."

"Trifles, my dear, mere tricks and trifles that I shall explain to you in due time."

"Then we can be united in matrimony and live openly and happily as man and wife as we dreamed of in Hampton?"

"Indeed, my dear, indeed, and the sooner the better for me. Yet I must explain two other matters before we consummate our happiness."

"And what matters are those?" Katherine asked warily. Your words affright me."

"They are matters fraught with no little embarrassment to me, my dear."

"Confide in me, my love. You know you may trust me."

"Well do I know that, dear Katherine, and the comfort it gives me is beyond telling. Yet the certainty of your love makes it no easier to reveal these matters to you. Rather the contrary."

"I promise you all the succor that lies within my power to give."

"Very well, but I shall beg you to think no less of me."

"That goes without saying, dearest Phillip, so tell on. My curiosity grows apace with my nervous anxiety."

"Then hear me out before you respond. To begin with, I departed in haste from England, so great was my desire to see you again. Nor would I do things differently did I again face that pressing but happy prospect. In consequence, I took not the time to put my affairs in proper order, but rather disposed of my ancestral properties quickly without due regard to their true worth. My thoughts were centered on my love for you and practical matters suffered accordingly. A distant cousin took advantage of my eagerness and purchased them for a trifling sum."

Katherine opened her mouth to speak, but Phillip put a finger to his lips to silence her.

"As you may easily imagine, therefore, my assets, modest to begin with, melted away as I made my way back to America. For reasons I shall explain, I had hoped to reunite with two maternal uncles of mine living on the island of Barbados in the Antilles and to Bridgetown in that place intended to bend my steps. I remembered in particular the benevolence and largesse of my Uncle William Woolsey, younger of the two, and though my memories of Uncle Alexander were fainter, for he had left England earlier in life to seek his fortune in the Antilles, I do recall that he was no less pleasantly disposed towards me. Providence had favored both and it came to be said latterly in our town that from comfortable circumstances in England they had risen to riches in Barbados. Unhappily, for a number of reasons I was not able to go to Barbados."

"My love, could we not continue on to Barbados and make our home there? Your uncles are established men of substance and if both feature a kindly disposition towards you, surely they would welcome us as a family, would they not?"

"Indeed, my darling, kinder, more generous men are not to be had in all the English realms. But the problem is their age. After half a lifetime spent away from Mother England she now calls them homeward. They wish to return to our town there to live out their last years. My uncles are dear to me, but once they have departed the island, I should not wish to subject you and the children to the backward conditions of Barbados. Only a few English families of means and class reside there, so I am told, and lacking books and instruction even they have sunk nearly to the level of uncouth sailors and tradesmen, and, indeed, only a bare margin above illiterate plantation workers. Barbados is an isolated island far from civilizing European influences and populated in the main by indentured Scots, Irish, and English, most of whom are brutish in the extreme. Charles Towne may seem little better at the moment, but the arrival of more desirable English folk will soon transform it into a civilized city."

"But that—", Katherine started to say. Again he put a finger to his lips to interrupt her.

"Allow me to conclude, my dear, for I must say on about what I intend to do in order to put an end to my lamentable state of near penury."

This time Katherine would not be silenced.

"You dear, dear man, there is no need to concern yourself with material matters. You have me, and I have estate and fortune aplenty for us both, enough for you, for me, the children, and more offspring if God so blesses us. For I confess I want nothing so much as to bear our child. Or children," she added as a crimson blush spread across her cheeks.

"Were our condition reversed, I should repeat your words with the same sentiments. For I share your high hopes for our family. But I am a man, my darling, and I cannot live on the largesse of a woman, not even the woman I love and intend to take to wife."

"You spoke of a plan, and if your heart is bent on fulfilling your manly aims, then explain them to me so that I may lend you my unstinting support in all possible ways. But understand well, my darling, that I deem those intentions needful only for your manly satisfaction, which I respect for your sake but do not urge because of any material want or desire on my part."

"Duly noted, my dear. The plan is this. There is a great shortage of building lumber in Barbados and neighboring islands where the tropical storms called hurricanes spawned off the African coasts are often especially destructive of buildings and human life. The native woods are soft and generally unfit for durable construction and, in any case, the best forests have been cut away for sugar and indigo plantations in all desirable sites, leaving only the stunted forest growth on mountain slopes. Very fine lumber may be had in Spanish, Dutch, and French dominions on the Southern Continent not greatly distant from Barbados, but the Spanish are arrogant and adversarial with the English, the Dutch greedy and deceptive, and the

French corrupt and treacherous. The great cypress and pine forests of Carolina produce excellent lumber that will fetch a handsome sum in Barbados and other islands. And though this commerce alone will be lucrative, it may be doubled or tripled by merchandise transported back to Charles Towne."

"What sort of merchandise is that? Sugar, indigo, or tobacco?"

"Slaves, my love, African slaves. The commerce of indentured servants from British realms is less dependable than it was in former times, and whites are ill-fitted for labor in tropical lands. Yet Barbados is the outermost of the Antilles and thus closest to the great African continent and the first port for the slave ships bringing their human cargo to the West Indies and the Americas. My plan is this: I shall, with your assent, hire crews to cut cypress lumber hereabouts in Carolina, then transport it along with sundry other goods—metal items particularly—on the *Kingston Elizabeth* to Bridgetown in Barbados. On the return voyage I shall bring a profitable cargo of slaves needful in Charles Towne and the plantations growing apace in the Carolina Colony."

"The vessel is yours, my love, for the purposes you describe and other uses that may arise later, but I confess it disturbs me greatly to hear it will be used to transport human chattel. Betimes I heard my father declaim against slavery, for in this particular he did indeed agree most cordially with the Quakers. More than I knew at the time, his opinions continue to have a compelling power over me, and even though I myself have owned servants, I treated them humanely and prefer not to think overmuch on the conditions under which they were brought to this land and came into my possession."

"Then if it causes you moral anguish, my love, we shall

forego the slave trade altogether. There are other commercial ventures in the Antilles that I may undertake in its stead. But now I must present the second and most painful aspect of my proposed enterprise. I am without funds to put my plans into play for the reasons I revealed to you. And while I am pained beyond measure to say it, I find myself in the embarrassing circumstances of having to appeal to your generosity to give them a beginning. I am newly arrived here and men of substance in Charles Towne who could give me backing know me not, though one day they shall, indeed they shall."

"My darling, all I possess is yours. Dispose of my funds, our funds, as you will."

"My love, you are the woman of my dreams!"

"More than a dream, my hope is to be the only woman in your life."

"And that you are, my love, and that you shall always be."

Few days passed before Phillip contracted with slave owners to send logging crews into the forests to cut and haul the giant cypress logs to the Charles Towne wharves.

Meanwhile, to Katherine's dismay, they were obliged to have a civil wedding in the office of a magistrate, for newly planted Charles Towne as yet had no church in which to formalize their union, nor a priest to conduct it.

"My love," Phillip assured her, "there are plans afoot to build an Anglican church here, and I hear it will be called St. Phillip, my namesake. When it is ready we shall solemnize anew our vows there, if that is to your liking."

"Oh, Phillip, yes, it is indeed very much to my liking!"

Due to repairs and a lack of skilled carpenters needed to convert the *Kingston Elizabeth* into a cargo vessel, Phillip's voyage to Barbados was delayed until October, time enough for Katherine to discover that she was carrying her third child. She was thrilled, but Phillip seemed troubled by her happy revelation. His unexpected attitude stung her.

"I hoped you should be happy with the news I bring you, my darling. We have spoken often of a child. Are you then displeased?"

"No, no, my love, of course not. The news you bring me is cause for great joy, but it renders all the clearer my meager means and my dependence on your estate and admirable generosity; and not least it is an unpleasant reminder that it came from Richard Blackwell, a man who wished my death. I am uncomfortable with my profitless state. I had hoped that by now my proposed commerce with Barbados would be thriving, but, alas, repair and restructuring of the vessel have been maddeningly slow."

"Do not concern yourself, dear husband. Materially we are well off, and think not of how my estate came to be. Richard is gone from our lives, and now that we are married, my property belongs to you. Henry and Mary are happy and soon coming to fulfillment is my greatest desire, which has always been to give birth to your child, our child. And now that God has blessed us, you can without concern delay the voyage until my time is up and I deliver God's gift to our union."

"No, my love, on the contrary, the added, "family responsibility makes it all the more pressing for me to place on firm footing my proposed commercial venture in Barbados, particularly since the storm season is nearly over and my uncles may depart any day for England. I have gathered a good crew and shall sail to Barbados and return before the child is born. And we shall make sure you have maids and help aplenty to attend you in every need and desire while I am at sea."

"My governing desire is to have you by my side always," she said with a pucker of disappointment.

"And so you shall, and so you shall, my love. I shall return soon."

But he did not return, late or soon. After the storm season was past, He sailed away of a morning in late October with a cargo of cypress and pine lumber and Katherine never saw him again.

She was disturbed when she discovered that Phillip had taken much of her jewelry and most of her funds. But she told herself that he took them as a precaution against what might chance unexpectedly on the voyage. Had she not assured him that all was his? Yet as the weeks lengthened into months she could no longer keep at bay a terrible suspicion of deception.

November passed and December came with its cold miasmic airs. Both children were ailing, suffering in their tender flesh, as she imagined, the affliction that was swelling in her heart. On warmer days she would walk to the harbor with her new black maids, Hannah and Ruth, to watch the vessels dock and put out to sea. Phillip may be marooned on an island, she told herself in moments of hope. Perhaps he lies wounded or captive, crying out for me as I send silent messages of love to him.

She sought information from seamen, but they had no knowledge of Phillip. Until finally a young Scottish sailor named Olgivie, newly arrived from Barbados after his indentured service, told her that the *Kingston Elizabeth* said to belong to a man by the name of Captain Stafford, as he recollected, had only a fortnight earlier sailed from the Bridgetown harbor.

"And this Captain Stafford, know you aught of him? She asked, trembling in uncontrollable nervousness.

"Why, ma'am, 'tis commonly bandied in Bridgetown that he lives as a principal gentleman on one of the French islands that neighbor Barbados—I disremember the name—residing thereon with a handsome estate, a great troop of servants, and a bonny wife. And though I saw his residence only through the glass as our vessel stood off becalmed in the sea lane, it was a pleasing sight indeed to the eye."

Katherine sagged in dizziness and her eyes clouded over. Stout Hannah had to steady her as Ruth fanned her with her hand. She had no memory of returning to her residence or of retiring for the night.

The next morning dawned clear and cold, for winter lingered long and strong that year. Not that she noticed in her befuddled state. Rare frost covered the neighboring rooftops. She went out on her veranda to look once more toward the docks, not to hope again for Phillip's return but to say goodbye and good riddance to his memory, and in bidding him farewell to think how she was to live the rest of her life. Unthinking, she had stepped out barefoot on the cold deck and finally became aware that she was shivering and her feet were cold. Then Sir Henry's oracular words came back once more to her in full force: "In a trice would hee traipse away to other adventures, leaving thee shivering barefoot on a frosty morn."

After much sobbing and tears generously shed, Katherine declared an end to her grief and stoically accepted her situation. She announced herself a widow, explaining that her husband had vanished at sea somewhere in the Lesser Antilles. She was concerned about her dwindling funds but by force of will determined to put the problem out of her mind until she should be delivered of child. Jeremy was born in February, nearly six months after Phillip's disappearance. He much resembled his father. Despite her determination to put Phillip out of her thoughts and heart, sometimes tears would come to her eyes as she lovingly caressed and kissed the handsome babe.

Hannah and Ruth were devoted and competent. Sharing Sir Henry's philosophy that no man had the right to enslave another, Katherine granted them their freedom but retained their services by paying them a small wage she could barely afford but which soothed her conscience.

To her good fortune she gained the steadfast friendship of several English ladies, especially Mrs. Elizabeth Clifford and Mrs. Sarah Bankhead, who attended her during her gravid state and helped to see to her needs at Jeremy's birth. Carpenters and masons were building St. Phillip Church and a growing Anglican congregation impatiently awaited its completion and the arrival of an English rector. In the meantime as best they could, they held informal prayer services in private homes, including Katherine's spacious residence.

Spurred by concern over her financial straits, it occurred to Katherine to act on an off-hand comment by Sarah Bankhead that Katherine's fluency in French was convenient for the community and perhaps could be profitable. Accordingly, she took steps to establish an academy that would offer classes in French for the children of English families and classic literary works for more advanced students. Back on her feet and fully active after a week, but down to a mere residue of funds, she interviewed and hired two young French Huguenot sisters, Claire and Beatrice Pontneuf to serve as teachers. English authorities barred French Catholics from Charles Towne but tolerated the French-speaking Huguenot Protestants. At first she set aside two large rooms in her residence as classrooms, but thanks to Sarah and Elizabeth enrollments quickly increased beyond her expectations, and as the school earned a respectable reputation with the better families, she leased a larger building. Within a year her income more than sufficed for her family and she was a much respected and appreciated member of Charles Towne society.

Even more beautiful as a woman than she had been as a girl, Katherine was obliged to fend off a queue of devoted suitors. Her broken heart mended, but she did her best to convince herself that there would never be a place in it for new sentiments. For the most part her life continued in this peaceful and prosperous way for nearly three years until an event beyond her wildest dreams again drastically altered her life. We shall hear that story at a later time.

Forefathers.com

I am searching for information about my GGGG grandfather Phillip Stafford, who also may have gone by name Phillip Sterling. I think he left England at an early age, distinguished himself as a soldier in France, and later resettled for a short time in South Carolina. He may have married there, although our family records list Dominique Desqueroux as his wife in Martinique. I am descended from the branch of his family that later resettled in Louisiana and points west, if my information is correct. I would like to make contact with any of his descendants, if there are any. I am not sure of the first marriage because the records are confusing, and I have not been able to find any Staffords/Sterlings still in the Caribbean islands. Any help will be appreciated. I would really like to verify the family tradition that Phillip Stafford/Sterling was a hero in the French wars.

--Andy Stafford, Pawnee, Oklahoma

...

Hi, Andy,

Sorry to give you this bad news, but your ancestor was, to put it as nicely as I can, a con artist. Apparently he did fight in France and later settled in Virginia under the false surname of Sterling according to family scuttlebutt to escape crimes and misdeeds in Europe. He then left a wife and several children in Virginia and showed up in the Caribbean married to another woman — probably the French woman you mentioned.

I am descended from Phillip Stafford's younger sibling, Martha Stafford Guildford. Our kin are scattered from Massachusetts to California. As you probably know, your ancestor Phillip was the twin brother of David Stafford who left Boston for Charleston, South Carolina. There David, not Phillip, married and had several children, some of whom later moved west through the Deep South and Texas. Some in our family still tell the story, which is a piece of nonsense in my opinion, that he married his brother's widow. Phillip, it seems, left a wife in Virginia, not in South Carolina. So the story does not tally with the facts.

Wish I could have had better news for you. But facts are facts. I suppose all this makes us distant cousins of some sort, so I wish you well.

--Harry Guildford, Peoria, Illinois

...

Chapter 3.
A Handful of Coins

Forefathers.com

[Early Virginians, Vol. V, p. 35: Matthew Stokesbury (164?-173?). There is no known record of his birthday or exact information about the year and location of his death. But Hamilton Stokesbury's family record appears to supply in part what public records omit in toto. It relates that he was born in Wales on Sir Henry Beaufort-DuCordier's Stokesbury Manor. That early employ earned him the position of butler and factotum to wealthy Richard Blackwell of Hampton in the Virginia colony following the latter's marriage to Sir Henry's daughter Katherine and the death of her father Sir Henry. For reasons that the early chronicles do not reveal, Blackwell angrily dismissed him from that position. Nothing certain is known about his later life, but years later several frontiersmen claimed contact with a one-armed white man by the same name living with an Indian wife in a Cherokee clan in the uncharted country across the Appalachian Mountains. The following narrative is built on Hamilton's account of his family history.]

...

Matthew Stokesbury regained consciousness on the forest trail to throbbing pain in his right arm and agony throughout his body. His forearm dangled at an unnatural angle. Sight told him it was broken and pain confirmed it. Blood, soggy and now cold, caked his once immaculate butler's uniform and stockings, and he could feel it squish as he flexed his toes inside the bright-buckled shoes. He was thankful for the pain that told him his feet were uninjured. He did not know whether other severe injuries, if any, imperiled his life, but only that his body ached so much that with the merest motion he groaned in spite of himself, alternating between praying in desperation and crying out in pain. He fought to hold back nausea. Though now fully conscious, for a moment the fear of moving and discovering more ghastly wounds checked the urgency he felt to stand. But stand he must, if he might. He counted only one advantage in his battered condition and broken right arm: he was left-handed.

Cautiously he stood and quickly he fell, astonished and frightened that his legs refused to move as he willed them. Face down on the damp forest leaves and heaving in unbearable pain, he rubbed his left leg with his good hand. There was feeling, yes, thank the Lord God, there was feeling! But was it in his leg or in his hand? Bracing himself against a tree, again he worked himself into a standing position. Now his legs were coming back to life and resuming their usual obedience to his will. He took steps, haltingly at first, and finding no breakage or bruises greater than those he knew, limped down the trail as darkness settled over the forest.

Master Blackwell had ordered the servants to flog Matthew for reasons not yet clear to him, and perhaps would never be, though he suspected that the beating came at Lady Blackwell's urging. She had never taken kindly to him, even though he could recall no lapses of proper conduct in her presence. He had always served Master and Lady Blackwell loyally, as earlier he had attended Sir Henry and his family, scrupulously fulfilling his duties as butler and never overstepping his bounds or acting out of turn. He knew many unedifying family secrets but kept them to himself.

Such behavior was bred into him. He was descended from a long line of serving folk in Wales whose pride and principles, transmitted over many generations, consisted in being loyal to one's master, and no less discreet than loyal in all circumstances relating to the master's household.

If the reasons for Master Blackwell's great rise in displeasure remained a mystery to Matthew, there was no doubt in his mind that the ferocity of Blackwell's lowly servants greatly exceeded the Master's orders. They acted with the perverse gleefulness of underlings given a rare chance to vent their anger at superiors who have lorded it over them. And the higher the rank the more ferocious their hatred: butlers they flog, captains they geld, kings they behead.

Master Richard's wrath had erupted so suddenly and disastrously that Matthew had no time to gather his few belongings, including a coffer of coins concealed in his room. His situation was bleak and a thrill of dread chilled his heart. Perhaps the other wounds would heal, but the broken arm meant that it would be weeks before he could work again. And who would take him into their service? After his calamitous fall from grace it was unlikely that any family in Hampton would allow him into their household and risk offending the rich and powerful Blackwells.

His first impulse, more like an instinct than a thought, was to return to his master's house and resume his duties. But slowly instinct yielded to logic: he could never again serve in the Blackwell mansion. Yet he could feature in his mind no other life, no other place. He was born to serve, but now there was no place left for him to be a servant. It was as if his corner of the world had suddenly fallen away under his feet, leaving him nowhere to stand. For the first time, America seemed completely alien to him, a bewildering welter of circumstances he had never experienced.

In his forlornness he thought of his boyhood home on the old Welsh manor. But he quickly shook his head and reminded himself that aside from deceptive memories there was nothing for him there, even if it were possible for him to return to the ancestral estate where generations of his family had lived and served. His parents were surely long dead, he reasoned, and a younger sister and two older brothers, should they yet be amongst the living, would no doubt shun him, fearful that he might ask them for help. The servant class he belonged to, sprung hundreds of years earlier from medieval serfs, could barely name their grandsires and in earlier centuries lacked surnames entirely. When in the late Middle Ages it became the custom for families to take a last name, they generally affixed for that purpose the name of a hereditary occupation or manor—Stokesbury for Matthew's ancestors. Parental tenderness towards offspring and kin soon withered in the severity and shortness of life. Service to them did not mean serving their own kind. Centuries of servitude to their masters had so stunted their familial affections that they thought little more of their mature offspring than a mother bear in the wild recalls her departed cubs of yesteryear.

Practical need soon dispelled his melancholy uncertainty. The immemorial tradition of his life was shattered. Suddenly everything was new and terrifying, as though he were seeing the world for the first time. Mere survival forced him to consider his situation as rationally as he could. As he limped along the forest trail, putting one foot slowly and gingerly ahead of the other, so he labored to arrange his thoughts in a similar logical progression.

First and most pressing, he must gain access to his old quarters in the Blackwell mansion in order to retrieve his money, clothing, and personal effects, including his brush and scissors. He was subservient to his masters, but he felt no conflict between obedience and the pride he took in his appearance. He was especially fond of his long blond locks and thick red beard.

He approached the Blackwell estate in the wee morning hours, carefully opened the rusty iron outer gate and warily listened for servants, once under his supervision, now his recent tormentors. Fortune was with him; all were asleep and the estate was silent.

But as he was awkwardly opening the window to his old quarters, Blackie, Master Blackwell's favorite hunting hound, suddenly put its cold, moist snout against his broken arm. Matthew moaned in pain, then caught himself, terrified of arousing the household. Not given to the sudden changes of affection peculiar to humans, Blackie recognized an old friend and whined in pleasure as Matthew stroked his back and head.

His room was in its familiar array for which Matthew whispered a quick prayer of gratitude. Even without light he found his precious coffer and other personal items. He quickly stuffed them in his trousers and a pillowcase. Then gathering his extra garments and a pair of boots, he pitched them out the window and dropped carefully to the ground where patient Blackie, head aslant in puzzlement, awaited him. At the gate Matthew gave him a final pat, closed the gate, and breathed a sigh of relief when he was clear of the estate. Blackie whined and scratched the gate with his paws, but Matthew did not look back.

Now he had coin but no food or water. He had not eaten or drunk in more than thirty hours, and hunger and thirst added to the misery of his broken arm and bruises. But he knew he must get away from Hampton and gain the main west road to Williamsburg as quickly as possible. Once out of sight of the mansion he replaced his blood-soaked garments and shoes with other clothes and foot ware. Bracing himself with his stout left arm, he drank copiously from a trickling forest stream a stone's throw from the road. He considered discarding the bloodied items, but clothing was hard to come by. Perhaps he could rinse most of the bloodstains away in the stream. At the moment, however, these were secondary concerns. Time was against him. The servants had repeated the Master's warning that another flogging—or worse—would be his punishment should daybreak find him yet in or near Hampton.

Suddenly fortune deserted him. As dawn was breaking Master Richard Blackwell came riding hard homeward after a night of cups, gambling, and wenching at the Red Sail Tavern hard by the Bay. He appeared so suddenly that Matthew had no time to hobble off the road and crouch behind the trees.

Already angry over his gambling losses and the bad luck to discover that his favorite girl was bedded with another patron, as soon as he espied Matthew he leaped from the saddle and unfurled a bullwhip of the sort that stockmen attached to the saddle horn to work their cattle.

"Well now, you miserable cur, I see you have made light of my warning! Were you not told to be out of Hampton before sunrise? Attend me, sirrah, and we shall see if my whip can teach you what my warning could not!"

The whip cracked and the whiplash bit cruelly into Matthew's already lacerated flesh.

"Mercy, Master Blackwell, mercy, I beg you!" Matthew cried out. "I am hastening as quickly as I can to obey your orders! But, sir, as you see, my arm is broken and my other wounds have held me to this slow pace. But have pity on me, sir, and soon you shall see no more of me!"

"I have already seen more of you and heard more of your lies than I can stomach! I will abide no more of your falsehoods! And what carry you there, brigand? Garments and shoes, I see! And do I spy coins spilling from yon coffer? So, you are both a traitor and a thief who has entered my house without my leave and made away with my property! For that you shall pay double for your treachery."

"But, sir, I took only the things that are mine, nothing more. The coffer of coins is mine, I swear it!"

"Nothing is yours! Everything on my estate is mine, and your wretched life is forfeit for taking my property! But I am done with talking. Now you will pay for your thievery and conniving! Stand before me and receive your punishment!"

With that he delivered a whiplash across his victim's broken arm. Matthew sank to his knees in screaming agony. The lashes continued to fall and Matthew continued to plead for mercy.

Richard came closer with his singing whip, drunk with fury and the lust of inflicting punishment.

In a red mist of agony Matthew knew Blackwell would not stop until he was beaten to death. Yet even in the midst of pain he was puzzled. He did not deserve to die. The Master had no reason to kill him, nor had he a reason to let himself be slaughtered. The injustice of it was monstrous and incomprehensible. At that moment Matthew espied Blackwell's saber sheathed and secured below the saddle. A whiplash nicked the horse as Matthew struggled to unsheathe the weapon and the panicked animal almost trampled him. Blackwell cursed the jittery animal and darted around it to get to the cowering Matthew. But as he lurched forward, raising the whip to strike again, Matthew met him in desperation, holding the blade erect with his good hand. Blackwell's charge caused the blade to run him cleanly through so that the steel tip emerged, blood streaked, from the small of his back. Blackwell fell backward, jerking the saber from Matthew's hand, his face settling into a death mask of agonized surprise and disbelief as life faded from his eyes.

Shaking and nauseous, Matthew could not bring himself to approach the fallen Blackwell, but it was plain he was dead even as he fell. Matthew looked down at him, horrified by the homicide he had committed and the ancient taboo he had broken. Sworn always to attend and obey the master, he had killed him instead. How had something so far from his intentions come to pass? It barely lessened the horror of the deed to argue to himself that his own life was in peril and that the master was unjust and abusive, indeed that he was no longer his master and thus had no claim on his loyalties.

"May God have mercy on me, I have done Master Blackwell to death! But he meant to kill me for reasons unknown to me. I was no longer bound to him, no longer a servant, not to him, not to any man, but on my own to live my life alone if I may."

So saying, he laid the sword gently across Blackwell's body and wiped the blood from his hands on the saddle blanket. Then leaving the now gentled horse to graze indifferently on the roadside grasses, he hobbled away as quickly as he could, warily watching the road in both directions lest early travelers should see him.

Eventually he would reach Williamsburg, where he purchased food and drink, but driven by guilt and fear he trudged westward, stopping only to sleep in deserted places and forcing himself to eat. His arm did not heal and he wandered in semi-delirium past the boundaries of white civilization itself. Matthew was a strong man in his prime, and though shattered in spirit and delirious of mind, he stumbled on. Many times he fell and rose along the mountain trails until finally he could rise no more. But that story is a later telling.

As for Richard Blackwell's death, it was common knowledge that he frequented the Red Sail Tavern and often lightened his purse in cards, cups, and chambering. The rough men who patronized the tavern and witnessed what happened related that at a late hour he paid the proprietor good coin for the replacement wench he led upstairs for his abusive play. But his purse was still far from empty when he kicked the bedraggled girl down the stairs and staggered out of the tavern after the night was far spent. The constables reasoned that one or several men must have followed and murdered him, even though it seemed passing strange that the assailants had not taken his half-filled purse. But that minor perplexity did not lessen the general consensus that among the tavern patrons were surely to be found the murderers. After all, they could have extracted coinage without taking the incriminating purse itself. But these were the merest suppositions. Without evidence and witnesses to gainsay the tavern patrons, who proclaimed their innocence with blasphemous oaths and swore alibis for one another, the authorities were obliged to enter Blackwell's murder into the colonial records as a crime perpetrated by a party or parties unknown.

Forefathers. Com:

I am descended, so I am told, from Richard Blackwell's only son Henry. The point I wish to make, and I hope the Stokesbury descendants read it, is that Richard Blackwell had good reason to punish Matthew Stokesbury. The problem, it seems, began during the Beaufort family exile in France. According to the version handed down in the Blackwell family, Katherine Beaufort, daughter of Sir Henry Beaufort, made an unfortunate reference to servant Matthew Stokesbury's long blond hair and red beard, comparing his features to those of a knight in one of her favorite old chivalric novels. The vain and puffed up Stokesbury imagined the worst—or for him the best—that Katherine had conceived an illicit passion for him, and he began to make sly insinuations to her about his own feelings. She rebuked him harshly when to her horror she realized that he had misinterpreted her innocent comment. She asked her father to dismiss him, but Sir Henry would not hear of it, and Katherine could not give him the real reasons for her request. From then on the relationship between lady and servant were strained and finally culminated when she gained enough influence with Richard Blackwell to force the issue. I think Ricard Blackwell

has been vilified long enough, first by an unfaithful wife and,
second, by an underhanded servant. I add this without further
comment: a suspicion persisted in later generations of the
Blackwell family that Matthew Stokesbury may have been
involved with Richard Blackwell's unsolved murder. There was
a report that a Stokesbury descendant once publicly admitted
as much.

    Sincerely,
    Dr. Thomas Blackwell, Tucson, Arizona
    ...

    Sir,
    Your insinuations are the purest slander full of evil
intention and minus any shred of truth. We of this branch of
the Stokesbury-Stokes family have read them with disgust
and rejected them with indignation. Matthew Stokesbury
was by all accounts a loyal servant to both the Beauforts
and Blackwells, and they repaid him cruelly for his loyalty.
Since he is not here to defend himself, we will speak for him.
What is true is that Matthew lost an arm and almost his
life because of a beating administered by Blackwell or his
henchmen. He owed his life to the solicitous care given him
by the Cherokees, particularly the Indian maid Agali, who
became his wife and co-founder of our line in America.
Please keep your fictions to yourself until you can first
admit the immoral conduct of your highborn Beaufort and
Blackwell families.

    Sincerely
    Reagan Stokes, Abilene, Kansas
    ...

Chapter 4:
In the Name of God

Forefathers.com

[Early Tennesseans, Vol. 1, p. 20: Agali Stokesbury (166?-175?). Early trappers and explorers acquainted with the mountain wilderness mention her as the wife and widow of Matthew Stokesbury, a white man said to have lived among a Cherokee clan in the Appalachian region of Western Carolina, later East Tennessee. (See Early Virginians, Vol. 5, p. 35.) Her name indicates a Cherokee pedigree. According to her descendants she was adopted by Chief Madok when smallpox decimated her own family. She was the mother of Lucinda, Hamilton, Nathaniel, and Evan. She died between 1750 and 1760, possibly at the hands of "Overmountain" white renegades, who around 1740 began to raid the Cherokee clans.]

...

From a distance Agali thought at first that she had come upon a dead or dying deer, or was it a bear, or maybe a wolf? So as not to disturb its departing spirit her first impulse was to turn away. But though respectful and wary, as the tribal elders had taught her to be with all creatures of the forest, she was also young and curious. She would take a quick look then run away. That impulsive decision was destined to change her life.

The dying creature had the general appearance of a man, but the likes of which she had never seen before. Long yellow and red hair grew from his head and face, concealing most of his features. His body was snugly clothed, but instead of the fur-lined skins and deerskin moccasins the men of her clan wore in colder months, torn black coverings of a material she had never seen covered his torso, and stiff black leather ware, now split and peeling, exposed his feet to the elements. He lay senseless on his left side in the shallow creek water. His right arm, monstrously swollen and purplish, dangled in the vegetation along the creek bank. Agali crept closer in fear and fascination. Now she could hear the rattle of its breathing. Everything about the being was strange, but she knew the sound; it was nearing death.

Now the manlike creature moved and uttered sounds, perhaps words, but Agali could not understand them. She saw that it was shaking with fever and cold. "*Duw, Duw, Tad, Tad,*" it murmured. For an instant he opened his eyes and she saw they were blue like the summer sky. No, this was not a man as she knew men. Fear overwhelmed her and she ran. She must tell the elders. They would know what to do. But she would have to tell them, too, that she had transgressed by disturbing the creature's spirit in its dying moments. She dreaded the scolding they would give her. The elders had reprimanded her many times for straying from the camp. Maidens were not allowed such freedom. Agali had always been different in her ways. She was the lone survivor of a neighboring clan devastated by the pox. Some in the tribe wished they had never taken her in to be one of them. They should have left her to the wolves and bears, they whispered behind her back, so that she could have gone to the spirit world with the rest of her family. But she was fairer than the other Cherokee girls and Kawani, second wife of the old chief, was childless. Agali would replace the daughter the spirits had taken from her. And so it was; Agali lived as Kawani's daughter, but she was always different. And some spoke ill of her.

"Lead us, girl, to where the man lies," Chief Madok said to the excited girl, "and tell the Medicine Man that I will need him and his sons to come with us."

Agali ran with the message, then eagerly led the men to the creek bank where the odd being lay.

The Chief nodded when he saw the man. "It is as I thought. He is one of the *unega*, the white ones. I saw hunters of his kind as a boy when I crossed the mountains with my father. Their bodies and faces are covered with hair of several colors, though many of the older ones have little hair on the crown of the head. Without sunlight their skin turns pale like new mushrooms. Many have hair the color of corn tassels and eyes blue as the sky or smoky like mountains in the far distance or green like early spring tree leaves. They are a strange, untidy tribe whose smell is a stench to the nostrils. But they are magically skilled and make many useful things of wood and metal like the little people of the deep woods told of in our old stories. And they possess a weapon that makes smoke and thunder and can kill at a great distance. This one is young but his blood is poisoned with great wounds. Death is upon him. We shall remove the body from the water so as not to foul the stream, but then we must leave him to die in peace with the spirits."

"He made sounds, or maybe words," Agali said timidly.

"What words, girl?" Chief Madok asked sharply.

"I-I could not understand them and he spoke little, but they had the sound of "*Tad* and *Duw*." It caused me to think of the cawing of a raven far off in the distance. Yet it was different. I cannot tell it in words."

Chief Madok quickly summoned Tlanuwa the Medicine Man and the two stepped out of their hearing to confer. After a time they returned.

"Pull the man from the water, Chief Madok ordered, but take care not to drag him by the broken arm." As they did so, the dying man mumbled again: "*Ein Tad...*"

Chief Madok and Tlanuwa waved the men away and knelt down to hear the whispered words. "*. . . deled dy deymas, . . . gwneler dy . . . ewyllys . . .*"

In wide-eyed astonishment Tlanuwa lifted Matthew's cross from his neck and whispered to Chief Madok: "He speaks the sacred words learned from our forefathers, and look, he wears the holy symbol around his neck. But his other words are barbarous and I cannot understand their meaning."

Head down and hands clasped around the Cross, the Chief sat silently for a moment. Then he stood and gave orders. "Carry the *unega* to our camp, Tlanuwa, and tell the old women to prepare healing herbs and potions. We must preserve his life if the spirits are willing to release their grip on him."

"Chief Madok, his arm is poisoned beyond healing," Tlanuwa reminded him, "and the corruption has spread through his body."

"Then you shall cut off the arm and see if he lives or dies," Chief Madok answered resolutely. "We must try."

The others did not understand why the effort was necessary. The man was not one of theirs and could be their enemy, but they did not openly question Chief Madok's decision. To them he was Chief Madok *yvni*, Madok the Great Chief, The Most Beloved Man, and they did not dare question his judgment or disobey him. But only Agali was glad in her heart as she sprinted like a young doe back to the camp ahead of the men.

With flint knives Tlanuwa and his two sons severed the unconscious Matthew's right arm above the elbow then stanched the blood flow and sealed off the open veins and arteries with burning hickory limbs. Agali hovered by day and stayed close by night to apply potions to his wounds and feed him herbs the old women prepared. For days Matthew lay feverishly between life and death, but finally the spirits relaxed their grip and withdrew. He opened his eyes and spoke.

"My arm is gone and my Crucifix is lost," he said simply, staring at the stub of his right arm, severed above the elbow. Nobody knew his words, but Agali understood his feelings. She pointed to his left arm and flexed her muscle to show him that now it must serve for both. Matthew understood the gesture, the first of many understandings between them.

When he had progressed and could drink the herbal teas and feed himself the venison, hickory nuts, chestnuts, herbs, and wild onions Agali brought him, Chief Madok and old Tlanuwa came into the tent and sat by his side. After a time

Chief Madok said words they had heard Matthew speak: "*Ein Tad. . . Deled dy deymas. . .*" Matthew understood and recited the Lord's Prayer in the Welsh tongue his mother had taught him as a boy.

Ein Tad yn nefoedd
Sancteiddier dy enw:
Deled dy deymas:
Gwneler dy ewyllys
Ar y ddaear fel yn y nef.
A maddau inni ein troseddau,
Ein herbyn;
A phaid â'n dwyn I brawf,
Ond gwared ni rhag yr Un drwy
Pjerwudd eoddpt to yw'r deymas a'r gallu a'r
Gogoniant am byth.
       Amen.

As Matthew recited the Lord's Prayer Chief Madok put his hands on his breast, closed his eyes, and rocked back and forth to the musical cadence of the consonant-heavy Welsh words. But all were frustrated at the end that no further communication was possible between the Cherokee and the white man. They understood only occasional words of the Paternoster and he knew none of the Cherokee tongue. They could not ask him about his silver Crucifix.

Agali set about to remedy their mutual ignorance. During his convalescence she patiently taught Matthew words in Cherokee and he, equally obliging and pleased by her presence, repeated the equivalencies, as he understood them, in English for her to repeat. He explained that the words to the Lord's Prayer were from another language. There were moments of hilarity over innocent but barbarous mistakes in both languages. They grew close and came to enjoy each other's company. When Matthew had regained much of his strength and learned to compensate for the lost limb, he and Agali spent hours exploring the forest where their lessons continued.

One day as she placed a dogwood flower in his hand and explained its curative power, he told her that the brown corners of the petals represented the nail wounds of the sacrificial Christ.

"What is Christ?" she asked.

"His name is Jesus and he is the Son of God, the Son of *Duw*, as Chief Madok remembered the name. Jesus died to save us from the Evil One, the Devil. The Prayer I prayed for the Chief is the Prayer of Jesus. He died but came back to life and lives in Heaven with *Duw*. One day he will come down to earth again and take us up to Heaven, too, if we have lived as he taught us to live—as good, obedient children."

"Who are these children?"

"You are one of them."

"No, Matthew, my people say I am bad, they say I do wrong things. They talk hard to me many times because I run far into the forest and want to see many things."

"We all do bad things. I do bad things, too. But if our heart is good and try to do good things, then Jesus smiles on us and we are his."

"Is this God, this Duw, a unega, a white man, like you, Matthew?"

"No one knows what he looks like or whether he has the form of a man. He does not show his face to people. He is too great for ordinary eyes to look upon him. The sight of him would blind and maybe kill a person."

"But if he has a son called Jesus, then he must be a man, or like a man. And what of his mother? Didn't Jesus have a mother? Was she a woman?"

"Yes, Agali, a young woman like you."

"I must think about these things. We will talk again of this Jesus, the son of *Duw*. It is hard for me to understand the things you tell me."

When Matthew spoke enough of the Cherokee tongue to talk with Chief Madok, he asked him how he knew Welsh words in the Lord's Prayer.

"In days long before the lives of our oldest grandfathers, there came among my people the *unega*, white men like you, from across the Great Water. In those days our people lived far to the north by the banks of a wide river. Our forefathers killed many of *unega* in a great battle, but spared a few of the young ones to be our slaves. In time they were not counted as captives but adopted as brothers. They brought no women from their land but the men my ancestors spared took wives from among our clan and became our people. The chief of the *unega* was a mighty warrior named Madok. My people tortured and killed him, but in time his son, who was mighty in battle, rose from slavery to become the first chief Madok. He told us of the great god *Duw* and taught us to kneel and pray to him in the words you know. Since then many times the count of my fingers the sons of Madok have borne his name and guarded the sacred emblem of the great god, even as I do."

"What is the sacred emblem?" Matthew asked him.

Chief Madok left the bearskin tent and returned with a small wooden case of rotting, splintered wood. The imprint of metal hinges, now reduced to rusted slivers, remained on the cover.

Making a curious motion with his hand that resembled the sign of the Cross, Chief Madok reverently extracted two objects from a deerskin pouch inside the case.

"It is this, like the one you wore around your neck," the Chief explained, cradling a small, blackened crucifix next to Matthew's in the palm of his hand.

"A crucifix and indeed like mine!" Matthew exclaimed. "Mother of God, how is this miracle possible? This, you say, your people have guarded since the days of Prince Madok?"

"So we have done. What do you know of Madok?" the Chief asked, returning Matthew's cross to him. "Was he of your nation?"

"As a boy I heard old tales of Prince Madok," he said, kissing the crucifix and awkwardly slipping the silver chain over his ears and around his neck. "But my father told me they were fables, stories to entertain children and witless folk."

"The story is true, for the son of Madok told our ancestors how their father gathered his warriors for a voyage across a great water to our land. But in the long count of time we forgot much they taught us, and the kindred clans and tribes of our Cherokee people turned us again to the gods and stories of our ancestors. Yet we still told the story of Madok and remembered a few of the *unega* teachings about the great god. And even though we forgot its meaning, we preserved the sacred emblem, passing it from one chief to another until my time. Now that you are strong, *unega* Matthew, and know much of our speech you will teach us again the things our ancestors knew and forgot."

Chief Madok's words allowed no refusal, and even though Matthew had no desire to obey, he knew he must. He remembered his childhood faith in Wales. Though the English overlords forbade it, his mother had secretly kept the old religion and taught it in the old Welsh tongue. But now it was a dormant memory nearly as distant from his life in America as the ancient teachings were to the Cherokees. But above all else, would it not be the vilest hypocrisy to teach what he had violated by killing Master Blackwell? He could only ask the question; there was no one who could answer him. Not even Agali. Least of all Agali, he thought. Sunk in doubt and indecision, he delayed the teachings as long as he could.

In Agali's eyes, Matthew could do no wrong. He came from a world she tried to imagine but could not. But the more she tried the more the mystery enchanted her. She pictured the eastern lands beyond the mountains and across the great sea as magical realms filled with wonders he described to her as much as their mutual languages permitted. For Agali, Matthew personified all that was grand and marvelous in the land of the *unega*, white people who possessed the happy truths of the great God.

But as Agali imagined the prodigies of the east, Matthew felt his life being restored in the wilderness of the west. With Agali by his side he climbed the higher mountains to enjoy the blue-hued vistas of valleys and ridges where streams gathered to form the great twisting torso of the Tennessee River. Then as the days shortened and foliage took on gold and yellow autumnal hues—Matthew had lost the calendar count of days—they came down from the heights to the creeks and caves of the lower hills.

Old Kawani no longer cautioned Agali about the yellow-haired *unega* and raised no objections to the time she spent with Matthew. She and the whole clan, including Chief Madok, accepted their relationship and began to think of them as man and wife. But Matthew and Agali had not consummated their union nor had they spoken of feelings at all. Their affections had matured as naturally as spring buds ripen into autumnal fruit. They felt no need to describe feelings as obvious as sunlight and already deeper than their imperfectly matched words could say.

But Agali did not forget the practical uses of her time with Matthew. Old Kawani and the other elderly women always needed herbs, berries, nuts, and roots from the deep forest. While Matthew sat captivated by the view or thought of old, unhappy, far-off times he could not tell Agali, she gathered her daily harvest and wrapped the herbs in a beaver skin for Mother Kawani and the old women. She explained as much as Matthew could learn of their properties and purposes.

One day as Agali rested from her labors and sat next to Matthew, he yielded to an urge to kiss her. She was startled and pulled away when he turned her face to his and pressed his lips on hers.

"Why did you do that, Matthew? I do not understand your touch. Does my face displease you? Are you hungry for the deer meat I brought for you?"

He laughed and pulled her close. "No, Agali. Your face is pretty, like a flower, and I am not yet hungry for food. It is called a kiss, and it is a sign of what we call affection in my language. It means love, joy, the feeling a man has when he is with a woman who pleases him."

"A kiss, you say. What a strange thing. I do not know of such things, for I am a maiden and no man has done them to me before. But Mother Kawani and other old mothers say that men must do such things to maidens so they can have children. Does it mean that now I shall give birth to a child?"

Matthew laughed at her innocence until his beard shook and tears came to his eyes. Never in his life had he laughed so heartily or felt so good. He could not remember a happier day. Agali was puzzled and concerned.

"Why do you laugh so hard, Matthew? I have not seen you laugh so much. Nor any other man. We Cherokee do not laugh much. The men think it not manly, and Mother Kawani and the older women tell us maidens we must be careful in our speech."

"Neither have I laughed much in my life, Agali. In my land the elders also taught that maidens and mothers must not smile too much and that loud laughter is not good. As for me, my life has not given me much cause for laughter. But now I am happy."

"Then becoming a father makes you happy?"

He laughed again and brushed back hair fallen over her face. "No, I am not going to be a father. I am happy just being here. With you, Agali."

"I am not with child?"

"No, Agali, not yet. But someday you could be."

"How?"

"How?"

"Yes, how do I become a mother? What must you do to me for me to have a child?"

His laughter faded. He knew no easy way in either of their languages to explain what a man could not, and according to his culture should not, put into words for an innocent girl.

"You must ask Mother Kawani or the other old mothers. They will tell you. A man must not say such things to a maiden."

"Is it a bad thing you must do?"

"No, it is not bad but a beautiful thing."

"Then you must tell me what it is."

"I cannot. Ask the old mothers."

She hardly spoke to him at all on the way back to the village. Was she angry or in some other mood? He wondered. There were still many mysteries in her Cherokee soul that he did not understand.

The next morning Chief Madok summoned Matthew to his tent.

"You spend much time with the maid Agali. We have watched you in the high mountains, by the caves, and along the water playing like children. Such is the way of children, not the way of a man. Take Agali if you need her to be your woman, but then you must teach us the meaning of the sacred sign of the great God."

"I am not a teacher, Chief Madok, and not even a good Christian. In my land we have men called pastors and priests who teach the people about God. I am not such a man, and I have not obeyed God since I grew to manhood."

"If the god of Madok is the great God, then why do you not obey him?"

"Like many men, Chief Madok, I have fallen under the power of a great enemy of God called Satan, or the Devil. He fights against the true God and tries to destroy his people. Many follow him."

"I do not know of this enemy called Satan. Is he stronger than the true God?"

"No, he once served God as an angel, a servant, but then he became proud of his great strength and wanted to be God himself. Many lesser angels followed him, though most remained faithful to *Duw*, to God. A mighty war took place between the good and bad angels," Matthew explained, pointing to the sky. "The good angels, the warriors of God, drove them out of Heaven. They fell to earth where they do all they can to harm God's people and turn their thoughts to bad things. They try to get us to lie, steal, and do harm to our brothers. They promise us many good things at first but give us only sufferings in the end. If we are true to his teachings, God takes us into his everlasting paradise, into his kingdom called Heaven, when we die. There," he said, pointing upward, "all good things come to us. But if we serve the Devil, then we go down to Hell, a dark, terrible land under the earth where fires burn us forever and there is no water for our thirst."

"Our ancestors told us stories of our old, old homeland in a land far away," Chief Madok said. "There smoke from these underground fires you speak of come from the tops of mountains. So what you say must be true. And if it is, then surely you must be a man without a mind if you serve this Devil instead of the Great God."

"You are right, Chief Madok, but under the Devil's influence I have done terrible things. Once I killed a man."

"Why did you kill him?"

"He was trying to kill me, even though he had no reason to kill me."

"Then you did right to kill him. If you had not killed him, then another would have. You must not be foolish enough to think you did a bad thing if he deserved death. It would not be the manly way. A warrior must fight if an enemy comes against him, and sometimes he must kill. It is better to live in victory than to die in defeat. It is the way of the world."

"Still, I was not happy to kill a man."

"The enemy of God you spoke of put the thought in your

head to trouble you and turn you from your purpose."

"And what is my purpose?"

"Our people believe the purpose of a man begins where he is. There is a saying among my people: "The oak must sprout where the acorn falls." And if the Great God created the world, as our own stories tell, and set the sun and moon and all the tomorrows of our lives in their pathways, then everything is by his order. You are here, Matthew, so it means that the Great God let you kill the man so you could come among us and teach us his way."

Matthew bowed his head in silence at the Chief's words. They rang true and he had no wiser ones. For a long time they sat in silence in the Cherokee way. Then Matthew spoke.

"Chief Madok, you are wise, much wiser than I. And your words are true. I accept that I am here not by my doing but by God's plan. I will teach you and your people all I know of the Great God. And henceforth I will be obedient to him so that I may teach obedience. From now on, everything must be in the name of God. From the French *unegas* who visit our village from time to time, I shall gather materials in their tongue or mine, books they are called in my tongue, so that I may have reliable truths and not just my weak recollections."

"You must say the right words so the right things may happen. And you must say 'our' people, for now you are one of us. We could have killed you or let you die in the old way, but the Great God had set before us another pathway."

"Our people," Matthew repeated softly under his breath. He thought of his life beyond the mountains, years spent serving Master Richard Blackwell and Sir Henry's family and before that, now almost dreamlike in time and distance, his earliest years in another world in France and old Wales. Could it be that what he thought was the set course of his life was a preparation for his true life? Was he meant to live among people whom his kind viewed as savages? Was his life just now beginning, finally beginning?

The next day dawned in autumn splendor and he was anxious to climb the mountains with Agali and think many thoughts. But her face showed concern.

"The season is closing and winter is coming, Matthew. Mother Kawani says that it will soon turn cold and heavy snow will fall in the higher mountains. She is wise and sees such things in her dreams. We must listen to her words."

"Surely Mother Kawani is mistaken this time, Agali. I have never seen a more beautiful day. Come, come, I want to go up to the mountaintop! You can gather your herbs and roots while I consider the things Chief Madok told me yesterday. Come! It's all right. The day is beautiful and the weather is fine."

Agali went reluctantly, often stopping to look back at the village. For a few hours it seemed that Matthew was right. The sun was warm but without being hot and winter was still far away. There was order and peacefulness all around. They had climbed above problems. Without being able to put it into words, Matthew knew at that moment that problems were mostly a point of view that vanished if one climbed high enough to have the right perspective. He could find no fault in what Chief Madok had told him. His words made sense, and for the first time since the death of Master Richard he felt free of dread. Matthew still felt something like fear, not the fear of his old mistakes but the uncertain direction in which the new truths beginning to appear in his life would send him.

Nature seemed to approve. He dozed in the peacefulness of the world. Agali shook him awake.

"We must go, Matthew, the storm is coming!"

"Storm? What storm?"

"There!" she said excitedly, pointing to the distant slopes. "There where the mountains rise the highest."

In the north a gray haze blotted out the fall colors, and behind it dark gray clouds climbed over the mountains like giant spiders.

"It is the storm Mother Kawani saw in her dream! Come, Matthew, we must hurry! Storms like this come faster than we can run!"

She was right. The gray haze sped towards them, leaping from one ridge to the next. Now Matthew could see the swirling snow and the first shock of cold air rattled the bushes, tearing yellow and golden leaves from the trees and sending them flying in wild disorder down the mountain. They ran, but it was several miles to the protecting cliffs and caves along the creek and much further to the village. By the time they reached the caves their breath was steaming in the cold and the snow was falling so thickly that they could barely see the trail.

The cave was comparatively warm and stocked with wood left over from their previous fires. They sat and waited for the storm to pass, but after several hours it was snowing as hard as ever.

"It is starting to get dark," Matthew observed, "We may have to spend the night here."

"We have food," Agali said hopefully. "You did not eat the meat I brought for you. And I can start a fire."

"It looks like it's going to come to that."

"I do not understand your words."

"I mean we shall have to stay here tonight. It's too far and cold to go in the dark."

They stayed. Agali conjured a fire from the charred limbs left from their last visit to the cave. But as the hours passed it grew colder and the fire was too small for much warmth. They had only their clothes and the beaver skin Agali brought to hold the herbs and roots. Matthew could see she was trembling from the cold and he was shivering himself. "Bring the skin and come here beside me. We will be warmer together."

They piled all the wood they could find on the fire. Then she snuggled up beside him as the winds moaned and snow fell throughout the night.

Morning dawned crisp and clear and their breath steamed in the cold air. The storm was over, the fire reduced to embers, and Agali was no longer a maiden.

Forefathers.com

When I was growing up, there were stories in my family, which is part Cherokee on my mother's side, about a Chief Madoc, or Madok (not sure about the spelling). Supposedly he was a white man, a prince, so the story goes, who, long before Columbus, led his followers to America. But there the story goes off in all directions. One version of the legend was that he became a chief of the Cherokees. Somewhere else I read, though, that he and his men married into an Indian tribe in the north called the Mandan, Menden, or Manten, something like that. Another version I read said he died in a battle near what I believe is the Ohio River. One of my uncles told me the whole story was a bunch of bull. But on the other hand, My Grandmother always swore that her grandmother told her old stories about Chief Madok of the Tennessee Cherokees. Can anybody shed some light on the story?

Marilyn Stokesbury Wilcox
Tucson, Arizona

...

Because I have Stokesbury ancestors myself, I have decided to respond to your request, even though normally I wouldn't deign to get involved in things of this level. Your uncle was right. The fable of Prince Madoc spread through several Native American tribes, but in every case it is the merest farrago. In the British Isles, the story grew out of an obscure and equally fanciful medieval legend intended to strengthen Welsh nationalism as Wales struggled against the English kings. It was revived later to support spurious English priority in North America over the claims of Spain and France. In point of fact, there may have been a Prince Madoc, as there could have been a local Romanized Celtic chieftain in much earlier times by the name of Arturius, whom we read of as King Arthur. It is even possible that

Prince Madoc sailed from Wales to escape a fratricidal conflict in his family following his father's death. But the story of Welshmen in America is pure fiction. If he sailed for America in 1170, as the myth claims, his primitive vessel was surely swamped and lost at sea. If he went anywhere, most likely he would have sailed for Brittany in France where Celtic people, fleeing the Anglo-Saxon invaders, had settled centuries earlier. In short, Ms Wilcox-Stokesbury, there is no evidence that a Prince or Chief Madoc visited America. I have come across the story many times in my work and take every opportunity to debunk it. It has no historical or scientific merit whatsoever, as any reputable scholar will tell you.

    --J. Stokesbury-Sinclair, PhD, Distinguished Professor of Archeological Studies, Department of Archeology, University of Danville

  ...

    With respect to the learned Professor Stokesbury-Sinclair, though maybe distant kin to us, he doesn't know his head from a hole in the ground. In my family we have old documents going back to the 1600s and, as hard evidence, an ancient Welsh Crucifix that once belonged to Chief Madok of our Tennessee Cherokee clan. (My family was originally from there and also has Cherokee blood.) It has been handed down in the Stokesbury family since the 1700s, and in earlier centuries before the coming of the whites, it passed from one Cherokee chief to another, all named Madok. They revered it as a sacred icon, which made it easier to convert our family's Cherokee clan to Christianity when our ancestor Matthew Stokesbury married into the tribe and explained the meaning of the Crucifix. At one time my Dad considered donating it to the Museum of

Tennessee History, but ran into the same attitude expressed by Dr. Stokesbury-Sinclair. After meeting with the curator, who yawned and looked at his watch during the interview, Dad realized he would probably toss it into the garbage heap the minute his back was turned. Dad, a blunt man if ever there was one, told the curator to go to hell and kept the Crucifix. Bottom line, Marilyn, you can believe the stories your Grandmother told you. (And by the way, judging by your hyphenated Stokesbury surname, perhaps you and I are related somewhere back in the line. If you wish and will give me a mailing address, I'll be happy to send you a picture of the Crucifix along with information about our family. Anyway, I would like to know more about your family line since I continue to gather information about the Stokesbury family in America and Wales.)

    --Jim Stokesbury, Sacramento, California

...

If Jim Stokesbury is so convinced that he possesses a rare historical artifact, why hasn't he submitted it to scientific tests to determine its age? The story sounds highly dubious to me. Stories are easy to concoct and take on an unholy life of their own. Real proof is harder to come by.

    --J. Stokesbury-Sinclair, PhD

...

For the same reason, Dr. Stokesbury-Sinclair, my Dad refused to leave it in the hands of the museum curator years ago. You have raised doubts about my integrity; I do not question yours, only your unwillingness to consider other possibilities. I am not a PhD, in fact not even a college graduate, but I know that things which don't fit into established theories have a way of being swept under the scientific rug and never seen again. I'll show you the Madok Crucifix if you are willing to come to California, but I will not let it out of my sight. Need I say more?

--Jim F. Stokesbury, Sacramento, California

...

Chapter 5.
The Foreshadowing

Forefathers.com

[Early Families of Massachusetts, Vol. III, Page 145, entry 17, 2nd column. It is not known if familial kinship existed between Horatio Stafford, stonemason, who was known to be residing in Boston as early as 1640, and David Stafford, first born of the twin sons of Daniel and Sally Stafford of Stafford, England. Their common craft and surname suggests, but does not prove, kinship. David Stafford bought a Boston property in 1668 and gained a reputation as a master mason in that city and later enhanced his standing as the wealthy owner of several major establishments. Sometimes mistaken in his native Stafford for his brother Phillip, who migrated to the Virginia Colony after a turbulent sojourn in France, David Stafford went to considerable pains to redress some of the misdeeds of his brother. No love was lost between the twins as young men, and as far as the matter may be surmised, they never saw each other again after their adolescence. Nevertheless there was a strange connection between them that is related in the following account.]

...

Four years passed and Katherine's French Academy for young ladies grew apace with Charles Towne itself. Her financial status was now secure and she was socially established and respected as owner and headmistress of her flourishing school. The turmoil she had endured in Hampton and in the first months of residence in Charles Towne, though it had left no outward effect on her remarkable physical beauty, inwardly moderated her inclination to fanciful, girlish dreams of love and romance. Despite her love of things French, she now felt herself to be more English than ever before, and hereditary practicality was the stabilizing feature of her life as her youthful sentimentality faded. The shock of Phillip's betrayal and desertion had scarred her too deeply for full recovery and was an enduring buffer to new attractions. She did not waver in her resolve to spurn all amorous overtures from her many admirers. She admitted to herself that many among them were upstanding men of truth and morality—though others were enamored also of her growing wealth—but she was still too disillusioned to risk courtship and entertain their hopes. Then there were married men with their sly but obvious insinuations of willingness to comfort her. But she was content without being happy; the respect she enjoyed compensated to a degree for the decline of her youthful hopes of love and romance. There was comfort, if not happiness, in resignation to the placid emotional life to which fate had consigned her. Furthermore, the maternal fulfillment she enjoyed with her three splendid children enriched her life in an entirely different dimension. The compromise was not happiness, and certainly not balanced, for she was still a deeply passionate woman, but it resembled happiness enough to be a passable substitute. She could go on with her life. Motherhood, the academy, and public standing, not romantic love, were now her destiny.

Or so she reasoned to herself until February 10, 1684 when petite and pretty Claire fairly rushed into her office to announce that a gentleman wished urgently to speak with her.

"And the gentleman's name, Claire?" Katherine asked her in French. "Is he the father of one of our girls?"

"No, Madam, and I neglected to ask him his name, but he is very handsome!"

"And what is the nature of the handsome stranger's business with me?" Katherine asked her sarcastically.

"*Je ne le sais pas*, I know not, Madam, only that he says it is urgent."

"Very well, Claire, show the gentleman in."

With that Katherine turned her back to the door and busied herself with other matters. She did not wish to seem eager to attend a total stranger, especially one who called unannounced. It had been a particularly trying day and she was not of a mind to waste her time with strangers. When Claire escorted him into the office, she waited a moment before turning to face him. Then upon seeing Phillip Stafford standing before her, she felt dizzy with rage and the room swam before her eyes. When she came fully to herself again, Claire and Beatrice were fanning her and rubbing her hands and face. Phillip kept his distance but concern registered in his features. Katherine waved the young women away.

"Thank you, ladies, but I'm all right, just a moment of lightheadedness. Will you bring me a glass of water, please? And give me a moment alone with this man."

As both girls ran to fetch it, Katherine turned with cold fury in her eyes to confront Phillip.

"How dare you show your face here, miserable cad and scoundrel that you are!" she hissed, rising from her chair, eyes and features ablaze with anger. "Remove yourself at once and never darken my door again!"

"Madam, Madam, please calm yourself, I beg you," he responded in his soothing and familiar baritone voice. "I am not Phillip. I note with sadness, though not surprise, that my brother has done you some great wrong, as he has to so many persons, including our family. I must confess to you the obvious: Phillip is, or perhaps was by now, my twin brother. For I know nothing of what has become of him. I am, madam, David Stafford, at your service and the Savior's, and it is urgent that you permit me to explain the purpose of my visit, which is obviously as disturbing to you as the reason is painful for me."

Katherine interrupted her imprecations in mid-sentence as a look of doubt and puzzlement came over her features. "You, you are not Phillip?" she said hesitantly. Then angry at her own momentary credulity, she resumed her indignation in even harsher tones but in French: "*Montrez-moi la main droite, monsieur, et nous verrons si ce que vous dites est vrai ou faux*" (Show me your right hand, sir, and we shall see if what you say is true or false).

"My French is poor, madam, but I believe you told me to show you my right hand."

He dutifully held out his hand. The livid saber scar she remembered above his thumb was not there. Her eyes widened in surprise and astonishment. "Then it is true, you are not Phillip! But this is impossible!" she said, befuddled by the conflicting certainties her reason and her eyes were telling her.

"Nor am I his keeper, madam, only the redresser of some of his wrongs. We are both victims of his chicaneries, as are others in uncounted numbers. But these are sensitive matters better treated in private. Might we arrange a time and place to discuss them without undue disturbance or inadvertent ears to hear what must needs be said between us but spread no further?"

Though still agitated and not yet emotionally convinced that the man was not Phillip, Katherine could not disagree with his reasoning. Yet she was mindful of the commotion and gossip his presence could cause if he remained unidentified, or worse, if the pose turned out to be yet another deception and he was, after all, the husband whose death she had announced years earlier. Who he was and a justifiable reason for his presence in Charles Towne were matters that urgently needed to be clarified. Before any private conversation, however, it had to be made clear to as many of her friends and acquaintances as possible that this was her brother-in-law come to pay his respects to his widowed sister-in-law and her children, most particularly his nephew Jeremy. The best way to proceed, she decided, would be to gather intimate friends for a tea that very evening. It would be risky to delay. David did not object but rather understood and appreciated her foresight and concern for their respective reputations.

Although he did not display the seductive charm and savoir-faire of his brother, David impressed Katherine's friends with his compelling honesty and gentlemanly conduct. Those who remembered Phillip—and the curious included Katherine most of all—could not help staring at him, for his features and stature were duplicates of his brother's, and his resonant baritone voice stirred disturbing recollections of Phillip. Katherine was pleased and relieved when her friends left her house completely persuaded, as was she, that David Stafford had shown himself to be a trustworthy gentleman, and in the unconscious manner of the wealthy, a man of substance. Several of the men expressed their hope that this visit would not be his last to Charles Towne and that he might see fit to establish commercial links with the Carolina Colony. Such men, they said forcefully, were needful for the Colony to flourish.

Even though it was an effort for her to trust the man, at least her fears of gossip and misunderstanding were alleviated by the favorable impression her closest friends formed of David. She had no qualms in inviting him for dinner, for not to do so now that she was surely to be under scrutiny would stir gossip, just as too much familiarity could injure the good reputation she had worked so carefully to build. She introduced him to her children, who warmed spontaneously to his affectionate way with them. Mary and Jeremy happily sat in his lap.

Leaning on his knee, Henry looked up at him and to Katherine's embarrassment, asked hopefully, "Sir, are you our father? I think I remember your face from when I was a little boy."

"No, lad," he replied, smiling and draping an arm across Henry's shoulders, "I am your Uncle David. But I hope we shall have other occasions to deepen our family ties and become good friends, for I see that you are a strong and handsome lad indeed."

By the time the children were asleep, Katherine was beginning to trust David. They talked well into the evening hours. Carefully choosing her words and artfully omitting complicity in any tawdry details, she explained some of circumstances surrounding her relationship with Phillip.

"I cannot express the sorrow I feel for the pain and unhappiness Phillip brought you, dear Katherine," he responded. "But neither am I surprised to learn of it. If I may speak boldly to the matter, Phillip's conduct deviates not in the least from the pattern of deception common to all his affairs I know of. In my particular case, I act principally on behalf of my two maternal uncles and two younger siblings but am mindful of other misdeeds, some directed against me, and no doubt ignorant of many others for which he must answer, in this life or the next. It is with great sadness that I must speak thusly of my brother, my twin. In physical appearance we exhibit only similarities, but God forbid that I should ever be tempted to tread the dark pathways he chooses. I am by no means a perfect man, but I try to act honorably in all my affairs."

"Phillip spoke of his uncles in Barbados and of their intention to take retirement in England."

"That intention, Katherine, innocently confessed to my brother, led him to commit one of his most despicable misdeeds."

"How so?" she asked, dreading to hear more of Phillip's misdeeds but moved by a morbid curiosity about a man she had loved deeply and now vehemently despised.

"It seems that Phillip began his deception by presenting himself as me, as David Stafford, to my Uncles. They knew something of Phillip's wayward life and being men of honor would not have allowed him into their confidence. But they had, I dare say, a favorable memory and impression of me. And this led to the calamity that I shall describe directly. My Uncles knew I had resettled myself in Boston and we maintained sporadic correspondence via distant kinfolk in England. But ignorant of Phillip's whereabouts, at first none of us had knowledge of you or the children. God only knows what fabulous tales he told my trusting Uncles Alexander and William to carry out his swindle."

"Although I am loath to learn of it, what swindle was that, David?"

"By an unhappy coincidence of timing, I had written my Uncles that I desired to see more of the world, the whole of my existence having been spent in Stafford and Boston. Keenest among my hopes was the prospect of seeing them again after so many years. Having amassed a comfortable estate and without binding family ties in Boston or England, I mentioned that a voyage to Barbados was foremost on my listing of desirable destinations, though I hoped also to visit other islands and perhaps the southern mainland as well. In time I received correspondence from them in which they expressed their eagerness to see me. In some manner that is still unclear to me, they learned about you. I surmise that soon after he met you in Hampton and before his later schemes were still immature, Phillip so informed them with some particulars about your family. It was there I learned of your remove to Charles Towne where, at last, I have happily found you and your children."

"And what has become of your uncles and their intention to return to England?"

"Insofar as I can determine, it appears that Phillip pilfered their fortune by offering himself as their agent, using the unhappy coincidence of his visit, his exact physical resemblance to me, and their desire to return to their old homeland. He then disappeared, perhaps removing to Martinique or one of the islands in that region, leaving them near impoverishment in

Barbados. The precise details of his mischief are unclear to me, but needless to say, their funds, placed trustingly in his hands, never reached England. Now I must with all possible haste proceed to the island to alleviate their plight as best I can."

"And what remedy do you foresee, if I be so bold as to ask?"

"If they are of a mind to return to England and have strength for the voyage, I shall see that they are comfortably reestablished in old Stafford. On no account shall I abandon them in backward Barbados. Perhaps they will choose to live with me and my siblings Garth and Martha in Boston where I have a spacious, near-empty house, though I fear the New England winters might prove overly rigorous for them."

"From your remarks, I gather you have no family of your own, David. Are you not married?"

"No I am not. When circumstances offered me a better chance at life in Boston I was engaged for marriage, but the lady who was to be my wife could not, at the final hour, bring herself to leave her parents and brave the ocean voyage and the uncertainties of life in America. She pleaded her youth and asked me for a greater grant of time. We parted in tearful sorrow and with hearty pledges of reunion and marriage in some happier day. But time eroded our young love and our pledges faded to melancholy memories. After some years we ceased to correspond and I suppose that neither of us wished to continue to entertain sentiments that belonged to our youth but not to our future."

"What became of her?"

"I confess my ignorance of her fate, as she surely became indifferent to mine. Forgive me for speaking of the matter at too great length."

"You must have cared deeply for her at one time."

"Indeed, so I did, or at least so fancied, which made our parting all the sadder for me. But after years of more mature reflection, I came to see that sentiments blinded us to an obvious truth: we both had many traits that did not promise a harmonious union. She was a gay girl, heartily fond of parties, dance and song, whereas I was concerned foremost with the work and responsibility of establishing myself."

"Stop me, David, if I ask questions that discomfit you, but were you ever again so deeply attracted to anyone?"

"No, not yet, but though I have not found love, I retain the hope that one day it will find me. But turnabout is fair play, Katherine, and surely your story is much more interesting than my plain life. From what I know and to judge by your handsome older children, I gather you were widowed before Phillip came into your life, were you not?"

"Yes, I was married to a man named Richard Blackwell not long after my Father and I left France for Hampton in the Virginia Colony. You will no doubt think me flighty, David, as indeed I was as a girl. In my young years my imagination was puffed up with vaporous sentimentalities, which prepared me only to be charmed witless by Phillip. I married Richard under protest only because my father pressured me into the union. But let me hasten to add, my father acted with the best of paternal intentions. Our family had lost almost everything meaningful in the Civil War, above all my two precious brothers, John and Pickford, may God rest their souls. After my mother's death in France when fortune and favor had long since abandoned him and he knew that he, too, must soon leave this world, my father had as his remaining desire to see me conveniently wed. I had not the heart to oppose him even if it meant sacrificing what I errantly believed to be my own happiness."

"I surmise, then, that the union with Mr. Blackwell was not altogether a happy one."

"No, not at first, though later it was bearable and at least I had my darling children Henry and Mary after his tragic death. And of my marriage to Phillip was born sweet little Jeremy. They and the Academy fill my life."

Not many days thereafter before Katherine and the children, David said farewell. All were teary-eyed, for during his short stay, mutual affections had grown strong. David took passage on an outbound ship for Barbados. Beyond that destination, plans were unmade and dependent on the wishes and health of his uncles. In any case, as soon as possible, whether measured in weeks or months, he must needs return to his affairs in Boston. Charles Towne had impressed him most favorably, particularly his conversations with town leaders regarding commercial needs and possibilities in the young colony. Nevertheless, when, if ever, he might make another trip to Carolina, though high among the hopes of all assembled, was unforeseeable and for the moment, unlikely.

Katherine soon resumed the former balance of life with the children, the Academy, and her circle of friends, but she could not so readily recapture the tranquility she had known before David's visit. The initial shock and anger that his physical resemblance to Phillip aroused in her soon gave way to cordiality and appreciation, though not without leaving a residue of agitation in her spirit. She cherished her female friends and coolly kept several respectable admirers at arm's length, but David reminded her how much her life could be enriched by trustworthy men—if such there were—who would offer genuine friendship and respect for her emotional boundaries. She had endured a loveless union with Richard and adored Phillip with a consuming passion in the other. Yet she remembered both marriages with hurt and humiliation and determined never again to open her heart to love. The world saw her as a wealthy and beautiful woman, and not even those closest to her could sense all the bitterness and hurt she harbored for the way life that had mocked her youthful idealism. The girl she once was still yearned to be cherished, but the mature woman she had become distrusted every romantic impulse. Not that she cast all the blame on others; her own impulsive sentimentality was foremost in fault.

The languorous summer of 1685 passed and autumn was nearly spent before a schooner brought to Charles Towne a post from David. Presently in England, he was arranging a comfortable living for his Uncle William Woolsey in Stafford. Sadly, his elder Uncle Alexander did not live to see his homeland again but died only a fortnight after David arrived in Barbados. From nothing David wrote, but by hints in his correspondence, Katherine deduced that as he feared, he found them reduced to near penury and too old and exhausted to rebuild their fortunes. David entreated his uncle William to remove to Boston so as to be with his closest kin, but though the old gentleman was grateful, Mother England made the stronger appeal.

"My remaining days in this world go dwindling in number, dear David, and I should like to complete the cycle of my life, ending it where it began, in dear old Stafford. Besides, from what I hear of the harsh winters of New England, I fear the cold would hasten my demise. At this point in my life I have no other compelling wish and but one regret: that Alexander was unable to share these last days with me."

David repeated how delightful it had been to meet her, Henry, Mary, and Jeremy, and to make the acquaintance of so many good people of Charles Towne. He closed with these words: "For me it was a delightful visit of which I preserve cherished memories and one I should like to repeat if God grants me time enough and chance. Were it merely up to me, I should as quickly as possible bend my steps southward again. So man dreams and proposes, but at the last God decides and disposes. In any case, I must complete living arrangements with my remaining kin for my Uncle William here in Stafford, then sail for Boston to put my affairs in good order before untried matters foremost in my mind may be contemplated."

She wondered what he meant by these vague words: '. . . before any untried matters in my mind may be contemplated'. What "untried matters" did he mean? But time passed and her curiosity diminished under the press of daily, mundane chores. In any case, she told herself, it was an idle matter without consequence. Although she would have welcomed him, she told herself several times that probably she had seen David for the first and last time.

But on a Tuesday afternoon in late May, petite Beatrice fairly ran in to Katherine's office breathless with the news: "Madame, Monsieur Stafford *est revenu*, he has returned! He is here!" Katherine barely had time to smooth her hair and compose herself before David stood smiling in the doorway. Later she would scold Beatrice for her undignified comportment in his hearing, but she could barely control her own excitement and pleasure upon seeing him again.

"Forgive me, dear Katherine, for arriving without giving you prior notice, perhaps warning would be a choicer word. No doubt you have perceived that calling unannounced is one of my many shortcomings. In my eagerness to see you and receive word of the children again, I hied myself directly here from the wharf. I should have taken lodging first and then sent word to you. I hope my presence is not a burdensome intrusion. And by the by," he added with a chuckle, extending his right hand, "as you can see, it has no scar. I am myself, that is, still myself."

"So I noticed, David," Katherine answered with a smile, "but I needed no such proof this time to know that you are the same dear gentleman the children and I met last year. And far from an intrusion, much less a burden, your visit is a most welcome surprise," she said, taking him by the hands and planting phantom kisses on each cheek in the French manner.

"I shall not long detain you from your tasks, Katherine. My porters await me outside with my trunks, and even now men are unlading my possessions from the ship. But to the main point: are all well? Are the children in good health, as you, by your appearance, evidently are?"

"Indeed, David, we are all well, thanks be to God. But what of you? We shall be eager to learn all the many things that have befallen you in your several destinations since you took your leave from us last year."

"And I with the same curiosity wish to learn what has happened here in Charles Towne, which I see has grown apace. But first, I must hasten back to attend to matters of lodging and storage. The porters will grow impatient if I tarry longer."

"You speak as though your visit will be long, as we hope."

"On that particular and others there is much to say. But I beg you, let us delay that conversation until we are at our leisure to discuss them."

The opportunity came that very afternoon. David was comfortably lodged in Travelers Inn and his possessions stored in Gilmore's warehouse near the wharf. Katherine invited him for tea and a reunion with her close friends, many of whom he recalled from his earlier visit.

"We are delighted to see you again in Charles Towne, Mr. Stafford," said haberdasher Bernard Clifford. "You will no doubt recall our collective hope that you might see fit to establish commercial links with Charles Towne. Remark how it has grown since your visit a year ago. May we now expect, sir, to hear the welcome news that you have favorably entertained our hope?"

"You may indeed, sir, if all do welcome the news," he responded with a quick glance at Katherine. "Not only do I intend to establish those connections but also to take up residence in this fair city."

"That is indeed good news to us all, Mr. Stafford," Mr. Clifford smilingly assured him. "Our community needs enterprising men of means to assure its future. I dare say I speak for all here that we welcome you and offer our assistance if we may be of service to you in any way."

"Hear! Hear!" said a chorus of voices.

"Katherine, we have not heard from you," said Mrs. Bankhead. "What do you think of your brother-in-law's intention to remove to Charles Towne?"

"I was thinking most directly of the children, and recalling how quickly they grew fond of David last year, I celebrate his return." Then turning to David, she added: "The children have asked me many times about you, David. And now that they have heard of your arrival, I doubt not that this evening you shall have a welcoming committee of eager small folk to greet you. It will be most convenient for them to have a man's influence in the family."

"I shall strive to be a good influence on them without being an inconvenience for you, Katherine."

Several of the women, though perhaps none of the men, noticed a slight tremor in his voice and a faint respondent color that came to her cheeks.

Rector Jonathan Meeks spoke to his particular interest and turned the conversation in another direction. "I shall welcome you into our worship at St. Phillips, Mr. Stafford. You are, I shall assume, a member in good standing in our Mother Church."

"Father Meeks, through no merit of mine but by the grace of God I am in harmony with the Church, and may God grant that I continue to be faithful in worship and service here as I was in Boston and have been since my boyhood in England."

It was evident from the frown that creased his face that Father Meeks was not pleased with something in the tone or turn of David's words. But he murmured perfunctorily, "I perceive, therefore, Mr. Stafford, that you acknowledge no obstacle that would hinder you from becoming a devoted servant of our Lord at St. Phillip. I shall hope that such is the case."

The comment, proper in words but cold in tone, chilled the easy cordiality that had prevailed at tea and replaced it with a tension with obvious effects but without reasonable cause. Not long thereafter the guests began leaving. David was taken aback by the Rector's oblique, frosty tone and wondered what he had said that could have offended the clergyman. Later, when they were alone he asked Katherine about it.

"Do not fret over the matter, David. Perhaps it will soothe your feelings somewhat to learn that Father Meeks has said similar things to many of us, myself included. There is a distressing coldness in his character that dismays many of us. In my case, the untidy circumstance of a having as a parishioner a woman twice a wife and twice a relict seems to annoy him greatly. We—and I believe I speak for all—have come to consider his peculiarities a sort of diffidence and a personal shortcoming of Father Meeks and for the good of the Church try to overlook it."

Before their bedtime, Henry, Mary, and Jeremy showed how delighted they were have an uncle in their midst and asked him several times as they climbed on his knees if he really intended to live in Charles Towne.

"Yes, I do intend to live here, and I know of no circumstance that makes me happier than to have about me two stout nephews and a pretty niece to bring enjoyment to my life. We shall have good times together. But you shall have to teach me your games. I am an old bachelor unused to fun but willing to learn. Will you then teach me how to play your games?"

"Yes!" they said as one.

"I shall show you how to play ball," exclaimed Henry. "It's not hard to learn."

"If you don't know how to play tag, Uncle David, Jeremy and I shall show you. Shan't we, Jeremy?" added Mary.

"Yes, but you're not too old to run, are you, Uncle David? Asked little Jeremy.

"Oh, I think I can still run a bit," David laughed, "but maybe not so fast as you, Jeremy. For I see that you are a good stout lad."

"David, you have won over the children in a masterful way," Katherine told him later when they were alone. "One would think you have had a long experience with children."

"Unhappily no, as you are aware, but with your blessing I intend to be a good uncle to these three."

"To all three?" she asked timidly. "I understand in the case of Jeremy, but Henry and Mary . . .?"

"I claim them all without distinction of blood relationship but with equal affection, if it please you, Katherine."

"Oh, David, it does please me very much, more than I can tell you. How generous of you."

"No, Katherine, you are the generous one to allow me to be an uncle to these beautiful little ones. But before I get carried away with that pleasant prospect, we shall have to see whether I really can run at tag and play ball," he laughed.

As the summer passed their conversations became more relaxed and intimate, though ever circumspect and respectful. David explained to Katherine that his circumstances in Boston had become increasingly stressful since his return from England. Garth, his younger brother, with whom he had partnered in various enterprises since their arrival in Boston, now chaffed under his directorship and felt a growing urge to control his own entrepreneurial fortunes, particularly in shipbuilding and shipping. In this their sister Martha sided with Garth, who was close to her in age and character. Finally, it became painfully clear to all that a change was inevitable. David then proposed a buyout much to the advantage of his younger siblings. They agreed and the transaction was completed without serious disruption of family harmony.

Meanwhile, as a transitional measure, David purchased two commercial buildings in Charles Towne for the purpose of leasing warehouse space to solid enterprises in order to provide himself a convenient and substantial income. But his eventual plans were more elaborate. He explained to Katherine and mentioned to some in her circle of friends that as soon as he was sufficiently at ease in Charles Towne and knowledgeable with the region, he intended not only to become a land broker but to set aside planation tracts for cultivation under his personal supervision.

"What sort of cultivation have you in mind?" Katherine inquired when they were alone.

"Rice, for one. With its mild climate, abundant water, and improving shipping facilities, this country is proving to be ideal for growing that grain."

"But, David, and I ask this with respect, have you the required experience? You have spent your life in Boston and England, and I cannot image growing rice in either place."

"Neither can I," he laughed, "but I am in a position and lately of a disposition to try new things. Rice farming is one of them, and I may also try indigo. It will require adjustments for me to become a planter, but I believe it will prove lucrative."

"Have you still other new ventures in mind?"

"Yes, several, but one above all others and indeed much more personal."

"If it is not an indiscretion to ask, what might it be?"

"Matrimony."

"Matrimony? Did I hear you correctly? I thought bachelorhood was a confirmed way of life for you."

"I long thought so myself. Yet you recall that in early manhood I proposed marriage to a young woman in England. Her rejection of my suit sent my life along a different course, which altered but did not displace my early conviction that marriage was a better state than the single life."

"Since you have affirmed your intention so directly, may I assume that you have a lady in mind?"

"Indeed you may assume so, Katherine. In my heart I have chosen the lady, but it remains to be seen whether she will have me."

"Do I know her?"

"Intimately."

"Are you willing to reveal her name?"

"I see no reason to keep it from you. Her name is Katherine."

"Katherine, but that is my name and I know of no other 'Katherine' in our circle of friends. She is then, I take it, a resident of Boston."

"No, I know no one by that name in Boston. But let me demur no longer. You, dearest Katherine, are the lady, and I shall be the happiest and most honored man on God's good earth if you will accept me as your husband."

She stared at him for a moment, then lowered her eyes as they moistened with tears. He touched her arm affectionately, but she turned her face and pulled away.

"Dear Katherine, I did not mean to cause you anguish, and I regret that without so intending, it seems that I have. My love for you took root a year ago and has grown without surcease since then. It is genuine and strong, and if there be any honor or truth in me, these are the qualities that move me to make this declaration of my love and petition of marriage to you. Yet poorly versed in matters of the heart and a mere bumbler in my treatment of women, I see that I have offended you. I ask your forgiveness."

"Oh, David," she said, daubing her eyes with a handkerchief, "you have not offended me. Stunned and surprised me, yes, but offended me, no. But marriage is out of the question. Our circumstances would not allow it even if I were worthy to be your wife. Consider the principal obstacle: we are family. Your brother was, and mayhap still is so legally, my husband. You know some of the unhappy circumstances of my life. I had my chances for happiness and either my poor choices or fate put an unhappy end to them."

"I respect your thinking but for good reasons soundly reject your objections. Everything you have said I have repeated to myself a thousand times. As for the 'principal obstacle', as you call it, I have dwelt on it longest. Leaving aside your first marriage, which has no direct bearing on the matter, there are two reasons that invalidate it. First, Phillip either married you under false pretenses or, second, abandoned you years ago. Either circumstance is enough to free you of any and all legal ties to him, living or deceased. Consider his relationship to you a foreshadowing, a false simulacrum, of a true marriage that I now propose to you. If I may speak even more boldly, the shadow he cast was empty and dark like all shadows, but our life together can be the substance his falsified life lacked. I have discussed all these matters with legal authorities and they corroborate everything I tell you. English law is clear on the point of abandonment provided the requisite number of years have passed, as indeed they have."

"But the Church would still view us as in-laws, which is as prohibitive a relationship as brother and sister, so I understand."

"No, dear Katherine, for the same reasons that our code of Common Law can set aside a marriage as I described, so the Church can similarly void an invalid union or annul it in cases of abandonment. In any case, a civil ceremony, while valid in the eyes of the Church in common practice, may in this instance with greater expediency be set aside, if need be. Strictly speaking, Katherine, at this late date you and I are not in-laws, which means that we may, as consenting adults, enter into the state of matrimony, which will be binding and permanent in the eyes of the Church so long as we both shall live. And it is this union that I propose and ask you to accept."

"I tremble to think what Father Meeks would say if we were to approach him on the subject. No doubt he would refuse to allow such a ceremony in a most fulminating and demeaning manner."

"Luckily, my dear, Father Meeks is Rector only of St. Phillip's, not the Church of England. There are other, wiser priests than that shallow fellow."

"David, would you really wish to marry a woman like me?" she asked.

"No, my darling, not a woman like you, but you yourself. And not only do I wish with all my heart to be your husband but desire further to be a father to your children."

"To all of them? Not just Jeremy . . .?"

"I believe we settled that question some time ago. What I said as their uncle, I repeat as their prospective father. I do not believe I speak in vain when I say that the children have rendered a verdict in my favor, albeit," David added with a chuckle, "stout Henry and spritely Jeremy make light of my clumsiness of foot in our games of ball and tag. And pretty Mary laments my dullness of wit because my memory falters at recalling the names of all her dolls."

Her eyes still glistened with tears but a smile brightened her face. "You joke of course; Henry adores you, as do Mary and Jeremy. But on the main point, David, I have determined never again to entertain thoughts of marriage. And there we must leave the matter. You have won my confidence and respect, and, yes, my affection and gratitude also as a friend, but my heart must remain closed to other feelings. Now, with all these feelings firm and foremost, I consider the matter settled and must ask you to leave me."

David rose at once, bowed, and with unusually curt words, "as you wish, Katherine," left after a few whispered words to Hanna as she opened the door for him. Katherine wondered if she had spoken too harshly and offended him. Another conflictive agitation, she sighed, to the many he had aroused in her.

But in the coming days and weeks, she discovered that if David was more circumspect in his methods because of her rebuff, he was undismayed in his eventual purpose. He pressed his suit with attentions paid her at every opportunity. She rejoiced in his affection for her children, for true to his word, he loved them generously and equally. Gradually her guard relaxed. In the abstract she still looked with horror on the thought of matrimony, but David loomed ever larger in her feelings. She was as adamant as ever against another marriage, but she had come to need and depend on David's steady support and friendship. As for her other suitors, she was less interested than ever in listening to their pleas and pledges. To make matters worse, Bernard Clifford, husband of her closest friend Elizabeth, was becoming so obvious in his sly insinuations that Katherine knew she must soon put a stop to them. But how? Elizabeth was devoted to her husband and would not believe the derogatory truth about him. To speak out would mean ridding herself of his advances but most likely at the sacrifice of her friendship with Elizabeth and the ugly possibility that the matter would find its way into public gossip. She did nothing at the time but fretted all the more in private.

One day the chilling thought occurred to her: what if David wearies of my rejection and leaves? Or turns to another woman for the affection I cannot give him? She spent a sleepless night with these bedeviling thoughts. To make matters worse, the very next day David told her that he must return to Boston and thence perhaps to England. His answers to her inquiries were so general as to be evasive, and Katherine was left with another cause for mounting agitation. She reassured herself that his departure was for commercial reasons, as he hinted, and that he should, God willing, make a timely return to Charles Towne. But then dark fears assailed her logic and she had to fight against the idea that he might never return. He had proposed honorable matrimony to her, and she, ever the fool, had rejected him. Would she never learn anything in matters of love? Already a matron in years, she berated herself for being sentimentally still a foolish girl half her age.

Four months later, an eternity for her, David returned, informing her that pending matters in Boston were finally resolved. The last commercial leases held in common with Garth had expired. With a joy she could barely conceal,

Katherine heard his pledge that from now on he would settle himself in Charles Towne and, undistracted, was more determined than ever to pursue his interests in Carolina.

Worn out by emotional turmoil, neither womanly modesty nor sentimental fear could keep her from asking him the tormenting questions: "David, have your interests changed? Do they still include rice and matrimony?"

For the briefest instant he was surprised by her bluntness. Then sensing victory in her obvious anxiety, he smiled, took her by the hand and kissed it. "More than ever, dear Katherine, more than ever. But before I plant rice in the fields, I hope to see it showered on my head in a wedding ceremony."

"Forgive my forwardness, David, but does your lady of choice remain the same?"

"For me there can be none other on earth. You, beloved Katherine, are, and always shall be, the possessor of my heart. How answer you now to my proposal of marriage?"

"The only answer I can give, dear David. In the days and months since we last spoke of the matter, my heart with its reasons has overruled my head with its logic, as Pascal forewarned. My world is upside down. But there is a higher logic to it after all. For plain reason and common sense cannot gainsay the fact that in the hierarchy of affections 'husband' has a far sweeter ring to it than 'brother-in-law'. Against my rational judgment and in despite of the alarums and caveats of my head and old sentimental wounds, Master Stafford, yes, I will marry you. It may seem immodest of me, but I shall confess to you that sentiments which began as cordial admiration of your qualities and affection for your person have deepened in these weeks and months into a love I cannot deny, nor do I have any reason to wish to do so. When I first confronted these feelings, I could not imagine life with you; now, dear David, I confess that I cannot bear the thought of life without you."

"Then save for pending particulars, dearest Katherine, the matter is settled. Surely you knew with the canny insight of your sex that I fell in love with you the first time I met you. You, dear Katherine, are now the resplendent light of my once solitary life, the joy of today and the happy expectation of tomorrow. Now I have a reason to live and to rejoice in life. I shall love you forever."

"And a day?" she smiled as she came to him to accept his embrace.

"Forever and a day," he echoed as he kissed her for the first time.

Ancestors.com

Notable South Carolinians. Vol. IV, pp. 374-379

Married life for Katherine and David appears to have been generally smooth and happy, though her independence of spirit and forthright manner at times bewildered him and tried his patience. But in other regards their wedding was for both a test of will and resolve. Records from that era and letters of their descendants reveal that as both feared, Rector Jonathan Meeks declined to allow the marriage ceremony to take place in St. Phillip Church, despite earnest entreaties by parishioners and sufficient canonical latitude. Finally, David hit upon a solution that coincided with another wish: to visit for a final time his Uncle William Woolsey and to prevail on his boyhood friend Benjamin Pearson, now Rector of St. Vincent's Church of Stafford to unite them in holy matrimony. Katherine named Claire as Acting Supervisor of the Academy in her absence, David appointed trustees to manage his accounts and properties, and they sailed for England on an unspecified date, but most likely in late spring of 1686. Katherine herself made no mention of the irony, but surely it must have crossed her mind, that for the second time she sailed abroad with a man not yet her husband. And not just any man but twin brother of her second. But there the similarities between the two brothers end. They found David's Uncle William happy in Stafford but so diminished in vigor that he lived only a few months, expiring not long before they were set to return to America. But the new couple had the great satisfaction and happy memory of beautiful Katherine walking to the altar on his arm. As for Rector Pearson, he cordially welcomed them and not only agreed to allow the wedding in St. Vincent Church but also to resolve any and all questions of residency and other possible canonical objections to their marriage. After all, David was baptized at St. Vincent's and regarded as a lifelong parishioner. Then during a year of travel in the British Isles they reacquainted themselves with the land of their youth, though Katherine declined to go near her family's expropriated estates in England and Wales. Nevertheless, it was a satisfying sojourn, which greatly enhanced the children's education and enriched their lives with imperishable memories. They returned to Charles Towne, as it was called in those days, in the summer of 1687 and began their long and successful rise to wealth and prominence. But by an unexpected turn of circumstances, only partly explained in the documents, it was not to be in Charles Towne. Nor are the records clear on another matter. Surmising by contextual documentation, it seems that Katherine gave birth to two more children whose gender and names for unknown reasons do not appear in the census records.

--Summarized by archivist P. Wayne Edderly from the <u>*Second Recension of Colonial Carolina censuses.*</u> <u>*Charleston, South Carlina, 1922*</u>

...

Chapter 6.
First Blood

Forefathers.com

[Stories of Old Boston. 2 Vols. "The Tragic Story of Susan Pickford," Vol. 2, pp. 34-38. Publications of the Boston Public Library, Boston, 1947.

Susan Pickford was the daughter and only child of the widower Henry Pickford who settled in 1750 in Waltham, Massachusetts. His family had been attached for many generations to the Beaufort-Essex estate in England. Susan was born in Waltham in 1757 and there her mother Lucy Shire Pickford died in 1759, leaving Susan in the care of nurses. Like his ancestors in England, Henry Pickford was an apple cider maker whose machine was set to wheels and hauled by horse team in due season to area farms whose owners could not justify purchase of their own apparatus. Henry fled England deeply in debt to the Beaufort-Essex family and in peril of imprisonment. But his fortunes reversed so spectacularly—and mysteriously—in Massachusetts that in 1768 he disposed of his machine and his yeoman past and established himself comfortably as a gentleman in Boston proper. Susan, now extraordinarily beautiful and well educated, was betrothed to Jeremy Atwater, once Henry Pickford's hired man. Lieutenant John Beaufort-Essex, philandering descendant of Sir William Beaufort-Essex, asked to be quartered in Pickford mansion. He soon saw in Susan's extraordinary beauty and his discovery of Henry's outstanding debts to his family a way to settle accounts to his pleasure and advantage. Such are the bare elements of the resulting tragedy, a summary of which follows]

On the morning of April 17, 1775 a fisherman saw Susan Pickford's corpse floating seaward in the Charles River. Her body was fully clothed but her dress was torn and there were bloody lacerations and gashes on the face and head. Investigating Constable Albert Stanley reported it as a homicide and the murderer most likely a thief surprised in the act of burglarizing the mansion.

"What about the soldier quartered in the residence? Have you questioned him for relevant information?" asked his sergeant, Milton Blackmore.

"Sir, you should know that Lieutenant Beaufort-Essex, though of a discredited reputation, so I am told, is nonetheless a British officer of one of England's noblest families. I thought it best to avoid antagonisms with the British militia under the tense circumstances of the moment, and to take special care not to impugn his illustrious family."

"Yes, yes, wisely done," the sergeant replied. "But in the interest of justice, we must at least get a statement from him. We are within our rights to do so in a matter this serious. What about servants and maids, and Mr. Henry Pickford himself?"

"Sir, Mr. Henry Pickford is insensible with grief and despite its size, the residence employs only two servants, an elderly female cook of Scottish extraction, Nattie McKenzie, and Miss Pickford's maid, Mary South, in age near to her mistress. The cook claims to have heard nothing, having retired early and slept soundly. As for the maid, she is beside herself with grief and unable as yet to give us a credible account of what she witnessed, or may have heard."

"What do we know about the Pickford girl's woman's normal activities and habits?"

"Sir, the neighbors describe her as a model of discretion and decorum, that she is—or was—betrothed to a young man by name Jeremy Atwater of the Lexington Township, and that her wedding was set for June."

"Aha, now we have information that may yield us results," the Sergeant said in a more energetic tone. "Love is mother to many tragedies. For where love is, jealousy stands beside it as its image and shadow, stirring hatreds and shaping devilish misdeeds, including murder. Bring that fellow to me at once! He bears careful questioning, and I shall do that myself!"

"Yes sir, and what should I do about Lieutenant Beaufort?"

"For the moment nothing. Fetch me the girl's lover, and when the maid has recovered her tranquility, we shall question her."

Jeremy Atwater broke down in despair at the news of Susan Pickford's death, sobbing and cradling his head in his arms. When he had regained a measure of self-restraint, he looked up at the Sergeant with tears in his eyes and rage in his voice.

"Sir, you must arrest that damnable Redcoat quartered in the Mr. Pickford's house! He's the guilty one! He's to blame!"

"Have a care with reckless talk, my good fellow. Your grief is understandable, but baseless accusations will get us nowhere. Why do you point a finger at the Lieutenant, Mr. ah . . . Atwater?"

"Because I know that he is responsible for my sweet Susan's death. That's why."

"And how do you know?"

"Because Susan told me."

"Jeremy, is it? To put the matter in plain words, Jeremy, Miss Pickford is deceased and can tell us nothing. Explain yourself."

"She told me not above a week ago that the Lieutenant had spoken to her in language that disrespected her modesty and bordered on lewd suggestion. Ask the maid; she will tell you the same, I am sure."

Later the maid denied any knowledge of what Atwater claimed.

"Were you not Miss Pickford's personal maid and privy to her affairs?" the Sergeant asked her.

"Yes, sir, I'll not deny it for truth's sake. But Miss Susan told me little. I know nothing about any of this."

"Let me tell you this, Miss South, we have a suspicious death on our hands, mayhap a murder. If you should by an unwise decision conceal information from city authority, which I represent in this instance, you may be guilty of complicity in a crime."

The girl's eyes, big and round, showed her fear. "What means complicity, sir?"

"Complicity in a crime means sharing the guilt for it. We do not assume that you had to do with Miss Pickford's death. Indeed, we do not know that she was murdered. That is why we are asking questions of all who knew her. But if her death was a criminal act and you should keep anything you know from us, then it would mean that you could be to some degree guilty yourself."

"Oh, merciful God! Then I shall tell you all I know and withhold nothing. I loved Miss Pickford and kept her daily in my prayers. And I shall miss her terribly. She was so good and kind to me, and likewise so to one and all."

"Did she have enemies, people who disliked her?"

"Oh, no sir, she becharmed all, young and old, men and

women alike. She was a saintly girl, kind and good to everyone."

"Tell me about her betrothed, Mr. Atwater."

"A kinder gentleman never lived, sir, and none could match him in devotion to Miss Pickford. When the Pickfords yet resided in the Lexington township, Mr. Atwater was but a lad, yet already he saw in Miss Pickford his one and only love. In those early days he worked for Mr. Pickford in the making of apple cider, hauling the mill from one farm to another in the country thereabouts. Then being of age and with a wish to establish himself in a livelihood when Mr. Pickford retired to Boston, Mr. Atwater arranged to buy the machine on generous credit terms offered by his old master. In this way, their friendship remained lively and in the case of Miss Pickford blossomed into a hearty wish to unite their lives and fortunes in marriage. They were to wed in June. Oh . . . how the thought of it doth grieve me now!"

"What can you tell me about Lieutenant Beaufort, lately quartered in the Pickford home?"

"Oh, sir, that is a harder task you ask of me."

"Why so?"

"Because so as not to be guilty of—what did you call it, 'complication'?—I shall have to say dreadful things."

"'Complicity', Mary, 'complicity; so you must tell me what you know, no matter how unpleasant it may be. Did Miss Pickford confide in you about the Lieutenant's attentions?"

"Yes sir, I must confess that she did, but the matter was not so simple as a gentleman's improper regard for a young lady."

"You must explain that remark. Tell me whole of it in your own words, Mary."

"Yes sir. Well, I know not whether the regard the Lieutenant had for Miss Pickford was an expression of honest sentiment. It was said that, though young in years, he was old in . . . worldly experience. That I cannot speak to. For all I know, it could have been the idle chatter of servant girls. But what is certain is that he was dashingly handsome."

"Mary, this sounds like the first page of a bookish romance, but what has it to do with Miss Pickford?"

"Their conversation, so she confided to me, advanced to talk of matrimony."

"But was not Miss Pickford already affianced to Mr. Atwater at the time?"

"Indeed, sir, and that was one cause of a great conflict in her sentiments. The other was that she was unsure of the Lieutenant's sincerity. Besides, she loved Mr. Atwater with a settled love nearly as old as they were. And she remembered fondly her young years in the country. But now she was older and educated in the best Boston schools. As she said, country life was a pleasant memory, but her life was now very different. The more she thought about it, the less sure she was that she could go happily back to the old ways. The Lieutenant was a fresh, exciting emotion and the pathway to a life beyond her grandest dreams. Or, as she feared, a nightmare of scandal and deception. Miss Pickford put it this way: Jeremy was the happy past; Lieutenant Beaufort dangled before her the promise of a greater future. Jeremy Atwater was a man of farms and forests, plain, decent, and devoted, whilst Lieutenant Beaufort was a man of the greater world, clever, of high aristocratic class and devilishly handsome."

"Are you telling me that Miss Pickford intended to break her engagement to Atwater and transfer her affections to the Lieutenant?"

"Sir, she was sorely tempted and I am afraid she so intended."

"Did she tell Atwater of her decision?"

"Sir, unhappily, she did, her sense of loyalty to Mr. Atwater demanded it, she insisted. For she was straightforward in all things."

"Unhappily, you say. I take that to mean that Atwater took the news badly. Did he?"

"Sir, I cannot speak directly to the question, for I did not speak again to Miss Pickford about it."

"When did their conversation take place?"

"Rather late in the evening before her death."

"And you did not see her afterwards, that is, after they had talked?"

"No sir, it was late and I was abed before he left the house."

"Was the Lieutenant in the house at the time?"

"No sir, that same afternoon he was called to duty. It was gossiped about that the Redcoats were about to begin a military action of some kind."

"Yes, so we have all heard. Mary is there anything else you have neglected to tell me that might have to do with Miss Pickford's death?"

"Oh no, sir! I swear on my mother's grave that I have told you all I know about the sad matter. Please do not think I am guilty of complica—complicity. I am an honest girl."

"So you are, Mary, so you are, and we are convinced of your truthfulness. You may go, but as this matter progresses, you may be called on to repeat what you have told me."

After she left, Blackmore summoned Constable Stanley to his office.

"Stanley, if the Pickford girl's death was a murder, pending the coroner's inquest, then we have our man. In the meantime, bring in the man Jeremy Atwater."

"You think he is responsible in some way for her death, not the Lieutenant?"

"I do indeed. As for Lieutenant Beaufort, a man of his standing would never offer an honest proposal of marriage to a girl of her class. It was simply a ploy to bed her. And the circumstances of the case incline me to believe that he succeeded in his purpose.

"How so, sir? I do not understand your reasoning in the matter."

"The young maid Mary South told me that Susan Pickford was exceptionally straightforward in all she did and said. I take that to mean that she was somewhat limited in her thinking and too rigid in her understanding to be aware that for safety's sake the truth must be shaded, softened, or silenced in certain circumstances. If she had simply told Atwater that she intended to break her engagement because she loved another man, he would have suffered and protested, but eventually accepted it. But if she rashly told him that had already given herself to his rival, he would take it as a betrayal that would so lower her in his sight that he would not scruple to take revenge. I have learned in this business that nothing is so protective as pure love, but nothing so murderous as pure jealousy."

"What do we do about Lieutenant Beaufort? If this is murder, does he bear any guilt?"

"I am afraid only a moral guilt. Lieutenant Beaufort is by all accounts a rogue and philanderer of the worst kind. But those same qualities would mean that he had no reason to kill the girl. If she resisted him today, he would find another woman to chase tomorrow. His feelings are of the shallowest kind. Atwater, on the other hand, is a simpler but deeper man who once he gives his heart to a woman, can never commit to another. His very steadfast devotion is his downfall, just as the Lieutenant's shallowness is his salvation. Bring in Atwater. As a formality I shall ask Lieutenant Beaufort for a declaration when his company returns from its maneuvers, but I am thinking at this moment that Atwater may be hanged for a crime of passion."

But events that transcended the death of Susan Pickford prevented any contact the Constables intended to have with Atwater and Lieutenant Beaufort.

On April 18, 1775 Lieutenant Colonel Francis Smith dispatched a force of seven hundred soldiers to Concord to seize and destroy a rebel arms cache. An irregular company of about seventy-seven Massachusetts militia intercepted them at Lexington but were under orders to withhold their fire. Nevertheless, a shot was fired and a skirmish ensued that left eight militiamen dead and one British officer wounded, a Lieutenant John Beaufort-Essex.

After considerable casualties, the reinforced British forces fought their way back to Boston where they were under siege for nearly a year.

"Who fired on the Redcoats," asked the annoyed rebel leader. "We had agreed to hold our fire. It does not help our cause for Englishmen to kill other Englishmen."

"Sir, it was the cider man Atwater well known in these parts.

He lies yonder dead under the tree. He was the first to fall."

"I like not to speak ill of the dead, but hotheads like him will set this land ablaze with war. His shot will echo far and wide, and who can say to what outcome?"

"Sir, he fired at the commanding lieutenant, then dropped his musket and ran, arms outstretched, toward the Redcoat line. A dozen balls at least struck him, but when we dragged him back in a moment of grace the soldiers allowed us, he still lived, though barely, and he spoke words with his last breath."

"A madman, no doubt. What did he say?"

"Nothing that made sense to us, sir. As best we could understand his dying words, he said, 'I have no reason to live and every reason to die. Dear God, forgive me my unforgivable deed'."

Lieutenant John Beaufort-Essex served honorably throughout the Revolutionary War. For though a man of dubious morals, there was never a doubt about his valor. Ironically he was unscathed in several major battles but limped from a wound he received in the first minor skirmish of that great conflict. (from a note in Jacob J. Filmore's History of the American Revolution, *Cambridge, 1927, p. 280.)*

...

Chapter 7:
The Prodigal

Forefathers.com

[Pioneer Tennesseans: Entry 68, Vol. II, pp. 12-14. Nathaniel Stokesbury (1803-1875), who shortened his name to Nathan Stokes, was a fourth-generation descendant of Nathaniel Stokesbury (1683-176?), the second son and third child of Matthew and Agali Stokesbury, Nathaniel was born in Blount County, Tennessee, formerly Cherokee territory, and died in Boston. Leaving his parental home at eighteen or nineteen, he fell into evil hands and was accused of a crime and sentenced to indentured servitude in Williamsburg, Virginia. There he mastered the first stages of ironwork and carpentry. He escaped from his Virginia master and made his way to Boston. With the help of a mysterious benefactor he established himself and perfected his twin crafts of metalworking and carpentry. A tragic affair drove him to the sea and eventually to service on a slave ship. He took part in a dangerous rescue mission. He was shipwrecked on the voyage from Africa and survived for a brief time on a bank off the Brazilian coast, where, so he wrote, a second miraculous intervention allowed him to make his way back to Boston. He visited his ancestral homeland in Tennessee, but no record of that phase of his life is found in his papers. It is to be supposed that his relatives had abandoned the site sometime before his return. This account is an edited version of a handwritten narrative discovered among Nathan's effects at his death in 1875. The Stokes papers were held privately by his widow Jane Olgivie Stokes until her death in 1880. The Stokes heirs then allowed them to be deposited in the Boston Public Library.]

...

"Nathaniel, son, come back!" were the last words I ever heard my father say. They still echo in my memory as they echoed in the deep forests and ravines that surrounded the Tennessee town of Maryville, built on the site of our ancestral Cherokee village. I recall clearly how he stood by our tent, waving and repeating his plea until I was out of hearing. I turned only once to wave. Then I rapped my horse smartly with the bridle rein, urging him into a gallop up the mountain slope. The years have softened the discontent I felt at the moment and increased my nostalgia for the old matters of life forever lost in the past.

I could recite by heart the stories and names of my ancestors and the romance of my great great-grandparents Matthew and Agali Stokesbury. True to his promise to Chief Mardok, Great great-grandfather Matthew gathered books and materials and taught the tribe all he knew of the Christian faith, and with it the English tongue. Chief Mardok's two sons, born to his first wife, were always hostile to my great-great grandfather Matthew Stokesbury and abandoned our village, leaving Agali, though adopted, as his only surviving child. Eight years after my great-great parents were declared married according to tribal custom, Chief Mardok, who felt the burden of years upon him, adopted Matthew as his son and relied increasingly on his counsel.

Other tribesmen privately grumbled that a white man, a *unega*, was their chief in all but title. But none openly challenged Chief Mardok, who reminded them that all the chiefs who had borne the name for many generations were descendants of Mardok's son, the first *unega* chief. Thus it was that my great-great grandfather acted as a sub-chief during Mardok's final years. Before he died in the winter of 1694-95, "old and full of years," as Matthew recited from the Bible in his funeral eulogy, none protested when he declared that Matthew would be the next Chief. But he added the stipulation that from now on his title must also be his name. Thus after many generations, another Welshman, bearing the same name as the legendary first Mardok, was again chief of the Cherokee.

But if *unega* was a revered word in old Cherokee legend, it became a curse when between 1740 and 1750 lawless whites began crossing the mountains to raid, plunder, and murder. It was, I am sure, a personal burden for my great-grandfather, also named Nathaniel. He was the fairest of his siblings. His green eyes told not only of his paternal ancestry but perhaps reflected his grandmother's ancient European lineage as well, if the old legends could be believed. He protested when children began calling him *unega* ("whitey") but soon it became his tribal nickname, used alike by children and grownups, who found his English name hard to pronounce. His siblings Mary and Hamilton had no noticeable European features but greatly resembled instead the other Cherokee children. From the first he perceived that he was different and the perception convinced him that he would never be taken for a true Cherokee, chiefly perhaps because he did not think of himself as such. He devoured all the books he could come by, but chiefly those about travel and geography. I inherited his bookish trait and read everything I could lay hands on, included a few that remained from his time.

It was a mystery to me why my Grandfather never left the village to explore the world beyond the mountains. He died before I could ask him, and the family would give me no reasonable explanations. On the contrary, they responded angrily when I asked, which caused me to wonder if some unhappy family secret was behind the mystery. All they told me was that no one in their right mind would leave their homeland to venture out into the strange and hostile white world. Perhaps they were right, but the white world was absorbing or annihilating everything in its path. Soon there would be no place of safety left for those who wanted no part of it.

With one notable exception, most of my Cherokee people had little to do with the war of independence from England. The exception was my father Nathaniel who served as a scout for the rebel forces at the battle of King's Mountain. He was immediately hailed for his accurate information about the movement of the British forces. But as soon as the battle was over, he was dismissed with indifference and no small amount of scorn. He returned to Maryville, as our village was called by that time, an embittered man who never again wanted anything to do with whites, British or American.

After the war with England and the news that the American colonists had formed their own nation, the over-mountain raids increased and the whites began to settle and intermingle with our Cherokee people. This and the susceptibility of the Cherokees to the alcohol and diseases they brought soon reduced the pureblood Cherokees to a small minority. In my own case I am certain that my blood is more white than Cherokee, even though I could not document the legitimacy of my ancestral line. To tell the unhappy truth, many of the Cherokee women were violated and the men killed or destroyed by alcohol and disease. Although my eyes are blue and my beard almost as thick as those of white men, I have black Cherokee hair and skin a shade darker than most full-blood whites. Our tribal history was quickly disappearing; only a few elderly Cherokees still remembered the old language, and the young, myself included, chose to speak only English.

My father's desperate pleas for me to return grew fainter, but I did not pause. I had my life to live and he had his to finish. In spirit I had separated from the family long before the day I rode away on the dead Frenchman's pony, and unlike my Grandfather, I meant to make the break, not to think uselessly about it until my life was too far spent. My father spoke often of the workings of Providence. I paid little heed to his teachings and had my doubts about a God I could not see and who responded with silence to the prayers father taught us. As for the old Cherokee teachings that I remembered, I dismissed them as superstitions and myths.

Likewise, I disbelieved the stories about the legendary Madok. To me they were also the fanciful product of ignorance, like others that some of the old people still told us around hearth and campfire. Yet I did not object to the convenient thought that God ordained the death of the Frenchman Trémont in our village, who by his dying words made it clear that my father was to inherit the mare and her colt was to be mine.

This seems to be as good a time as any to say that should any of my family chance to read this account of my early life and wanderings, let them do so knowing that it is flawed in irremediable ways. The man I am now only partly continues to be the youth I was when most of these events occurred. It has always been a mystery to me—and another reason why I once had doubts about an all-wise God—why our most life-defining events seem to occur before we have the knowledge and skill to deal effectively with them. In the midst of youth and ignorance, we are obliged to deal the great perplexities of life. Perhaps our ancestral pagan gods still live and take delight in our confusion, tormenting us as children sometimes torture small animals. We claim the love of divine origin, but is that only because we fear to describe the real nature of things? At that time I had no answer to the question, nor have I yet, though my assertions have grown stronger, as they tend to do with old men.

And there is another problem. Many years have passed and while my faith has returned in great strength, I am not sure whether some of my toils and troubles were at all as I recall them. Instead they may consist of invented memories. Truth weakens like a drying stream as it stretches back into the past, and time often betrays memory with stronger fancies. With much time and much altering, perhaps like the Madok legends, stories sprout branches, roots, and fruits that were not part of the original, but now seem truer than what was real at the earlier and actual time. I claim no peculiarity for myself in these misgivings, for I see my friends and acquaintances with very different histories experiencing similar lapses, if indeed they can be called that.

But before I become hopelessly bogged down in soft-brained sentimentalities, let me return to the tale of my life. After a day's ride into the mountains, I entered unfamiliar terrain. As yet I had discerned no trace of white settlements, but guessed from what travelers had told me that they lay not far ahead of me. A thrill of fear and excitement gripped me. What would I find there? Danger? Fortune? None of the stories I knew prepared me, and as I learned later, none could have. For I was already past a point of no return and was soon to be subjected to dangers for which my most extravagant daydreams could not have forewarned or prepared me.

An hour before dusk, these and other idle thoughts came to an abrupt end. Suddenly three white men emerged from the trees. Before I could react, one jerked the reins from my hand and two others pulled me from the frightened horse and threw me to the ground. I looked up to see a musket aimed at my head.

"Could be Cherokee or a half-breed from the looks of his hair," said the tallest of the three. "Shoot him, Jake, or cut his throat and throw the body in the bushes, and bring the horse along. It's young and looks to be in good condition. We can sell or trade it or maybe keep it for our own use."

"But Jarvis, do you think that Harry Bradmore would give us money for the boy?" asked the shorter, thin-faced Jake.

"I doubt it. What would he be good for? When they're mountain bred and scrawny like this one they're not suitable for regular service or work."

"But he was riding a horse, and that's peculiar in itself," said the stocky, gray-bearded third man. "These mountain Indians don't have horses. Why don't you ask him how he came by the animal? There might be more where this one came from. You speak some Cherokee, don't you, Jarvis?"

"Some, but nowadays most of these mountain Cherokees, pure or mixed, speak some English."

The tall man started to ask me in butchered Cherokee, but I answered him in English. "A Frenchman, a fur trader on his way west, died in our village four years ago and left me the horse, then a colt. It is mine."

"Well, what dya know! He does speaks English," said the

gray-beard, shaking his head.

"Yeah, and better than you, Frank," laughed Jake. "How come you speak such good English, boy? And what's your name?"

"I learned it from my folks. We're white. My name is Nathaniel Stokesbury."

"Big name for such a scrawny kid. But you know, Jarvis, he could be telling the truth. His skin is whiter than any Indian I ever saw, and now that I look at him up close, his eyes are blue and he's sprouting some beard. Who ever heard tell of a blue-eyed, bearded Indian?"

"Where was you headed when we caught you?" Jarvis asked, prodding me in the side with his boot.

I gave no answer.

"Boy, I asked you where you was heading," he said angrily, giving me a swift kick in the ribs.

"To Hampton," I gasped out the name of the only city that popped into my mind. By this time I fairly shook with fear that they would kill me, as the tall one called Jarvis had first threatened.

"And what's your business there?"

"To apprentice myself for a trade," I said, unable to think of a better answer. "I cannot live any longer in Cherokee country with the fighting and sickness. I am a white man, as you can see."

"I'd say you ain't no kind of a man yet," Jake laughed. "Hell, you ain't nobody, are you boy?"

I did not answer him.

"And mayhap never will be after we finish with you," Jake threatened.

"Tie him up," Jarvis ordered, "and tight so he don't run away while we're deciding what to do with him. Bradmore might take him off our hands at the Cumberland Camp. It's worth a try. And keep your eyes open, in case there are more of them out in the bush."

Jake tied my hands and feet with buckskin thongs. They talked out of my hearing for a while as my dread built up into near panic. Then gray-bearded Frank came back, untied my ankles, and ordered me to my feet. "You'll walk tied behind the horse, and you better hope he's broke good so that he don't spook. If he does and runs away, he'll drag you to your death over these rocks or leave you so battered that we'll have to do it for him."

"Why can't I ride my horse? You could tie him to your mount."

"You'll walk because that's what Jarvis says, and what he says goes. Don't cross him, boy. If he says jump, you better make like a jackrabbit."

"Where are you taking me?"

"You'll know when we get there. Now no more questions, because you'll get no more answers."

I walked for hours until the mounted whites camped for the night, chewing on dried venison and sharing water from a buckskin bag. Once the bearded man called Frank got up to offer me a cut of meat and a drink, but Jarvis stopped him.

"Frank, give him a drink but don't go wasting vittles on the boy. We're running short. He'll last till we get to the Cumberland Camp tomorrow or the next day, but if he drops aforehand, the forest varmints can feast on him."

"Why drag the kid along?" Jake said, "He's more trouble

than he'll ever be profit to us. But I've been thinking about that horse and I sure could put it to good use."

"You leave horse and kid to me and stay a distance away if you know the good of it for you," Jarvis answered in a menacing tone. "I'm head man here and working out the profit is my business. And don't you forget it."

"I was just making talk, Jarvis," Jake whimpered.

We reached the Cumberland Camp around the middle of the third day. I was hungry, thirsty, and scratched but not really the worse for wear. In happier conditions I had walked much farther in the mountains. Frank tied my hands around a birch tree and served himself a sizeable piece of venison, grinning at me as he chewed but offering me nothing. Meanwhile Jarvis negotiated with two men in a large white tent. The tantalizing vapors tortured me with images of food and water.

Later Jarvis told me that I was to be hauled in an ox cart to a city named Williamsburg where I would appear before a magistrate to answer to a criminal charge.

"What crime? I have committed no crime."

"Oh, but you have, boy. What about the horse you stole from me? There it is, plain as day."

"But, sir, the horse is mine!"

"I have two witnesses that will swear it's mine. Can you prove them wrong? You got documents proving ownership of the animal?"

It happened as Jarvis said it would. After two and half days of bouncing overland in an ox cart and four more locked in a Williamsburg jail, a black-robed Williamsburg magistrate declared me guilty—of stealing my own horse—and sentenced me to a public whipping and six months of incarceration.

"You got off light, boy," a constable whispered in my ear. "Maybe because you're young and mostly white, so they tell me. You could have received a hanging sentence."

At that moment a tall, corpulent man rose in the attending public and asked to address the magistrate.

"Sir, I shall hear you only if it pertains to the matter with which we are presently occupied."

"It does indeed pertain to the matter at hand, your honor. With respect, I am Harry Bradmore, son of John Bradmore, of the Hampton Bradmores. I come in representation of my father who regrets that ill health prevents him from appearing in person before you."

"The esteemed Mr. John Bradmore is favorably known to this court, and as his son and representative, you are received cordially in his name. Please explain, sir, the business that brings you before us."

"Your honor, if it please the court, on behalf of my father I am instructed to pay all fines and public expenses incurred in the arrest, incarceration, trial, and conviction of the felon Nathaniel Stokesbury yonder seated and request in consequence that he be turned over to my father's estate in indentured servitude for a period of time that this court in its wisdom will see fit to set. My father has authorized me to declare on his honor as a gentleman that the fellow shall be treated humanely and shall do honest labor to compensate for the crime committed, all the while obeying the principles and rules of Christian behavior."

"The court so rules, taking into account the disposition of Mr. John Bradmore and stipulating the following conditions. Let the court records show that the prisoner is hereby sentenced for a period not less or more than five years to the service and supervision of Mr. John Bradmore or his agents subsequent to payment of fines and costs, as Mr. Harry Bradmore has stated. The prior sentence is accordingly set aside, subject to re-imposition of the same or to graver punishment should this court become cognizant of further unlawful acts by this person."

The following months now appear to contract to a much shorter time. Yet for nearly a full year I labored with a baker's dozen of indentured Irish and Scottish servants on the Hampton plantations belonging first to the elder Bradmore and, upon his death several months later, passing by inheritance to his son Harry Bradmore.

An incident during my second year of servitude that set the course of my life on a new and unexpected pathway. As son and heir to the Bradmore estate and fortune, Harry Bradmore set about ambitiously to reorganize his plantations and servants. Having proved myself to be an adept worker, I was released from my dull task as herdsman in the back pastures and plantations near Hampton to join an experienced cadre on a vast plantation near Williamsburg where Bradmore himself had resettled his family in an opulent residence. There he named me apprentice to his blacksmith Hiram Hardin, a squint-eyed, emaciated man who drank rum constantly and paid little attention to me. The work was much more to my liking than the lonely work in the pastures, and only a few months passed before I surpassed my indolent master in working with iron, brass, and other metals, and showed considerable skill in woodwork. Far from resenting my emerging skills, the indifferent and steadily weakening Hardin heaped more work on me and devoted his time to his rum bottle, his only friend and consolation.

It so happened that Mistress Brenda Bradmore, wife of Harry Bradmore, prevailed on her husband to install at the entry lane to their estate an elaborate metal gate with family insignia. For she claimed that the Bradmores were descended from English aristocracy. Obligingly he ordered Hardin to proceed with the design and installation. But now sunk in nearly permanent rummy drunkenness, Hardin's design was a flawed travesty of competent workmanship. Bradmore was irate when he saw the work and ordered his overseer to summarily dismiss him—with a flogging if he resisted. The drunken Hardin went quietly, but now Bradmore was in a quandary, lacking a craftsman and further than ever from having a presentable gate. Daily he suffered vain Mistress Bradmore's unrelenting hysterical outcries that their social standing must become subject to ridicule when the gentry and authorities from Williamsburg saw the rubbish that Hardin called a gate.

In desperation Bradmore turned to me as the only possibility in the short time left. "Think you, Stokesbury, that you could design and install such a gate? I am mindful that you have shown skill in working with metal and wood. But mind you, we have only a fortnight," he reminded me. Then, turning away, he added almost in a whisper under his breath, "Not that I shall live so long unless something is done to soothe her harpy temper."

I assured him that I could, and in a bare ten days I produced and installed a princely gate complete with the family coat of arms that greatly pleased both skeptical Bradmores. In my impatient, youthful hope, I dared think that in consequence of this triumphant work and the favorable display of my talents, Bradmore might release me from further servitude and even offer me Hardin's position, which carried, as I believed, a modest stipend. But his natural avarice and meanness of spirit proved stronger than any impulse of gratitude. I was told by one of the older servants that it was a Bradmore trait, evident in earlier generations of the family. He offered not a word of thanks or hint of recompense. I saw my fate handwritten on the wall. Years of unappreciated, unpaid labor lay ahead of me. And perhaps more, for my disillusioning experience with Williamsburg justice fed my suspicions that new accusations could be leveled against me at any time with the same ease as in the first false charge, so that my servitude could extend for as long I proved profitable to Bradmore and the dishonest magistrates. I was learning the hard way to foresee in the character of men a prophetic chart of their future acts. From the moment that realization settled into my thinking I began making plans to slip away from Bradmore's greedy grasp. For the briefest moment I entertained the thought of running back to my family in the mountains. But the thought quickly faded. The world now belonged to the whites whose dominion was broad and tyrannical. But surely, I reasoned, somewhere in it a better destiny awaited me.

My best chance for escape was even now upon me and I was obliged to move hastily. The inaugural ball drew all attention and ordinary surveillance ceased in favor of the great event. I gathered my meager belongings and a few coins that in his drunken haze Hardin had neglected to pocket. Then, having packed away as much food as I could lay hands on, I slipped out into the night, leaving by the new gate after the last arriving carriages had rumbled past. For a moment I was tempted to unhinge the gate and drag it to the middle of the lane as a vengeful gesture to embarrass Bradmore and his frivolous lady. But then I thought better of it; anger was a poor reason to damage my own good work. Perhaps my father's teaching legacy had a greater weight than I knew, for even at that young impulsive age I was already persuaded that vengeance is but a second helping from the menu of wrongdoing.

I had daydreamed much but thought little in concrete of a better destination, but I recalled that one of the indentured Irish servants, by name Owen O' Farrell, had told me of the docks and great ships he had seen upon his arrival in Salem, Massachusetts. His descriptions stirred my imagination. My mind could not yet feature the unbounded sea, yet from there, I reasoned, I could travel to the farthest reaches of the world. I had never sailed, but for everything there is a first time. I would head for Salem, and from there circumstances yet unborn would determine my next step.

Daylight brought with it the fear of recapture. I was now a fugitive, and recalling the magistrate's warning of harsher punishment should I fail to abide by the terms of my sentence, I decided to shorten my names from Nathaniel to Nathan, and Stokesbury to the simpler Stokes. It was a feeble disguise for anyone bent on discovering my true identity, but all I could think of under the circumstances.

I shall omit several phases of my journey to Massachusetts, but what happened to me in Boston bears telling. Two weeks later, hungry and cold, I fairly staggered into that city. I had slept in forests and abandoned buildings and eaten roots and berries, and cadged carriage rides when I could. For once I was grateful for the forest lore my Cherokee relatives had taught me. Would that I had listened more closely to my elders!

It was too late in the season to reach Salem. Autumn was far advanced, winter soon to descend, and I knew not when, if ever, the next morsel of food would touch my lips. I could go no further. To my inquiries framed in complete ignorance of Boston and its people and in a strange accent, I received curt dismissals from passersby and warnings by the alerted constables to cease molesting decent folk.

My appearance was also a curse on my cause. My clothing was now dirty and beginning to fray and my hair too long and black to win me a sympathetic hearing from the prosperous fair-skinned and tawny-haired Bostonians. During a respite from their unfriendly scrutiny, I wandered about city's forty-acre Common, desperately hungry and anxiously considering my circumstances. Late in the day, a Monday if I recall rightly, I passed a corpulent man with a shock of red hair sitting on a bench and amusing himself by tossing nuts and grains to a veritable tribe of raucous, fluttering birds and chittering, scampering squirrels. His clothing was of an elegant but antique cut. On his right ring finger a large gold ring with a magnificent blue turquoise caught my attention, for the Cherokee and other native people believe it to be a lucky stone. I thought to myself how grateful I should be to join the beasts and consume some of the precious grains and nuts myself. The first time I passed by, the man gave me not the slightest glance. Then on my reverse circuit, he called after me in a deep baritone voice.

"I say there, Nathan, attend me!"

"Sir?" I responded, astonished that he knew me by name but

fearful, judging by his sharp tone, that I had in some manner either offended him or been discovered as the fugitive I had become. Not far behind me strolled a pair of constables eyeing my movements.

"Step this way, I would have a word with you."

"Yes sir, but how is it that you know my name? I have never seen you before. But how may I be of service to you?" I asked as I watched the constables out of the corner of my eye.

"How I know your abbreviated name is of no consequence. You cannot serve me in any way you could imagine, but I may be of some aid to you. What are your intentions in Boston?"

I hesitated but saw no reason to ignore his request. He seemed to know everything about me already, and knew the answers before he asked the questions. "I hoped to apprentice myself as a metal worker and carpenter in Salem, but the weather and circumstances obliged me to stop here in Boston."

"From the looks of you, I venture to say hunger was the main one," he laughed. "So thin have you become that you fain must stand twice to cast a single shadow."

His words annoyed me and too hungry to entertain frivolous commentaries about my condition, I said nothing in response. For a long moment neither did he as he eyed me intensely. Then he extracted from a vest pocket three small coins—gold by their look—and proffered them. "Take these coins; the first will be more than enough to have your hair and whiskers trimmed in yon barbershop by the upper Common, and the return change will suffice for several day's lodging and board in the neighboring inn. On the morrow when merchants open their doors for business procure for yourself decent clothing. The remaining coins shall do you until you earn your first wage."

"Wage? Sir, what wage?" I said irritably. "I have no employment, nor prospects of any."

"Be patient, Nathan. Betake yourself thereafter to the wharf address I shall give thee and speak to owner Gaylord Stafford. He rises early and attends to many matters, so do not delay, lest the opportunity pass you by. You must speak to owner Gaylord himself. Be not dismayed by his assistant who delights in bullying all such as you. Understand you my instructions?"

"Yes sir. But why, I ask, are you doing this? You are not known to me, even though in some manner that is a mystery to me you know my name."

He smiled broadly and tossed another handful of feed to the fluttering birds and scurrying squirrels at his feet. "Indeed, your knowledge is limited, yet it is important that you follow my instructions. Now see to your tasks, lad, as I have described them to you, as I must see to mine."

So saying, he handed me the bag of grain and nuts and walked away quickly across the common as the constables reached me. I turned to go also, but one of the men called to me.

"A word with you, fellow. What have you in the bag?"

"Why the grain and nuts the gentleman seated here was tossing to the birds and squirrels."

"Gentleman? Look about you, fellow" said the older constable. "There is no one on the Common save the three of us at this late hour. Nor has there been in the past hour. We have been watching as you gestured as though speaking to someone. Are you drunk with grog? We must know your business. You appear to be an idler without worthwhile purpose here. Let me see what the bag contains."

"Certainly. The gentleman was, as I said, tossing grain and

nuts to the birds and squirrels. And as for me, I am Nathan Stokes, and I am in Boston for the purpose of apprenticing myself as an ironworker or carpenter."

He opened the bag, and seeing that the contents were as I described, frowned and returned it. "Now, do you have lodging or money to arrange it or shall you be our guest in our jail?"

"Indeed I have money, good sirs, and will straightway attend to the matter if you will give me leave to do so," I responded, showing the officers one of my three gold coins.

They looked at each other, apparently in disbelief that I had money, but finding no reason to query me further, instructed me not to appear again on Boston streets in such shameful array. I was more eager to comply than they could have guessed.

I hoped to thank the benevolent stranger, but he was nowhere to be seen. I dared not linger on the Common lest the annoyed constables lose patience and carry out their threat to jail me. In any case, surely I would see the gentleman again under better circumstances and thank him for his charity. Meanwhile, making my way to the barbershop, I munched on the nuts and grains as ravenously as the hungriest members of the feathered and furry tribes had done not long before me.

After my hair and whiskers were properly trimmed—not without unwelcome commentary by the barber—I ventured with considerable trepidation into the inn. I was unacquainted with such places and my appearance, though improved by the barber, inspired little confidence. The innkeeper looked me up and down with suspicious reluctance, but persuaded by a shiny gold coin, gave me room and board in his establishment, returning several lesser silver coins in change. After devouring a hot chowder and scrubbing my body, I slept the sleep of death.

The next day was well advanced when I awoke with a start, and remembering how the redheaded man had described the busy Mr. Stafford, I hastened to a nearby clothing store and quickly purchased new garments for myself. By midmorning I presented myself to his establishment only to be confronted by his officious assistant who ordered me to leave. But I stubbornly held my ground, having been forewarned by my benefactor and determined to speak only to Mr. Stafford.

Angered by my obstinate refusal to depart, the assistant raised his voice and threatened to expel me by main strength, for he was bigger and better fed than I. At that moment the inner door slammed against the wall and a large, red-haired man entered.

"What is all this commotion?" he said to the assistant in a rumbling, baritone voice. "I could hear your shouting from the far end of the shop."

"Sir, this fellow will not quit the premises, even though I ordered him to do so."

"And why, lad, do you make an obstinate ass of yourself?" he asked, turning to me.

"I am no ass, sir. I was told to come here and to speak only to you."

"Who told you such? I do not know you. What is your name?"

"He would not state his business, Mr. Stafford," the assistant said angrily, "and to be sure he has none worthy of your attention."

"Sir, I am Nathan Stokes, at your service. The name of the

gentleman who so instructed me is surely known to you, though he did not give his name to me. I can offer you only a description of his person. He is a hefty, well-dressed man with very red hair like yours who spoke of you in familiar terms. By the resemblance, I now see that possibly he is your kinsman. He summoned me to him on the Common as he was feeding grain and nuts to the animals."

"What other particulars about this man can you give me? What you have told me could variously describe a hundred Bostonians."

"I recollect only that on the fourth finger of his right hand he wore a gold ring with a large turquoise mounting. And his voice was deep like yours, sir."

Mr. Stafford paled at my description and spoke words under his breath that I could not catch.

"Sir?" asked the assistant, whose name I learned later was Steadman Fuller.

"Never you mind, Fuller. Leave me alone with this young man. I will hear him out."

Fuller gave me a hateful look and took his time leaving as ordered. Once we were alone, Mr. Stafford queried me at length about the redheaded man. But I could add little to what I had told him earlier.

"That will do, Stokes," he said abruptly, holding up his hand to stop me. "Why did you come to see me?"

"Sir, I would like to apprentice myself to you as a metalworker and learn what I can of carpentry."

"I myself am proficient in neither of those crafts. But to conclude the matter, for reasons I will not explain, I am willing to take you on as apprentice in my shop under the conditions that commonly pertain in these arrangements. These include food and an occasional wage. For lodging you may accommodate yourself in the loft over the shop. Heat from the forges will keep you warm enough in winter, but you must take your meals elsewhere, for the space has neither heating nor cooking stove. Showing up when you did is strangely convenient. We are in need of a helper, and it is possible I know the man who sent you to me. His recommendation, for such I take it, must serve. You shall begin at once under the guidance and instruction of Master Thomas Olgivie. But bear in mind, Stokes, if you prove to be indolent or talentless I shall be obliged to dismiss you forthwith. And now that we have finished our talk, I have other tasks. Come, I shall take you to Master Olgivie."

"Sir, I cannot thank you enough and promise that I shall obey faithfully all that you and Master Olgivie instruct me to do. And I would like to thank the gentleman who sent me to you. Can you tell me his name and where to find him?"

"I could tell you only who I believe he is, but for reasons you would not understand, I shall not do so. In any case, I could not tell you how to find him. But if he is of a mind to do so, he will find you."

"I don't understand, sir."

"Be grateful for his help, but to the little I have told you, Stokes, I will add no more. Now come with me and make the acquaintance of Master Olgivie."

Master Olgivie, a tall muscular Scot of middling years with a close-clipped red beard, stern look, and intense blue eyes proved to be a man of balanced disposition, yet exacting to a fault in all things pertaining to his craft. It troubled me that prudence would not permit me to provide him details of my experience on the Bradmore estate in Virginia, but I assured him in Mr. Stafford's hearing that even though I could not claim a high level of mastery in metallurgy and carpentry, I promised to be ready and willing to learn.

"He seems fit," he said to Stafford, and turning to me, added, "now, lad, let us see if your work proves to be as good as your words."

Although it will come as no surprise to readers acquainted with my full account, Master Olgivie and Mr. Stafford, knowing nothing of my servitude in Virginia, marveled in the following days at the speed with which I demonstrated skill in both metals and wood. Not many days passed before Master. Oligivie, now my advocate, assigned me the task of forging precisely dimensioned iron bolts and shaping matching planking for the skeletal hull of a two-masted schooner rounding into shape in a dry dock adjacent to the workshop.

Despite further queries and searches in Boston, I learned nothing more about my mysterious redheaded benefactor. But years later in a land half a world away I was destined to meet him again, and to be as baffled by our second encounter as I was mystified by the first.

Master Thomas Olgivie and his wife Sarah, were the parents of seven children, in ages when I first met them from eight to twenty. Frederick, 20, the eldest, soon became my good friend and working companion in the shop. Master Oligivie, the son of Matthew Oligivie and Nattie Mckenzie Oligivie, made no distinction between us insofar as the quality of our labor was concerned; on the contrary, only the very best we were capable of was acceptable. And our best was never singularly praiseworthy; invariably he pointed to some minute flaw that only his eagle eye could see. Yet because his hard exterior could not hide a much nobler heart, I came to respect him all the more.

Mrs. Oligivie was a highland Scottish lady. At first I missed the meaning of some of her oddly intoned words. But her maternal warmth and concern for my welfare were unmistakable. She all but adopted me as another chick in her brood and thought it a tragedy of nature that I was separated from my own family. (I said little of the circumstances.) Only a heartless person could have failed to respond to her warmth. And even if her motherly affection had failed to win through, her food and table would have tamed the stoniest heart.

I believe Master Olgivie, as she always called her husband in public, felt obliged to maintain a certain patriarchical severity lest the whole family risk dissolution into a saccharine maternal mush. But it was not lost on any of us that he adored his wife.

Jane, newly turned eighteen when I met her, captivated me from the start. Tall, redheaded, with sky-blue eyes, delicate features and pearl-white complexion, she was the most beautiful girl I had ever seen. She did all things with a happy exuberance that never failed to lift me out of my customary silence and cause my face to crease in unused smiles, though often I was tongue-tied in her presence. I could not at that inexperienced age give my feelings their rightful name, but from the higher elevation of advancing years, I now recognize it as love of her at first sight, as the Romantic poets call it.

In even numbers but alternating sexes came Kevin, 16, Alice, 14, Joseph, 12, Madilyn, 10, and Ramsey, 8. Though I spoke little of my life in the southern mountains, the little I said stirred their curiosity. They plied me with questions and as my affection for the family grew, and in a special, secret way for Jane, so did my trust. I revealed more of my history to them.

One night as Mrs. Olgivie was serving us a rich pot roast, Frederick laid his hand on my arm and asked, "Nathan, from what you say, your family must have Indian ancestry."

Mrs. Olgivie stopped and waited for my response. I would have preferred to remain silent but knew now I could not. With a measure of annoyance and an admixture of fear, and excepting my full name, I opted for honesty.

"Not Indian, which includes a variety of peoples, good and bad. My family is of white and Cherokee descent, and the Cherokee consider themselves to be what you might call the most advanced of the original Americans. My Great grandmother was Cherokee, my great grandfather Welsh, born in the old country," I said, looking at Jane as I spoke. My grandfather, after whom I am named, married a Whitcomb of English ancestry. "But whatever that makes me, I am myself in all plainness and without pretense, Nathan Stokes."

Mrs. Olgivie put down her serving ladle and walked around the table to give me a hug with kind words I always treasured. "You are our friend, Nathan, and I am pleased that you are supping with us. The Lord's blessing be on you now and always, for your being here is his holy doing. We are all his sons and daughters, and we must take pride in our ancestry and honor our forefathers. For God created all the races of man for his glory and purpose."

"Mother Olgivie, as always you speak the truth," said Master Olgivie. Then he went to say, "Nathan, your heritage be one thing, your craft another, though there be connections not visible. See that you continue to work earnestly. Mr. Stafford has placed a trust in you and put you under my guidance for instruction. If in any way you see your heritage as a hindrance, conform to what Mother Olgivie said. And look all the more to your craft so as to honor and fulfill the trust placed in you and thereby to praise your Creator and raise yourself in the eyes and esteem of men."

"That, sir, I shall try to do in every way," I answered, ill at ease.

"Now, having said what must needs be said," Master Olgivie declared in a lighter tone, rare for him, "Mother, please serve your excellent pot roast! And note ye well, Nathan and Frederick, and all present besides, if ye should learn to do your tasks as well as Mother Olgivie knows her cooking, ye shall indeed be deemed masters of your craft!"

We all broke into spontaneous applause and cries of "Hear! Hear!" Mother Olgivie's happy face blushed pink with pleasure as she rounded the table to hug and kiss each and all in turn.

Dark, wintery Boston at length began its spring surrender to light and warmth, in joyful cadence with my own radiant and rising happiness. I was in deeply in love with Jane and everything bright and beautiful reminded me of her. The center of my life moved away from my old morbid thoughts about myself and settled in her. Boston was beautiful because she was there to make it so. The plainest streets and shops took on an afterglow because she had walked along them. I had never dreamed before that life could be so good, and caught up in her magic, everything I once saw as dreary and dead now sparkled with magical meaning. For the first time I sensed that I was coming into my own. By some wonderful, paradoxical magic, by centering my life in her I was becoming myself. And I forgot my old quarrels with God.

But there were fearful, tormenting questions: Did Jane love me? Could she love me? What would she say if I became bold enough to confess my love to her, as I knew I must sooner or later? She was my friend, of that I could have no doubt. All the Olgivies, modeling themselves on Mother Olgivie, lavished friendship in all the noble, magnificent range of sentiment the word could contain. But was that friendship destined to be a boundary, perhaps even the enemy of my love for Jane? I dreaded a fallback from the full grace of her love, a retreat to lesser glories and a compromise with what I foresaw as perfect happiness.

The schooner was in the main completed, wanting only the completion of the upper decking being shipped down from Portland in the Maine territory and a dozen cannons in transport from England. In the meantime, our shop carpenters and mechanics, reputed to be the best in New England, constructed a handsome pinnacle to serve as the schooner's boat.

Frederick and I could not keep our eyes and hands off the smaller princely vessel, and as soon as it was seaworthy he began to implore his father to let us take it out for a shakedown cruise in Boston Bay. As first Master Olgivie simply ignored his son's pleas, but at length, wearied of Frederick's requests, he called us to him and explained that since the pinnacle was not his, he could not authorize its use.

"You must approach Mr. Stafford on the matter, though were it up to me, I should say no to entrusting such an expert craft to inexperienced hands. And prepare ye for a like response from Mr. Stafford. If he denies permission, as most assuredly he will, the matter shall be settled without further ado."

But Mr. Stafford had a better idea.

"I believe the young men have hit upon the right idea," he said to Master Olgivie, "but perhaps without providing sufficient crew and passengers for the excursion. Let us declare this very Saturday a day of recreational pleasure to celebrate the pinnacle and the schooner. And even though for the latter, which stills lacks its finishing touches, the festivities are a trifle early, the weather bids fair to be ideal and spirits are high because of labor all but finished and, if I do say so, expertly done. We shall staff the pinnacle with family, employees, a pair of expert sailors, and with abundant drink and food take a gay turn about the Bay. What say you?"

We were delighted. Even stern Master Olgivie smiled at the pleasant prospect. As for me, I was eager to be close to Jane. Perhaps, I smiled to myself, I could arrange matters unnoticed to sit next to her. I could imagine nothing more ideal.

The day turned out to be more pleasurable than we could imagine. The pinnacle responded deftly as we sailed smartly past the inner islands, waving or shouting to fishermen on their way to the Outer Banks. In the outer bay the swells and waves were larger, and as they struck, as though to test her, the pinnacle lifted and plunged through the watery valleys and peaks, involuntarily throwing us together. Mother Olgivie raised her frightened voice in prayer. Of her own accord, Jane had seated herself next to me, and though we said little each to the other, the feeling of her body pressing against me at those exciting moments was a heady sensation I shall never forget. As for Frederick, he was so thrilled with his first experience at steering and learning the intricacies of sailing that he spent nearly every minute learning what he could from the sailors.

The pinnacle stood a short distance off Point Allerton as the sailors, with Frederick's help, secured the vessel with two ship cables fore and aft tied to an old dock. This was to be the midpoint of our circular trajectory. Then we waded ashore with Mother Olgivie, all loaded with baskets of food and drink she had prepared for the crew and passengers. The salt air had so sharpened our appetite that we ate and drank until it seemed we would never again relish the smell and savor of food. Afterward, Jane and I, joined by her excited younger siblings, went along the shore to explore and look for seashells. At one point she took me by the hand as her brothers and sisters called me to explore a small cave they had discovered several hundred yards down the narrow peninsula.

"Forget that muddy cave, Nathan," she said with an impish smile. "Today you belong to me."

I thought my heart would pound through my breast at her words, and it is doubtful whether at that moment any human force could have pried me from her side.

It would take a volume to recount all the events and sensational emotions of that day and of many others in the long, lovely Boston spring and summer. To a casual observer they would have no doubt seemed trite, the trivial recollections of ordinary lives. But experienced from within, they were magical.

But pleasure pursued past the bounds of legitimacy has a way of turning nightmarish. With these ominous words as prologue, let me summarize what happened next.

In late July, Mr. Stafford purchased another shipbuilding enterprise in the town of Essex, and in the company of the expert Master Olgivie journeyed there to inspect and regulate it to his satisfaction. Master Olgivie gave us detailed instructions about our tasks and responsibilities. But as it was likely that they would need to spend several weeks in Essex, we readily agreed to our tasks while secretly reserving ample time for more pleasurable activities. Steadman Fuller was given the general charge of overseeing the shop during their absence. But since I loathed the man for the way he had treated me, and Frederick believed he surpassed him in standing because of his father's position, we promised to comply but perhaps not to obey fully.

Would that we had made a stronger resolve to see to our responsibilities! But as soon as Mr. Stafford and Master Olgivie were out of sight, their instructions were all but out of mind, replaced by Frederick's consuming passion to take the pinnacle out for another go in Boston Bay. I protested feebly against the idea, but secretly I was nearly as eager as Frederick, though concerned that a day at sea would mean a day away from Jane.

Two days later, a Wednesday, after stowing food and drink aboard the pinnacle, we slipped out of the harbor at first light. The "Rover," as Frederick had privately christened her, unburdened by the weight of so many people this time out, fairly skipped to a good breeze over the rippling bay. Distant clouds sat low on the eastern horizon but the sun was warm, our masters far removed, and the pinnacle's double sails as responsive and nimble as a thorough-bred horse.

Then standing off Point Allerton we debated turning back or racing ahead toward Cape Cod.

"But Frederick," I protested, "Cape Cod is too far to reach and return in a day, if I read the charts aright. Let's not press our luck. I don't have a good feeling about it."

"Feelings, smeelings! Don't be a chicken, Nathan! We'll race down and back to Boston and no one will be the wiser that we did. It will be a grand adventure!"

Seeing that Frederick had his mind firmly made up and aware of his Scottish stubbornness, I said no more. For several hours it appeared that he was right, but as we swung round and tacked north, the low lying clouds to eastward suddenly seem to awaken and move toward us like living things. The wind picked up and the pinnacle shook with the gusts. Hourly they grew in intensity and by midafternoon, as I judged the time, they reached gale force. Neither of us knew how to deal with the storm, and our ignorance was to be our undoing.

The clouds turned the day into darkness and soon rain came with such blinding volume and force that we lost all sense of direction. The pinnacle began to take in water faster than we could bail it as the gentle waves of the morning became the roaring monsters of the angry afternoon.

The occurred the worst. The wind and waves worked themselves into a simultaneous coordinated fury, capsizing the pinnacle and hurling us into the water. I saw Frederick go under an instant before the waves rose and smashed me into the deep. Fighting my way back to the surface and spitting mouthfuls of salty water, I called for him. But I heard no human voice above the screaming din of the storm. Unlike Frederick, an expert swimmer, I could barely swim at all, having learned to stay afloat in the freshwater creeks of my native Tennessee. But with great effort I made my way around the overturned craft. There was no sign of Frederick and no response to my cries. A cable from the toppled mast sail lashed about in the water. Grabbing it, I then ventured out as far as its length permitted, but still I heard nothing and saw only one of our two wicker food baskets being quickly carried away in the roiling current. The other was nowhere to be seen. Tiring and in danger of sinking into the deep myself, reluctantly I swam back to the capsized pinnacle, its keel barely visible a few inches below water level. Frederick, I concluded to my horror, had surely drowned.

Unbeknownst to me, overcome by panic, despair, and the howling gale, all the while the wind and surf were carrying the wreck and me shoreward. Thus it was that perhaps no more an hour passed before, to my surprise, my feet touched bottom and I waded out and collapsed on shore.

As morning dawned and the storm passed, I discovered myself to be on a fair sandy beach from where not far inland I espied wagons and carriages passing along a main high road. I inquired of a black-clad driver who stopped his team to stare me up and down, still wet and dripping salt water. But before giving me an answer, he desired to know how I came to be there. I pointed to the capsized pinnacle and spoke of the story, but gave only enough details to satisfy his curiosity and without mentioning the tragedy with Frederick, lest he should inform authorities. He said I was not far from the old town of Plymouth, famous, he proudly added, as the site where the English had first landed in New England.

He took me to Plymouth, pointed me to the northward running road to Boston, and drove away. I stood there undecided and mulling my options for a time. I was torn by powerful but opposing impulses. On the one hand, I desired above all else to see Jane again. But on the other, I dreaded having to tell Mother Olgivie and the family about Frederick's drowning and my irresponsible part in causing it. If I had stood firm, he could not have sailed alone in the pinnacle. There was no way I could stay in Boston. Even if the family and Mr. Stafford could forgive me for my part in the tragedy, I would be a daily reminder of their loss. I had lost my best friend, and now I must lose the girl I loved with all my heart. My world had capsized, as surely as the pinnacle, and everything was upside down. I thought of simply vanishing without telling the Olgivies, but conscience would not let me cowardly slink away. Besides, even though I bore a responsibility, I was not guilty of Frederick's death. As hard as it was, I must face the family and admit my complicity. I was aware that very likely their grief would be so much greater than mine than they could have no spare compassion for me, even if I had deserved it. I would be the living reminder of a brainless act that took Frederick's life. I could not stay in Boston, but for that same reason I must not leave without facing them like the man they once thought me to be.

And so I did the very next day. Mother Olgivie, frantic with worry before, now paled and with Jane's help stumbled to her bed at the news. I could hear her sobbing. At first the younger children did not understand what was wrong. Later they cried in a mixed confusion of disbelief and mourning for their beloved elder brother. Half an hour later Jane came out and gave me a long searching look but said nothing at first. Finally she asked me for details of the tragedy.

"We shall have to give an account to father and Mr. Stafford when they return," she said quietly.

"I can lead them to the beach where the pinnacle beached itself."

"That won't necessary, Nathan. By the time they return likely either the sea will have carried it away or salvagers taken it. Simply tell me the location and I shall relay the information."

"I want to do all I can to help."

"There is no real help any of us can offer now. Frederick is gone, and life must go on for those who remain."

"Jane, I want you to know that I did all in my power to find him."

"Nathan, no one doubts your good intentions and earnest efforts, but the fact remains that my brother is dead. Please pardon me for saying it, for it sounds cruel, but we will be reminded of his loss each time we see you."

"I have thought hard on that point, Jane, and I believe the best thing for all concerned is to remove myself so as not to be a painful reminder."

She nodded and after a silence spoke words that pierced my heart. "We had many things to tell each other, Nathan, and the time had not yet come for us to say them. Now they must never be said but silenced as things that can never be."

"Please do not hate me."

"I shall never hate you, Nathan, but instead always think of you as our friend. There is no room for hatred in this family. We shall, each and all, pray that your life be long and happy. I speak for Mother, Father, and all the family. But that is all I can say and all that should be said. Now, as you said, it is best that you leave Boston—and us."

The air was heavy with dampness as I stepped out into the dark street. A carriage rumbled past, iron rims and horseshoes harshly striking the cobblestones. There was no softness left in the world, and my destiny was as unknown to me as the destination of the carriage disappearing into the gloom.

Rather than spend the night in my quarters over the shop, I

gathered my few possessions and lodged myself in the same inn on the Common where I had stayed upon my arrival in Boston. If it had a name, I cannot remember it.

I awoke to a monumental melancholy, but at least my unhappy obligations in Boston were settled and the thought of them almost tranquil, as though belonging to a time already long past. It steadied me that I had resolved my doubts about my next step. I would try my fortune in Salem, which had been my original destination.

In the course of my life I have come to the conclusion that by comparing them each city will reveal a peculiar nature that colors and outlives the personal character of its mortal inhabitants. So it was with Salem. Compared to proud, firmly planted Boston, which gave the appearance and had the feel of a much older city than its calendar date, Salem, though of nearly equal history by year count, rested uneasily on its foundations, and one could not escape the impression that about it hovered an atmosphere of furtiveness and a stronger presence that I could only describe as shamefulness. I knew something of its nefarious history of witch hunts and superstitions, and no doubt that intelligence of the place colored my impressions. I sensed a collective guilt. On the other hand, I do not discount the possibility that I simply misread circumstances and again fell victim to my usual tendency to exaggerate. My knowledge, sparse as it is, is not rooted in formal instruction and thus lacks the necessary correction that wise schoolmasters can impart, but is instead the fruit of a disorderly and desultory assortment of readings and unguided philosophies. It is as though a library had crumbled at my feet, strewing books in wide disarray without sensible transitions or connections. Simply put, my thinking links concepts that have no business being lumped together.

The wharves buzzed with the busy hum of men as great schooners, whalers, and clippers disgorged cargoes and took on provisions for voyages to the ends of the earth. The bustle worked to my advantage. When shipmaster Eric Johnson, Captain of the clipper *Chesapeake*, learned that I had apprenticed under Master Ogilvie of Boston in the double crafts of iron work and carpentry, he quickly added me to his shorthanded crew without asking many questions about my skills and experience. It struck me as odd but suited my purposes. Officially the *Chesapeake* was bound for Jamaica, but secretly also had a second destination, as I learned later.

The readers of this account will understand my melancholy sentiments, especially as long as we were in Massachusetts waters to remind me of the pinnacle disaster. But the *Chesapeake* with its two rakish masts and rigging was famed for its speed and with steady winds and good seas in three days we were far down the coast. But to my wounded sentiments another problem was added: *mal de mer*, or to call it by its humbler English name, seasickness. Despite my lies about experience at sea, the veteran sailors quickly discerned by my gait that I lacked sea legs. Aboard the pinnacle we were never, or perhaps only briefly, out of sight of land. But on the open seas all such fixed terrestrial points were lacking and I was at the mercy of that other earth, the greater, unfixed world of the seas. For the better part of two days I was forced to endure not only vomiting miseries that seemed only a step from death itself but also the jokes and humiliations generously heaped on me by the hardened, callous sailors.

Chief among my tormentors was our Portuguese first mate Manuel Furtado, who from the first took a perverse pleasure in humiliating me in front of the others. But I soon discovered that I was not the only target of his vicious temperament. Many of the sailors despised him for his brutal ways and told unflattering stories about him as we gathered for water around the scuttlebutt. But six or seven of the fifteen-man crew were loyal to him for reasons I could not understand, for only four of them were Portuguese or Brazilian. It made even less sense to me that Captain Johnson would take on such a man as his first mate. To my sorrow I was to discover later the reasons and consequences of the decision.

Several times I inquired about our cargo, for during my inspection tours as carpenter's helper I was shown only our ship's stores in the hold. Durward Mason, the stooped and gray-grizzled ship's carpenter, took me aside and cautioned me to curb my curiosity.

"Lad, take some friendly advice. Word got up to the Captain about your questions. He's an able captain but hard, and he does not like a questioning crew. And Mate Furtado even less. God help you if that one finds you poking around below decks without good reason, there's no telling what he might do to you, maybe clap you in irons until we dock in Kingston and leave you there when we sail. I'll be honest with you, Nate, we've got us a bad situation on this ship. Furtado's as much master of her as the Captain. And don't ask me how or why. As for our real cargo, we'll take it on in Kingston and if talk around the scuttlebutt talk is true, deliver it to Vera Cruz. But what it is I don't know and I don't care. I just keep my mouth shut, and I advise you to do the same."

I said no more openly about the cargo and my thoughts were distracted days later by the sights, colors, and sounds of Kingston, but above all by the people. I had almost no experience with Africans, having seen a few Blacks, usually from afar, working the Virginia fields. I was rendered slack jawed by the cadence of their songs and agile rhythmic movements. Unlike the grave demeanor of my Cherokee relatives and the discordant gestures of my white kinsmen, the Blacks seemed to me to do everything with an effortless sinuosity. Nor was it the special talent of a few. They all seemed attuned to a spontaneous rhythm of movement and sound that they all unerringly sensed by some mysterious instinct imperceptible to other races. As far as I could tell, only the very old Blacks seemed to lose the African rhythm. But then I have observed that in old age all people leave behind most of their differences and sink to a lower, common level in appearance and attitude. Toward the end of their life once bitter enemies have only affection or indifference for their former adversaries. The very young play in harmony and the very old live in peace. It is in their middle years of greatest strength and ambition when men fight and kill one another under the prod of great lusts and strong causes. Why is it that when men are strong they are most prone to wrong? I have no answer to my question and make no claim to any particular insight. It is only as I grow older that I reflect at all on such trifling matters. In youth I was more impressed by what I saw than what I thought.

What I saw in Kingston impressed me overmuch. Before I realized what was happening, the African drums and rhythms had so hypnotized me and drink had done the rest that I lost consciousness. Mason and other sailors mockingly told me that they had to drag me back to ship. When I came to my senses, I felt the swaying motion of the vessel and the shuddering of strong wind in the sails. But of purse and money I had none. God knows what furtive black hands—male or female—had made away with my modest funds.

"Let it be a lesson to you, lad," laughed Mason. "Next time it could be a slit throat or a dagger in the belly. The Blacks will bow and call you 'Massa' and 'Governah', but they will rob and kill you for your valuables as readily as the common footpads of London or New York. And like all subservient people, they are usually cleverer than their masters about such things."

"What of our cargo?" I asked.

"The Black stevedores took it on board while you were drunk and the rest of the crew were amusing themselves with the girls."

"And what was the cargo?"

"As I told you before, it's best not to ask. All I can say is that New Spain, or Mexico as they are calling it now, has risen in revolt against Spain, and I suspect that our cargo has something to do with the war. The Captain and Mate kept us in the dark. That's why they wanted all hands off the vessel last night."

In contrast to Kingston, if you ask me about Vera Cruz I will tell you that I never saw the city. With trimmed sail the *Chesapeake* made her way slowly up the deserted New Spain coastline. All I could see of human presence was smoke rising above palm fronds. Whereupon we dropped anchor and Furtado or one of his men signaled with a mirror. Soon a large boat emerged from the tropical foliage and came toward us.

Furtado's followers had trundled ten sealed crates on deck as we looked on under the Captain's orders to stand clear of the transaction. "Guns and ammunitions I'm guessing," mused Mason, and the men around us nodded in nervous agreement.

"If that's so," said ship cook Hiram Benson, nervously rubbing his gray chin whiskers, "the sooner we get out of here, the better our chances will be. This ship is swift, but my brother's been to Tampico, which is not far north of here, and he tells me the Spanish have a garrison there with naval support. As defenseless as we are, a broadside or two from one of the two San Ildefonso class battleships my brother saw there would send us to the bottom. And even if some of us survived and made it to shore, they would execute us for aiding the revolutionaries."

Benson's words quickly turned prophetic. Barely had the boat come within hailing distance than a sail cleared a promontory on the northern horizon and a vessel came into full view. "A San Ildefonso warship!" yelled the sharp-eyed Captain Johnson. "All hands to posts! Weigh anchor! Step lively!"

The Spanish vessel was at full sail and closing rapidly as our crew weighed anchor and scrambled to set our sails for full running speed. At that moment we saw a puff of smoke and then heard a distant detonation. The cannon ball came nowhere near our vessel and instantly we saw that it was not meant for us, but for the boat. The first ball fell harmlessly in the water, but a second caused the boat to rise from the waves, spilling crew members. We could see them flailing in the choppy sea only to disappear one by one as the ship hove within musket range to dispatch the unfortunate wretches.

Another cannonade then sounded but passed over our prow and splashed harmlessly in the water a hundred yards ahead of us. It was understood as an order to drop anchor and await the warship. Naturally, Captain Johnson had no intention of obeying. The *Chesapeake* swung smartly around in response to Furtado's expert seamanship, and as the full deployment of sails filled and strained in a good wind, we surged southward.

Meanwhile the warship was pulling within cannon range of the *Chesapeake*. Training his spyglass on it, Captain Johnson told Bosun Adkins in a low but emotional voice that it was the *Asia 64*. Commissioned in 1789 with 74 cannon but now modified to carry 80.

"I know the ship and if Alberto Moreno still captains her, we face an experienced seaman who neither gives quarter nor asks it. If he gets within range, he'll make splinters and spars of our vessel and rags of our sails! Get down there with Hurtado and do everything you can to get us more sail! We are doomed if we cannot outrun her!"

A sailor working with the cables overheard the conversation and spread the word. We were petrified by panic. And with good cause; despite a gallant effort, the flying *Chesapeake* could not escape entirely our pursuer's early favorable momentum and fell briefly within cannon range of the *Asia 64*. Fifteen or twenty of its cannon fired on us. Most of the balls fell harmlessly into the water, for we were now too far ahead for consistent accuracy. But two found their mark amidships and by ill luck carried away Captain Johnson, Bosun Adkins, and Hank Filmore, the sailor working with the tangled cables.

There was no time to waste. Durward Mason yelled for me to follow him to assess the damage. It was even worse than we dreaded. Water was pouring through two breaches in the hull and quickly rising in the hold.

"Quick, Nathan," yelled Durward, "nail the timbers

lengthwise across the two breaks! They're close enough together to cover with a single double-ply set of braces! Then we can reinforce them with crossing vertical boards!"

Though still with only partial mastery of ship carpentry, I remembered some techniques that Master Oglivie taught me and reasoned that the patchwork that Durward intended would be too weak to stand the turbulence and pressure and might instead cause the whole section to tear loose and sink the ship.

"Your pardon, but I don't recommend it, Mr. Mason. If it doesn't hold then that section of the hull will break loose and we'll be under water in a matter of minutes."

"So what would you, sir, with your long experience, recommend?" he asked sarcastically.

"Two things: first, we have timbers and oakum, and metal sheeting wide enough by my calculations to go from rib to rib. After we put wedges in the breaches along with all the oakum we can push in around them, we will need to lay on double layers of the metal sheeting and secure each end to the ribs with iron bolts and, second, reinforce it with all with the best timbers we have, and not just the area around the breaches but that whole side of the hull. That way I think it will hold so that we can pump out enough water to get to the nearest port outside of Spanish waters. All that provided the Spaniards don't overtake us and finish the destruction."

Durward started to object, but thought better of it and muttered grudgingly: "It might work."

Durward naturally resented my youthfulness, but he was wise enough to see the advantage of my strategy. He yelled for two men to come down to help us. With their help on the pump and the oakum, in thirty minutes we had the worst leaks stanched to a controllable degree. If all went according to plan, the leakage would diminish as the wood swelled and compressed the oakum. Everything depended on the integrity of the hull. But if it was not further compromised we had a chance to save the vessel and ourselves.

During all this time we were ignorant of the pursuit. When finally our repairs were done and I was able to go on deck to get water and inquire about our situation, I learned that despite her wounds, the *Chesapeake* had safely raced ahead of the ponderous *Asia 64*. But instead of elation, the mood of the crewmen was subdued because of the loss of Captain Johnson and their shipmates.

We all assumed, at least the crewmen I talked with, that Furtado would put us into port at Kingston in order to make more substantial repairs than our patchwork measures at sea. But Furtado, others cautiously advised us, had his reasons for avoiding Kingston.

I knew little about life and law on the high seas, but enough to be aware that the death of a ship captain was a serious business that would require a formal inquiry. Add to this important circumstance the ominous fact that his death occurred far from the announced destination of the *Chesapeake*. Naturally, this would raise suspicions of mutiny, piracy, or contraband that once spread abroad could implicate us all. As for Furtado himself, those who disliked the man hinted that he had a turbid and perhaps criminal past, though they revealed no details to me.

For three days we limped along the north coast of Cuba, giving a wide berth to Havana, which was certain to have Spanish vessels in port. Even more fearful were the British warships on the lookout for slave runners bringing human cargo to work and die in the sugarcane fields of "the Pearl of the Antilles". Some of the English captains had a habit, I was told, of shooting first and asking questions later.

Here I cannot pretend a courage that was completely lacking in me at the time. I was terrified that the combination of a long voyage in rough seas infamous for sudden gales and destructive winds would overwhelm our repairs and sink us, for I knew better than anyone aboard how flimsy they were. Surely, I reasoned, we would have to put into a port, but where that would be no one could tell me, and for reasons that only later became clear, Furtado and his henchmen seemed recklessly indifferent to the fate of the *Chesapeake*.

A nightfall later found us almost becalmed but drifting with drooped sails close to the Cuban reefs some miles from a place called Cruz del Padre. Now seasoned sailors amongst us were also becoming alarmed. Our fears were soon justified as the swift tropical night descended. There was a sudden scraping noise, followed by a crunching shudder and a pop of snapping timbers, as the *Chesapeake*, pierced and pivoting on an up-thrusted pointed rock, swayed to a scant four feet of water in the shallow reef.

Furtado ordered us ashore. But we soon discovered the folly of his command. Mosquitoes descended on us like a biblical pestilence. The men screamed curses and beat futilely with rags and branches. It occurred to me that I could escape the torment by burying myself in the sand and covering my head with a shirt. Some of the men tried to go back to our stranded vessel, but Furtado would have none of it. Then seeing the measures I was taking to protect myself, most also tried the ploy.

Durward Mason, his exasperation with me finally overcoming his good sense, declined. Instead, he preferred to immerse himself in the water and cover his head with a shirt like the rest of us. Hiram Benson cautioned him.

"Durward, I wouldn't stay down there in the water if I was you. There's sharks and caimans, they call them, along these shores and danger aplenty for all of us here. Why don't you come up here and dig under the sand like the rest of us? I had my scullion Pete slip out a couple of muskets and some spare blankets I keep in the scullery. It's better if we stick together."

"I'll be just fine," Durward said testily. "I know a thing or two and can take care of myself. You just go along there with Mr. Stokes. He seems to know everything except how to wipe his butt and keep his mouth shut."

Hiram sighed and shook his head. "That cussed stubborn streak will be the death of him yet."

And in a way it was. We never saw Durward again, although the next day a piece of his shirt was floating close to the *Chesapeake*. At first we thought he had slipped back on board and had not thought to look for him, but later when it was apparent that Durward was nowhere to be found, Benson described his probable demise.

"Caiman musta got him. I tried to tell the damn fool, but he wouldn't listen. He's probably out there somewhere on the bottom. The big caimans and crocs—and gators up in Florida they say—will grab a grown man, pull him under water, and then spin him till he's good and dead. Later, when they get hungry, they'll come back and eat their kill, one chunk at a time. To them we're just another piece of meat, and they like it better half rotten than fresh."

"You sure about that?" asked Porter Foreman, "I thought these Cuban caimans didn't bother people."

"I guess somebody forgot to tell that to the caimans, didn't they?" said Benson. "When they get hungry enough they'll go after anything that moves, man or beast. And they say these Cuban caimans can jump up and grab birds and animals in low hanging tree limbs."

"Leastwise, we won't have to bother with burying him," laughed Milford Tapscot.

"Before all this is over, Tapscot," scolded Benson, "you may be hoping there are still some of us left to say words over your own carcass."

"You could be right," Tapscot answered in a subdued tone. "But tell me, do you know something you're not telling us?"

"No, I don't, Tapscot, and you can stop your questions right there. I don't know any more than the rest of you. It's just a feeling I get about Furtado's bunch of cutthroats. They're two-legged versions of that caiman that drug old Durward to his death."

"Well, I have one question I've been mulling over that I'm going to ask all of you anyway," Tapscot said, "and I don't give a damn what you say, Benson. Why did Furtado order us off the vessel and into this hellish jungle?"

"What are you thinking, Tapscot?" asked Foreman.

"If what I'm thinking is about to happen, I'm for striking out for the interior. I don't like Spaniards and they sure as hell don't like us, but I think we'd have a better chance with them than with Furtado's bunch. On that point, I'm with Benson. I'm getting a bad feeling about all this."

"But what is it?" asked Foreman. "Furtado's gonna need us

to get the ship off that rock on the sandbar. He can't do it with just the five or six that follow him."

"Maybe he's got more men on the way."

"More?" laughed Benson. "Look around, Tapscot, this place is deserted."

"Well, I don't know about that. The other day I heard them talking Portuguese, and while I don't understand the language, it's a lot like Spanish that I know a little. They stopped talking when they saw me, which is a little suspicious in itself, but they were saying things like '*chegada*' and I think I heard something like '*nossa outra tripulacao*. I got to thinking about it, putting two and two together, and I believe it means 'arrival' and 'our other crew'. I'm not saying it does, because all I know is a little Spanish, and the words may not match and mean what I think. But, men, the more I think about it, the more I believe we're in one hell of a dangerous situation."

"Meaning what?" asked Benson, suddenly taking Tapscot's fears very seriously.

"Meaning that Furtado may have another ship and crew on the way here, and if he does, we could either be abandoned to starve in this godforsaken place, or, possibly shot on the spot. Furtado has all the guns and ammo we were supposed to deliver to the revolutionaries, and we're sitting here covered with mosquitoes, no food, and with only a couple of old muskets."

"But how could he have set up such a scheme? I can't imagine Captain Johnson being involved in anything like you're talking about," said Benson.

"Maybe he wasn't, but he was willing to run contraband to the Mexican rebels, wasn't he? Anyway, he was only one man, and Furtado could have killed him when the time came. This may be something Furtado has been planning for a long time, even before we left Salem."

"Or maybe it's your imagination running wild, Milford. Why don't we wait and see if this mysterious crew shows up before we run off half-cocked into wild country we know nothing about? Even if we made contact with Spanish officials, they would arrest us on whatever charges they please."

"True, true," admitted Tapscot. I say wait to see what happens but be ready to run inland if they show up."

Meanwhile, to my surprise I was summoned on board. "Mr. Furtado wants you to start working on the repairs," a gaunt Brazilian by the name of Lenheiro explained. And he wants you to find Mason and bring him along."

"We think Mason is dead. Caimans got him last night."

Lenheiro shrugged his shoulders dismissively. "Then you are now our carpenter. Furtado was going to name you so anyway."

Upon inspection, I saw that the massive rip in the Chesapeake's hull was beyond our capability to repair. I told Furtado so.

"Don't worry. This vessel is not going anywhere. Help is on the way and soon we shall be gone from this miserable place."

His words all but confirmed the fears of my crewmates. I said nothing to Furtado or the other sailors, but to myself, I vowed, if possible, to alert my stranded companions. I asked permission to go ashore to retrieve my shirt, but Furtado, suddenly suspicious, refused. Later he sent Lenheiro and another man ashore armed with muskets. I heard a shot but within the hour they returned emptyhanded.

Reasoning among themselves, our stranded shipmates must have concluded that summoning me aboard meant that my services as ship's carpenter would be needed and theirs would not. In any case, my companions waited no longer; evidently they had decided to strike out for the interior. The next day there was no sign that any remained on the sandy beach.

I never saw any of them again and must leave their story unfinished. I wondered if they died of starvation in the wilderness or made contact with a Spanish outpost or patrol. I feared that if any among them was careless enough to let slip intelligence of our clandestine voyage to Vera Cruz, then the lives of all would be in danger. The Spanish would be within legal rights to condemn them as piratical *filibusteros* and execute them by firing squad or hanging. And the same would be true for the entire crew of the *Chesapeake*, myself included. When the full realization of the danger struck me, I went from dreading the arrival of another vessel to hoping it would show up quickly and remove us from Spanish territory.

In this hope I was not disappointed. Late that same afternoon a dashing, arrow-shaped ship known in Caribbean waters as a "slaver" hove into view under a Portuguese flag. But since the Spanish distrusted the Portuguese as much as they detested British, French and American freebooters, we were hardly better off than before.

Furtado knew far better than I how perilous our circumstances were. For unbeknownst to me, the craft had been purchased and refitted at the Casa Blanca of Havana and cleared for the Madeira Islands. The latter ploy deceived no one, least of all the Spanish officials versed in the all tricks of the illicit slave trade. But they were willing, for a price, to turn a blind eye long enough for the vessel to clear the Morro channel. After that, it was up to the *Dourada*, as it was renamed, to fend for itself against patrolling English warships in open waters.

Furtado wasted no time in ordering the crew to transfer the cargo of guns, powder, ammunition, timbers, cables, stores, water, tools, and anything else of use and value from the stricken *Chesapeake* to the sleek *Dourada*. When this was done to his satisfaction, he gave a signal to an expert swimmer remaining on the *Chesapeake* to torch it in several places and quickly come on board. By the time we stood two miles off the Cuban coastline the *Chesapeake* lit up the dark skies with its spectacular funeral pyre.

The next day I marveled at the lines and workmanship of the *Dourada*. At forty-five tons with a culverine amidships and the trim, rakish dimensions mentioned previously, it seemed to my carpenter's eye a thing of high craft and beauty. On the other hand, the requisites for the transport of slaves puzzled and disturbed me. I could hardly imagine how human beings could survive in conditions that by my measurements allowed almost no movement or personal space. But since it was all still vaguely abstract and untested by real experience on my part, I put it out of my mind and paid attention to practical matters as ship's carpenter.

Four days out a gale roiled the seas and the waves rose to monstrous size. But for all his human faults, Furtado was an excellent seaman. Some of crew grumbled in fear when he ordered up more canvas, for they were hoping instead that he would bring down the foresail and turn the vessel to the wind with bare masts. Instead, Furtado chose to match sail with sea and so sent the *Dourada* scudding mightily through the storm until by noon of the following morning both sea and human spirits were again placid. Afterwards, no one questioned Furtado's orders or doubted his seamanship.

Without other incidents worthy of recounting, thirty-nine days later with favorable tide and wind, we ended our voyage at the mouth of the Rio Pongo south of the great bulge of West Africa and hard by the squalid river settlement of Bangalang and its *barracoons*, or slave pens. I found myself in a world magnificent and savage beyond anything I knew or could have imagined. And beautiful? I am tempted to add it to my impressions, except that it is too soft and dainty a word to describe what I saw of Africa.

It had become known to me to my great surprise that Furtado's daughter Catherine was married to Englishman Reginald Brighton, who claimed de facto lordship of the Pongo and costal territories extending inland to the lower reaches of the Mandingo kingdom.

Furtado was disturbed and angered on three counts: first, he could not understand why his daughter had accompanied her husband on what, at a formal level, Americans or Europeans would call a state visit to the Mandingo ruler, who annually sent hundreds of "Bush Blacks" to Brighton's barracoons. The visit was an extraordinary event. Seldom did whites—and never white women—venture inland, especially this close to the rainy season. But lately word got out that the Mandingo King Ben Ibrahim was secretly negotiating with French slavers and considering sending his annual roundup of slaves to their factories down the coast. Gifts and guile were quickly needed on a vast scale to avert the catastrophe, and the wily Brighton was best suited to the task. A meeting was arranged on the loosely defined border between the costal territories and the Mandingo Empire.

Second, Furtado was distressed to see that Brighton's *barracoons* were less than a third full of serviceable slaves, though another score of old, useless Blacks had been released to save food. These were too spent to make their way back to their inland homeland. Instead, they shambled about Bangalang, begging and enduring kicks and insults by the exasperated villagers, black and white.

Third, Brighton's house guards inexplicably denied Furtado and his officers lodging in the "Big House," as it was called, forcing the Portuguese Captain and our entire crew to sleep aboard the *Dourada*. Furtado was in a murderous mood but the guards were adamant and uncharacteristically tightlipped. Short of storming the residence, there was nothing to do but wait until Brighton's return with wife Catherine and the news, so it was hoped, that negotiations had been successfully concluded and the Mandingos would soon be driving hordes of new slaves—the currency of Black Africa—coastward.

That very night, however, every assumption and perspective changed. A young Spaniard named Miguel Astorga, in Brighton's employ as secretary and factotum, asked and received permission to come aboard the *Dourada*. There he told a horrifying story of betrayal. Brighton, he explained to Furtado, having succumbed to the lax African customs concerning marriage, had abandoned his Christian heritage and taken multiple Black wives since his marriage to Catherine. The closely guarded harem in the Big House accounted for the refusal to offer accommodations to Furtado and his officers. But the worst part, Astorga said, unable to hold back his tears, was that Catherine herself was the prize that Brighton offered King Ben Ibrahim in exchange for a new pact. And given the sexual lust of African despots for young European women, she would be a gift the King could not refuse. Thus it was expected that an agreement would be reached and new slaves would be herded into the *barracoons*. As for Brighton, once rid of Catherine's daily screams of protest, could settle into the indolent life of a petty African despot. On the other hand, Catherine herself, Astorga said despairingly, would be the target of unthinkable cruelties inflicted not by the King but by the jealous and vengeful Black wives in his seraglio, to say nothing of being forced to foreswear Christianity and convert to Islam.

"Unless she is rescued quickly, don Manuel," he added tearfully, "your daughter will have a short and painful life without friends or protectors."

Instead of ranting and cursing, as we all expected him to do, Furtado grew strangely silent and his face was expressionless, save for his eyes that flashed with mountainous passions.

"And you, young Miguel," he asked after a pause, "did you have a part in arranging Brighton's atrocity? And why do you tell me this about my daughter? What do you want from me?"

"Sir, I could not stoop so low as to betray my condition as a Christian and a man. I had nothing to do with Brighton's treachery, and my only concern is Catherine's welfare and happiness. I will offer my life for her if I can help rescue her from the horrors that await her and may have commenced already."

"What, then, are your feelings for my daughter?"

"Sir, I shall not withhold from you that I have loved her in silence since you brought her to Bangalang two years ago to marry Brighton. And though she has never said so in words, I believe she would love me if she could. As far as circumstances permitted, I have been her friend throughout."

"Then she shall be your wife if we live and accomplish two things: first, kill Brighton for his villainy and, second, rescue her from the Mandingo King. Now tell me, are there other men in Bangalang that we can enlist to help us?"

"Only two that have my complete confidence, an Englishman named Michael Brownley, who holds grudges against Brighton for several wrongs done him, and my cousin, Primitivo Astorga, who is unconditionally loyal to me."

"Then collect them at once and bring them here so that we may plan our strategy. Know you the country well enough to lead us to the Mandingo encampment?"

"Not I, I have been no more than a league upriver in my three years here, but the English hunter knows the country far and wide, all the way into the Mandingo highland."

Within the hour Astorga returned with his kinsman Primitivo, a short but strongly muscled Castilian of twenty-five, and Brownley, a rangy, blond-bearded Londoner above thirty-five. Both pledged to aid our band in any way they could.

"We must move quickly," Furtado said to our motley band of twenty-four. "The Mandingo, though somewhat civilized in the Muslim way and considered the aristocracy of Black Africa, love long festivals and music as much as the bush Blacks under their dominion. So it is likely they will celebrate for a week before beginning their return journey. And if I know anything about the Mandingo, courtesy demands that Brighton remain until the festivities are over. If we can take them by surprise before they withdraw out of our reach, we may rout and scatter the lot of them. So dreaded are the Mandingo by the savage tribes around them that they fear no attack and take few precautions. A single Mandingo warrior can inspire panic in a whole band of the bush people. But if this is a sign of their strength, it may also prove to be their weakness. And we shall exploit it in a way they will not soon forget. Now, tell me, Mr. Brownley, where and how shall we find their camp?"

"No doubt Brighton met them at their accustomed lowland post where they customarily deal with whites. And for a transaction of this magnitude the King himself, not one of his princes, will be present. If my supposition is correct they will not yet have decamped, even if an agreement has been reached in principle. The Mandingo are a people of much formality and ceremony in all their affairs and scrupulous in obeying all the precepts of their religion. They know that whites are an impatient people and for this reason prolong their negotiations with them to an extreme in order to gain advantage. They regard haste as both a sign of weakness and an unpardonable breach of ethics, and have a secret scorn of whites because of it. As for the camp, it lies in the foothills of the Fouta Djallon Mountains at a three-day journey, two by river and another by land. The place is purely ceremonial and unfortified, and usually uninhabited, unlike their strongholds beyond the mountains. If we are act boldly, we can take it."

Furtado nodded and repeated, "We can take it," then added, "We must, and we leave at first light to do so."

Supplied with enough guns, ammunition from our undelivered contraband stock to arm a troop thrice our size— we loaded ourselves into three capacious boats, leaving room for food and water. Obvious to all, but commented by none,

Miguel Astorga prepared a special curtained space for Catherine. I knew, as I think we all did, by the grim set of his features that he would not return alive without her.

For a moment his anguish and my melancholy memories of Jane Olgivie merged in a wrenching conviction of life's futility. What was I doing? Why was I here? What was the meaning of this or of anything, for that matter? At that instant I had the horrifying feeling that my life was not only pointless but might soon be over before I had a chance to live it. I was grateful that Hurtado, displeased with my momentary idleness in the midst of our frantic preparations, sharply ordered me to be alert and busy myself with the loading.

As our boats pushed off upstream, the jungle protested with the raucous cries of hidden birds and shrill screams of monkeys that mocked our desire for stealth and silence. The night with its duels of death and devouring was lifting and nature was conducting its indifferent morning requiem for the slaughtered. I struggled in vain to recall my hereditary Cherokee understanding of nature. It was no use; there was no match. I had grown up in a gentler nature, a creation of the kinder climes of earth's higher latitudes.

We proceeded apace, now used to the jungle cries but molested occasionally by monstrous bugs and hungry mosquitoes and alert to motionless crocodiles watching us from the banks or eyeing us like submerged logs in the narrowing river.

After two days the Pongo had shrunk to the size of a wide American creek. The jungle was now sporadically interspersed with broad stretches of attractive grassland. At an unmarked spot known only to Brownley, he instructed us that it was time to leave the river and strike out overland. We took great pains to conceal the boats and cover the extra supplies with heavy canvas.

Furtado and Astorga were of a mind to push on at once, but Brownley cautioned them that we must rest and take sustenance so as to be at full strength for the assault. "Besides, now that we are leaving the jungle and entering the savannah, we may encounter big cats ahead."

We heeded Brownley's advice and camped near the boats. The next day, we saw nothing of the great felines but were roused to alertness several times in the night by their roars. The next day around noon we began to hear the steady, unnerving throb of tom-toms.

"We are now six to eight miles from the encampment," Brownley told us. "From here on we must be doubly vigilant. The Mandingo themselves do not often venture into the jungle or the grasslands, but their slave scouts keep them informed."

"You did not tell us this before," Furtado chided him.

"If we considered every possible danger beforehand, Captain, we might be too discouraged to take the first step. There are always perils we cannot foresee, and some we know of are best left uncommented. I have lived in Africa long enough to believe that spoken words often summon the things we fear."

Furtado nodded. "I cannot disagree, Mr. Brownley, so lead the way. I will brave the jaws of Hell itself for my daughter."

We had not gone a mile further when a painted warrior rose from the high grass, screaming and brandishing a lance. Astorga raised his rifle, but Brownley pushed the barrel aside with his left hand and with his right let fly a twelve-inch steel knife. The weapon whistled and buried itself in the man's back as he turned to flee.

"A Nalu," said Brownley, turning the corpse over to look at the face and body markings. "They do not usually range this far south of their homeland. The Mandingo must be expanding their empire."

"Search the area widely and carefully," Furtado ordered several of his men, "but if you find other scouts, use your knives if possible. And fire your weapons only as a last resort. Our whole strategy depends on stealth and ambush."

Now doubly cautious, we advanced slowly toward the camp. The tom-toms grew louder and before long we perceived distant music and faint voices.

"What is your advice now, Mr. Brownley?" asked Furtado. We are here and in place for the assault. What say you? Where is Catherine most likely to be?"

"You can see the central tent, larger than the others. In it all the principals of the festivities will be congregated, including most assuredly your daughter, Brighton and the Mandingo leaders, perhaps the King himself. The Mandingo protocol does not vary. There we must strike, suddenly and lethally. This is no time for sentimentalities about sparing human life. Only your daughter matters. There is no reason to delay. Are you then ready and does everyone understand the plan?"

"We are ready and on my count of three we rush the tent, killing all in our path: one, two, three!"

We rose as one and screaming pent-up cries of death and defiance rushed the compound, firing as we went. For an instant, the human tableau was frozen in utter stupefaction and bewilderment, then scattered in terror before our charge. In a thrice ten valiant Mandingo warriors died with spears in hand. The less courageous fled with two of the Mandingo princes. We never saw the King or knew what became of him, but supposed that he was spirited away to safety by his guards. Three of Brighton's white guards closed protectively around him, but they fell under our withering fire. Brighton himself was down from a bullet but conscious and trying to crawl through his own blood to safety. Furtado checked him with a saber to his stomach.

"I will not waste words with you, for we have other killing to do. But this is in payment for your treachery!"

So saying, he drove the saber through Brighton's stomach and left him to lie and die.

Meanwhile, as the killing and screaming continued among the Blacks, Miguel came from behind a curtained area, escorting the terrified and trembling Catherine. One of the braver Mandingo warriors, witnessing the outrage of a Christian touching a consecrated Muslim bride to be of the King himself, rushed to defend her. But Primitivo felled him with a single shot.

In less than five minutes the carnage ended with all the assembly either dead or fled. Forty Mandingo warriors and nobles and eight whites, including Brighton, had fallen in the onslaught. Of our men, two had been cornered and hacked to death by the bravest Mandingo warriors. But Catherine, the object of our raid, was alive, if not exactly well, and only death itself could have removed Miguel Astorga from her side.

Now our circumstances were reversed and perilously magnified. Without the element of surprise, we faced the prospect of having to fight our way step by step back to the

Pongo pursued by the King's fanatical warriors, outraged by the surprise attack.

"We must march all night," said Brownley, "before they can gather their warriors and allies. We are doomed if we cannot reach our boats or if the Mandingo or their allies should happen to discover them first."

"Our advantage," observed Furtado, "is that we have superior arms and a head start. And best of all, we have Catherine. So let the race begin."

"Catherine is a precious prize to us, but her rescue is a consuming shame for the Mandingo," said Brownley. "When word spreads that we have snatched her away under the very noses of the Mandingo, they will be mad for revenge. For if they cannot punish us, their prestige among conquered and allied peoples will suffer. Black Africans are quick to abandon sworn loyalties and servitude if they perceive a loss of strength in their masters."

"Is it not the same with all people?" wondered Furtado. "But we waste time in idle talk. Let us move out while there is still daylight. And God has favored us with a full moon tonight."

Both Miguel and Manuel Furtado were worried that Catherine appeared to be in a stupor. But compliantly she marched as her father ordered, occasionally stopping to rest but saying nothing to their solicitous entreaties. Her condition slowed our progress, but by midmorning the next day, we espied the Pongo ahead—and awaiting us, a mixed troop of Mandingo and their allies.

We did not await their attack, but as we had done at the encampment charged toward the main body, shooting as we went. Against the the superiority of our weapons and ample supply of ammunition, their primitive arms could not prevail. The concentration of men on the river, which at first appeared to be to their advantage, soon turned into their second downfall. As our firepower mowed down their forces, the survivors had nowhere to run and many were gunned down as they fled laterally upriver. Three of our men were wounded by a sprinkling of ancient French muskets, but their wounds appeared to be—and so it turned out—healable.

Either the Mandingo had discovered and destroyed one of our boats, or it had sunk for other reasons, taking food and supplies to the bottom. But two proved to be sufficiently water-worthy to get us back to Bangalang. We arrived tired, triumphant, and speaking for myself, glad to be alive.

Although our men were exhausted, Furtado and Brownley posted a watch. But the night passed peacefully. The next morning they gathered our troop for a council on the fate of Bangalang. We noted with relief that Catherine, who had rested in her father's quarters aboard the *Dourada*, appeared much more alert to people and her surroundings.

"The first order of business for us," said Furtado, "should be the dismissal of Brighton's women and remaining guards. But the fate of Bangalang is not my affair."

"If it please you, Captain," offered Brownley, "I believe I can direct things here with a few trusted men until the British patrol pays its scheduled visit."

"And what will you say to them about what has transpired in our time here?"

"The truth, but perhaps not all the details," laughed Brownley. Bangalang has outlived its time and usefulness, if ever it had any. I, for one, would like to see the *barracoons* closed and the human trafficking stopped. In this regard, I am in agreement with the will and actions of the English Parliament."

"Then the place is yours to do with it as you see fit. But I came here for slaves," Furtado asserted, "and I do not intend to leave without them."

"Then with misgivings I say take aboard your vessel the sixty-odd poor devils that remain and be on your way to Cuba or Brazil or wherever you will. And keep your specie, or whatever you intended to use as payment. After the *barracoons* are emptied I intend to close and burn them."

"And what will you do with yourself afterwards, Mr. Brownley?" asked Miguel.

"I have no clearly formed idea, Miguel, only that I have been in Africa long enough, maybe too long. Perhaps I shall return to old England after all these years, or try my luck in America or Australia. I am still young enough to make a new start. These past days have reminded of something I had forgot: this is not my land."

"You may sail with us if you are of a mind to leave this place," said Furtado. "We head first to Brazil with our cargo. It is also a great land for fresh starts. But from there you may go where you will."

"Father, may I say something?" said Catherine to our great surprise and delight. For she had said nothing audible since her rescue.

"Of course, my dear, say on."

"Miguel and I have talked, and he has confessed to me his feelings. My recent ordeals weigh too dreadfully on me to make decisions of any sort, especially sentimental ones. But..."

"But what, dear Catherine?" Furtado asked with a gentleness

we had not seen in him before.

"When things return to normal, if ever they do, he will be foremost in my life. We hope to start a new life in Brazil and that one day you and his cousin Primitivo will join us there."

"I understand and have given Miguel my permission to marry you in due time. But what is your point?"

"Only that you, father, treat Mr. Brownley and the other men with honor. I know they helped gain my freedom at the risk of their own lives, and I shall always be grateful to them for it."

"As shall I, dear daughter. You did not need to make the request for me to keep it always."

On that happy note our meeting ended. The remaining guards were dismissed with stern warnings not to return, and the women Brighton had collected were released with instructions to return to their villages. Some loudly protested how wronged they were, as they scooped up all the clothes they could carry. Others begged recompense for their suffering and gloomy marital prospects, tearfully assuring us that their families would not take them back and no man would have them. None of the eight betrayed any remorse that I witnessed for their late husband. Brownley gave each one a handful of coins and trinkets from Brighton's collections—a double portion to two that appeared to be pregnant—which brightened their dispositions considerably.

The next morning Furtado ordered us to attach interlinked ankle chains to all the able-bodied slaves, sixty-two in number, and herd them aboard the *Dourada*. They whimpered in wide-eyed terror, imploring us in their several tongues, which I could not understand but supposed from their tears and the tone of their voice, to be merciful. It was not from dread of slavery, Brownley told us, which all understood as a normal human condition in the world they knew, but in fear of boarding the ship, which they believed would drop them to their death in the ocean.

"That myth started decades ago," he explained, "when a ship under a Captain Daniel Stafford foundered near here and some of the slaves made it back to land. Since then they look on all slavers as murderers. And in a sense, they are not far wrong, are they?"

The next day, after taking on water, wood, and what supplies were still available, we bade farewell to Brownley, weighed anchor, and hoisted sail bound for Brazil. Reluctantly, Brownley allowed us to attach one of the remaining boats to the *Dourada*. Never again did I see or have news of him, but I always remembered the blond-bearded Englishman kindly. An hour later we saw smoke rising from Bangalang. We surmised that Brownley had made good on his promise to burn the *barracoons*, and we, for the second time, marked our departure with a fiery conflagration.

For twenty-five days all went well. Having overcome their fears of being dropped into the water, the slaves, most of whom were young and strong, had settled into a peaceful docility. Because they were fewer than the vessel was equipped to accommodate they were more comfortable and almost free of the infections and diseases that traditionally condemned many to death before they reached the Americas. On Furtado's orders, the slaves were put to work cleaning their deck of human filth. And also following his orders, we obliged them to strip and bathe every two days in a huge vat or tub brought out on deck for that purpose. At first, the sight of the bare-breasted females unnerved me, but since the uncommon often seen soon becomes commonplace, so it was with me. By our navigator Joaquim Pessoa's calculations in another week approximately the *Dourada* would be approaching the friendly port of Recife on the great Brazilian bulge. We had not seen a single British warship in the crossing and already we were beginning to breathe easier and feel festive.

But our celebration began too soon. The next day at six bells a sleepy crewman coming off his morning watch spotted what appeared to be a squall line coming rapidly at us from the east. He ran to alert Furtado who made his customary decision to run in full sailing regalia before it. But this time his luck—and ours—ran out. It was no ordinary squall but a hurricane ranging well south of the normal Atlantic storm track. Mountainous waves soon rose, swamping the slender *Dourada*, and before other maneuvers could be tried she was reduced in a half hour to a helpless derelict. Both masts snapped low in the shrieking wind and fell in full canvas and cable, one amidships, the other cleanly into the water, dragging cables and at least one man, maybe more, with it. Faintly, above the whistling din of the storm, I could hear the slaves screaming. One second I saw a dozen men running and yelling across the upheaving deck, the next they were all carried away as a monstrous wave swept it clean. Before the next arrived, on an impulse that I did not fully understand, I ran and unlocked the slave deck with a key I had devised, for Hurtado kept the master. Then the next wave, twin to its killer predecessor, struck and carried me with it. I hit the water headfirst and plunged so deep that I counted my life as finished. But then with bursting lungs I was thrown in a somersault into the air long enough to draw new breath and prolong my fragile lease on life. Up and down the water tossed me, draining me of sense and strength. Then I came down a final time and my hand struck a solid object. It was a broken timber from the dying *Dourada*. I clung to it with the last strength I could muster and watched the vessel describe a mad pirouette, whirling ever faster as it stood almost perpendicular to the water before sliding into the depths. I caught sight of a few bobbing black bodies and shipmates circling the sinking ship. For a terrifying moment the sucking vortex created by its demise threatened to pull me down with it. But then the funnel closed and the debris scattered at the mercy of other forces. The rain was now became so dense that I could see nothing.

For what must have been several hours I drifted in stunned semi-consciousness, nauseous from exhaustion and the salt water I had swallowed. But my arms remained locked in a death grip around the spar.

When things began to come back into focus I found myself bobbing within swimming distance of a low shoreline and kicked off towards it, pushing the timber before me. The Brazilian coast! I thought with rising hope.

But no; later I discovered I was on a bank or island of limited dimensions, as best I could make out in the uncertain light and low-flying clouds, perhaps a mile in irregular circumference and rising to a modest peak near its center. The windswept eastern slope where I had come aground in ankle deep mud was almost bare of vegetation, but later as I made my way just past the central hill I espied palm trees and a profusion of other trees and shrubs surrounding a lone manmade structure. There I hastened, hoping to make human contact.

In this second hope I was also disappointed. The building was an abandoned hacienda of the Spanish or Portuguese style, and from the looks of the few dilapidated items of furniture and rotted draperies, abandoned for many years. Water lines on the walls spoke of many floods.

None of that mattered very much to me in my condition. I had reached the limits of my endurance, and my disappointment at finding nothing of what I hoped for on the island completed my dejection. Water dripped through many holes in the broken tile roof, but there were dry areas where it still held. On one of these I piled my wet clothes and making a crude bed next to them of frayed linens and draperies, I slept uncounted hours away.

I awoke at dawn sore in body but with hunger pangs that were more bothersome. I had lost count of time, but judging from the near dryness of my clothes and the early morning sun, I calculated that I had slept close on to thirty hours. Unless, as I wondered, I had lost another day entirely. I dressed quickly but had trouble getting into my leather boots, which were shrunken and stiff. I was eager to venture outside to see whether the world into which I had fallen might contain something edible. Though food was not readily available, water was plentifully collected from the storm in clear puddles and small streams. I drank my fill, which eased my hunger a bit, then headed toward what appeared to be the remnant of an ancient orchard.

It was, but unsuited no doubt for the tropical climate and saltwater flooding, the apple and pear trees barely clung to life and bore no fruit. I saw nothing that would provide me nourishment and after circling the island, returned to the ruined hacienda frightened and despondent. Was I, then, destined to starve on this deserted island?

But I slapped my forehead for my stupidity as it suddenly occurred to me that if there was no food on the land there would be nourishment in the sea, if I could contrive a means to catch fish or other sea creatures. I searched through the house and found a rust-encrusted knife in the cupboard. I whetted it on the hard masonry and soon had a serviceable tool with which to make a wooden spear.

I fashioned a crude spear from what I thought was a species of hardwood that resembled an ash. But spearing fish was a skill I had not yet acquired, and dozens of awkward misses discouraged me, already weak from hunger. Eventually, however, a foot-long, unnamed subject of Neptune's kingdom swam by, and even clumsier than I, became my first victim.

Now what to do with my catch? I could eat it raw, and in truth, the idea was much less repugnant than it would have been with a steady diet. On the other hand, the art of starting fires had been handed down from my Cherokee ancestors, and a cooked fish had a much great appeal than a raw one.

To sum up the matter, I started a fire with dry straw and other material in the hacienda and cooked it over the open fire, as I cooked several others in the coming days. It was a monotonous diet, and I had never especially like fish. But as a saying I learned in New England goes, "hunger makes any broth delicious."

My thoughts then turned to escaping from the island. I guessed that I was less than a hundred miles from the Brazilian mainland, stranded no doubt on one of the low-lying banks I had heard of from experienced sailors. Obviously humans had once inhabited the island but it had subsided to such dangerous levels that storms sometimes submerged it. No wonder, I thought, there appeared to be no animals except a few birds on the island.

After considering my options, I proposed to put together a raft from whatever materials and cloth I might strip from the hacienda and the few trees still standing. I still had the ship spar as a beginning. The risk was great, but the distance to the mainland was minimal. Later that morning after an auspicious breakfast of red snapper and mollusks—I was becoming more proficient as a fisherman—I began work on the raft. After finishing off the snapper for lunch, I took my knife and headed out to collect or cut what branches I could. I was in luck of sorts. The storm had torn several substantial limbs entirely from the tree trunks, while others dangled weakly. I returned, dragging my best trophies, tired but happy with my labors. But never in a million years could I have expected to see what—or better, who—was waiting for me in the hacienda.

"You!" I blurted out in astonishment. It was the red-headed gentlemen from the Boston Common comfortably resting in the only chair left in the place.

"And a good day to you, too, Nathan. Each time I see you it appears you have found some new means of distressing yourself," he chuckled in his deep baritone voice.

"How in God's name, sir, did you get here?"

"You have said it, my boy, in God's name. I am here to help you again. The way I got here does not matter, only my purpose."

"Sir, perhaps I have lost my mind. I understand none of this."

"Your mind is raw but sound enough, young man. My

understanding of the matter will prove sufficient to rescue you, but only if you follow my instructions."

"I am building a raft to get to the Brazilian coast."

He held up his right hand to stop me. I noticed his gold ring with the magnificent turquoise.

"Forget the raft. You must not go there. Your salvation lies elsewhere. Besides Carib folk live along the coast, and some of them have a taste for human flesh. You are too thin and wiry to be truly delectable to them, but they would roast you nonetheless if nothing better falls into their pot."

"You, sir, guided me before. I was not able to express my gratitude then. I do so now. I thank you from the heart. Tell me what I must do."

"You will find a strip of white sail on the east beach. Attach it to a pole, one of those you are trimming, and stake it on the highest point on the island. And take care it does not fall. In a few days a whaling vessel will see it and take you aboard."

"Yes, sir. Now will you answer a question that weighs heavily on my heart?"

"You may ask."

"Many went down with our vessel. Did any besides me survive?"

"Some did. I see that your concern is mainly for Catherine and Miguel. You have no cause for grief."

"Does that mean, sir, that they and others survived the storm?"

"That is all I can tell you."

"Is there anything else I should know?"

"More than you can imagine, Nathan, more than you can imagine. But this only I shall tell you for the moment: sail no more. A survivor of three shipwrecks ought to learn to stay on land," he chuckled. Then he added with a sparkle in his blue eyes, "Your life is elsewhere. Live well and trust the Creator, as wise men say."

For the briefest instant I turned to look at a large tropical bird with brilliant red and green plumage that suddenly perched unexpectedly on the window ledge. When I turned back to my guest. He was gone, and so was the bird. I would see him once more. But that telling belongs to another time.

I followed my strange guest's instructions to the letter. The sail was where he said, and attached firmly to the pole, was soon erect atop the central hill. Three days later a whaling ship returning from the southern ocean passed by my island and dispatched a boat to fetch me aboard. I told my story in detail to Captain Braddock and the assembled crew, but the looks on several faces told me that not everyone believed me. Captain Braddock, however, was not among the skeptics. He had known Captain Johnson and had encounters with Manuel Furtado.

"Furtado was a wanted person in several countries. It is said that his backers, shadowy financiers in London seeking to profit illegally from revolutions in the Spanish American countries and slavery in Africa, supplied him capital to buy his way into partial control of the *Chesapeake*. It may be better for humanity if, indeed, he went down in Brazilian waters. In that regard, you may be asked to appear before a maritime inquest to tell what you know of Captain Johnson's fate and Furtado's activities. As far as I know, Johnson was an able seaman and it would not surprise me to learn that Furtado, not a Spanish cannon, did him in."

"I was not in any way involved in the decisions that doomed

both vessels. I was obliged to serve as ship's carpenter after the man under whom I served died in Cuban waters."

"All the better to get an impartial version of what happened from someone who had no axe to grind, profits to make, or misdeeds to conceal."

"Where most likely will the inquest take place, sir?"

"Probably in Boston, but possibly in Salem."

We docked three weeks later in Boston. I thanked Captain Braddock profusely for my rescue and promised to be available as a witness if the need should arise within a reasonable time. I was safe and free but only a few coins which Captain Braddock had given me jingled in my pocket. I would not sail again but must soon find some sort of livelihood on land.

Sad memories of the city burdened me. Nevertheless, an irresistible curiosity led me to walk the streets where I had known Jane, Frederick, and all the Olgivies I had loved in a time that now seemed far distant from me but forever near in sentiment. Thus it was that I chose to visit Mr. Stafford's workshop. But to my surprise the sign now featured the name Thomas Olgivie & Son.

Even as I stood puzzled at the change, a door opened and out walked my dear deceased friend Frederick Olgivie. He saw me before I could react, called out, and rapidly approached. I was skittish and turned to flee; persons from other spiritual realms were becoming too frequent in my life.

"Nathan, wait, it's me, Frederick!"

"But Frederick, I thought you were . . ."

"Yeah, dead, I know. Just as I thought you were. We tried to catch up to you and tell you I was alive, but you were too far ahead of us. By the time we traced you to Salem, you had already shipped out."

We hugged each other and questions poured forth about where I had been, what had happened to the Olgivies, Mr. Stafford, and the shop. He explained that Mr. Stafford had branched out into other enterprises and sold the shop to Master Olgivie. But the one question I could not bring myself to ask was about Jane. Frederick guessed my perplexity and teased me about it.

"Just on the wee chance that it may be of minor interest to you, Nate, Jane has a fiancé who is pressuring her to marry him. He's nice enough, but she, for reasons that may have something to do with you, is unenthusiastic about the whole thing. You have returned just in time to right the ship—or maybe sink it for good—and put things in their proper order. I'm on my way home and you're coming with me. So no argument; Mother, Father, brothers and sisters, and perhaps even Jane, will want to see you."

I protested in vain—no good clothes, no haircut or shave, nothing but a long list of misadventures.

"Who cares about any of that, Nathan? The real thing is that like the Prodigal Son, you have returned to us. So come along, Mother will, so to speak, surely kill the fatted calf, and Father will put a ring on your finger and order a party in your honor, and all of us will celebrate the happy occasion. So you're coming home with me, even if I have to drag by the heels."

So with misgivings I went along. It turned out to be one of the happiest days of my life. The Olgivies all but smothered me with love and food. Master Olgivie, stalwart, kind, and firm as ever, asked me many questions about my travels and work as ship's carpenter. And with a few discreet omissions, I described them to the rapt attention of the entire family — except Jane.

Mother Olgivie, gentle and loving as ever, observed that I looked as strong as a young horse but as thin as a rail and promised as quickly as possible to remedy my excessive slenderness, which translated into her familiar terms, meant that she would ply me with food. As she began to do so that very evening.

The younger Olgivies had grown considerably but were as lovable and happy as I remembered them. I am afraid, however, that I did not pay them as much attention as they deserved. The reason for my distraction was, of course, Jane, who still had not made an appearance. Perhaps she was with her fiancé in another part of the house or on the grounds, or maybe my presence was now a matter of indifference to her. I wondered but could not ask any of these things.

After half an hour the door to her room opened and she stepped forth. I felt weak-kneed by the woman I saw. More beautiful than I remembered her, Jane came forward without hesitation, but instead of greeting me with a hug and a kiss, as her younger siblings had done, she shook my hand and asked formally about my health.

For the rest of the evening, I talked and asked questions distractedly, agitated and mystified by Jane's cool distance and aloofness. As the hour grew late and I was about to leave, Master Olgivie brought the conversation down to hard facts.

"Nathan, what are your plans now, if you can tell me?" he asked.

"Sir, all I have at the moment is a firm resolution never to go to sea again. As someone recently pointed out to me, three shipwrecks and naught to show for my voyages should be proof enough that the sailor's life is not for me. But so far that is my only firm decision. It remains to be decided where I'll go and what I'll do for a livelihood."

"There is a position open at our shop, and I imagine that with all the practical experience you have had at sea, even though you deem it profitless, will prove to be valuable knowledge. The employment is yours if you are of a mind to rejoin us."

"Master Olgivie, I am, and always will be, grateful to you and your family for all you have done for me," I preambled, watching Jane out of the corner of my eye. "But I would not want to be a bother in any way."

"Sleep on it, Nathan, and we can discuss the matter tomorrow. Perhaps by then your way will be clearer."

As I was leaving, Jane finally called me aside and the family filed out to give us privacy. "Nathan, I know I seemed a bit standoffish with you, but as I imagine Frederick has told you, I am engaged to be married."

"Yes, so he said, but he also hinted that you do not seem to be really enthusiastic about setting a date for the wedding. Is there any chance that I may have had something to do with that?"

"When you left, I doubted I would ever see you again," she answered obliquely to my direct question.

"Does it bother you that I have come back, as Frederick says, like a returning Prodigal?"

"I am glad to see you again, Nathan."

"Only glad, nothing more?"

Her face reddened and I perceived that I had touched on a sore point and that her Scottish temper was on the rise because of my prodding questions. I was unsure of how things were going, but I felt an urgency and wanted to push as far as I could with her feelings. It might be the only chance I would have.

"Nathan, you remember enough about me to know that I don't like subtleties and indirect speech, but neither do I like being pushed."

"But indirect answers are what you're giving me."

She stared at me for a moment, then laughed and the tension between us eased a bit. "You're right, I was being evasive. I don't always practice what I preach."

"Then, Jane, let me say this: I will tell you my feelings honestly if you will then tell me yours under the same conditions."

"Fair enough, Mr. Stokes, but I must hear first what you have to say before I make any promises."

"That's fair enough for me too. I know you are engaged, and Frederick describes your fiancé as a good man. Be that as it may, I am sure you know that I love you, and I believe we were on the verge of telling each other how we felt months ago when it appeared that Frederick had died in the pinnacle disaster. My feelings for you have not changed, but instead absence has made my love grow stronger. Here's the heart of the matter: I want to marry you, to be your husband, to spend the rest of my life with you. Now, there, I have said my say; now it's time for you to say yours."

"Nathan, that's about as direct as it gets. So why deny the obvious? I promised to tell you my feelings in response to yours. You silly goose of a man, don't you know that I have been in love with from the start? All that time you were away. I prayed for you every day. My love never faltered, but finally I realized that my life had to go on and that I might never see you again. I was not even sure you were still alive. My family did not need a spinster to deal with. That's when I met Aaron. And now you show up and . . . Well, darn it, man, yes, I love you. And I don't apologize for my language. But now I have the complication with my fiancé and his feelings."

"Can't you explain to him that we knew each other before he met you? Or would you like for me to talk with him?"

"Nathan, I'm a big girl, a woman, and I can take care of my own problems. You leave the talking part to me and do something more gainful. Get yourself to work in Daddy's shop. You'll need steady employment if you plan to be my husband and the man in my life." Then with a lovely smile she added, "And for God's sake, don't you and Frederick slip away on another boating adventure!"

I left walking on a cloud. Of course, I took Master Olgivie's offer. Of course, I asked him a few weeks later for newly unengaged Jane's hand. Of course we were married in Boston. Of course, as everybody knows, six children were born to us in the first dozen years of our marriage. But whether we lived happily ever after, as the fairy tales go, I can't say for sure, for the "ever after part" is still happening with no end in sight.

But I have a witness that things were off to a good start. A week before Jane and I were married in June, eight months after my return, I asked her to go for a walk with me on the Boston Common. The day was warm and Bostonians were out in force. I noticed a familiar man of substantial girth and a shock of red hair dressed elegantly in the old style doling out handfuls of nuts and seeds from a bag to a troop of scurrying squirrels and fluttering birds. As before, his gold ring with the magnificent turquoise caught my eye. He smiled and waved his hand which I took as a gesture that all was well and on the right track. I stopped, bowed in his direction, and thanked him in my best manner.

"Darling, did you speak to someone just now?" Jane asked.

"Yes, so I did, my darling, to the gentleman sitting on the bench back there feeding the birds and squirrels. I've had some dealings with him."

Jane looked back and frowned. "Nathan, all I see are birds and squirrels. There's no one there."

I looked too and was not surprised to see that he was gone. "My friend is a very busy person," I explained to her. "He has a way of rushing off suddenly like that to take care of things."

Forefathers.com

I am trying to trace a Scottish ancestor of mine by the surname of Olgivie. I believe he immigrated to Virginia around 1790. The only tangible link I have in my possession is a property deed issued to a Benjamin Olgivie in Williamsburg in 1796, but of his marital status I have only family stories. According to my Grandmother, whose memory was fading when she told me, Benjamin married a Blackmore woman and moved to Baltimore where they raised numerous children some of whom, so she claimed, resettled in Illinois, Iowa, and perhaps in Nebraska. She also said that his younger brother came to Virginia around 1800, but I have no other proof of his existence. I am an amateur in genealogical research and would appreciate any guidance or leads.

--Havard Olgivie, Fredericksburg, Virginia

...

Dear Havard:

I can believe you when you say you are an amateur. You obviously don't know that you are living in the state with the richest genealogical information in this country.

Just google "Virginia Genealogical Sources" and you will find enough stuff to keep you busy for months, maybe years. A good place to start would be to check passenger lists to find out about the younger brother, that is, if he came into a Virginia port. Anyway, good hunting!

--Arnold Olgivie, Boston, Massachusetts

P.S. my ancestors came directly to Boston, but no doubt there are clan links to your family back in Scotland.

...

Chapter 8:
The Lady of Shiloh

[In his journal article, "The First Indiana Rangers at Shiloh," <u>Hoosiers in the Civil War</u>, No. 11, Nov., 1954, pp. 34-39, Seymour Murphy comments briefly on an incident that for reasons that are obvious on the one hand but mysterious on the other does not appear in military reports or scholarly histories of the battle. There are, however, indirect anecdotal references to it in several known memoirs of both Northern and Southern veterans. None claimed to have witnessed the disputed incident themselves but knew men who had.

What is well documented is that the battle did not go well for Union forces the first day of great conflict, the first major battle in the Western theater of the war. But with the arrival of General Buell's army by boat at the Tennessee River Landing, the combined Federal armies were able to push the single Confederate host back to Corinth and ultimately to Tupelo under General Beauregard and secure the Union victory. Dr. Murphy writes that under the leadership of Lieutenant Hiram Stokes of Muncie, the First Indiana Rangers dislodged a Confederate force in a pivotal action that initiated the Confederate withdrawal from Shiloh. His twin brother, Second Lieutenant Hamilton Stokes, was killed in the third uphill charge.]

...

The sharpshooters from Tennessee and Kentucky were generally acknowledged as the best riflemen in the Confederate armies. But even they had to admit grudgingly that the First Indiana Rangers were their equals. Before the War, many of the future Rangers, themselves the sons of resettled Southerners, honed their skills not only hunting in the forests of lower Indiana but also in friendly but spirited competitions across the Ohio River with their Kentucky and Tennessee cousins. When the war came the elites of both sides often knew one another by name and blood kinship and though deadly in battle, admired the skill of their adversaries and praised them as worthy foes when they fell.

To hear his men tell it, no rebel and only his twin brother Hamilton could match Hiram Stokes shot for shot. If it had been possible, they claimed, in a contest they would put their money on the Stokes brothers against the best marksmen the Confederates could field.

Meanwhile, General Buell and his staff, along with over thirty thousand reinforcements, were impatient to reach Shiloh. The boats were maddeningly slow with breakdowns and conflicting orders. The urgency grew by the hour. It was no secret to any one on board that there was a good chance—or a bad one—that they would arrive too late to save General Grant's forces from a major defeat. Nor was it lost on the men that a Confederate victory would strengthen the rebel cause in the West and could persuade populous and prosperous Missouri to join the Confederacy. It was an accepted fact on both sides that with evenly matched forces, the Confederates were the superior soldiers because they were fighting on their home ground.

But high policy and grand battle plans quickly break down into the private hell of each soldier who loses sight of the bigger battle. He sees only the smoke and dust, and hears the screams around him. The lines break, men charge and fall, run and regroup, and all sense of order and plan is lost in the mayhem. At close quarters friend and foe are not always distinguishable and a man may die at the hands of either.

Hiram's unleashed Rangers charged twice up the slope, but Rebel fire withered their resolve and they had to fall back, leaving fifteen of their two hundred men dead or wounded on the hillside.

"Drink and reload, men," he panted, "Then on my count of ten we go at 'em again, and this time all the way!"

But at the high count of ten," nearly twenty of the men froze, including Hamilton.

"Wait, Hiram" he yelled, "not yet! Don't fire!"

Hiram turned to his brother and the wavering men. "Wait for what? In God's name, it's now or never!"

"Hiram, wait, there's a lady up there on the slope right in front of us! See her? She's wearing a white dress. We can't shoot! We might hit her! I don't hold with shooting a woman, even if she is a Rebel!"

"What woman? I don't see a woman! Come on, we've got our orders, and I'm giving you mine. We have to take out that Rebel nest! So move!"

"We see her, too, Lieutenant!" said several of the men holding back with Hamilton. By quick count he estimated seventeen or eighteen.

Hiram cursed for one of the few times in his life, as much in shock as in disgust with his reluctant Rangers, especially

Hamilton. His brother had never faltered before. What had gotten into him and the others? A woman that nobody could see? Was it a cover for cowardice? Whatever it was, he couldn't let it contaminate the whole company.

"I'll count again. We go on ten, and those that don't will be subject to court-martial!"

Reluctantly, they fell in with the others and the charge began. This time it carried over the Confederate trenches and in hand to hand fighting they took the hill. Sergeant Bob Jones reported that they lost eighteen men.

A young Confederate gasping for breath as his blood poured out on the ground, looked plaintively at Hiram. "Lieutenant, I didn't think you'd come up the hill with that woman standing out there. Did you kill her too?"

"No, soldier, we didn't shoot her. We don't kill women, and I'm sorry we had to kill you. What's your name?"

"Jimmy Stokesbury, lieutenant."

Damn all war, Hiram thought to himself. Older version of my surname, maybe even a cousin, so young, his life wasted. Jimmy's breathing stopped.

"Jones," Hiram called out as he closed Jimmy's eyelids. "Where's Second Lieutenant Stokes?"

The Sergeant hung his head. "Sir, I'm sorry, he . . . he's wounded real bad."

They all saw the woman, or whatever it was, Hiram said under his breath. Like the young Rebel Jimmy Stokesbury lying there. It must have been a signal that they were going to die. I've heard of such things.

"Sir? I didn't catch what you said."

"Nothing. Take me to Hamilton."

Hamilton was on a stretcher, and two men were treating him. But Hiram saw at once that his wounds were mortal. In a detached, military space in his mind, he saw and accepted that Hamilton was dying, another casualty. But then the military veneer vanished and he was simply Hiram staring at his twin brother so like him, so constant, so close, so much a part of himself.

"Hamilton, I can't let you go unless I go too. We were born into this world together, we have to leave it together."

"No, Hiram, you have to stay here and live for both of us. You were always the leader, but this one time I'll take the lead and wait for you on the other side. I know you'll have a family and a good life, and you'll do it for both of us. But now I have to go. I can see people I recognize gathering to welcome me. I love you, Hiram."

He expelled a deep breath and was gone.

"And I love you, Hamilton," Hiram said as tears flooded his eyes."

After a while and back in his military role, he called Sergeant Jones.

"Yes sir?"

"See to it that my brother and the others have a proper burial. And do the same for the young Rebel."

"Sir?"

"Is there a problem, Sergeant?"

"No sir, I just thought that being a Rebel and all, you wouldn't want to bother . . ."

"Sergeant, someday when we've finished with the killing and the dying, we'll have to get back to the living and respecting one another again. Just think of this as a small step in that direction."

"Yes sir," Jones said with a puzzled frown, wondering to himself if the Lieutenant was about to break down on them.

Hiram fought on till the end of the war, taking part in a dozen major engagements and winning many commendations and medals for valor. And when finally the guns went silent at Appomattox he hung up his guns and vowed never to fire another weapon. Later his resolve would be tested.

Forefathers.com
I am confused by Hiram's instructions to Sergeant Jones, if what is reported here is correct. It doesn't compute to me that only minutes after his twin brother Hamilton was killed by Confederate gunfire Hiram would show concern for a Rebel soldier, who could have been the one who shot him. Did the surname have something to do with his order? Stokes and Stokesbury are fairly common surnames but doesn't necessarily mean kinship. Or did I miss something?
--Arthur Purefoy, Portland, Maine
    ...

Arthur,
I think you would understand better Hiram Stokes' reasons for doing what he did if you knew what happened to him after the war. Please reserve your judgment. I think you would discover that he was an uncommon man and that his behavior in this instance was characteristic.
---Sean Stokes Olgivie, Terre Haute, Indiana
    ...

Chapter 9:
The Cordele Ghosts

*[As far as this research genealogist has been able to
ascertain, the following accounts are not included in any extant
genealogical records of the states involved: Florida, Georgia,
and Texas. There is, however, ample documentation of the
Southern branch of the Stafford family itself and a reasonable
amount of evidence regarding their westward migration across
the Deep South beginning in Charlestown, South Carolina. Less
is known about the Blackwell family that was prominent in
Virginia in colonial times. Land records show that David and
Katherine Beaufort Stafford, representing the original Southern
Branch of that family, sold their rice plantation and city
properties in the Charlestown area in 1714. Since this
transaction occurred not long after the devastating storm of
1713, it is likely that they first resettled somewhere in what
later became the Georgia Colony. Subsequently, they moved
again, establishing a cotton plantation near the town of
Cordele, Georgia where their descendants lived until 1865. The
narrative about Mary Bankhead Blackwell, whose husband
was descended from the Virginia Blackwells, is based on
correspondence with her older sister Katherine (née Bankhead).
The two sisters never saw each other again after Mary married
and moved away from Cordele, but they wrote each other until
Katherine's death in 1904 in Lufkin, Texas. It is not known to
this genealogist when Mary passed away. The following
narrative (retold by an unknown Alabamian with explanatory
material by Katherine's descendant) is set in Cordele in 1865
amidst the devastation of the Civil War.]*

...

Mr. John Thomas Johnson, who used to hire us for assorted jobs on his small farm, liked to tell us the story of "The Cordele Ghosts." Well, to be completely accurate, neither he nor we called them "ghosts" but "haints" back in those days. Mr. John Thomas, as we always called him respectfully, had grown up in Cordele, Georgia before resettling in Alabama as a young man. And the older he got, the more he relived his fondest days back in Cordele.

"Did you ever see any haints yourself, Mr. John Thomas?" we children would ask him as we rested after dinner, taking care not to crowd him too closely and get splattered by his chewing tobacco juice.

"Well, I can tell you young'uns that I saw a lot of quair things back in old Cordele when I was just a lad. Why if I was a mind to, I could tell you things you wouldn't believe if you saw them with your own two eyes. But as for spirits, the colored folks always said there were haints aplenty up in Boney Hill Graveyard by the old ruins of the Stafford Plantation. But generally speaking, we white boys didn't go up there ourselves, you understand, unless we were drinking a bit or daring one another to do crazy things. That was the colored graveyard that'd been there since back in slave times. We respected it, just like the colored folks respected our white graveyard."

"What did they see, Mr. John Thomas?" we asked, crowding in a little closer and risking the tobacco juice.

"Why, the colored folks would tell how they had seen the haints running and prancing around in white sheets, little'uns, big'uns, all sizes, so they told the tale. But the scariest thing was the lights and the chains a-rattling and other commotion. Their eyes would get as big as half dollars when they told us about it.

It was plain that had seen something that was more than flesh and blood out there in that old graveyard."

By the time I got to ninth grade and knew most everything, one day I dared ask him, "Do you believe there really are haints, Mr. John Thomas, or were those colored folks just imagining things?"

Mr. John Thomas gave me a withering look, as if I had uttered a blasphemy.

"Why, child, of course there are haints. All the old folks in olden times knew about them. Haints, witches, spells, evil eye, and all such things as that, and more besides. The old people of long ago knew a lot more than we do about stuff like that." Then he added pointedly, looking at me, "You see, they were not in the habit of disbelieving like some people are today."

Mr. John Thomas always talked of going back to Cordele, and his voice would take a tone of lonesome sadness and his eyes had a faraway look. But as far as any of us knew, he never got the chance, even though he lived to a good old age. As we grew up and scattered, we mostly lost touch with him. He eventually retired from farming, but we would see him sitting on the front porch of his little white frame house on the main road. We would wave to him, and he would wave back, but it always seemed we were too busy to stop and say hello to him. I regret that now, and for the life of me can't remember why we couldn't spare a few minutes for an old friend.

I thought of him when I chanced to drive through Cordele once on my way back from Florida. I didn't see any "haints," nor, the truth be told, not much of anything else that got my attention in that small town. But I remembered the name and all the old memories I learned from Mr. John Thomas. Maybe it was better he never went back, I thought to myself. Some places are made to be in only once in life.

As for the Cordele "haints," I dismissed them as fancies of his imagination that existed only in his reworked memories. That is, until many years later I learned that the Cordele ghosts were more real than even he knew. Let me tell you the missing part of the story, as Dr. Leland Stafford, IV, of Lufkin, Texas told it to me.

Colonel David Stafford, great-great grandson of the original Englishman David Stafford, and his two older sons, Wadsworth and Geoffrey, died in the battle for Atlanta, leaving Mrs. Katherine Wadsworth Stafford with a ruined plantation and three younger children to care for: daughters Mary Hope, 14, and Alice Beatrice, 12; and son, Leland Wadsworth, 10.

Food was a pressing problem, but not the most urgent one facing Mrs. Stafford. With the advance of General Sherman's Union forces, which came burning everything in their path, and the waning Confederate resistance near the end of the Civil War, the slaves either fled or were forced to flee, taking with them most of the remaining food, animals, carriages, and implements. In the end Mrs. Stafford was left with one old farm wagon and a half-starved mule team decrepit with age.

Worst of all, word came that some of the ex-slaves had formed themselves into a marauding band out to rob and kill their former masters or anyone else unlucky enough to be in their pathway. There had already been atrocities in east Georgia, so it was reported. The matter was desperate. Mrs. Stafford was alone and unarmed, but like the ancestral women in her family, she was no weakling. If she had held things together in good days, she would do her best, with God's help, to do so in bad times. But what could she do to save her remaining family? The thought obsessed her day and night as she prayed to God that he would show her a way.

Then pushed to the limit and fearful that the marauders could show up at any moment, she suddenly had an inspired idea. Immediately she called the children and gave them their orders.

"Leland, hitch the team to the old wagon. Can you do that, son?"

"Yes, ma'am. But what for?"

"You'll know soon enough, but be quick about it. We don't have much time. Now, Hope and Alice, you come with me. We've got work to do."

As Leland hitched the team, she and the girls packed all the clothing and everything of value, ripped up the remaining bed sheets, and gathered all the candles and lanterns they could find. At dusk, ever fearful of the vengeful marauders, they headed in the old wagon for Boney Hill Graveyard. The girls were so frightened they could barely speak, and little Leland, trying to make a brave show of courage, trembled with fear.

"Why the colored graveyard, Mommy?" whispered the terrified Alice Beatrice. "I'm afraid of that place."

"And so are a lot of other people, Alice Beatrice, including the servants. Right now it's the safest place for us. Now here's what I want you all to do. Are you listening to me, Leland and Mary Hope?" When we get to the cemetery, you take these sheets and . . ."

When the Black riders arrived at the Stafford plantation that night all was dark and deserted and nothing of value was left. Infuriated and many of them drunk, they torched the house and buildings, danced and sang as it burned, and finally rode on, the lurid crimson fire lighting up the sky.

But as they came within sight of Boney Hill Graveyard they saw a terrifying sight: Mary Hope, Alice Beatrice, and Leland Wadsworth marching in white sheets, each with a bobbing candle or lantern. Leland had loosed a trace chain, which he rapped on the stone markers. Behind them the taller, sheet-draped figure of Mrs. Stafford, arms uplifted, cast a flickering, gigantic shadow in the pale light.

The riders panicked in superstitious terror and raced away. Some people said later it cut short their destructive rampage. What is certain is that the next day and for days thereafter no one dared go near Boney Hill Graveyard, which was time enough for Mrs. Stafford and her children to make good their escape from the devastation in Georgia and reach areas where there was still a semblance of order and, best of all, food from sympathetic families for the family and the tired old mules. They survived and eventually made it all the way to Lufkin, Texas where she had a brother and former neighbors.

Dr. Leland Wadsworth Stafford, IV chuckled as he ended his story. "Thank God for the 'Cordele ghosts'," he said. "Without those good spirits I wouldn't be here today. So the 'Cordele Ghosts' were real just as your Mr. Johnson said, but not exactly what he thought they were and not yet in the spirit world. We still talk about the will and determination of my great-great Grandmother. They say that when they finally reached Texas the hands of that genteel, beautiful lady were as calloused and rough as a farmer's from handling the reins. You have to wonder if they still make women like her in this day and time."

History of Angelina County
Entry 35, p. 67, 1956

Leland Stafford became a prominent planter and, later, wealthy businessman in Lufkin, Texas. He ran unsuccessfully for state senator in 1896 and 1898 and supported the failed "Bull Moose" presidential bid of Teddy Roosevelt. He commented humorously near the end of his life that given his poor political judgment and few likeminded friends, he ought to be permitted to wear a .45 publicly to defend himself.

...

Chapter 10:
Mary Blackwell

[Early Settlers in North Florida, Avery Scott and Mary Dougherty, The University of Florida Press, VI vols. 1962-66 (Vol. II, p. 20).

As authors Scott and Dougherty point out, the history of northern Florida is closely linked to the adjacent Southern states, especially Georgia, and to a lesser extent Alabama and South Carolina. The settlement of Anglo-Americans in northern and central Florida is a dimension of the Anglo expansion generally overlooked or relegated to a footnote in the westward march. It occurred after the initial westward surge had reached the central states and Texas.]

...

In 1852, Jeff Blackwell, 21, and his new bride Mary Bankhead Blackwell, 20, along with fifteen other families moved down from Cordele, Georgia to frontier territory in north central Florida. Jeff and neighbors felled trees, burned stumps, limbs, and underbrush, and helped one another erect log cabins on their homesteads. They named the settlement Providence and built a small church, Providence Church, on the Jacksonville Road, just north of the community. South of their settlement stretched primitive pine forests that gradually merged with the tropical vegetation of lower Florida. War bands of young Native Americans still ranged north of their customary hunting grounds in the southern swamps to forage and steal from the white frontier settlements. The screams of panthers were common at night, and Jeff and his neighbors kept shotguns loaded and ready to protect families, mules, cows, pigs, and chickens from both human and animal predators.

If Georgia summers were hot, Florida's were sweltering, but Jeff and Mary adjusted and survived. The "crackers," as they were called, were hardy and fiercely independent. In letters to her sister Katherine back in Cordele, Mary told of the bears, panthers, and unfriendly Indians that roamed the forest but boasted that the Florida winters were usually like perpetual springs. Though she could do without the snakes, spiders, and alligators around the creeks.

Their son Henry was born in March, 1853 and in April of 1855 daughter Agnes. Mary was a tall, strong woman who delivered without undue labor or distress. Old Hattie Philpott, the Black community midwife, said admiringly of Mary, "She could drop a half dozen more babies with no trouble at all." Mary's strength was a good thing, which was more than could be said of some women in Providence. The nearest physician, Dr. Hansford Humphry, was sixty miles away in Jacksonville, much too far to save Sally James, wife of Arnold James, from fatal childbirth hemorrhaging. Their child, Tom, survived on goat's milk and Myrtle Simmons' loving care. Devastated by Sally's death, Arnold moved back to Georgia, leaving little Tom with the widow Simmons, who renamed him Tom Simmons for her deceased husband and raised him as her own. A few years later Arnold moved west and as far as anyone knew, never saw Tom again.

With the secession of Florida and other Southern States from the Union in 1861, the Blackwells had a decision to make. Jeff and Mary discussed it after the children were asleep.

"Mary," Jeff said, taking her hands in his, "I feel it's my duty to fight for my country, but I can't rightly leave you and the children here all by yourselves. So I was thinking that I'll take you back up to your sister's in Cordele. That way you'll have people to help and look after you. But if you're not of a mind to do that, then I'm not going."

Mary withdrew her hands and placed them firmly on his shoulders. "Jeff, I have just two things to say about it. First, I would be ashamed to be the wife of a man who wouldn't fight for his country. And second, this is my home now, not Katherine's house in Cordele, and this is where I mean to stay. You go on and do your duty like the brave man you are, and I'll stay here and do mine. We didn't move down here to turn back the first time things got rough."

"But I'll be worried about you and the children here all by yourselves."

"And I, dear husband, will be worried about you. We'll pray

to the Good Lord that He will guard and protect you and bring you safely back to us. And don't you worry about the children and me. We have neighbors I can call on if things get rough. Just leave me the mule team, the shotgun and plenty of shells, and we'll be just fine. I'll educate Henry and Agnes as best I can. All I have is God and the Bible, but with them we are strong enough to face any enemy. The children are smart, so I'm sure they will learn quickly all I can teach them. When will you leave?"

"This Saturday, I reckon, he said with a faraway look in his eyes. A couple of the men here, Jeb Bennett and Levi Stevens, were saying they'd walk over to Jacksonville and join up there. I'm hoping I'll get assigned to brother-in-law David's company with your nephews Wadsworth and Geoffrey. David's a colonel, I hear, and has raised his own company, so he must have some influence. But I don't really know where the army is liable to send us. Anyway, I don't think this war will last long, and I'm hoping to be back by spring. And this I promise you, Mary, I will come back."

"I believe you will, and I'll hold you to that promise. Now then, I'll fix up some food and water for you to take on the road."

"But what about the crops, Mary? That's a worrisome matter. The corn will need gathering in two months and the potatoes will be ready about the same time. It's a lot of work for a woman."

"And a lot for man, too, Jeff. You always told me I was a strong woman. I guess it's time to find out just how much truth there is in your words. Remember, Jeff, I won't be alone. Henry is strong for his age and works like a man, and he'll try all that much harder while you're gone. And Agnes can already cook and clean just about as well as I can. Besides, we've all worked shoulder to shoulder in the fields, and I know just about as much about farming as you do. We'll get it done."

Jeff's eyes were aglow with admiration for his Mary. And a lump formed in his throat when he thought how lucky he was to have a wife like her.

Two days later, In June of 1862, he left.

Jeff was wrong about the war. At first his occasional letters were cheerful, but by 1863 Mary could sense his fatigue and discouragement. Levi Stevens, he told her, died in Tennessee and Jeb Bennett was missing in action on a Confederate raid across the Ohio River into Indiana. Of his original Florida platoon, the two men left were reassigned to a Georgia company. From comments he made about tobacco fields, she guessed he was now in North Carolina or maybe Virginia. In his last letter he mentioned the Tennessee River and the Smoky Mountains. That's Tennessee, she thought. At least he's a little closer to home.

Things did not go all that well for Mary either. A few weeks after Jeff left, she discovered she was pregnant. Now we're in a pickle, she thought. Harvest time was upon her, and she had to take extra care of herself to protect the life of her unborn child. She did not dare tell Jeff, even if her letters reached him. If he found out, he might desert and rush home, and the roving "home guard" of Northern Florida, as it was called, had a reputation for hanging or shooting renegades and Confederate deserters, or anyone else who crossed them. Anyway, she was sure she could work until the corn and potatoes were gathered, but her dresses were already becoming too tight and restrictive. A big baby, she thought, with joy and worry, probably another boy who would be big and tall like his brother Henry.

Then an idea occurred to her. Digging into Jeff's clothes, she found one of his old shirts and a serviceable pair of pants. Since she was nearly as tall as Jeff they fit fairly well and much more comfortably than her dresses. Although she had washed them before she put his clothes away, she imagined they still had his aroma. It was a comfort to her.

But her solution did not last long unchallenged. One Sunday afternoon she was surprised to see half a dozen neighbors standing at her front door when she opened it to a loud knock.

"Good evening, Mrs. Blackwell," said Matthew Glover, a short graying man in his fifties who did the preaching. "We thought we'd all come over and see how things were coming along for you."

Mary was surprised by the formality of his greeting. The Glovers, former Virginians, had been their nearest neighbors since moving to Providence five years earlier.

"Why, doing just fine, Matthew. You'all do come on in. I don't have chairs enough for everybody in the fireplace room, but you are welcome to sit on the bed or take a seat at the kitchen table. Agnes, run and fetch a pitcher of water and some glasses for everybody. It's hot out there today."

They talked about the war, crops, illnesses, and other matters, but it was obvious to Mary that they really had other things on their mind. She was a patient woman and knew that eventually they would get around to the real purpose of their visit. After a while Matthew did.

"Mrs. Blackwell" he said with obvious nervousness, "some of us have noticed lately that you've been working in the field wearing men's clothing."

"Why, that's right, Matthew, Jeff's old clothes. I imagine

most of you know that I'm . . . in a family way, and dresses are just not suited for that kind of heavy . . ."

"You know, Mrs. Blackwell," Glover interrupted her, "that women aren't supposed to dress like a man. The Bible speaks against it."

Mary was stunned and angered as the meaning of his words sank in. After a pause, she responded. "Well, I tell you what, Mr. Glover and you other men, if you'll agree to come down here and do the plowing and field work that has to be done, I'll be happy to wear a dress and take my ease in the shade of that oak tree out there."

"We meant no offense, Mrs. Blackwell, and you have no call to speak in such a tone to us. Our intention is to be a God-fearing community," Matthew offered, hastily getting to his feet. "The Scriptures teach that a sharp tongue spawns many evils."

"In that case, Reverend Glover, I'll keep my words short. We won't be back to your church. Now I bid you all good day."

Some of the embarrassed women mumbled offers of sympathy and help as they left, but Mary made no response. Still smarting from Mary's rebuke, none of men offered to help her with the fieldwork. And none did.

Not that she needed help until it came time for her to give birth. Henry, growing stronger by the day, gathered most of corn, and she and Agnes managed to harvest the potatoes and vegetables. The rains held off until the most demanding work was done, and for every fair day, Mary gave thanks. At night they prayed for God's help and Jeff's safety.

Then one morning in late March of 1863 her contractions began.

"Henry, you run over to Miss Hattie's house and see if she

can come. And hurry, son! You know who she is and where she lives, don't you?"

"Yes, ma'am, the colored woman. I pass by her house when I go fishing in the Santa Fe fork. She always gives me a drink and a cookie and asks me about you when she sees me."

Henry ran all the way, and within an hour old Hattie was there. And a good thing, too. For the delivery was harder than the earlier ones. And for a good reason: twin boys.

"Twins, Miss Hattie? I knew I was bigger this time and the thought occurred to me, especially one night when I guess both were kicking. I thought to myself, this boy is going to be born half grown."

"No, but they're full term, judging by their eyelashes. Both look fine, and they're identical, like two peas in a pod. You think you're gonna have milk enough for the pair? If not, maybe we can get some goat's milk from Myrtle Hardin's old nanny goats."

"I usually have plenty for one baby. We'll just have to see about two, specially two boys."

Agnes hovered over the twins like a guardian angel, which freed Mary, on her feet after a couple of days, to attend to urgent farm matters. Henry was now measurably stronger and fiercely committed to being the man of the house. Mary was convinced that with his help they could get the spring planting done on time.

And so they did. The 1863 crop was good, and Mary's milk held out until the twins, Daniel and David, were able to supplement it with table food.

But on another front, Mary was troubled as the weeks and months passed without word from Jeff. By the winter of 1864 she had not heard from him in over a year. Word reached Providence of heavy casualties as the tide of war turned against the Confederacy. Was Jeff among them? He had promised to return, and she refused to let go of the assurance. You promised me, Jeff, and I'm holding you to that promise, she told herself as she wept almost nightly on her pillow.

Worms, drought, and parasites took a heavy toll on the 1864 corn crop. The potatoes did better, but then another calamity happened. By the winter of 1865 Mary had used up all her shotgun shells and she had no way of getting more. Hawks and foxes made off with most of their chickens and thus their supply of eggs. Mary sensed it was the beginning of the end for them on the homestead. In spite of her oft-repeated assurance that Jeff would return, her sense of realism was eroding her confidence. But where would they go if they had to leave? Cordele did not seem to be an option, and as far as anyone in Providence knew, it might not even exist, and Katherine might have moved her family. Sherman's Union army had destroyed Atlanta and cut a sixty-mile wide swath of destruction through Georgia.

Henry and especially Agnes were beginning to forget their father. They asked their mother about him, where he was, what he looked like, the kind of man he was, and when he would come home. She did all she could to keep his memory alive for them, even sketching a picture of him that Henry hung over the fireplace. The actual likeness to his features was casual, but affection made up for the artistic deficiencies.

Then word came that the war was over, and not long afterwards weary Confederate survivors, many lame, began to straggle home. Jeff was not among them. Nobody could tell Mary anything about him. Yes, one remembered a man by that name in Tennessee, another thought he was sent to Virginia, and still another said that he was lost defending Atlanta.

Summer passed and fall was upon them. The harvest was better, but Mary's situation was increasingly stark. The twins were healthy but always hungry, Henry and Agnes were outgrowing their clothes and no new ones were to be had. Mary began cutting and redesigning her old dresses for Agnes and restitching Jeff's remaining garments for Henry. They were running low on food. Since that fateful day when the church delegation came to reproach her, with the happy exception of Miss Hattie, Mary had little contact with her neighbors, most of whom, persuaded by Matthew Glover's sermons, now warily regarded her as a heretic.

One afternoon Mary and her children were sitting under the oak tree. Mary was thinking about what she had to do—and soon. The twins squealed as they chased each other around the yard. Henry was jumping to reach a low branch of the oak, happy that he was able to touch it. Soon a man, he thought to himself, and then I'll reach it for sure. Agnes was placing strips of cloth together in a pattern on the lush grass. It won't look too bad, she thought, if I can get the right thread. Maybe Miss Hattie has some I could use.

Suddenly Henry stopped his jumping. "Momma, look yonder. Who's that man coming down the road?"

"Why I don't know, son. I can't make his features out from this distance."

Agnes abandoned her cloth strips and turned to look.

All at once, Mary jumped to her feet so swiftly that her children were alarmed. Even little Daniel and David stopped running for a moment and looked at her in puzzlement.

"What is it, Momma? Do you know the man?" Henry asked.

"I'm not sure, son, but there's something about him . . . the way he walks. He's limping, but even so . . . I don't know, but I think . . ."

Mary usually kept her feelings under control. But all at once she screamed, "It's him! It's him! Children, it's your father! He said he would come back! And he has! Oh, children, it's your father! Your father!" she cried as they ran to meet him, all that is but the twins, puzzled by the affair and wary of the stranger.

"Oh, Jeff, it's you! It's really you! You said you would come back, and you did!" she cried out, lavishing hugs and kisses on him.

"Not all of me, Mary, just what's left of me," he said wearily, his face deep wrinkled with fatigue. "Let me rest a minute and have a drink of water, then I'll tell you about it."

Agnes ran to bring water.

"I lost my left arm at the end of the fighting to a Yankee cannon south of Atlanta and messed up my right leg. A doctor at the Macon hospital where they took me told me the only way they could save my life was to amputate the bad leg. I told him no, that I would need that leg for farming. He shook his head and said I would never make it back to Florida. I told him I would because I had to, because I had promised you I would. I just asked him to clean and dress the wound, soak it in alcohol or turpentine or whatever they had around the hospital, which wasn't much of anything, then push me out into the sunshine to die of gangrene or live by the grace of God, and go tend to men worse off than I was. I lay there for nearly two months. Then one day I felt better and the next, better still. The next day I got up from that bed as shaky as a new-born calf, and a couple of days later started limping my way back towards Florida. So here I am. But, Mary, tell me, who are these young people, this big stout boy and this girl as pretty as a picture? Are these Henry and Agnes? I can't believe they've grown so much."

"They are, Jeff, these are your children and better ones you won't find anywhere. I couldn't have made it without them. Children, come and hug your daddy."

They did, a little unsure how to behave with a man they barely remembered, especially Agnes. Henry was unsure whether to hug his father or shake his hand, so he did both.

"But Mary, I see two little ones standing off over there like little deer, twins by the looks of them. Who are they?"

"Ours boys, Jeff, our twin boys, Daniel and David. They were born in March of 1863. Do the arithmetic, if you have any doubts."

"Arithmetic?" Agnes asked, what are you talking about, Momma?"

Jeff laughed, and the wrinkles softened a bit. "Nothing, darling, just something that grown people worry about sometimes. Bring the boys to me, Agnes, if you can catch them. They don't know me from Adam. But, Mary, you never told me about them in your letters. Why not?" he asked as Agnes chased them down and brought them squirming and protesting for Jeff to hug.

"Because you had enough to worry about with the fighting. I didn't want you to come home and risk meeting the Home Guard."

"Yeah, I heard about that pack. I respect the Yankees. They fought and died like men, but not these cowards and murderers. Our fighting may not be over until we rid Florida of that vermin. But tell me, Mary, what shape are we in as far as the farm is concerned?" He said as he released the squealing, twisting twins.

"I'm sorry to say that things are not in good shape. We managed to plant and harvest every year you were gone. But last fall I ran out of shotgun shells and the foxes, hawks, and panthers killed off our chickens and so our egg supply, and made off with all but one of our pigs. These last few months I have to say I wasn't sure what we would do next."

"What about our neighbors? Did they help out?"

"Some did," she said, thinking about Miss Hattie. "But it was hard on everybody." She thought it best to keep the matter with Matthew Glover and the church to herself for the time being.

"Well, I'm afraid a one-armed man is not going to be that much help."

"Daddy, I can plow and work like a man in the fields," Henry offered proudly.

"And I can take care of the twins," said Agnes, "I just love them to death. And I can cook and do other chores Momma taught me, and work in the field too if I have to."

"Jeff, you may have just one arm," Mary broke in, "but it's the strongest one in this family. I have two that I can use pretty well, Henry has two more as strong as mine, maybe stronger, and Agnes can do nearly everything I can. And now that we're all together again, now that we have our husband and father with us, I'd say we make a considerable work force, able to take on just about any problem that comes our way. What say you to that, Jeff?"

Jeff stood and hugged Mary with his good right arm. "Children, I say your mother's right. Come tomorrow, we get started working on whatever it is we're up against. But today let's just be happy and thankful to the Good Lord that we still have all that is dearest to our hearts. And one more thing, Mary, something really important."

"What's that, Jeff? Mary asked with a worried look on her face.

Jeff laughed. "Is there anything left to eat around here? I'm about half starved!"

"Not much left, Jeff, to be honest about it, but I think I can still fix up something fit for our family hero!"

"Man, I can't tell you how glad I am to hear it. I have missed your cooking like you can't believe. But you're wrong about that hero business. Children, let me tell you right now, the real hero of the family is this lady named Mary Blackwell."

"Well, we could argue the point, Mr. Blackwell," she said, planting a kiss on his forehead, "but I can tell you ahead of time that you'd lose. If you don't know it yet, I imagine folks will tell you soon enough that I've been wearing the pants in this family. And there's a story about that, too, that I'll get around to telling you one of these days."

Henry jumped higher than he ever had before and finally brought down the limb.

Because of lingering animosities in Providence and Jeff's restrictive war injury, not long after the Civil War the Blackwells abandoned cracker farming in North Florida and moved their family south to what later was named Winter Haven. There they established one of the early citrus growing plantations. Many of their descendants still live in the area.

...

Chapter 11.
Duel in Abilene

[<u>Kansas Genealogical Records</u>, Vol IV, pp. 81-82; VI Volumes. J. Robinson Brown, General Editor. 1976-1984.

There is some uncertainty about the surnames Stokes and Stokesbury, entered hereinafter as Stokes. According to records in the Boston Public Library, the founder of the family line in Massachusetts was Nathan Stokes, or perhaps Nathaniel Stokesbury, which he may have shortened for unexplained reasons, but which was common in that era. As far as the family history can be traced, he apparently came from the South, perhaps an area of Tennessee once considered Cherokee land and was said to be partly of Native American ancestry on his father's side. He was related by marriage to the Scottish Olgivies of Boston who were prominent as machinists and shipbuilders. A sailor in his youth, Stokes left a copious account of his voyages. In later life he rose to economic prominence as part owner with brother-in-law Frederick Olgivie of a shipyard and owner of a marine machine and carpentry shop. His older son, Frederick Stokes, migrated around 1840 to Indiana, settling near Muncie. Frederick was the father of twins Hiram and Hamilton Stokes, as well as three younger children, Jane, Jeffrey, and Michael. Hamilton was killed at the battle of Shiloh (1862). Hiram returned to Indiana after the Civil War, married, and after the death of his wife in 1876, resettled near Abilene, Kansas. He died in 1910, leaving many descendants.]

...

Nobody in Abilene, Kansas knew much about Hiram Stokes. Despite the best efforts of town gossips, the only things for certain they could discover about him was that he was from Indiana and had fought in the Civil War before homesteading a few miles north of Abilene in 1876. From land records he filed they learned that he was thirty-eight and that his full name was Hiram Frederick Stokes.

His two children were more talkative than their father. Daughter Betsy, 16, confided to her new friend Kathy Schultz, 17, that their mother had died of typhus a year earlier in Indiana. And at a Thanksgiving turkey shoot in Salina son Daniel, 15, boasted to Kathy's twin brother Bernard that if he could be talked into it, his father could outshoot any man present.

But Daniel's claim would have to remain unproven: Hiram refused to fire any sort of weapon, including a sidearm he possessed but kept locked away. When pressed on this peculiarity, all Hiram would say was that he "had seen enough killing to make him sick to his stomach for a lifetime." He vowed to his children, as he had to his wife, that would never again pull a trigger.

Maybe it was destiny's decree that Hiram's resolve would be tested by the Blackmores. As soon as the Civil War broke out, Big Bill Blackmore had foreseen eventual disaster for the Southern cause. Not that he cared one way or another. His only cause was his own wealth. He managed to sell his estates around Williamsburg, Virginia at a good price and head west to Abilene, Kansas, with stops in Kentucky and Missouri on the way.

His timing was, as always, nearly perfect. At war's end Texas cattle herds began to pour into Abilene and other Kansas towns. Now he was the richest man in town and father of a numerous clan. Like his Blackmore ancestors, Bill was a huge muscular man who on election days and other liquor-flowing occasions customarily challenged all men present to enter a circle he traced on the ground. Any man still standing after five minutes inside the ten-foot radius could earn twenty-five dollars. If he lost, he forfeited the five-dollar entry fee. At first many men accepted Big Bill's challenge. All lost, and later few dared to face his ham-hock sized fists. Bill was simply too strong for ordinary men. Rumors persisted that he had beaten at least one man to death in a Kansas City saloon brawl.

Bill's sons Vester, 21, Jack, 19, and Graham, 17, strutted in the glow of their father's reputation. Nearly as powerful and profane as Big Bill, they bullied the Abilene boys and disrespected adults. And the two Blackmore daughters, Tressie, 16, and Florence, 14, were nearly as foulmouthed and arrogant as their brothers.

Privately, merchants and other townspeople complained to the sheriff and his deputies, who found it convenient to look the other way where the Blackmores were concerned. For Bill and his sons were not only dangerous with their fists but also quick and proficient with their sidearms. They laughed at a city ordinance forbidding the wearing of pistols inside the town limits. Finally their behavior became so flagrant, however, that Sheriff Norwood McGraw, hat in hand, appealed to Bill to control his sons.

"I know they're good boys at heart, he said, nervously twisting his hat brim and looking at the floor, "but sometimes maybe they get a bit too feisty. You know, just like fun-loving boys will do. So I would appreciate it, Mr. Blackmore, if . . ."

"Don't you bother my boys," Bill interrupted with a frown

and a thud of his mighty fist on the table. "I'll take care of my folks. And don't let me hear about any of your deputies mistreating them."

"Oh, no sir; you have my word on that. My men are always respectful of our Abilene people."

"Well, just see to it that it stays that way. So you just be on your way and remind them of their civic duty and I'll see to my boys. Understand, sheriff?"

"Yes sir, I sure do. So I'll not take any more of your time and I wish you a good day."

Bill spat contemptuously as McGraw closed the door.

On Election Day in November Big Bill drew his customary circle on the ground and issued his usual challenge, but the only taker was a drifter half Bill's size and down on his luck. Driven by desperation, he proved to be surprisingly gritty and agile. Bill was embarrassed by the sweat he had to work up on a cold day trying to catch him. Finally, just before the five minutes expired, he caught his tiring victim with a crunching left hook to the chin. The drifter collapsed like a sack of rocks and lay motionless for several minutes as Bill calmly wiped away the sweat with a towel and collected the five dollars from crony Fergus Hanley. Some wondered if the man's neck was broken, but finally he moaned, rolled over, and sat up, shaking his head.

"Mister," he pleaded to Bill as he staggered to his feet, "that was the last money I had in the world. Could you see your way clear to let me have a dollar back to eat on? I'm trying to make it on out to Colorado."

"You think we run a charity ward here?" Bill sneered. "Give you a dollar back? I'll tell you what I will give you if you don't get your scrawny ass out of Abilene. I'll beat you into sausage meat."

The drifter headed for his horse, head down. Hiram Stokes stopped him and pressed a dollar bill in his hand.

"Take this and stay out of trouble. There are better ways to live than getting your brains knocked out."

"Thanks, mister. I'm obliged," he mumbled, massaging his swollen chin.

"Hey! Hey! What the hell is going on?" bellowed Big Bill, elbowing his way toward Hiram. "I thought I made it clear that the drifter gets nothing!"

"I heard what you said," Hiram said calmly, "and that's your business. Helping him a little is mine."

"What I said, sodbuster, goes for everybody around here."

"The name is Hiram, Hiram Stokes, Mr. Blackmore. And I make my own decisions."

"Hiram-skiram!" Bill thundered. "I don't give a rat's ass what your name is! If you don't want to end up like the drifter you'll take back that dollar!"

"As I said, I make my own decisions, and this one's been made. He keeps the dollar."

The veins bulged on Big Bill's neck. "Step inside my circle, sodbuster, no charge for this one, and you'll learn what it means to cross Bill Blackmore!"

"That's not my way. I have things to do, so I'll be going."

"You talk big for a man no bigger than you are, but I'm thinking it's all bluff. Here and now I'm calling you out for what you are, an outright coward afraid to fight."

"Call me what you will, Blackmore, but I'll not get in that circle with you."

"I don't have to beat you like a drum to show everybody

what a coward you are, clodhopper. If you won't fight with your fists, do you know one end of a sidearm from the other? I'll give you the choice, fists or firearms, if you're man enough to face me."

"I see no reason to accept either option. I have no quarrel with you or anybody, much less a reason to hurt or kill a man over a dollar. Good day to you."

And with that he walked away to the jeers and taunts of Big Bill and his crowd.

The next day Daniel came home from school with one eye swollen shut and his face bruised and bleeding.

"Paw, it was Graham Blackmore," Daniel confessed to Hiram's questions. "He insulted you and I couldn't let him do that. But he's a lot bigger than me and . . ."

"Daniel, I appreciate your spirit, but I've told you before not to get involved in fights. I don't need you to defend me. I can take care of myself."

"But, Paw, he said some awfully insulting things about you."

"I imagine he did. He picked them up from his father. But you stay clear of the Blackmore boys until things quieten down. You hear me, son?"

"Yes sir," Daniel said through swollen lips, secretly beginning to wonder if his father really was afraid to defend his name and honor.

Daniel stayed clear of the Blackmore boys for the next few days, but Betsy was not so lucky. Two days later she came home from school in tears, barefoot and with her best dress ripped down the back.

"Daddy," she wailed, "Tressie Blackmore knocked me down and her brother, the one they call Jack, threw my shoes in

Schultz's pond! Then she and that nasty little sister of hers tore my dress! My best dress, too! Now I don't have anything decent to wear to Church! And I was supposed to sing in the choir."

Hiram was silent for a moment, then sighed, got up, and knocked the ashes from his pipe into the fireplace. "You'll be all right, Betsy; as soon as I can, I'll see to it that you get a new dress and shoes for Church."

"But, Daddy, the Blackmores have got it in for us. The next time they see me or Daniel, it'll happen all over again. They've told us both we had better not come back to school if we know what's good for us."

"Well, you're not quitting school. So put that idea out of your head. I'm going into town now to settle the matter. You get supper ready for you and Daniel. I'll be home in a couple of hours."

"But what are you going to do, Daddy? You can't fight the Blackmores. They're too strong."

"You leave that to me, honey. I'll take care of things," he reassured her as he opened his gun case.

Betsy's eyes widened in surprise when she saw what he was doing. She ran to tell Daniel.

Big Bill was holding forth as usual with his cronies in Eastland's saloon when Hiram walked in with his .44 strapped to his side. A hush came over the drinkers, and no one was more surprised than Bill.

"I came to speak to you, Mr. Blackmore, more to the point, to accept your challenge unless we can come to an agreement. I can deal with insults about me, but I can't let you or your family mistreat my children. Now if you'll issue an apology for the things that have happened here lately and give me your word it won't happen again, I'll go my way and leave you in peace. What say you, sir?"

Big Bill knocked over several chairs getting up from the table, his face turning purple with rage.

"Apologize? Me apologize to a sorry excuse of a man like you? Hell will freeze over before Bill Blackmore apologizes for anything. What I'm going to do is break some bones and teach you some manners. So clear the tables, boys, and let the lesson begin!"

"You misunderstand, Blackmore, I came here to accept an apology or to challenge you to a duel. You do recall, don't you, that you gave me the option of fists or guns. I choose guns."

A faint trace of uncertainty crossed Bill's broad face. "Guns? What do you know about guns, sodbuster?"

"Enough."

"You did give him that choice, Bill," Fergus Hanley reminded him. "We all heard you."

Bill hesitated for an instant before pounding the table with his fist. "I know damn well what I said, Fergus, and Bill Blackmore stands by his word. Guns it is. You pick the time and place. We can do it right now, if you're man enough to face me."

"Not now, Blackmore, I have more pressing things to do first. Let's make it a week from now, next Monday morning at 7 a.m. at the cemetery. That satisfactory with you?"

"Suits me fine, sodbuster, that way they won't have to carry your sorry carcass far to your grave," he chortled.

Subdued laughter ran through the group. The men were puzzled and some noted that Hiram's gun belt was worn smooth and his .44 nicked as though by long use. What they didn't know but some were beginning to guess was that Hiram was a good judge of character honed by his years of leadership on the battlefield. He knew that a week was a long time for a man like Blackmore, long enough for doubts to eat away at his bluster.

"All right then. Pistols at twenty paces, one shot each. Now let me give you two things to think about in the meantime: first, we can avoid this confrontation if you decide to apologize and get your children under control; and second, it may interest you to know that in the war I served as Lieutenant and then Captain of the First Indiana Ranger Battalion, Indiana's crack marksmen. By my count I have killed upwards of a hundred men, many in close combat. Killing men was my business and I'm good at it."

With that he turned and walked out of the saloon.

It took Big Bill a few minutes to regain his swagger, but by the end of the evening and fortified by a dozen drinks he was promising quick death and destruction to Hiram. But his companions were not so confident. Several of them had heard of the First Indiana Rangers, said to be as good as the best Kentucky and Tennessee sharpshooters on the Rebel side.

"I don't know, Bill," Fergus said shaking his head, "if that man's who he says he is, he may be as dangerous as they come. If you noticed, that pistol and gun belt of his looked like they had seen a considerable amount of use."

Bill responded by kicking Fergus's chair from under him, sending him sprawling.

"Don't any of you ever doubt Bill Blackmore! Sharpshooter or not, and I say not, that was a long time ago if what that sodbuster says is true to start with. He could be the biggest liar and worst shot in Kansas."

"Or the best," Luther Foreman whispered.

"What did you say, Luther?"

"Me? Nothing, nothing at all."

Rumors circulated fast and furious in Abilene that week. Soon people were saying in bug-eyed excitement that Hiram Stokes had killed close to two hundred men in single-hand combat. Others recalled or invented stories of his legendary bravery, and most of the townspeople were secretly hoping that Hiram could take down Big Bill and end the Blackmore oppression.

For all his public blustering and boasting about what he would do to Hiram, Big Bill could not shake a gnawing fear. By midweek it was keeping him awake at night. Damn! Why did he give Stokes an option? Why didn't he just beat the hell out of him inside or outside the circle and be done with it? Why was he dumb enough to give the farmer a chance? And what if Stokes as good at killing as he said? But try as he might, he could not think of a way to get out of the duel, and the clock was ticking toward the fateful hour. He considered ambushing Hiram, or burning his house at night, or hiring a gunman to kill him. But no, everybody would guess immediately it was his doing and his reputation would be tarnished, and if proven guilty, his life could be at risk. In Kansas murder was a hanging offense. Bill still remembered but never talked about the trouble he got into in Kansas City.

By Sunday Bill could no longer hide his nervousness. His eyes were red from sleeplessness and the unbelievable quantities of whiskey he had drunk. Meanwhile Hiram's reputation continued to grow. Now the gossips were claiming he could shoot out a candle at forty paces, or a match at twenty. By now the men he had personally dispatched were counted not in dozens but hundreds.

Early on Monday, fortified by a fresh pint of bourbon, Bill

rode out to the cemetery with a dozen of his followers. There was scant comfort in whiskey or cronies, but at least they momentarily deadened the fear tying his stomach in knots. The only real comfort was a risky strategy he had worked out with Fergus.

Hiram was waiting when Bill rode up and dismounted.

"You still have time to save your hide, sodbuster," he said to Hiram.

"And you still have time to apologize and settle this matter like civilized men," Hiram answered.

"When hell freezes over, sodbuster, when hell freezes over."

"Then let's get it over with. These are the rules as I understand them. See if you agree: we stand back to back, step off twenty paces to Fergus' count. From that point, we turn and fire once.

Bill looked at Fergus. "That's right, Mr. Stokes. Bill's .45 has one bullet. What about yours?"

"My .44 conforms to the rules. Only one shell in the chamber. You can check it if you like."

Fergus shook his head. "Mr. Blackmore will take your word for it. Now if you men will line up, I'll count off twenty steps."

Fergus began the count as Bill and Hiram began their march. But after "eighteen" he skipped nineteen and called out "twenty."

Bill turned and fired as Hiram was turning. Hiram went down and Bill threw up his arms and shouted gleefully.

"I told you I'd take him down! Didn't I tell you? Didn't I? Huh? Huh?"

But Hiram was not dead. As Bill was bragging he slowly got to his feet, left shirtsleeve was red with blood. His .44 came out and with practiced, steady ease lined up with Bill's ample torso. Bill panicked and screamed at Fergus.

"Fergus, give me another bullet, quick! I need one more shot to finish him off!"

Fergus shook his head. "No more, Bill. You had your chance. I broke the rules once for you, but I won't do it again. You're on your own now."

Hiram took a step toward Bill, his .44 steady, lethal, the weapon that had killed a hundred men, maybe more. Bill turned away to avert the menace, then he took a step backwards, then another. Then dropping his weapon, he fell to his knees and began to plead for his life.

"Don't kill me, Mr. Stokes! Please don't kill me! I have a family! I apologize for what they did to your children! But let me live! Please don't kill me!"

"Blackmore, I'll spare your life on one condition: that you leave Abilene before the sun sets today and never come back. What you and Fergus did here today dishonors you both. And these men with you will tell everybody. You are both finished in Kansas. Nobody here will ever respect you again. If you stay you'll be the laughingstock of Abilene. And remember that by the rules of dueling I still have the right to take my shot when and if I choose to. And I could decide to exercise my right any time, day or night. What say you?"

"We'll be gone by sundown, Mr. Stokes."

"And you, Fergus, what do you have to say for yourself?"

"My apologies to you, sir, for my part in this trickery. I should have never listened to Bill. I'm leaving and you won't ever see me again in this town."

The townspeople were jubilant as the three Blackmore

wagons lumbered away westward in late afternoon. Fergus had slunk out town earlier. Word quickly spread about Bill's cowardice and Fergus' complicity in the treachery. Everybody wanted to shake Hiram's hand and ask him to replace irresolute Sheriff Norwood McGraw. A grateful merchant saw to it that Betsy got her new dress and shoes.

As for Hiram himself, he wanted no part of being sheriff, and all the public adulation was an embarrassment. As soon as he could slip away to his farm he took off a curiously padded vest that had slowed or stopped more than one bullet. Then cleansed his flesh wound and treated it, as he had treated his own and those of his Rangers, with a strong, burning ointment, which he said was an herbal remedy handed down from Cherokee ancestors. Most of all he wanted to put away his .44, this time forever. The weight and feel of it had brought back old memories of gore and death. He still thought of Hamilton every day. Daniel and Betsy watched as he doubled the thickly padded vest and stuffed it deep in a trunk.

"Pa, what kind of vest was that you were wearing? I've never seen it before."

"One I made back in the war. It won't deflect a direct hit, but it will absorb a lot of the force and maybe keep it from being a killing shot. It saved my life a couple of times."

"And today, too."

"No, Blackmore's bullet only grazed my arm and side. He was too drunk and shaky to shoot straight. It was no worse than a hornet's sting."

Hiram removed the shell from his weapon and doubled up the belt. Something caught Daniel's eye.

"Pa, can I see the bullet?"

"You can keep it if you like, son."

Daniel gasped when he saw the empty shell. "Pa, this is a shell casing. Where's the live ammunition?"

"There wasn't any, son. I told you children and your mother I never intended to fire another weapon, and I've kept my word. Not that I was dumb enough to face Blackmore without any kind of protection. There's no rule that says you can't be smart even with an empty weapon. I figured Blackmore for treachery but also counted on cowardice and liquor to have him so rattled he couldn't think or shoot straight. But the point is, children, don't ever give your word lightly and never for things and people that aren't worth it. But once you do, always keep it. A man's word, or a woman's pledge, is sacred, and if you break it, you dishonor yourself and God. And let me just say here and now, Daniel and Betsy, in case I haven't told you before, that you two are the most precious things in my life."

Betsy rushed to kiss her father in love and admiration. Meanwhile, Daniel put the empty shell casing in his pocket and kept it all his life to remind himself of his father's courage and example.

Ancestors.com

I am a direct descendant of Hiram Stokes—great, great grandson—and needless to say, very proud of my brave ancestor. I am not sure if my great-grandfather was aware, or even if the story is true, that his own ancestor, Nathan Stokes, was once—may late 18th or early 19th century—an indentured servant of the early Blackmores back in Virginia. If true, the twist would be truly ironic. Can any of you cousins or genealogists set me straight, one way or another?

--Michael Stokes, Spokane, Washington.

...

Not a cousin, Michael, and maybe not even anyone you would welcome in this discussion when you see my name and the information I pass on. I am William Blackmore, descended from the Virginia and Kansas Blackmores. I inherited old family papers going back hundreds of years that contain the name not of a Nathan Stokes, but a certain Nathaniel Stokesbury. If he was indeed the same Nathan Stokes you mention, then I have to tell you that according to these records, he ran away from his sentence as an indentured servant for my family and became a fugitive from Virginia justice. Maybe we all have black sheep—or at least some with black spots—in in our families. My Kansas forebear certainly was of the black sort, if the stories are true, though I'm told he became a quiet alcoholic man in his later years in Sacramento, California where I grew up a few generations later. In any case, I hold no ill will toward anyone for what their ancestors may have done, as I hope no one will hold me responsible for the misdeeds of my forebears. I dare say we are all descended from sheep that have gone astray and all of us are in constant need of the Good Shepherd.

I pray God's blessings on you.
--Reverend George Blackmore,
Christ Church, Corvallis, Oregon.

...

Chapter 12:
Uncle Homer's Umbrella

[Frontier Families of Nebraska. Vol. II, p. 44; III Volumes. Edited by Priscilla Truax, MA, The Pioneer Society of Nebraska, Lincoln, Nebraska, 1935-37.

These volumes contain not only genealogical data of families and individuals but also interesting anecdotes submitted to The Pioneer Society of Nebraska from many sources. We cannot presume to verify all the latter as being objectively faithful to the dates and facts of history. What we can attest to is the general spirit of pride in Nebraska evident in those items the society has judged worthy of inclusion, even though in some instances lacunae and unanswerable questions may persist. In cases where these were too many to ignore, the item was omitted. "Uncle Homer's Umbrella" is, however, a persistent legend with enough verifiable data to earn it inclusion in these Nebraska documents.]

...

Before it burned down in 1954, the Swanton Lutheran Church exhibited Uncle Homer Stafford's umbrella in a prominent spot in the Narthex. We grew up hearing the older members tell the story.

They explained that back in 1910 farmers in Swanton had never seen it so dry. Except for a sprinkle in January, it had not rained since December, and now in mid-May the corn was yellow and wilted and the wheat that had even bothered to sprout was stunted beyond all hope. Streams had stopped running, and the livestock gathered to drink from stagnant pools full of gasping, dying fish.

Uncle Homer Stafford, now past seventy and one of the oldest men in the Swanton community, compared it to the legendary drought of 1851 in his native Indiana when farmers around Muncie lost their crops and many of them their farms to boot. He remembered vividly the long line of wagons piled high with furniture and farm implements and the tearful farewells as kinfolk and neighbors began their trek along Kilgore Road bound for destinations in the west.

Though he said little about it, he never forgot his farewell to his sweetheart Sally Henson, as his own family joined in the migration. Usually Homer was a talkative, animated old man, but his face took on a somber cast and he grew silent whenever somebody or something reminded him of Sally. They had made their plans to marry, and Sally, seventeen at the time, cried bitterly when she learned that Homer and his family were moving to Nebraska.

Homer worked hard to make a go of it in Nebraska. His aim was to return to Indiana with enough money to marry Sally and bring her back with him to Nebraska. But a year after their move, Homer's father died, leaving twenty-two-year-old Homer with an ailing mother and his father's debts. Then his mother's lingering illness and subsequent death delayed him still more. Three years passed and one day he got a letter from Sally, explaining that she was marrying another man. Homer's hands shook but he said nothing. Folks in Swanton still talked about his sad love story when they ran out of other gossip. But more than fifty years had passed and most people dismissed old bachelor Homer as a curiosity, a one-woman man whom practical folks could not understand. After all, they reasoned that there were other girls in Swanton and he could have married one of them like any normal man.

Homer kept his grief to himself, never complained about his life, and his faith in God never wavered. He would have been the last person to reproach Providence with the customary, accusing question of most mortals: why me, Lord?

By the end of May people were hauling water for their families and livestock from the deeper wells in Saline County, some going as far as Big Blue River fifteen miles to the east. The current was down to a trickle but there were still deep pools of good water. At first their neighbors were generous, but as the water table lowered they became concerned and cut them off. Hard feelings ran high and anti-Christian accusations against those with water were heated. Old friendships suffered and families divided. Even mild-mannered Purvis Maywood took to guarding his well at night with his double-barreled shotgun.

As the drought reached biblical proportions, it became a theological topic. Preachers told their congregations that it was the wrath of God unleashed on sinful humanity, as in the days of the Prophet Elijah, and that repentance and prayer were their only hope. Reduced to desperation, the churches suspended most of their usual dogmatic differences and agreed to come together as a community to pray for rain at the Swanton Lutheran Church, the largest in the town. But since some denominations could not bring themselves to set foot in another church on Sunday, they agreed to meet on a Thursday.

And so they did. It was the biggest gathering Swanton residents could remember, far exceeding the crowds that came for Sunday service or summer revivals. Buggies and farm wagons overflowed the church grounds and stretched for a quarter of a mile up and down the dusty road. Father Marlow Thornburg welcomed his neighbors and preached an opening sermon, describing the three-year drought in ancient Israel and telling how Elijah triumphed over the prophets of Baal.

"Now brothers and sisters," he concluded, "we must likewise call upon the same God who responded to Elijah and brought rain to the parched land. For God hears the pleas of his servants and as the Scriptures say, 'the prayer of a righteous man availeth much.'"

"Amens" chorused throughout the church and prayers for rain began. Eloquent and mighty words resounded, first from the assembled ministers, then from the elders, finally from the overflowing congregations.

But no rain came. The sky was as spotlessly blue and cloudless as it had been when the meeting began. As noon passed and the afternoon wore on, a pall came over the assembly. What else could they say? What prayer had they not prayed? Had God turned a deaf ear to their pleas? The consternation of doubt began to overwhelm the people. Father Thornburg and the other preachers conferred and decided to dismiss the people with the promise that the Lord had heard their prayers and would respond in his own way and time.

At that moment Uncle Homer rose and asked to say a word before the dismissal prayer. It was out of character for him to speak, for though talkative outside the church, he seldom spoke inside it, preferring to listen and remember what he heard. Surprised by the unusual request, the Reverend Thornburg invited him to come forth. He did so, carrying his old umbrella, which in late years had also served him as a walking cane.

"Friends," he began, "I just want to ask you, how many of you brought umbrellas today? Would you raise your hand?"

Only three did. Most of the congregation probably thought it was a silly question, since there was not a cloud in the sky that Thursday. But those alert enough to catch the ironic implications of the question lowered their eyes sheepishly.

"Friends," Uncle Homer went on, "we came here to pray for rain, but if we pray in faith, shouldn't we have brought our umbrellas or raincoats?"

Then Uncle Homer said his last words. "Friends, let's all go home, feed the livestock, milk the cows, eat a bite, and come back here around suppertime. And this time bring your umbrellas and raincoats."

There was a moment of stunned silence. Then Father Thornburg jumped to his feet with a loud "Amen!" The other ministers joined in and before long the old church fairly shook with renewed faith and excitement.

That night an even larger crowd gathered amidst a sea of umbrellas and raincoats. But Uncle Homer was not among them. "He doesn't see well at night," somebody explained. The prayers began anew and continued into the night. The moonless night was still and star-spangled.

Then far off across the prairie there came a faint rumble and an excited man came in to report flashes of lightning in the southwest. A half-hour later the wind whipped up and enormous dust-laden raindrops started to fall. Thunder rattled the windows, wind lashed the trees, and lightning lit up the night. The rain came in driving sheets and continued through the night. The drought was broken.

And by a convergence of events, either coincidence or Providence, so was Uncle Homer's life. The next morning they found his body on his front porch, his clothes soaked with rain and his umbrella clutched in his gnarled hand. Among his few possessions—the deed to his farm, a few old letters, a Bible beside his bed, and an ancient, faded portrait of Sally in a small box—was a letter from Sally's granddaughter that apparently had arrived in the Thursday mail. It read as follows:

July 17, 1910
Mr. Homer Stafford
Rural Route 3
Swanton, Nebraska

Dear Mr. Stafford:
It is my sorrowful duty to tell you that our Grandma Sally Henson Stokes passed away on June 6th. We buried her at New Bethel Church. I'm sorry I didn't write sooner, but since I'm the only member of the family that still lives around here, it was my job to sort out her things and settle her affairs.

I imagine it will seem strange that I am writing to you at all, since we've never met. I'm doing so because Grandma asked me to, and I promised her I would. I hope this is the right address for you.

As she got older, especially after our Grandpa Stokes died, Grandma talked a lot about her early life and mentioned you along with other friends and family. She was a good Christian woman and the best mother and grandmother in the world. As she aged, her mind would wander sometimes and she forgot, I think, that some of the people she talked about as though she had seen them yesterday had moved to Nebraska and other places many years ago. In her last hours, though, her mind was as sharp as could be, and we even got our hopes up that she might get well. But her time had come and she passed away peacefully in her sleep.

Grandma told me to tell you this, Mr. Stafford. These are her exact words: "I didn't forget, Homer, but life had to go on. It doesn't wait for us." She said you would understand their meaning.

I close with respect and best wishes for your health and wellbeing.

Mrs. Irma Mae McGuire
Rural Route 1
New Bethel, Indiana

...

His neighbors had no way of knowing how Uncle Homer took the letter, but many thought Sally's passing was a sign that he was now free to go on himself. Maybe his personal drought was finally broken too. Some even imagined it was Sally's call for him to join her. But that may be stretching things too far.

However, there was no mistaking the church members' feelings about his umbrella. Nothing would do but that it should be displayed prominently in the Church Narthex. If the Church were Catholic, it would probably be an icon of sorts. But in any case, it remained there for many years as a mighty testimony to unbreakable love and faith.

Today the only visible reminder of those events is a small commemorative plaque in a corner of the new Lutheran sanctuary.

Forefathers.com

Is there anyone still alive that actually saw the old geezer's umbrella? I was born in nearby Lincoln, Nebraska, lived there until my college years, and never heard the story. I suspect it is an American version of the "pious myths" and so-called holy "relics" that one finds in many European cathedrals and religious sites. In the Middle Ages they were pitched to the ignorant and simpleminded masses to entice them to go on pilgrimages to these places and, naturally, spend their money on religious trinkets.

Harmon Glover
Omaha

...

Harmon,

I was born after the Swanton Church burned, but my grandfather, who was as truthful a man as you could ever hope to meet, saw the umbrella and assured us that the story of Uncle Homer was true. Your unflattering description of Uncle Homer as an 'old geezer' is disrespectful. You, sir, come across as another member of that numerous tribe of skeptics who are wiser than God.

Marlene Schmidt
Madison, Wisconsin

...

Marlene:
Not smarter than God, if he exists, but infinitely smarter, if he does not. But in any case, I stay a step ahead of simpletons such as you who believe such cock and bull stories about miracles.
Harmon

...

Harmon,
This will be my last post on this topic with you, for I see that you are an arrogant person with a distorted outlook on things. I simply point out that the story of Uncle Homer's Umbrella is not a tale of miracles like your so-called "pious myths" but of a simple man's firm faith. If it appears to be a matter of ignorance to you, it seems admirable to me.
Marlene

...

Marlene,
Your sniveling personal attack and defense of the indefensible is duly noted. As my final word on the matter, I remind you that no one has yet come forth as a bona fide witness to the famous umbrella, which is all I asked for in the first place. Until I have better proof, I shall, as an enlightened person, reject the account as a fable.
Harmon

...

Chapter 13:
Jane Olgivie Shoots
Jack Stafford

[Tales of Old Colorado, No. 15, December, 1895, pp. 67-80.
The following account is included in this narrative because
it involves descendants of two families variously interwoven
over several centuries before they came together again in
frontier Colorado. No attempt has been made to verify the
accuracy of the events, or even if they are partially or wholly
factual.]

   ...

Grandpa Asa Olgivie used to say that the Staffords and the
Olgivies had been feuding ever since ole Methuselah was a pup.
That may be stretching the truth a little, but even so the feuding
had been going on so long that nobody still in the land of the
living could remember how or when it started. Grandpa Asa
always said it was over a prize fattening hog the Staffords stole
and barbecued back in his grandfathers's day when both clans
still lived in the Texas Panhandle. But the Staffords claimed it
was because Obadiah Olgivie, Asa's granddaddy, cussed out
Miss Arizona Stafford when she turned down his marriage
proposal with the comment, "I'll bet every time your mother
looks at you she's sorry she didn't stay a virgin." (They say Miss
Arizona was a caution in her day and had a tongue sharper than
a razor. Some said she was mean enough to pour water on a
drowning man.)

Since I don't know what really happened way back then, I'll

just tell you how things turned out when Jane and the younger generation of Olgivies matched up against Jack Stafford and his pack. Things had been peaceful between the two clans for more than a dozen years. Of course there were the usual fistfights, slapouts, window panes shot out at one house or the other, and other minor differences to be expected, but no serious ruckuses since 1885 when Rooster Stafford and Arlon Olgivie got into a humdinger of a fistfight and Rooster ended up chewing off a piece of Arlon's ear. When they sobered up, Arlon said he worried "about catching mad dog rabies" and Rooster claimed he had a middling case of food poisoning.

But the peaceful times ended when Grandpa Asa and Grandpa Abe Stafford had their little tiff in Looney's saloon over in the town of Stonewall. For about the hundredth time Grandpa Asa was holding forth about his heroic exploits in the Civil War when Grandpa Abe, about half way to the bottom of a bottle of bourbon, slammed his fist on the table and called him a liar. "If Asa is awake and his lips are moving, you know he's lying! Everybody knows that when the Indiana Rangers topped that ridge at Shiloh he ran off like a dog with its tail betwixt its legs! It was the rest of us that held our ground and sent the blue devils skedaddling!"

Now Grandpa Asa took Abe's words to be a bit unkind, and since the topic of conversation had gone to the dogs anyway, it seemed a good time to remind Abe of his canine pedigree on his mother's side. Of course he regretted that he couldn't say much about Abe's daddy, since nobody knew for sure who the man might be. At least, he gave him the benefit of the doubt and called him a man, but on further consideration, it could have been some other kind of varmint.

Thereupon, Abe staggered to his feet with an anger terrible to behold, let loose some of the foulest cuss words you ever heard in Stonewall, plus a few never heard anywhere, and hit Asa upside the head with his whiskey bottle, spilling half a pint of good bourbon on the sawdust floor. Naturally Grandpa Asa was offended by Abe's impolite act, what with his honor and lineage being called into question and his head all bloody and such. So he pulled his sidearm and probably would have shot Abe if a deputy hadn't run in about that time and grabbed the .45 out of his hand. At that point all Grandpa Asa could do was shove Abe down on the red-hot potbellied stove over in the corner. There Abe sat befuddled for the merest instant before jumping up screaming like a stuck pig and clawing at his pants that were scorched and his backside starting to fry like a rasher of bacon. Then, drunk, lightly fried on one side, and his pants smoking, ole Abe stumbled out into the street yelling bloody murder and after considerable mismanagement forked his horse, and rode off—standing up in the stirrups—to gather his clan for war.

Grandpa Asa turned philosophical when he heard what happened to Abe on his way home. "Not my fault that he fell off his horse up on the Kid Branch Road and just about froze his fool self to death. I tell you, if brains were water, Abe Stafford would die of thirst in a cloudburst."

Well, that set the two clans off and they went at each other again, and even though nobody got killed that anybody could remember go-around, there were enough bullet wounds, stabbings, broken legs and arms, knocked out teeth, lost fingers and toes, and general mayhem to keep the womenfolk in both families tending to miseries day and night.

"I swear," said Grandma Sarah Olgivie, "if these fool men don't stop trying to kill one another and get back to ranching, we'll have no cloth scraps and bedsheets left and no food to put on the table! I'm thinking the next one that comes in here with a broken leg or arm, I may just take a stick to him and crack his head wide open. I'm disgusted with the whole lot. There's not a lick of sense in either bunch!"

Even though Abe and Asa had kindled the fires of conflict, both claimed too many assorted ailments to do much riding and fighting. So the actual feuding fell to the younger men like Jack and his brothers, cousins, and uncles. And if the chance presented itself, sometimes even to the young women like Jane Olgivie, as I will tell you directly. But first I need to talk a bit about the two. Let me just put it this way: if pretty were money, Jane Olgivie would have been the richest woman in Las Animas County, Colorado. And if manliness were gold, then Jack Stafford could have claimed Fort Knox.

Just about every single man in and around the lower end of the county had tried to court Miss Jane, 19, but she had no patience with their pleas of love and sent them all packing. She was as strong willed as Miss Arizona of earlier times, but Jane broke male hearts with a sweet voice and an icy rejection. The difference between her and Miss Arizona was the difference between a dagger and a sledgehammer. But both got the job done.

"I have considered your offer, sir," she would say, "and I find nothing of interest in your proposal or your person. I will thank you not to call on me again." (Miss Jane had three whole years of schooling back in Amarillo, Texas and it showed in her polite way of speaking.)

Jack Stafford, 23, was about the only man Miss Susan had not run back to the pasture, and that was only because he had never had any dealings with her to start with. Of course he would have had to be blind not to notice how beautiful she was, but being a practical man, he also knew he would have the whole Olgivie clan after him like a swarm of mad hornets if he tried to approach her. And as Jack always said, "Shooting Olgivies is about the same as shooting coyotes, and I don't like wasting my bullets on either set of varmints." He caused the hearts of Callahan lasses to do a stutter step when he walked by, all six feet three of him. But asked what she thought of him, all Jane Olgivie would say was "I may have seen worse looking men on the outside, but he's a black hearted Stafford and I wouldn't give him the time of day if he was the last man on earth."

Jack did his part in the feud, sending Frederick Olgivie home with a bullet hole in his leg and Love Benefield, cousin to the Olgivies, to his bed moaning with bloody contusions and a nose repositioned on his face after a knockdown drag-out fist fight over in Stonewall.

Not that Jane intended to do any actual fighting. She spent most of her time helping Grandma Sarah bind up wounds and do the cooking. But once she did draw a bead on Luke Stafford, uncle to Jack, when she caught him trespassing on Olgivie land. She might have shot him if Luke hadn't politely removed his hat and explained that he was rounding up strays that had wandered onto Olgivie property. Then he wheeled his horse and flew home like a buzzard late for lunch. She could have plugged him, for she was handy with her carbine, but Susan didn't think it was ladylike to shoot a man in the back, not even a lowdown Stafford.

I suppose that for its own perverse amusement fate had already decided that one day Jack and Jane would meet face to face. As I said, Jack was a practical man, and when not feuding, did his best to keep the ranch running and food coming to the kitchen. The feuding families had cut the fences between the two ranches in several places and now the herds strayed back and forth, interbreeding and eventually dropping calves all over the place as if they knew nothing about boundary lines and feuds. Each family blamed the other for the promiscuous commingling of the herds, which each swore bastardized their prized bloodlines.

"I'll sue Abe Stafford for every dollar he's got," Grandpa Asa ranted, "if I don't shoot him first!" And Grandpa Abe promised a similar horror for Asa and the Olgivies.

One day in early summer Jack was riding fence and doing what he could to sort out the confusion of the herds. Pondering the problem and possible solutions, he rode up a ridge in Olgivie property to size up the herd spread out over the valley. Pausing, he took his hat off and wiped his face with his bandana. At that instant a shot rang out and he felt something tear through his left shoulder, knocking him out of the saddle and sending his hat spinning several yards away. He lay motionless, slowly inching his .45 into an accessible position.

Miss Jane Olgivie rode up in near hysteria. She had meant to fire a warning shot in front of Jack, but just as she was pulling the trigger, a bobcat jumped out of the bushes and startled her palomino. Oh my Lord, she had shot Jack, maybe killed him! She jumped down to see and her worst fears were realized. Jack lay motionless with his eyes closed and blood oozing through his shirt.

Jack opened his eyes and looked on the most beautiful face—and eyes to boot—in Las Animas County.

"Mr. Stafford, I didn't mean to shoot you! I swear I didn't! A bobcat spooked my horse and he bolted and threw my aim off! I was only going to warn you that you were on our property! Oh, my Lord, what have I done?! What have I done?! I didn't mean to shoot you!"

"It's all right, Miss Jane, don't you fret. We all have to go sometime, and I think my time has come."

"Oh, don't say that, Mr. Stafford! You'll be all right. Here let me help you. We'll get you home and then send for Dr. Howard in Trinidad. Are you hit bad? Can you stand up?"

"It's all right, Miss Jane, it's all right. Don't try to move me. It wouldn't do any good. I can feel the end coming. Just let me rest here as my life drains away. I know you didn't mean to shoot me and I don't hold it against you." Just sit here with me, if you will, and hold my hand till it's over."

Now Jack was playing his part like a professional actor and Miss Jane took the bait like a catfish swallowing a grubworm on a hook.

"Is there anything I can do, Mr. Stafford, to ease your pain and make you more comfortable?"

"Miss Jane, would you mind calling me Jack in my last mortal minutes? I came into this world as Jack, not as Mr. Stafford, and that's how I want to leave it. And, Miss Jane . . .?"

"Yes, Mr.—uh—Jack?"

"I've never seen a girl as beautiful as you, Miss Jane. I always thought it, but knew I could never tell you, not with our families being what they are. But now, would it be asking too much of you to give me a goodbye kiss, so that I can meet my

Maker with a last pleasurable memory of this life?"

"Why, I don't know, uh, Jack, I-I don't know what to say."

"I understand, Miss Jane. That's all right. It was too much to ask, so I'll just say goodbye to you and go on to the next life and ask the Good Lord to bless and keep you in this world."

It was too much for Jane. Tears came to her eyes and ran down her cheeks. She cradled Jack's head in her arms and gave him a long, lingering kiss well-watered by her tears.

Of course, Jack still had some life left in him. The minute she put her arms around his neck and their lips met, he embraced her with his good arm that was so strong that a mountain lion could not have broken his grip. Susan screamed, struggled, and scratched until finally Jack laughed, relaxed his grip, and received her stinging slap. He said later that she hit him harder than Love Benefield in their fight.

Then in language she did not learn in her Amarillo school or her church in Trinidad, including some words she was not even aware she knew, she compared him to the vilest varmints of the forests, the ugliest vultures of the air, and the foulest fiends of the infernal regions. If words could kill, as they say, Jack Stafford would have died a dozen times over that day. In fact, the thought occurred to him as Jane ran to her palomino that she might really take aim at him this time with her carbine. But instead she rode away still spewing verbal venom at him.

Jack got to his feet, sore and bloody around his left shoulder and lightheaded from loss of blood and flooding emotions. But overall he was pleased with himself and feeling at least ten feet off the ground because of the lingering sensation of her lips on his. What a girl! What a day! And as he rode back home he wondered, and what next? For Jane had bewitched him and he would have her or die trying.

Jane was livid, but what she didn't know at the moment was that Cupid's amorous venom had seeped into her system as surely as it had infected Jack. That kiss had done them both in. The anger would pass but Cupid's arrows were firmly embedded in both young hearts and in time would work its magic.

Days passed and Jane continued to fume and sputter. She was mad as a hornet at Jack but also angry at herself for being so gullible. To Grandma Sarah's questions, all she would say was "those damned Staffords!" Grandma Sarah scolded her for such salty language. "Jane, don't let these crazy men and their fights drag you down to their level. You're a lady and ye have to be ladylike through thick and thin. That's how we raised you since your Momma and Daddy died and why we gave you all that education back in Amarillo."

Then Jane's mood shifted from anger to concern. Despite his trick, Jack really was wounded and plainly he had lost a good amount of blood. Was he healing? Had he made it home all right? She had heard nothing. What if the wound had become inflected? Did they get the bullet out? She had to know, and when Miss Jane made up her mind about something a herd of buffalo could not change it. That Saturday morning she saddled her palomino, stuck her trusty carbine in the scabbard, and rode off without answering any of the family's questions.

Now some things are just contrary to the order of nature, and one of them has to be an Olgivie showing up at the Stafford Ranch, or vice versa for that matter. But that's exactly what happened. I don't have the words to describe the surprise, the consternation, the disbelief, when Jane Olgivie rode up, dismounted, and tied her palomino to the hitching rail. The

Stafford men down by the corral were slack jawed.

"Jane Olgivie?" said Ma Stafford, "You mean Asa Olgivie's granddaughter? No that can't be," as one of the youngsters came in wide-eyed with the news. But rushing to the window, she saw that it was true. Ma met her at the half-open door.

"Mrs. Stafford, I'm Jane Olgivie."

"I know who you are, girl. What I want to know is what your business is with us. Have you come here to finish killing my boy Jack?"

"No, ma'am, I'm here to find out how he's doing. The shooting was unintentional, and I'm sorry, but my concern is real."

"He's doing just fine, thank you. Now is there anything else you want to know?"

"May I talk to him? Just to offer my apology in a proper way, if he's well enough to hear it."

Ma stared at pretty Jane, then sighed wearily and opened the door to her. "Come on in and take a chair there while I go get Jack."

Jack lit up like a lantern when he saw Jane. He was bandaged up and sore but, he assured her, just about ready to get into working harness again. Jane apologized for the shooting. But it was apparent that both had other things they wanted to say, and since everybody in the house was trying to eavesdrop on their conversation, Jack invited her to go out to the shade tree swing. You never saw so much curiosity in your life, but every time the children or grownups edged too close, Jack shooed them away.

To tell what they said would be pure guesswork on my part, but we can get the gist by what happened later. Susan came away from their handholding chat with a blush on her pretty cheeks and a smile she was having a hard time hiding as she rode out past the incredulous Stafford menfolk. As for Jack, he made no bones about his feelings.

"Ma," he said, forgetting his sore shoulder and swinging her around the room, "Jane's the girl I mean to marry! And you can't deny she's the prettiest girl in the county!"

Ma Stafford was horrified. "Marry an Olgivie girl? No, no, son! Now I grant you, she's a pretty one all right. Everybody knows that. But pretty or not, your daddy might shoot you himself if he hears such loco talk from you! And Asa Olgivie may if your father doesn't! Half our family are laid up because of the Olgivies, and here you come spouting off about marrying Jane Olgivie! Why that would be like marrying into the Devil's family! You just better get that notion out of your head this very minute!"

"Momma, I've always minded Pa in everything when I was tending to his business as his son. But now I'm tending to mine as a man, and neither Pa nor anybody else can tell me who I can or can't marry. I've only got eyes for Jane! She's the one, Momma, the only one for me!"

Jack stuck by his guns and Jane by hers. Asa and Abe ranted and raved like two banshees, and Asa threatened to lock Susan up until she came to her senses. It was easier for Jack. After all, he stood half a head taller and was twice as strong as any man among his kinsmen. In the last year or two he had become the natural leader of the family. He was goodhearted and easy going in ordinary business, but in matters of honor and principle men soon learned—some the hard way—that it was better not to cross him.

To pleas, threats, and arguments of every flavor from their families, the two sweethearts met nearly every evening out on the ridge where Susan shot Jack. It became their rendezvous spot. Their romance so distracted both families that they almost forgot about their feud.

Seeing that threats would not work on the pair, both Asa and Abe resorted to more subtle methods to derail their romance. Asa swallowed his pride and found an opportunity to offer Jack a thousand dollars if he would forget about his granddaughter. Surprisingly, after mulling over the offer for a couple of days, he accepted.

"That's exactly what I figured that lowdown snake would do," Asa declared.

Abe made a similar offer to Susan, although he could muster only five hundred dollars. She also accepted the money.

"She's just as underhanded as all the worthless Olgivies," groused Abe with a grim satisfaction.

Both families thought the romance was over like a bad dream, but a month later the sweethearts rode in a buggy down to Trinidad where Reverend Milton Copeland married them in the Baptist Church. After a few days and frantic searches for their whereabouts or, God forbid, their bodies, Jack drove the buggy back to the Stafford ranch and with Susan seated beside him, proudly announced that they were now Mr. and Mrs. Stafford.

"Now, Pa," he told Abe, "you and Ma and all the family have to understand that our feuding days are over. The Olgivies and Staffords are joined, and if the Lord blesses us with children someday we'll need two sets of grandparents and kinfolks to help us raise them. And another thang, Jane turned the money you gave her over to me, and with what her Grandfather

Olgivie gave me we bought the old Varner spread. But we aim to pay you both back as soon as we get able."

A similar conversation and transaction took place at the Thomas Ranch, and for the first time in his life, Grandpa Olgivie was speechless. His world had truly been turned upside down. For his part, Abe groused and sputtered for a few days, but in time both old men started thinking more and more about the possibility of the couple's offspring.

It took time for the reconciliation to take hold, but by the following spring when Jane was expecting her first child, the two families met in an awkward reunion at the Thomas Ranch. At first Abe and Asa glared at each other, but as liquor flowed and food was devoured, they began to recite the tales of olden days, and the two old enemies warmed, then glowed with friendship and sentimentality.

"You remember, Asa, when the Yank Rangers topped that ridge at Shiloh?"

"Lord help us," whispered Grandma Sarah to Ma Stafford, "it's all about to blow up again. Those two don't have the gumption God gave a billy goat."

"I do, Abe; as I recollect, you boys in Company D gave them hell."

"Yeah, we did, but the Yankees had us two to one. We couldn't have held them back for long if you and your rangers hadn't circled around and got the angle on the Bluecoats. That's what we needed to drive the blue devils back!"

"Yeah, and if our general officers had had any sense, we could have driven them all back into the river."

"You know what they say, Asa, it's the foot soldiers that pay in blood for the generals' mistakes."

"That is the pure truth. You know, Abe, we were lucky to get out of that battle alive. Lots of our boys didn't. We talked about it later and it seemed that every man that saw the woman in white died on the field that day."

"Yeah, I never did see her myself, but men around me were pointing and swearing that she was right there between us and the Yankees. And they say the Yankees that died saw her too. What do did you make of it?"

"To this day, I can't explain it. I've heard of the Angel of Death. Maybe that's who she was."

"I don't know of a better way to understand it."

"Glory be," Grandma Sarah said under her breath, "I wouldn't have believed it if I hadn't heard it with my own ears. Those two agreeing on something."

"That's what comes from working together." Abe was silent for a moment, then he added, "Maybe that's the way we ought to do business now. Working together, I mean. Don't you reckon?"

"Well, yeah, I guess so. It's about time. We've battled each other long enough. Now that some people claim we're both getting a little long in the tooth we need to help each other, Abe, like we did back in theWar. You understand what I'm saying, so we can show these young people how it's done."

Jack slipped an arm around Susan's expanding waist and they smiled at each other as the two old men chattered on in their memories. At the end of the day, mellowed by food and rendered expansive by drink, Asa and Abe allowed that the proper thing to do with the rejected bribe money would be to call it a late wedding present. Jack and Susan could use all the money they could get, they agreed, to fix up the old Varner spread. As for stocking it with cattle, well, that would be a lot easier. The two herds had been dropping calves something furious ever since the fences came down and were running together.

But there still some fractious moments. One day Asa and Abe were sitting out under the shade tree at Asa's house whittling and spitting tobacco juice when Abe had a pleasurable thought.

"It'll be right pleasant having a little Abe running around the place."

"What do you mean, 'a little Abe'? Jane's my granddaughter and she's going to name him Asa, after me. Ye can mark that down for a fact."

"Well, Jack's my son and he'll have the final say-so. And you can bet he won't let his son have an ugly old name like 'Asa'."

"Are you going to sit there and tell me that an old-timey Bible name like Asa is not fitting for a Christian boy like little Asa's going to be? What are you, some kind of heathen?"

Their rising voices got Grandma Sarah's attention. "Lord have mercy! Those two old goats have got into it over something, probably fighting the War again," she said to Jane and Ma Stafford who were busy sewing baby clothes. "Sometimes I think we just ought to take them out yonder somewhere and knock them both in the head! First thing you know they'll have the menfolk stirred up and shooting at one another again!"

But what Grandma Thomas feared didn't happen. The two old men didn't settle their argument, but Susan did by giving birth to a beautiful little girl she named Madelaine Marie.

"What kind of name is 'Madelaine Marie'?" Asa wanted to know. I can't recollect any girl in my family by that name."

"In mine either," said Abe, "though I recollect some on the male side of your clan that deserved some names I can't mention in front of womenfolk."

Asa was about to light in on Abe when Jack stood up to full height and raised a big hand for silence. "Pa, Ma, Mr. Asa, Mrs. Olgivie, everybody, Jane tells me that Madelaine Marie was the name of a brave, good girl she read about in one of her schoolbooks in Amarillo. And if my Susan likes the name, then I like it just as much. So that's the name our little daughter's will have. Does everybody understand what I'm saying? Anybody got a problem with it?"

Everybody understood and nobody had a problem, especially when Jack got a certain look on his face. In fact before long neither Abe nor Asa could imagine a better name for Jack and Jane's darling little girl. In fact the old warriors were in complete agreement: Madelaine Marie was the prettiest little girl with the prettiest name in Las Animas County, Colorado, and they would fight any man who dared to say differently.

Note from the Colorado Cattleman, *No. 7, 1946:*
The Olgivies and Staffords established the biggest ranches in Southern Colorado in the years following the Civil War. Both families left the Texas Panhandle after a prolonged drought in the 1870s, driving their herds westward to the Purgatoire River. Their family feud continued until events in the accompanying narrative resolved it. But both ranches prospered and still exist in altered form. Their improved breeds mixed with the semi-wild herds of Spanish longhorns to produce a particularly hardy and disease resistant strain.

    ...

Chapter 14:
A Man of his Word

[Louisiana Genealogies. Vol. VIII, pp. 41-44. XII Volumes. Edwin Laplace, editor. Compiled from various biographical and genealogical sources in Natchitoches, assorted private papers and memoirs, Tulane University Library, Louisiana State University Library at Lafayette, and other materials. 1970-1980. Baton Rouge, Louisiana.

For an extended period (1753-1759) during the hostilities known as the French and Indian Wars, Hiram Stokesbury acted several times as a guide and scout for the forces of General Braddock, Colonel George Washington, and other English and colonial military leaders in various expeditions and battles beyond what later became known as the Proclamation Line of 1763. He was the son of Hamilton Stokesbury and grandson of Matthew and Agali Stokesbury of Cherokee Territory (later incorporated into Blount County Tennessee). Stokesbury saw for himself the vast wildness beyond the Appalachian Mountains and learned much from French trappers, travelers and scouts. Because his Cherokee homeland was increasingly subjected to the depredations by renegade "Overmountain Whites," he conceived a plan to lead his people westward. Though of mixed blood, he considered himself Cherokee. He first led a half dozen families, including his own, to a site on the Tennessee River a hundred miles east of present-day Memphis, but poor land and scarcity of game caused them to abandon their settlement after a few years and remove further west. Ultimately they resettled in the Cane River district of Natchitoches at the invitation of planter Henri Trémont, whose ancestors had once trapped and traded in Cherokee country and were on friendly terms with the mountain Cherokees, particularly Hiram's clan. Hiram's people lived peaceful and prosperous until the territory passed into American hands with the Louisiana Purchase in 1803-04. The arrival of Anglo-Americans put new pressures on the old settlers, including Hiram and his people. The records show that in his extreme old age he and a few followers moved once more, probably around 1820, this time resettling either in far West Texas or Northern Mexico where they faded from history, leaving no recorded trace. Most of the original Stokesbury settlers, by this time integrated and intermarried with the French and Anglos, chose to remain in and around Natchitoches.]

...

On a Wednesday afternoon in mid-April, 1922, Wesley Stokesbury, 21, waited as usual for teacher Helen DuMont, 20, to dismiss her first-grade class at the Natchitoches Elementary School. Then together they strolled the short distance to the gate of her two-story, white-columned house at the edge of town. After lingering as long as she allowed, he said goodbye and with her lovely image flooding his thoughts, headed happily toward his house a half mile north of the River Road. Down the road a way he climbed under the barbed wire fence and took his usual shortcut across the pasture, first making sure that "Ole Romper," Fulmer DuMont's prize bull, was nowhere around.

Wesley and Helen had been friends from childhood and classmates until they both finished ninth grade in 1917. Helen went on to High School and then spent a year at College in New Orleans before returning to teach first grade in her old elementary school. Further schooling was out of the question for Wesley. By that time his father James was hopelessly alcoholic and Wesley had to work their thirty-acre farm east of

Natchitoches.

Her image abruptly vanished as he reached the north fence without any sign of the bull and heard his mother screaming and his father cursing. There was a dull thud followed by a second, weaker cry of pain and terror. Wesley knew what was going on and what he had to do to stop it. It was an old, ugly story, repeated many times before, but today enough was finally too much. He would not let it happen again. He scrambled under the barbed wire, ran through the open back door to his bedroom, grabbed a double-barreled, twelve-gauge shotgun, loaded both chambers, and kicked open the door to his parents' bedroom.

He saw a grisly scene. Mildred Farley Stokesbury, 44, was fetally curled up on her side, her arms crossed defensively across her battered face, while husband James Stokesbury, 45, waved a blood-splattered, straight-back hickory chair over his head ready to hit her again.

"You hit her again and I'll shoot," Wesley said quietly.

"You get outta here, boy! This ain't none of your business!"

"You hit her again and I'll shoot," Wesley repeated in the same quiet voice, leveling the shotgun at his father's midriff.

Something in Wesley's tone got through to the drunken James. In earlier years Wesley had pleaded with him not to hurt his mother. But in his violent drunken rages James paid no heed to the boy, or anyone else. Several times city constables or parish deputies had arrested him for assault and destruction of property, but Mildred always refused to press charges. She blamed herself; in some way she could not understand or correct, she had failed James. As for James, nothing was ever his fault. "I do as I damn well please," he said, "and that goes double for my own house!" But this time it was different. Instead of a boy, a man's voice was now speaking to him, and even in his drunken fury James knew there was lethal intention in Wesley's words. He hesitated, then slammed the chair against the wall and stepped away from his wife. Mildred groaned and got to her knees. Blood dripped from her nose and her right eye was already hideously blue and swollen shut.

"She ain't hurt, just putting on a show. But next time, by God, she'll know better than to spend my money! Anyway, I didn't aim to hurt her. It's just that she makes me mad with her whiny complaining and the way she hides my money. On top of that, a man takes one little drink, and she's on him like a chicken on a June bug. I'm the man of this house and what I say goes!"

"Not this time! What goes is you! Get your things and get out of this house! And don't come back! Don't ever come back!"

"Wesley," his mother pleaded, "put the gun down! He's your father! You're his son! Please, Wesley, don't even think about doing what you're saying! You can't have your father's blood on your hands!"

"I don't want his blood on my hands. I'm sorry it runs in my veins. But he can't stay here. One of these days he would kill you, or I would have to kill him. How many times has he promised to change, and how many times has he gone right back to drinking and beating you? Momma, get his things together and put them out on the front porch, or throw them out in the yard. I don't care which. This man is going to leave or I'll have to shoot him. He'll decide, but he's not going to stay here!"

"Son, you can't . . ."

"I can, Momma, and I will if I have to. Now get his things or he'll leave without them."

"Wesley, put the shotgun down," James said with a travesty of a smile. I promise I won't ever hit your momma again. And I swear I'll never touch a drop of liquor again. I'll quit drinking. I swear it!"

"Wesley, put the gun down and listen to him. We're supposed to forgive. That's the Christian way. Anyway, it's all my fault. I said some things that made him mad. I'll try to do better."

"Momma, you always say that but you didn't do anything wrong, and I want you to quit saying you did. He's to blame. He's made that same promise a thousand times and you still believe him? No, Momma, he's got to go. He's never kept any promise he made to us. But I can tell you one thing. I will keep my promise. If he ever shows up here again, I'll have to shoot him. I can't let him stay here, not now, not ever again."

"Son, please . . ."

"No, Momma, no! Quit trying to defend him and go get his things! He has to go!"

"Mildred, you just go ahead and get me my damned things and see if I give a good goddamn! I don't aim to stay here and be insulted by this sorry boy of yours! You always took his side anyway, and look what it got you, a boy who's got no natural respect for his father! What mother would let her son take a gun to his father and throw him out after he's agreed to every goddamned thing y'all want him to do?"

"It's too late for talk, now it's time to walk. So get out, with or without your things. And I'm telling you right now, don't show up here again!"

Wesley trembled with rage and conflicted emotions as tearful Mildred gathered James' clothes and pleaded in vain with her son to put the gun down. James blustered and threatened, then promised to change and asked for another chance. But Wesley kept the shotgun leveled at him. In the end James cursed both of them and the world in general, slammed the door so hard that the windows rattled, and disappeared from their life.

Less than two weeks later he was dead from a brutal beating and knifing by an unidentified assailant, or assailants. Only the murderer ever knew who killed him. Mildred and Wesley, Fulmer, Martha, and Helen DuMont, Reverend Buford Yates, Tom and Marie Bougeois, Louis and Inez Tremont, and a few other townspeople attended the funeral on Saturday in late April. Several of the Catholic mourners were a bit tense being in a fundamentalist Protestant church, but in human tragedy and friendship they all overcame their differences. Reverend Yates of Christian Assembly Church preached a short sermon on God's forgiveness and his firm belief that in his final minutes James repented of his sins and was restored to heavenly grace. "Remember, brothers and sisters," he reminded the small congregation, "we believe that once saved, always saved, and for much of his life James was a faithful member of this church." Wesley was empty of feelings and could think of nothing meaningful to say to his weeping mother. Racked with sobs and with a world of grief and pain in her voice, she bent over the body in the open pine-plank casket and asked softly, "Why, James, why couldn't you have changed back when it would have mattered to us?" Despite his resolve not to show his emotions, tears gathered in Wesley's eyes as the pine-plank casket was lowered into the grave and the first shovelfuls of red dirt and gravel rattled on the boards.

The following Tuesday Fulmer DuMont drove his buggy out to the Stokesbury place and informed Mildred that a week earlier James had sold him their farm. The tract was once a part of the 300-acre half section his great great-grandfather Jacques DuMont had bought in 1796, and Fulmer had always wanted to restore it to the original DuMont estate.

"Mr. DuMont, this is the first I've heard of it. I didn't sign any papers, and I would never have agreed to the sale. This land and house were all Wesley and I had left. And I don't see how James could sell the place without my agreeing to it. I thought there was something called 'community property' law."

"Well, Mrs. Stokesbury, I thought so too, and I guess there is. So I asked lawyer Ben Boudreau about it. He looked into it and told me that in his opinion the sale is legal and binding. Seems that there was some confusion about the original sale and deed, and ownership was never clear to start with, whether my family or James had title to the land. In any case, James had claim to the land before you married him and his is the only name on the 1890 deed. You have to understand that James came to me with the offer, otherwise I wouldn't have approached him. Now I'll be glad to take you into town to talk to Mr. Boudreau if you want."

Mildred sighed and shook her head in resignation. "No, it wouldn't change anything, and I don't have money for lawyers and legal stuff like that. So we'll just have to leave things the way they are. It's true that James had the farm when we married. He told me his granddaddy bought it from your folks way back yonder in the 1800s and that there were some questions about the transaction that were never settled."

"That's the way I understand it, too. Some of the old deeds are confusing because of the differences between the French and English languages and land measurements—*Arpents* and acres, things like that. Anyway, I wanted to come out and tell you about it. I'm real sorry about the troubles you've had and now this."

"I just don't know what we'll do now. All we have left are the team, wagon, and plows. I reckon there's still a few bushels of corn in the crib. James didn't leave us any money and had none on him when he died, they tell me. Did you pay him in cash money, Mr. DuMont?"

"I did, $1,000 in ten new hundred-dollar bills, but I guess we both know what happened to it. I'm sorry I couldn't turn the money over to you, but legally it was his. And I hate to tell you, but the team, wagon, animals, and farm implements were part of the deal. James threw them in with everything else."

Fulmer didn't tell Mildred that James had offered to include the house furniture, but he wouldn't accept it.

Mildred shook her head. "I understand, and yes, we both know there's no question about what went with the money. Every penny James could come up with always went for liquor or gambling—or worse things. No reason to drag all that up again. My problem is that we don't have anywhere to go. The folks I have left don't live in this part of the country and couldn't help me even if they did."

"Look, Mrs. Stokesbury. This is part of what I wanted to tell you. I'm not asking you and Wesley to move out of the house. For the time being I don't have any pressing need of it, though

Cyrus Hardoin, my overseer, may want to keep some farm implements in the barn. You and Wesley can live here rent free if you want to, at least until you figure out something better. You can have the corn that's left in the corncrib and the use of the outbuildings just like always. I'll leave you and Wesley the cow, hogs and chickens. Go ahead and tend your garden spot, too. And I was thinking that since this year I'll be needing more field hands, Wesley could work for me like he has in his spare days for the last few years. You tell him to come by the house tomorrow evening around five or so. I want to talk to him about it. He's the man of the family now and needs to hear it from me, man to man. And if you're willing, Mrs. Stokesbury, Martha tells me she may ask you to help some with her housework. I guess you heard that her colored maid Hannah Meeks has moved out to her sister's in Dallas and left Martha without housekeeping help. But I reckon she'll talk to you about all that. I know all this is hard on you and we want to be fair with you."

"Mr. DuMont, you don't know how much I appreciate what you're saying. Wesley and me, we need the work, and we want to do whatever we can to show our appreciation. Thank you and God bless you both for your good intentions. I don't hold what James did against you. You and your family will be in my prayers."

"Well, I'm glad you feel that way and thank you for it," Fulmer said with some embarrassment. "Now, I'll say good day to you and be on my way."

When word spread that Wesley had run his father off with a loaded shotgun people forgot his many reasons and remembered only the single threat to shoot. Before he was murdered, James told a twisted version of what happened that put all the blame on Wesley and Mildred. That plus the normal gossipy exaggeration of events persuaded some people that Wesley was probably directly responsible for James' death.

"I know James Stokesbury was a drinking man and could be mean as a sore-tailed bear when he was drunk," storekeeper Tom Bourgeois said, "but that don't give that boy the right to pull a gun on his daddy. I reckon he's twenty or twenty-one and nearly a grown man, but if my boys Robert or Joel had done that, grown or not, why I would've taken that shotgun away from them and broke it over their head."

"I see it the same way you do, Tom," cane grower Louis Tremont said as he trimmed his last wedge of chewing tobacco with his pocket knife. "James used to be a good worker when he was sober but mean as hell when he got to drinking, which is about all he was fit for these last few years. But then again we don't know what aggravations he had to put up with, do we? People tell me there's more to the story than what Mildred and her boy are telling. I do feel sorry for her though. She seems like a good, soft-spoken woman and all in public, but then again we don't know what she's like when the doors are shut, do we?"

"No we don't, Tom, and that's the thing. James Stokesbury was not a perfect man. Hell, no mortal man is—except me of course," Tom grinned, "But a man's got a right to have the say over his own household. Folks are saying now that the boy might even have been the one that killed his daddy."

Tom shook his head. "I've heard that talk too and that's why I've told my kids to stay away from him. I don't want them around somebody like that. Why, even if he didn't kill James, he was just one pull on the trigger from being a murderer. And his own daddy, too. Riotous living, as Father Vincent said in his homily last Sunday, runs in that family and trouble follows them like their shadow. You remember old Henry Stokesbury, James' daddy, don't you? He was as much of a wino as James was, maybe worse. And somebody told me that the family was prosperous way back before the Civil War. Now I don't like to speak ill of the dead, but old Henry, and maybe some before him, started that family down the road to ruin and I guess now James has finished the job."

"Yeah, and alcohol got his daddy killed just like it did James. They never did find out who knifed old Henry either, did they?"

"No, they didn't. You remember that all kinds of rumors circulated about money he owed to some gamblers down in Baton Rouge but nothing the law could use as evidence. There was talk that Ben Judson, that lumberman up in Mansfield could've been involved. That man's as mean as a Mexican scorpion. But could've been anybody. He ran with bad company just like James. He cheated and gypped everybody he could in Natchitoches and other places around this part of the world. And I was one of the ones he swindled way back when I was just starting out as a young storekeeper. Never saw a penny of what he owed me, and it was considerable. The only good I got out of it was a lesson to be more careful with credit. I reckon he ended up with more enemies than fleas on a dog, and to tell the truth, James turned out to be just as sorry. And I'll bet you money that boy Wesley will be just like them. I heard a doctor say one time that drinking runs in families. And besides all that, I was always told that the Stokesburys have Indian blood, and it shows with their black hair and darker skin and all, and they say Indians can't handle liquor."

"Well, hell, Tom, you don't have to be a doctor to know that stuff. You can see it in families all the time. But I reckon you're right about the Indians. I remember my great grandpapá on my mother's side, Antoine LeBrun, saying they couldn't hold their liquor, and he would never offer them wine. Some of them and a few of the Natchez tribe still lived in this part of the world way back yonder when he was a boy. That was before they were killed off or the government sent them out to Oklahoma Territory. Speaking of Indians, while you're up there by the counter, Tom, hand me another pack of that Red Man chewing tobacco, yeah, that's it, the one right there on the right, and then I'll be getting on back to the house."

"What's the story on the Stokesburys anyway, Louis? Wasn't your family connected with them in some way?"

"I was told it started way back with my great great-grandfather. He started out in Quebec, so they said, and then sorta turned wild after his first wife died and lived for several years as a trapper and hunter back in Cherokee mountain country. I think they called men like him "coureurs de bois" or something like that. My grand papá said it mean "wood runners." I guess that's where he first met up with the Stokesburys. Later he moved down here, settled, and married again. When he heard the Stokesburys were looking for a new place to settle, he had them move here. Great Great-Grandpapá must have been a pistol in his day. My *grandmaman* told us that he ran away from Quebec with a girl from a high class family. And she told me, too, that a long time ago, back in France, that the Tremonts, or Trémonts, as the old folks used to call it, were high society folks and members of the nobility. So Tom, you don't have to bow, but you need to be more respectful when you talk to me."

"That'll be the day. But ain't it always the same story? Women just keep a young man's life in an unholy mess. What did the old folks used to say every time a fellow got in trouble, *Cherchez la* woman, or something like that."

"As I remember, it was *Cherchez la femme*. Look for the woman."

"Yeah, that was it. Look for the woman. Too bad we forgot all our good old French language, ain't it, Tom? My Grand *Maman* could still speak it and tried to teach me, but I didn't want to learn. But anyway, women get a man into more trouble than he can ever get out of."

"And if you think about it, don't we do the same for the ladies?"

"I guess so. Seems like that's the way God set up creation. Well, I'd best be getting on. I got me a man coming over to look at my cane harvest and a couple of fattening hogs and I'm hoping he'll make me an offer to take all of it. How much do I owe you for the tobacco?"

"Fifteen cents."

"Fifteen cents? That's three pennies more than last time."

"Yeah, prices have gone up a little."

"I don't see how common folks are going to make it with prices going up all the time. But things are always against plain folks. Anyhow, stay in the traces, Tom and I'll see you next time."

"Same to you, Lou, er, Sir Lou, I reckon I should say."

Wesley showed up at the DuMont house at five the next afternoon. Fulmer opened the door and told him to come with him down to the barn. Helen was nowhere to be seen.

"Wesley, I'll say again that I'm real sorry about your father,"

Fulmer said, fumbling with the Georgia latch on a stable door and more nervous than he wanted to show.

"Momma said you wanted to talk to me," Wesley responded, ignoring Fulmer's comment.

"That's right, Wesley. She probably told you that James sold the place to me."

"Yes sir, but she said you would let us stay on in the house."

"I did tell her that, but I wanted to talk to you about that and some other things, now that you're the man of the house."

"We're obliged to you, Mr. DuMont. Daddy didn't have any right to sell the place without telling us. But I guess what's done is done. Anyway, if you'll let us stay on, we'll take good care of the place."

"I know you will."

"Momma said you might want me to work for you."

"That's right, Wesley. You may have heard that I'm planting a lot more cotton acreage this year—nearly two hundred fifty acres—plus my usual acreage in cane, and I'll need more field hands. What I'll want you to do mainly is tend the thirty acres your family has farmed over the years. You know the land and the team, and the plows are already there in the barn and outbuildings, so that makes it easier for you. Now then, if you have time to spare, I'll ask you to help out in my cane fields. As you know, Cyrus Hardoin is my overseer, so you'll be working under his supervision. Of course you've worked under Cyrus before."

"Yes sir, when I could these last five or six years, both in cotton and corn, and some in the cane. I always tried to put in an honest day's work for him. I guess you know I've already planted early this year and was lucky enough to miss the late frost. I've got a good stand of cotton and corn already. Momma and me had just enough money to cover the fertilizer with money she saved up last fall and kept from Daddy. He beat her up when he found out about it. That's why I had to run him off, to keep him from killing her."

"I know, Wesley, and that's a shame. But here's what I can offer you to make things as right as I can with you. The land and everything planted on it is mine by right of ownership. That was the agreement I made with James. But I don't know if you and Mildred knew about it."

"No sir, he didn't tell us anything. We didn't know the first thing about it."

"That's what I figured. But to be fair to you I'll hire you on come Monday when the main planting starts. And, as I said, you and your mother can stay on in the house rent free. And like I said, you can keep the hogs, cow, chickens, and the garden spot for your use. I believe that's a fair arrangement, not perfect but the best I can do under the circumstances. You're a hard worker, and I want you to see to it that the land gives us a good crop. That's why I want you to work for me again. Cyrus speaks well of you, Wesley. As for the money, I'll pay you the going wage for a man, two dollars a day in the growing and gathering seasons, except Sunday and rainy days, just like all the other hands. And I keep short accounts—pay off every Friday. You check with Cyrus about anything you need and help with the chopping, hoeing, and gathering. Does all this sound fair to you?"

"Yes sir, Mr. DuMont, and I'm much obliged to you. I promise I'll do my best. Now if you don't need me for anything else right now, it's late so I reckon I'll be on my way, Momma being the way she is after . . . But again, I thank you for the chance. I'll do what Mr. Hardoin tells me."

"Uh, yeah, Wesley, that's good. I'm glad that's settled, but now there is one other matter I have to talk to you about before you leave."

"Yes sir?"

"Wesley, I know that you and Helen played together when you were little kids and that here lately you've been walking her home from school after she's finished her teaching. I need to talk to you about that."

"Is something wrong?"

"Not with you, Wesley, just the circumstances. I hate to say this, but I'll have to ask you to keep your distance from Helen from now on."

"Is it because of the drinking in my family? Or our religious differences?"

"To be honest with you, Wesley, it's the drinking, not the Church. Helen likes you. As far as that's concerned, we all like you, but you both are getting on toward marriageable age and . . ."

"You don't want her to end up with a man from a family like mine. Is that what you're telling me?"

"Wesley, I've got nothing against you personally. You have proved yourself to be a hardworking boy—young man—and Helen tells you were a smart student back in your schooling days. But to be honest with you, the family reputation is against you, and I can't run the risk where Helen is concerned. She's my only child since our baby girl Betty passed away in the flu epidemic in '17, and I have to do all I can to protect her and give her every chance at a good marriage. So, I hate to do it, but I'll have to ask you to stay away from her. Now Wesley, this is what I'm asking you to do: give me your word that you'll do what I ask. And I believe you are a man of your word. That's the one and only condition I place on our agreement to let you and your mother stay on the place and work for me like I said before. Now if for some reason you can't agree to it, then I'm afraid I'd have to ask you to move out. As I said, Wesley, I have nothing against you personally, but my first obligation is to my daughter. I hope you can see things from my side. I try to be fair to everybody, but my daughter comes first."

Wesley was silent for a long moment as he stared at Ole Romper stalking back and forth by the far pasture fence next to his house.

"Wesley, what . . . ?" Fulmer started to ask.

"Yes, sir," he interrupted, turning back to face Fulmer, "I understand your reasons. Mr. DuMont, and I give you my word that I won't talk to Helen any more. But just let me say one more thing."

A flicker of concern wrinkled Fulmer's broad face as he closed the Georgia latch. "And what would that be?" he asked cautiously.

"I just want you to know that if there's ever anything I can do for you or your family, Mrs. DuMont and Helen, I promise I'll do it. You have all been good to us and I would want to do what I can if ever you are in a bind. I want you to know that."

"I appreciate that, Wesley," Fulmer said with relief and a condescending smile, thinking to himself that such a circumstance would never come about. "I don't like asking you to do this, and let me say here and now that I hope life is good to you. You've had a hard life and Lord knows you and your mother may be in for more hard times down the road—for that matter, who knows what we all may be in for—but I hope you always stay on the right course. If you keep the faith and work hard, I believe the Good Lord will see you through. Wesley, I know what I'm talking about. I had it pretty hard myself growing up in Henderson Swamp down south. But no need to go into that story now."

They shook hands and went on their way. Wesley took his customary shortcut across the pasture and for once he didn't look to see whether Ole Romper was close by or not. Today was different in a lot of ways. There was a finality in his life but he did not know exactly what it meant or what would follow, only that it was painful. A lot of doors had slammed shut and the world was closing in on him. He was having to pull back in retreat on all sides. Now, suddenly, Helen was beyond his reach. Wesley meant to keep the promise he had made to Fulmer. But despite his resolve, his eyes teared over and he clinched his fists in anger as he silently said goodbye to her and surrendered his boyhood ideals and the future he had dreamed about. From now on, he thought to himself, he would have to take care of his mother and face the ugly world as a man. His young life was over in everything but years. Despite all, though, the transition had a certain upside. He needed the full strength of manhood. What hurt—and probably always would—was losing the girl who had always been the center of his world.

At that moment he saw the yellow glow of the kerosene lamp Mildred had just lit. The lamp and emerging starlight were the only lights left. Ole Romper watched him from his favorite spot by the fence, but except for a snort and a swish of his tail made no hostile move. For once Wesley felt no fear of him and perhaps the animal sensed the change in him.

With few exceptions, his former friends and schoolmates kept their distance. True to his promise to Fulmer, Wesley stayed away from Helen. He wondered if Fulmer had explained the situation to her. It would be years before he spoke to her again, though at times he yielded to the overwhelming desire to sneak a glimpse of her from a distance.

Helen was always on his mind, but loneliness drove him to talk to other girls. Judith Fontaine twice invited him to escort her, first to a picnic and then to a party. She was pretty and talkative, but afterwards Wesley did not follow up and Judith turned to other boys. Months later she married Brian Bordelon of Colfax. News of her wedding saddened Wesley, not because of any feelings for her but because it was another reminder life was passing him by.

A similar isolating separation happened at Christian Assembly Church that Mildred and Wesley had attended since he was a child. James was a member until alcoholism replaced his religious faith. After a few Sundays of stares and cold treatment, Wesley pleaded excessive farm work and told Mildred that he would not be going back to church, but urged her to go for both of them. She said she understood, but her eyes glistened with tears. Wesley was everything she could desire in a son and it grieved her to see him entering manhood without the normal youthful entertainments and friendships. He did not speak again of Helen, in fact spoke little about anything, but she guessed what Fulmer, or maybe Helen herself, must had said to him and with a mother's wisdom understood his silence and sensed his pain.

Wesley devoted all his time and energy to the fields, and the crops prospered. At first Cyrus balked when Wesley asked for extra guano for the fields.

"Son, we've never used more than three or four hundred pounds to the acre and that at spring planting, never any extra in the middle of summer. This stretch of land, especially this side of the Red River, is pretty rich to start with. You use more than that and you'll burn the corn up and the cotton will be all stalk and no bolls. I don't recommend it."

"Mr. Hardoin, I understand what you're saying, but along about the first week in July I'd like to try about a hundred and fifty pounds of fertilizer an acre extra and see what happens. I could be wrong but I believe it'll pay off."

Wesley had read about the beneficial effects of extra fertilizer and the negative thinking of Southern cotton farmers about its use, but he thought it best not to mention book knowledge to crusty old Cyrus.

"Well, I reckon I can spare you that much. Fulmer told me to give you what you asked for. But if it don't work, we'll both have to answer to him."

Wesley applied the extra fertilizer in July. Rains came three days later and by laying-by plowing at the end of the month both the cotton and corn had taken on a deep green, vigorous luster and sagged under the weight of bolls and ears. As the cotton field began to turn white in the last ten days of August it was apparent that Wesley was right about the extra fertilizer. Old Cyrus shook his head in disbelief when he came out to have a look.

"Well, *sacré bleu*, just look at that field, would you! I wouldn't have believed it, son, but you have the best cotton and corn in this part of the Valley. They say old dogs can't learn new tricks, but by George, I'm ready to take back what I said to you in the spring. If this works, and it looks like it will, next year I'm going to recommend to Mr. DuMont that we do to two hundred acres what you've done to thirty."

When the final harvest was over, Wesley's twenty acres of cotton yielded forty-six bales of cotton, over twice the average harvest. And the corn bushel production was equally impressive. The following year, Fulmer took Cyrus' advice and added the midsummer fertilizer following Wesley's example. Even though the rains did not come at the best times, the cotton yield was still fifty percent higher than normal. Fulmer was delighted with both the profits and his enhanced reputation as the top cotton farmer in that end of the parish. Wesley's field yielded thirty-nine bales in a drier season than normal and nearly the same bumper crop of corn as the year before. On a late October Saturday Fulmer came out in his brand-new Model T Ford to talk to Wesley.

"Wesley, I just want to tell you how pleased I am with what you've done. For two years in a row you have had the top yield around this part of the parish, and our overall production is over half again as much as it was two years ago."

"I'm real pleased it turned out that way. I'm glad you and Mr. Hardoin let me use the extra guano, and the credit goes to him. I believe it more than paid for itself."

"Man, you bet it did! Now, Wesley, is there anything else you know of that will let us get even bigger yields?"

"Well, Mr. DuMont, I've been thinking about that, and I do have one thing we might try?"

"Yeah, and what's that?"

"I don't know much about cane, but I wonder if we're not

thinning out the cotton and corn too much. Now that we're using more fertilizer, maybe we could leave more stalks. I believe it might pay off."

"But what if it didn't? Wouldn't too many stalks crowd too much and stifle everything?"

"Maybe, but what if we tried it on just a couple of acres? Then if it didn't work, it wouldn't affect the harvest that much. But if it does work, then the next year we could do the same thing to more acreage."

"Well, it sounds reasonable, but I still have my doubts. But I guess we wouldn't be taking a big risk if we first tried it on just a few acres."

"The way I figure it, eventually we might not have to chop by hand at all."

"I don't follow you. What do you mean?"

"We could just put a different plate in the planter, one that it would spread the seeds apart a little more. If it worked, just think of the money and time you could save if we didn't have to pay for all that chopping."

"But they don't make planter plates like you're talking about, do they?"

"No sir, not that I know of, but why couldn't we make our own?"

"What do you mean? How could we make our own?"

"Well, sir, I don't mean make them from scratch, but we could modify the factory-made ones, maybe plug every second hole or third hole in the rotation, something like that. If you want me to, I have thought of a way to rig up one for you and Mr. Hardoin to look at."

"I wish you would. But first, Wesley, I need to talk to you

about something else."

"Yes sir?"

"I'm not going to keep it from you that you've made me a lot of money with your idea about the extra fertilizer and I'm beholden to you."

"Well, I'm just glad it turned out that way, and I give credit to Mr. Hardoin for letting me do it."

"What I'd like to do is offer you the job of working directly under Cyrus. It would mean more responsibility but a higher pay, too, three dollars a day instead of two. Cyrus has been my right hand man for a good many years now, but he's getting a little long in the tooth and can't put in the hours he could when he was younger. I know he likes you and I believe you could work together, under his supervision of course. What do you think?"

"I respect Mr. Hardoin a lot, and if you ask me, he seems to still be much of a man. But if it's something you want me to do, I'd be glad to give it a try. But I have to say I don't have any complaints about doing what I've been doing."

"And you're good at it, and that's all the more reason to tighten up your traces a link or two. So unless you tell me different, come next Monday, you'll be working with Cyrus. You can think of yourself as 'underseer' to my overseer," he said, a smile creasing his face, "something like a deputy overseer."

"I have just one question, Mr. DuMont. Is Mr. Hardoin okay with me? Like I said, I respect him a lot and wouldn't want to do anything that puts him in a bind."

"Wesley, I've talked with him already, and he's happy with the idea. There are older men, good men, who work for me, but you seem to have a special knack for seeing new ways to do things, ways that make money and do us all a lot of good. That new Model-T Ford car you see sitting out there in the yard is one result of your good thinking."

"I'm glad."

"Tomorrow, me, Martha, and Robert Bourgeois, Tom's son, are driving Helen in it. She's having a reunion with some of her old classmates down in Alexandria. It's a long way, forty or fifty miles at least, but that's a fine automobile."

Wesley nodded without comment, but the mention of Robert Bourgeois was like a stab wound. Long after Fulmer left, he felt residual emotional tremors. He had not spoken to Helen since James' funeral and had seen her only from a distance, but he reasoned that eventually Robert or someone like him would come along and that in the natural unfolding of life someday she would marry. Still, his heart rebelled against what his head told him. Helen was ever present in his thoughts as he worked in the fields, her image undimmed by separation and time. But he had given Fulmer his word not to see her any more, and he would die before breaking it. It was all he had left. Even though he did not say so in words, not even to himself, there was a wounded pride in him. He was determined to prove to himself and everybody else in Natchitoches that even though he was the son and grandson of drunkards, he was his own man who lived by his private code of honor. But to say so would seem like dismissive arrogant boasting that nobody would believe. Only in the slow pace of life would he be able to show it. He could not foresee what it meant, only that it did not include the happiness with Helen he once dreamed of, at best only a grim, silent satisfaction. But that he could endure, or at least told himself he could. He sensed rather than reasoned that a day might come when his determination would be put to the test. He had set his life course for the years ahead, patiently living them one day at a time. But even at that early stage he was aware that someday the wild card of chance could trump his well-laid plans. But it was nothing to be concerned about. He was too still young to see it as anything but a time too distant from the present to be real. His life appeared to be still too spacious and his days too many ever to be overtaken by the slow approach of remote years yet unborn.

The events leading to James' death, which many in Natchitoches first attributed to the same ancestral flaws in Wesley that had brought the family to moral and alcoholic ruin, in time were reduced in the collective opinion to a small blemish on his growing reputation as a successful farmer and man of influence in his job as Assistant Overseer to Cyrus Hardoin. Just as his perceived defects were once exaggerated, now in the fickle swing of public opinion so were his virtues.

"You know, Tom, I never did believe all those tales they were telling two or three years ago about Wesley Stokes," Louis Tremont said as he cut a slice from his Red Man Chewing Tobacco with his Barlow knife. "That man was always a hard worker as a boy and now as a man he's just about the best cotton farmer in this parish. I reckon if he had to get tough with his daddy, why it was to defend his momma. James was a mean one when he took to the bottle, which was every chance he had."

"Yeah, I agree with you, Lou. People talk out of turn and make mountains out of molehills. Wesley comes in the store a lot, always friendly and never late in paying for what he buys.

I've never heard him use swear words and doesn't drink at all. And you remember when everybody was saying he would follow right along in the tracks of his daddy and grandpa? Shows you how much judgment some folks have. Not a thimbleful of sense, as my grandma Marie-Agnes Meuniere used to say."

"Somebody told me yesterday that a farm agent and some agricultural experts along with some bankers, have been out to talk to him about how he manages to get so many bales to the acre."

"I don't doubt it. He's just about made Fulmer DuMont a rich man. And done all right for himself, I reckon. Did you see that new car he bought?"

"Who, Wesley?"

"No, Fulmer, it's some kind of truck, not a car, a Chevrolet I think. I saw it yesterday. Shiny as a new silver dollar. And he's still got his Model-T Ford. I doubt you'll catch Wesley Stokesbury spending money on motor cars. They tell me he saves about everything he makes. Somebody at the Bank let it slip that he's got an account with over a thousand dollars in it."

"Speaking of the DuMonts, what's this I hear about your boy Robert and Fulmer's daughter breaking up? Last I heard they were about to get married."

"Well, that's what we all thought. They've been going together for two or three years. Robert wanted to get married some time ago, but Helen wanted to teach school a little long. So one year turned into two and still no wedding. Times have changed, but the school people still don't want married women for teachers. That makes it hard to keep teachers; they keep marrying and leaving the teaching business to start families of their own. Oh, here comes Mrs. Cora LeBlanc Let me wait on her."

"You go right ahead. Well, *bonjour*, Mrs. LeBlanc. How's your family getting along?"

"*Tres bien*, I reckon, Mr. Tremont. Bill has the miseries again. Gets them every year about this time. Coughing, sneezing, runny nose, and all."

"What do you reckon it is?"

"We don't have the slightest idea. Last year we took him to Doctor Bentley down in Baton Rouge and he told Bill he probably had what they call an allergy."

"A what?"

"An allergy, they call it. I really don't know what it is, Mr. Tremont. Dr. Bentley said it was a kind of irritation caused by plants or animals that affects the breathing passages. I told Bill it might be the cedar trees out in the front yard. He likes to sit out there on the porch with that old dog of his when the weather's good, and that powder and stuff comes blowing in the house. I told him he ought to cut the cedars down just to be on the safe side."

"Did he?" asked Tom.

"Lord no! You know how stubborn Bill is, as hardheaded as a balky mule. He got mad and said that Dr. Bentley didn't know his head from a hole in the ground—and some other things I can't repeat."

"Is he taking any medicine?" Tom wondered.

"Well, he claims he isn't, but he's got something hidden out in the storage shed. I see him slip out there every now and then when he thinks I'm not looking. That's why I've come down here to the store, Mr. Bourgeois, to see if you might stock something that could help him."

"The only two things I can think of right off hand are garlic powder, which I have on the shelf, and honey, which I don't stock. Directions on the powder will tell you how to fix it, but do add a dash of Cayenne pepper to it. But I would advise you to go over to Delbert Brown's. He just put up about fifteen jars of fresh clover-based honey, as pure and clear as it can be. But do what you can to keep Bill out of the smokehouse. I imagine we all know what he's got hidden out there, and you don't want him to get in the habit of nipping that stuff too often."

"Well, I'll try it. Bill coughs and sneezes so much that nobody can get any rest at our house."

"Have you thought about locking him and his old dog in that shed you talking about?" Louis asked with a grin.

Cora stared at him for a few seconds before catching the humor. "You know, Mr. Tremont," she said laughing, "that's not such a bad idea. It might make my life a lot easier if I could put him and that old hound of his in there together. They're both too old to hunt anyway. About all they're fit for these days is to get in my way. How much do I owe you, Mr. Bourgeois?"

"Nothing for the advice about the honey, Mrs. LeBlanc; thirty-five cents for garlic powder and a penny tax. Got to keep the government in business."

"Yeah, they've always got their hand out, don't they?" Louis commented, "For all the good they do us."

"Uh huh, well, I best be getting along. Good day to you both, and do give my kind regards to Inez and Marie."

"Yes, ma'am," Lou and Tom said in unison.

"Mrs. LeBlanc is a fine woman," Tom said as the door closed behind her, "maybe a bit hot-tempered, though, so I hear."

"Yeah, that she is so they tell me. Horace Dutreau is neighbor to them, as you know, and he told me once that she and Bill have had some arguments so loud they could damage your eardrums."

"I guess we all have our faults—except me, of course," Tom said with a grin.

"Yeah, you wish. Well, I'd best be getting back to the house. But I just remembered, you never did tell me why your boy and that DuMont girl broke up. Inez couldn't tell me."

"Well, Marie and I couldn't get much out of Robert," Tom said, his grin fading, "but as best I understood it, they had a falling out over Wesley Stokesbury."

"Wesley Stokesbury? What did he have to do with it, if you don't mind telling me?"

"I don't know for certain. Robert never has liked him for some reason. Maybe jealous of him. You know the Stokesbury boy used to talk to her before Fulmer DuMont put a stop to it. Well, I guess Robert said something about him that the girl didn't like and she took up for him. That made Robert mad. One thing led to another and first thing you know they broke up."

"Don't you reckon they'll patch things up? Young people say just about anything that pops into their minds these days. It was different back in our day."

"I have my doubts that they'll get back together any time soon. Robert's already talking to Cyrus Hardoin's granddaughter Margaret. She's been after him for the longest."

"I guess she's a good girl, if you can stand the Hardoin clan. You reckon he's just trying to show the DuMont girl that other girls like him so she'll come a running back?"

"It could be that, but I'm thinking there's more to it. The fact that the girl kept putting off the wedding tells me a lot. Anyway, me and Marie are staying clear of the whole thing. I've got enough worries without trying to settle young people's spats."

"Probably the smartest thing to do. Well, I better be getting on back to the house. Stay in the traces, Tom, and I'll see you next time."

"Same to you, Lou."

Tom was relieved that Lou had not asked him for a Coca cola that he never paid for.

In the fall of 1924 Mildred started coughing and losing weight. Wesley was concerned but she insisted that nothing was wrong. "I always get a cold in the fall."

But then one day her coughing worsened. She began spitting up blood and was too weak to do housework for Mrs. DuMont. Over her objections, Wesley hitched the team to the wagon and took her to see Dr. Bentley. His preliminary diagnosis was ominous. "Mildred, Wesley, I'll be honest with you. I'm afraid it could be tuberculosis, consumption the old people call it, and I've seen several cases lately. I'll be in a better position to say for sure when we've had a chance to examine the specimens I took. I don't have the equipment here in my office, but the hospital across town does. It probably will take the better part of the week to get the results."

To nobody's surprise but contrary to everybody's hopes, Mildred's tuberculosis was confirmed. Dr. Bentley was vague about possible cures.

"You might think of moving to a place like Arizona," Dr. Bentley advised. "The desert climate seems to help some people, and then there's the coast. Others report that the salt air is beneficial."

"I can't even think of such places," Mildred said, "I can't afford to move away, and even if I could, I wouldn't. I've lived here most of my life, and here is where I'll die."

"No, momma, you're not going to die!" Wesley protested, disturbed by her fatalism, "We'll get you well and strong. You'll see."

But Wesley was wrong and Mildred's mortal premonitions were right. She could not keep her food down. She lost weight and declined rapidly and within weeks took to her deathbed. But the cause was more than tuberculosis. When Dr. Bentley responded to Wesley's desperate request and drove his Buick up to see her, he found the symptoms of stomach cancer. As she edged closer to the end, her mind wandered and several times she was delirious with high fever. But one day when her mind was clear, she confessed her feelings to Wesley.

"When James died, I started dying too. Until then I hoped he would come back and we could live together as a family. I know, son, Lord God how well I know, that he was a bad husband and father, but I loved him anyway and was never meant to live without him."

She silent for a moment, staring into space. Then she turned and placed her hand on Wesley's arm. "Son, there is one more thing I need you to do."

"What's that, momma?"

"I want you to write to my folks back in Blount County, Tennessee. Let them know about me. Tell them I'm sick but happy and that I've had a good life. There's an old address in there in the dresser drawer. I don't know if any of the family still lives there or not. But maybe a letter will get to them. Just put it in care of Harris and Dicey Farley. They're your grandparents, if either one is still alive."

Mildred had never talked about her family, and after several years Wesley stopped asking her about them. He guessed that over their objections his mother had run away and married James.

Many weeks later the letter returned unopened. "Dead," I guess, Wesley thought to himself.

Wesley second guessed himself as Mildred grew weaker. "Maybe I was the one that should have left," he thought. "But then he would have killed momma. I thought I was doing the right thing, but maybe I was wrong. Maybe I should have just walked out and left them together. Maybe I didn't have the right to do what I did. But then I couldn't leave momma."

After obsessing for several days over the contradictory options, he convinced himself that an ideal resolution of his dilemma was out of the question and in any case the consequences could not be undone. He had done what he thought was best under the circumstances and so eased his conscience and put the matter to rest, though sometimes at night he would wake up and rehash it.

A week later when he brought in her breakfast, Mildred did not respond. He touched her arm and knew by the alien feel of her skin that she was gone. He sobbed but after a while was comforted by the realization that she had died in her sleep and her suffering was over. Then, suddenly, the temporary relief gave way to a feeling of absolute and utter loneliness. Mildred was the remaining tether that had tied him to the world, like those he sometimes attached to the young mules to keep them from jumping the low barnyard fence and wandering into the fields. Now he felt the subdued dread of abandonment, which unwise people mistake for freedom.

Unlike James' funeral, Mildred's was packed with church members and townspeople. She was praised as a faithful Christian woman whose life was hard but her example was inspiring. Preacher Yates spoke of her many acts of kindness and charity and assured the congregation that Mildred was now at peace in the Heavenly Kingdom. "Brothers and sisters, this parting sermon is sad for us in this sinful world yet easy in a way to preach. Mildred already preached it for us by the Godly way she lived." With that and many condolences to Wesley from the congregation, she was laid to rest beside James. But Wesley bought her an iron casket.

As for Wesley, he was far from any peace of mind in the following days. Helen and her parents attended the funeral, and at the sight of her and the sound of her voice—the first time she had spoken to him in over two years—his old feelings rushed forth like a reopened wound. She was lovelier and more mature, transformed in ways he could not describe from the pretty girl of former times into the beautiful woman who told him how sorry she was for his loss. She meant Mildred, of course, but for Wesley even at that moment of grieving he was aware of an even greater loss. He loved Helen and despite his promise to Fulmer, could not imagine not loving her, even though now she had moved beyond him and his small world to higher circles he could not reach. Everything separated them— money, church, social class. There was only one possible remedy and it was clear to him before the funeral had ended: everything that had been meaningful had left him, and now he must leave Natchitoches.

But then, as Wesley once idly speculated, fate now chose to play the wild card. The very day Wesley had made up his mind to tell Fulmer of his decision to leave Natchitoches, word came that Cyrus Hardoin had suffered a debilitating stroke and could not stand or speak. Two hundred fifty acres were snowy with cotton, and Wesley had to do what he could to bring in the harvest. His plans went unmentioned in the urgency of the moment. Fulmer, genuinely concerned for old Cyrus, was more frantic with worry than any of his men had ever seen him. After considering his options, he had no real choice but to entrust Wesley with the supervisory job even though he may have felt secretly it was still too much for him. The men liked Wesley, but he was young and Fulmer had reason to doubt his leadership.

Fulmer's distracting worries proved to be near fatal. He pitched in and personally hauled cotton to the eastside cotton gin. But on a hurried late afternoon run in his Chevrolet truck, top heavy with an overload of cotton, it tipped over while crossing a shallow ditch at too high a speed. Fulmer was thrown across the cab, banging his head and side on the passenger door. He was groggy and bleeding when the men got to him. They stretched him on some of the loose cotton until he roused himself. Wesley gave him a dipperful of water, then deciding that his injuries were not life-threatening, asked Les Chaney to take him home in one of the wagons. Fulmer protested that he had to get the cotton to the gin, but Wesley would have none of it. "We'll haul it to the gin first thing in the morning, Mr. DuMont, and if the weather holds, we'll have this field picked clean in another two to three days. Just rest and leave it to us. That's what you pay us to do. And we'll do it."

After Les had driven Fulmer away in the wagon, Wesley ordered the cotton unloaded on a tarpaulin and with a dozen strong men and some stout ropes tied to the sideboards and through the cab they uprighted the truck, undamaged except for a few scratches. "It's quitting time," he told them. "Leave the cotton on the tarp and we'll reload it first thing in the morning. It's too late to do anything else today. Go on home and sleep well. Tomorrow we'll make up for lost time, and remember Mr. DuMont and Mr. Hardoin in your prayers, if you are praying people and your good wishes if you aren't."

After the hands left, Wesley walked to the DuMont mansion to check on Fulmer and to ask about Mr. Hardoin. Fulmer had painful bruises but was not permanently injured. Mr. Hardoin's condition was unchanged. "I'll go over to his house after a bit," he told the DuMonts. "Is there anything I can for you while I'm here?"

"No, Wesley—" Fulmer started to say before his wife Martha interrupted him. "Yes, there is, Wesley, you can accept our thanks for sending Fulmer home. He needs to rest. It's a wonder he didn't break his neck when that truck turned over."

Helen came downstairs to offer her thanks. "Wesley, let me thank you too for helping Daddy. We're all worried about Mr. Hardoin, but do try to get Daddy to slow down a bit."

"Helen, Mr. DuMont is the boss and we're all out there to work for him, and to be honest about it, I don't think he would take kindly to my telling him how fast or slow to work. You can, but I can't. What I can say is that we got the truck back on its wheels and everything looks fine."

Fulmer chuckled. "Wesley, you're wiser than you are old. These women boss me around all the time, and there's not much I can do—or want to do—to change it. But seriously, I thank you for what you did. I was worried about the truck, and more so about Cyrus. I promise one and all that I'll be more careful. And I will say, too, that I'm pleased we're getting the cotton ginned as fast as we are."

"We all miss Mr. Hardoin, though, it's not the same without him. I'm going over to his house to check on him. I hope I find him better."

Helen walked him to the door. "Thank you again, Wesley," she said softly. He turned as though to say something to her but thought better of it, nodded in acknowledgment, and left in silence.

Cyrus could move his hands, and his eyes were expressive, but he was still mute. "Dr. Bentley says it will take time for Cyrus to recover," Mrs. Hardoin said, her eyes glistening with tears that she tried to hide.

"We all miss you, Mr. Hardoin, and we want you back as soon as you are able. We're holding the place down for you, but we need you and we're all pulling for you to get well soon."

Cyrus looked earnestly at Wesley and responded with a slight hand motion. Then he closed his eyes.

After the way Wesley had handled the overturned truck and the injury to Fulmer, nobody had any doubts about him—least of all Fulmer. The three dozen men and a few women worked with a renewed zest, the weather held fair, and in two and a half days the fields were bare except for a few late-opening bolls that some of the women would pick in late November.

When the harvest was over and four hundred fifty cotton bales had been ginned and sold, Fulmer DuMont had sixteen thousand dollars in the bank, of which he cleared fourteen thousand after wages and expenses came out of it. He was delighted and asked Wesley to come by his house for something he had ready for him.

"Here, Wesley, this is for you," Fulmer said, gingerly handing him an envelope.

"What is it?"

"Open it and you'll see."

It was three crisp one-hundred dollar bills.

"Mr. DuMont, you've already paid me. You don't owe me anything."

"I know that, Wesley, but this is not wages. It's what you can call a bonus. You got us through while I was bruised and laid up and Cyrus was down with that stroke. This is in appreciation for your good work."

Wesley hesitated, uncertain of what to do.

"Take it, Wesley," Mrs. DuMont urged, "you earned it and more from what Fulmer tells me."

"Now, Martha, don't you go getting too generous with my money," Fulmer laughed. "I get nervous every time you and Helen get that spending look in your eyes and decide to make a round of the stores."

"Our money," Martha corrected him, "and I vote we offer it to Wesley with our heartfelt thanks."

"Did somebody mention my name?" said Helen who had just come downstairs. "And what's all this talk about money?"

"We're talking about a bonus I'm giving Wesley. He worked like two men to get the cotton picked, ginned, and sold."

"So I heard, Wesley. I'm pleased but not surprised. You were always that way. But thank you."

"Now I say again, don't you two brag on him too much and

give him the big head. I'll need him to be his normal hardworking self, come spring planting."

"I appreciate the bonus and the bragging, as Mr. DuMont says, but you may not be so happy with me when I tell you what I'm fixing to do."

"And what's that?" Fulmer asked in a more serious tone.

"I guess I'm going to leave Natchitoches. I've been thinking about it since Momma died. I don't have any family or things to tie me down here now."

"But do you have family elsewhere?" Mrs. DuMont asked.

"No, ma'am, not any close kinfolks, and I don't really know the ones I do have. But on the other hand, I don't have bad memories in other places either."

The tone had changed and all were silent for a moment.

"Wesley, I was going to talk to you later about this," Fulmer said, "but I'll just go ahead and tell you now. I'm offering you the overseer job. The doctors have told Cyrus that it looks like it'll be a long time before he can come back to his old job, if he ever can."

"Mr. DuMont, I appreciate your confidence in me, but I wouldn't feel right taking Mr. Hardoin's place even if I stayed in Natchitoches."

"Then you have made up your mind to leave?" Mrs. DuMont asked.

"I think so, ma'am. I believe it's time."

"Wesley," Fulmer said, leaning toward him to emphasis the point, "if it's Cyrus that's bothering you, I can tell you that he is not going to be hung out to dry. I aim to take care of him and his family and see to their welfare. He was worked for me all these years, and now I want to help him. He means a lot to us."

"I'm glad to hear that and I hope he'll be able to come back and work for a long time to come."

"Where will you go, Wesley?" Helen asked, "Have you decided? And what about your things, the furniture and all?"

"No, I can't say I have. I guess I still have some kinfolks back in Tennessee and some others out west somewhere. One I heard of went north a long time ago, but we never heard from him again. Some of the Stokesburys that used to live around here moved out to West Texas many years ago, I'm told. Maybe I'll try to find them. As for the house things, I guess I'll sell whatever I can and give the rest away to anybody that can use them."

"Well, Wesley, you think about my offer before you do anything one way or another. I didn't tell you that you'll be making more money. The overseer job pays four dollars a day, and it's year round, not just in the crop months. It's hard to beat that kind of money in this day and time."

"I do appreciate it and I will think about it before I decide anything."

"You do that and we'll talk again."

Early the next morning, a Saturday, Les Chaney knocked on Wesley's door and told him that Mrs. DuMont wanted to talk to him.

"Mrs. DuMont? She say what about?"

"No, just that she wants you to come up to the mansion as soon as you can."

"You tell her I'll be right over," Wesley said, looking for his other shoe and wondering apprehensively if something was wrong.

"No, nothing is wrong, Wesley," she said in response to his

first question thirty minutes later. "Please take a seat. I'd like to talk to you about what you told us last night."

"You mean about leaving?"

"Yes, about leaving."

"Well, ma'am, as I told you all last night, I will think seriously about the offer Mr. DuMont made, but to tell you the truth, I haven't had time yet."

"I know that, but there are some other things you might want to take into consideration before you decide."

"Yes, Ma'am?"

"Let's go back a ways. I know in a general way what you agreed to when it came out that your father had sold Fulmer the farm and all. But Fulmer never filled me in on some of the details. A part of the deal was that you would not see Helen any more. Isn't that right?"

"I gave him my word."

"Not to see Helen anymore?"

"Well, yes, ma'am, and I guess you know his reasons."

"Yes, I knew that. Did you care about her?"

"Yes, ma'am."

"Then why would you agree to such a thing, if you cared for her?"

"Mrs. DuMont, I have to say with all due respect to you that the things we talked about that night were, as I saw them, confidential, and since I gave my word, I feel I can't say much more than I have without putting Mr. DuMont on the spot and betraying his trust."

"Then let me ask you this, Wesley: do you still have feelings for Helen."

"Yes, ma'am, you know we were friends from the time we

played together as little children."

"I don't mean childhood friendship, Wesley, but feelings between a man and a woman, which is what both of you are now."

"What can I say, Mrs. DuMont? I have to keep the promise I made to Mr. DuMont, and so far I have."

"I know you have, but tell me the truth, Wesley. Do you love Helen? Tell me the truth."

He looked around, searching for another evasive answer, but the truth she had asked for broke through his defenses: "The truth is, Mrs. DuMont, I love Helen more than my own life. She means everything to me."

She drew back at the quiet intensity of his words and stared at him for a moment before adding, "Then you must tell her, Wesley, for she cares for you too, how deeply I don't know. She has never told me. But this is not something you can keep bottled up. You need to resolve it one way or the other. How you have managed to keep all this to yourself until now is something I find hard to understand."

"Because I gave my word to Mr. DuMont, ma'am, that's why."

"Your word is that important to you?"

"My word is my bond. I come from a family with a reputation for broken promises and I told myself that I would never break mine."

"I understand, but what if I gave you permission to override that promise?"

"With all due respect, ma'am, you can't. Only Mr. DuMont could do that because I gave my word to him."

At that moment Fulmer came down the stairs, still favoring

his right leg, a reminder of the overturned truck. "Well, hello, Wesley, I didn't know you were here."

"I asked him to come over, Fulmer. I had something to ask him."

"Is that a secret or can the simpleminded man of this house know what it is?" Fulmer asked with a note of irritation in his voice.

Martha sighed and rolled her eyes, then realizing there was now no going back, she plunged full bore ahead: "It's about that promise you asked Wesley to make back when you bought the place from his father. I want you to release him from it."

Fulmer's reddened. Wesley had never seen him really angry, but now he was afraid he was about to see the first demonstration.

"What Wesley and me talked about that day was between us. He promised me he would keep his word."

"And so he has. He won't tell me anything because he is a man of his word, but you, dear husband, have gotten no such agreement from me, nor will you ever as long as I am your wife," she retorted, her own temper ticking up a few notches. "Wesley has honored his word, and now I want you to honor him by releasing him from what you agreed to and the conditions you placed on him."

"And if I don't?"

"Then I'll think less of you and that will bring on consequences that you don't want. That's all I can say."

"But why, woman? What Wesley and me agreed on was between two men. Why are you asking me to disregard it now?"

"I have my reasons, Fulmer, and that's all I'm going to say at the moment."

"Hell fire and damnation!" Fulmer exclaimed in a rare outburst of profanity, "I'll not agree to anything until I can think it through. But I know that now that's it's started, I'll never hear the end of it. A woman can wear a strong man down to a nub quicker than a snowball melts in August. Wesley, you don't need to hear us arguing. I'll talk to you later."

"Yes sir, and thank you both," he said over his shoulder as he hurried out the door.

Later that morning Fulmer drove up in his Model-T.

"Wesley, you got time to talk over some things?"

"Yes sir, I'll bring us some chairs out and we can sit under the magnolias. That way you won't have to climb the porch steps."

"Wesley, let's get right to the point. You heard what Martha asked me to do and that's why I'm here. I didn't want to say what's on my mind in front of the women folk."

"I understand."

"Wesley, I asked you to stay away from Helen when we made the agreement about you and your mother staying on in this house and you working for me."

"Yes sir."

"Well, you proved to be a man of your word, and then some. You got us through the harvest this year with the best profits I've ever had. I have nothing but praise for what you've done. But I also have a riled-up wife, as you know, and that's about the most miserable thing a man can deal with."

"I hate to be the cause of that."

"It's not your fault. Fact is, I don't think it's anybody's fault. It's just the circumstances."

Wesley squirmed uneasily in his chair, not knowing what to say and not sure the direction Fulmer was taking.

"Wesley, let me be up front with you with a couple of questions. First, do you ever get the urge to drink?"

"No sir, never tasted the stuff and never wanted to!" he said so forcefully that Fulmer pulled back in his chair.

"Second question, what if right now I asked you to have a glass of wine with me? Would you do it?"

"With the respect due you, no, Mr. DuMont, absolutely not. I know that liquor or wine in itself is not the problem; it's some of the people that drink it. But you know about my family, and I don't want any part of it. I don't condemn men who can have a drink and go on their way, but as for me, I made up my mind a long time ago that I would not tempt the Devil, so to speak. I never have felt the urge to drink and never intend to go down that road."

Fulmer stood up with difficulty and extended his hand. "That's good enough for me, Wesley. Consider that part of our agreement over, contract null and void, as the lawyers would say. And any friendship you may have with Helen is something between you two. The rest of what I offered you still stands, including the overseer's job I told you about last night. What do you say to that? Can we shake hands in agreement?"

"I'll willingly shake your hand, Mr. DuMont, but I need another day or two before I can give you an answer about the overseer job."

"You've got the time, and I hope you come to see it my way."

With that, they shook hands and Fulmer left.

That afternoon as he was trimming some new replacement rails for the low fences one of the mules had kicked down, he sensed someone behind him. It was Helen.

"Helen, I didn't see you come up."

"You weren't supposed to," she said laughing. "I slipped up on you so I could see what you're up to."

"Well, one of the mules knocked the fence down and I was trying to fix it."

"I hear you've been knocking down a few fences yourself."

"You mean what me and your parents were talking about this morning?"

"'Your parents and I', or have you forgotten what Madame Meuniere taught us in sixth grade about proper English syntax? But yes, Mr. Stokesbury, it is about that little matter. I happened to hear part of it up past the stairwell. We schoolteachers have to have good hearing, you know."

"And what did you hear?"

"Something about promises and keeping your word."

"Nothing else?"

"Nothing I will admit to hearing. Were other things discussed?" she asked with wide-eyed pretended innocence.

It was Wesley's turn to play coy. "Maybe."

"Like what?"

"Nothing I will admit to saying. What else did you think we were talking about?"

They both realized that they had resumed the playful banter of their earlier years and delighted in it. It was the eve of their happiness, which already was sprinkling joy, like first drops of rain before the main downpour.

"Did Daddy come over here a while ago?"

"To that I will give you a straight answer. Yes, he did."

"For?"

"To talk about certain matters that me and him—pardon, he

and I—needed to clear up."

"And did you?"

"Did we what?"

"You know what I mean! Clear up those matters."

"Well, yes, I guess you could say we did."

"Was I one of them?"

"Yes, I guess you could say you were."

"And what did you say about me."

"Nothing directly, and that's the truth, Helen, but it made me a free man."

"Free man from what, or for what?"

"Free from a promise I made years ago; but for what, I still can't say. It's not up to me to say."

"You mean the promise you made to Daddy not to see me anymore? Momma told me about it."

"Well, since you already know, yes, that was it."

"Was that how you felt about me at the time, so little that you could just walk away and let Daddy decide for you? I was so angry with you."

"Is that when you started dating Robert Bourgeois?"

"Don't start answering my questions with another question. But yes, to be honest as I want to be about it. I had to get on with my life."

"I'm sorry about that, but there were things I couldn't say or do. I am glad, though, that you broke up with Robert."

"I had my reasons, he's a nice person but I was not in love with him. But since you seemed to lose interest in me . . ."

"Helen, you have to know that was never the way I felt about you, not then, not now!"

"Then tell me this, Wesley, how do you feel about me?"

"The truth?"

"The truth and nothing but the truth."

Wesley's hands were sweating and shaking and his throat was dry. His whole life was packed in a confession he once thought he could never make: "Helen, I love you, always have and always will. I just couldn't tell you before."

"I know, Wesley," she said softly, putting her hand on his arm. "I overheard you tell Momma this morning how much you love me, and they were the most beautiful words I've ever heard in my life. But I wanted you to tell me in person. A woman always needs to hear the words from the man she loves. I thought I would never get those words out of you, words I've wanted to hear—and waited to hear—for as long as I can remember." Then she laughed and added, "And even then I had to corner you in a barnyard to get them out of you. Just wait till I spread that story around Natchitoches. Now, Mr. Wesley Stokesbury, will you make your declaration of love a promise and give me your word to keep it? If so, I'll be happy and secure in the certainty that you will never break it, for everybody knows you are a man of your word."

"I promise."

"Then put that ax down before you hurt somebody and kiss me. You have told me how much you love me. I'll need a lot of time, my darling, to tell you how much I love you."

They sealed their love with that barnyard kiss. He accepted the overseer job and they married in Helen's Catholic Church with Fulmer's blessing in December, 1925. Cyrus Hardoin was able to attend. His speech was slurred and steps were unsteady, but he insisted on being there for Wesley and the DuMonts. After the ceremony, people lingered to talk, among them Tom

Bourgeois and Lou Tremont.

"Tom," Lou said in a low tone, "don't you reckon Wesley Stokesbury's head is swimming a little over all the money and property Helen is due to come into some day?"

"I wouldn't know, Lou, but it'd be human nature not to think about it. That's what my boy Robert keeps saying that's the real reason he's marrying her. He never did like him, you know."

"Could be for good reason. I don't know if you can really trust the Stokesburys. Now is Robert going to marry the Hardoin girl? I notice she was at the wedding with her grandpa Cyrus, just as happy as a fox in a henhouse."

"I guess that's because now with the DuMont girl married she's got Robert all to herself. They probably will get married, but I think it's more her idea than his."

"Speaking of Cyrus, you think he'll ever get over his stroke and back on his feet? He looked awfully shaky to me."

"I have my doubts. You don't get over things like that. Why he was completely paralyzed there for nigh on a week, they tell me."

"Nearly two weeks the way I heard it. Well, he's lucky that Fulmer's going to take care of him and his family, leastwise, says he is. People promise things sometimes and end up doing something else."

"That's the truth. But he's got the money. I will say this for Wesley Stokesbury, he's twice the overseer and cotton farmer lazy old Cyrus ever was. The way things are going, Wesley's going to make Fulmer the richest man in Natchitoches Parish."

"Yeah, no telling how much money he's got already, and Wesley will come into it someday. Who would have thought that the son and grandson of the most worthless men in this parish would end up being maybe the richest? You just never know how things will turn out, do you? Well, I guess I better go over yonder and pull Inez away from those gossipy old women and go tend my canefields. My cotton didn't do all that well this years, but a feller's got to make a living. I'm having a hell of time getting that sly old Enos Filmore to give me a yea or nay on my cane. Ain't nothing easy in this world, is there? Anyhow, you stay in the traces, Tom, and I'll be seeing you."

"Yeah, you too, Lou. I need to get back and open up the store for two or three more hours. People like us that don't marry into money have to work for a living, don't we?"

"You got that right."

Four children were born to Helen and Wesley in a long and happy marriage in which they enjoyed riches, respectability, and the greater wealth of many grandchildren and great-grandchildren.

Chapter 15:
The Undoing

[<u>Prominent Residents of Redding</u>, California 1887-2010;
Entry 74, pp. 167-174.

*Like thousands of other European "War Brides" who came
to the United States with their GI husbands at war's end in
1945, Madelaine-Marie DuCordier-Stokes (1922-1992) followed
Captain Dan Stokes to Redding, California. Though typical in
most regards, Madelaine's case differed in at least one decisive
way the importance of which becomes clear in the appended
narrative. In her biographical sketch, "The Life of Madelaine-
Marie DuCordier Stokes," Jennifer Stokes Blackwell offers a
sympathetic mini-portrait of her beloved but enigmatic
"imported" mother, as Madelaine sometimes described herself.
Jennifer's forty-page account, filed in the biography section of
the Columbia Public Library, is an important complementary
component, but Madelaine's own diary, written in French
before 1975 and English for nearly seventeen years thereafter,
reveals thoughts and dimensions of her life that even those
closest to her and loved her best probably never suspected and
would not have interpreted them as Madelaine did, even if they
had known of them.]*

...

Madelaine-Marie DuCordier-Stokes described her first impressions of the American soldiers at several family gatherings after her marriage to Captain Dan Stokes. She was not quite twenty-one when the first American tanks rolled into Rouen followed by lines of soldiers behind each one. At first the French populace, weary of German oppression and wary of all soldiers, was not sure how they should react to the new invaders, although word had reached them that the Yanks, though heavy drinkers, had a reputation for benign treatment of the civilian populations. Nevertheless, at first the French were sullenly resentful that aside from the good or ill intentions of the Americans, foreign forces still controlled the destinies of France.

It was not only a matter of pride and humiliation. The retreating Germans not only had taken with them almost all available goods and food but also in obedience to vindictive orders had destroyed the means of distributing any that were left. Rouen faced starvation. The Nazi crime was the final outrage in a list too long and shameful to report. Would the Americans now repeat those atrocities?

French apprehensions were soon laid to rest. The loud, boisterous Americans quickly began to distribute food, water, clothing, blankets, and basic commodities to the hungry citizens with smiles, shouts, and incredible largesse. The French, though heirs of a thousand-year-tradition of Gallic skepticism, were soon won over and came to look on the Yanks not as conquerors but as liberators in the noblest meaning of the word. With few exceptions, the Americans behaved more like oversized, playground boys than grim soldiers. Most knew only a few catchphrases of French and almost nothing of French history.

They drank not to enjoy the wine but to get drunk and ate not to appreciate the cuisine but only to fill their stomachs. Refinement was not their calling. Compared to the Germans, even the common foot soldiers, they were as oblivious as children to the old European canons of art, music, food, and culture. But they compensated for their vast ignorance and exuberant barbaric behavior by their much greater human qualities of generosity and optimism. And the French could only marvel at their creative ingenuity.

Madelaine had nodded in agreement with the words of an admired French intellectual of that era who said of the Americans, "The Germans, like other despotic nations before them, set out to conquer Europe and the world. Were the Americans imbued with the Nietzschean will to power, they might really accomplish what other great tyrants tried but failed to do. Yet the idea is self-contradictory: for if they were to set their mind on world conquest, it would cost them their youthful freedom of spirit, which is the secret of their ingenuity and true power. Let them be as they are, and as long as they are so, we shall all be the better for it."

Young Madelaine was as *éblouie*, as dazzled, as her countrymen by these brash, irrepressible Americans who appealed to the youthfulness of each person, lately forgotten by young and old alike under the duress of war and oppression. Matronly and grandfatherly French faces etched by care, smiled again. Once more light reached corners of the French soul sealed up for years. It is true that some French smiles concealed secret scorn primped to imitate a friendly face. Their ancestral skepticism held on tenaciously. The Americans did not notice, did not care, and would have taken it as a thing of no consequence if they had known the difference. They had no talent for nuances, and least of all for delicate jabs inspired by secret animosities.

Madelaine, who had read much, saw in the young Americans a kinship to the extinct heroes of old Europe. Once medieval knights and champions had strutted with the same unconcerned abandon. Like the Americans, they had sat, spat and pissed where they pleased and walked the world with the fierce, unpretentious happiness of being themselves. They knew and generally respected larger laws, but their first loyalty was to their own self-worth. Later ages would give it the coded, abstract names of honor and integrity, but at the primal, unrefined level of early times it was simply the unfeigned pride and privilege of being free men and the willingness to defend it under all circumstances.

Madelaine saw old Europe reincarnated in a new generation of large, loud and lusty barbarians from the West. In America, Europe's offspring, she believed herself to be a witness to the revival of the European spirit, not in refinement of the cultured taste and appreciation of modern times but in the primitive energy of its medieval warriors and champions that undergirded later refinement.

But as she was to discover later, there was a danger in giving free rein to her grandiose philosophic comparisons. These soldiers were comparable but not identical to her idolized old European knights, and young America was not Europe reincarnated, though an ancestral bond between them remained that neither continent could safely sever. Madelaine recolored her world with idyllic images, for tarnished after years of warfare, it was too sordid and horrific to command her full loyalty. She took to heart and expanded a conviction rooted in her readings that no world and no person is fully real without their poetic dimensions, and she luxuriated in the soothing conviction that every human life is a new metaphorical creation. It gave dignity to everything human teetering on the brink of annihilation, yet required of her no vast commitment in return. Madelaine did not like sudden strenuous efforts of mind or body, nor things that came uncomfortably close to her private world of ideals and fancies. Hundreds of years earlier her DuCordier ancestors had intermarried with English aristocracy, and she wondered if Anglosaxon genetic remnants had something to do with her need for withdrawal and ample personal space and silence. These moments alternately thrilled and frightened her, for they seemed to threaten her Latin side that lived and longed for company and conversation. It was a conflict she chose not to explore or resolve, preferring the mystery of uncertainty to the rulings of clear-headed thinking. Like all Frenchmen, she understood and claimed as her own the diamantine reasoning of Descartes, but she was too much a child of the Nordic world to be an ever faithful disciple of his logic. Stranded between two worlds—or so she imagined herself—she did not worship nature like a true Romantic, or even less as a rational Deist. Her favorite vistas were not lofty physical mountains or actual seas—though she had a respectable artistic appreciation of such sights—but insights and voyages on oceans that flowed from her spirit.

She had grown up amid luxuries, music, literature, art, and sophisticated philosophies of a bygone world, and though these had been stripped from her life, she saw no reason to the confine herself to the commonplace, though she accommodated it. Insofar as she could, and as long as she could, she held her conflictive inclinations in a kind of tentative balance. She was too wise to hope for a definitive truce, much less a clear triumph of one dimension or the other, instead she reconciled herself to the inevitability that everything human falls apart, as it must, so that, as she believed in happier times, it can be recreated, or, as she feared in gloomier moments, it can revert to nothingness.

In a less definitive form, these were some of the general patterns of her existential thoughts when she met and, at the urging of her fearful father, married Captain Dan Stokes in August of 1945. She did not try to explain her thoughts to him for she knew that he would not understand them, any more than one of her medieval knights would have understood the subtleties that developed centuries after his life. Their only common ground was his desires and feelings flowing in high hormonal flood. Dan Stokes desired her as only a young, hot-blooded man can lust for the evasive beauty of an exotic woman who seemed ever just beyond his grasp. Madelaine was younger, yet he thought of her as older than he. She did not avoid him, yet did not offer herself entirely then or later. He regretted angrily, yet manfully kept his hasty promise to respect her virginity until they could live together as husband and wife in California.

Language was an incidental problem in their relationship. All the DuCordiers spoke a degree of European English, especially Madelaine, who had studied piano and literature in England for two years. But at times the two versions of the language did not mesh, and Dan, who knew no French, was too limited in his own language and education to grasp some things they told him.

He left for America a week after their wedding. Claude DuCordier, Madelaine's father, was in frail health and lacked the stamina to confront and resolve convoluted matters of the family's several estates, including defiant squatters on some of them and foreign accounts in London and Switzerland. Her mother Madame Angélique, whose father taught her that women did not concern themselves with business matters, took his teaching as dogma. This left Madelaine herself, Louis, her underage brother, 17, and older brother Marc, 26, who when last heard from had settled in Algeria and vowed never to return to France. The agreement was struck: Captain Stokes would return to America and Madeliane would attend to pressing family matters and follow him within the year.

And so she did in October of 1946. After three days of train travel from New York she reached San Francisco. There, fatigued from lack of sleep and bewildered by the strangeness of everything she saw, she found her way to a bus station and completed the four-hour ride to Redding.

Danny was nowhere to be seen as she scrutinized the welcoming crowd. Her arrival was something of an epiphany for the thirty-odd townspeople on the platform. Dan was a much decorated local hero, and the townspeople, who had heard exaggerated stories about Madelaine's links to French nobility, were ready to treat her as visiting royalty. Immediately they offered to show her the town and points of interest. Madelaine was astonished at their apparent indifference to her fatigue and need to rest. Since they were not tired, it did not occur to them that anyone else would be. Someone had remembered that one of the local men had married a German girl named Helga and trotted her out to meet Madelaine as though they had everything in common. The two women shook hands and mumbled pleasantries that neither felt, then turned aside to the disappointment of the sponsors who expected them to bond like two long-lost sisters. Weren't they both from Europe?

Jasper and Henrietta Stokes made their way through the crowd to greet and rescue their mysterious daughter-in-law. Jasper was shorter than Captain Dan but with some of the same facial features. Henrietta was nearly as tall as Dan and probably as heavy as her husband, blue-eyed and fair with once-blond hair now fading into gray.

"And Dan, Madame Stokes, is he here?" asked Madelaine.

"Oh, we didn't get your message until late yesterday. Danny's enrolled in the University of Oregon, up in Eugene."

"I didn't know," Madelaine said softly, wondering why Dan had not mentioned it in his brief letters.

"Well, he just started this fall," she said as though it were the most natural thing in the world. "He was expecting you in November, but he'll be home in two weeks. Or you could join him in Eugene. It's not too far. He has a nice little apartment close to the University. I think the two of you would be comfortable there. And Eugene is a nice university town with a lot of things to see and do."

Madelaine was unsure where she stood. Henrietta seemed nice enough, but Jasper was not as welcoming. A thought occurred to Madelaine: two people can love each other, but their cultures may not have any love for each other. She thought of Helga and wondered if they would ever be friends, or if Helga would be happy with an American. Maybe she and Helga did have something in common: the negatives of their circumstances.

She was several years older than Madelaine but seemed lost and forlorn, like a sheep separated from its herd. As for Dan, yes, it would be better if she went to Eugene, wherever that was. Her sense of direction had abandoned her, but her usually reliable intuition alerted her that her presence was disturbing to Henrietta, and more so, to Jasper. What had Dan told them about her? Or hadn't told them? Her discomfort was growing and she had not experienced any real sensation of welcome.

She was beginning to understand American roads and directions better. Finding Dan's apartment was fairly easy after New York, Chicago, and San Francisco. After the false start in Redding, maybe things will start coming into focus. She liked the idea of being close to a University. Maybe she could enroll in an English class to acquaint herself with American speech patterns, some of which continued to mystify her.

Madelaine was about to experience one of the rudest shocks of her life. For reasons that she could not have explained in any reasonable way, she did not knock on Dan's door right away. Instead twice she walked around the block, hesitant, almost afraid to see a man whose face she had trouble remembering. A year was a long time for two young adults. She had to remind herself that Dan was her husband but not yet her lover. They were married on paper but there had been no intimacy to bond them. And what little they remembered, at least what she remembered of him, belonged to another context. In France he was the handsome, uniformed Captain Dan Stokes; in California, the diminutive told a different story: he had reverted to Danny Stokes. It was as though the man she married had evaporated. She had looked up to the Captain. Would she now look down on Danny? She was not sure she would have anything in common with Danny, a college freshman. How could a Captain become a freshman? Madelaine did not think of herself as a snob. There was no need to. She accepted class differences and social position as unquestioningly as she accepted eye color or stature. All her doubts came down to one as she circled the block. Who was the man behind the closed doors down the street?

On the last turn about the block Danny seemed to answer her question when he came out of the apartment with a girl on his arm. From her look and gestures Madelaine knew intuitively they had been intimate.

Embarrassment was etched in Danny's features, and he was too unsophisticated to conceal it. He was at a loss, unlike his companion who looked at her rival with a contemptuous smile.

"Madelaine," he blurted, "I didn't expect you today. Alice, this is Madelaine, my wife. She's French. Uh, Madelaine, meet Alice, she's my classmate in accounting. We were working on some problems together. Class problems. The class is hard."

Madelaine bowed slightly, while Alice gave her a miniature wave of the hand. Neither woman made a move toward the other.

"Uh, Alice, I'll see you in class. See if you can work out that last problem, will you?"

Alice delayed a few seconds, then nodded and said, "Will do. See you tomorrow, Danny. See you later, Mrs. Stokes," she said with a certain deliberate emphasis on 'Mrs.' "Bye now," she added as she sauntered off.

Madelaine was not yet familiar with some nuances of American English, but she recognized in Alice's tone the timeless scorn and challenge that one woman directs toward a rival.

Madelaine's felt no jealousy, only shock and disillusionment. She had never loved Danny to begin with. Although she had not said so in words, hers was a *mariage de convenance,* a convenience her father had urged partly in order to save her from possible abuse and suffering, but mostly to make her another man's problem. She had read somewhere—was it in Rochefoucauld?—that good intentions commonly pave the road to evil results. For the first time in that revelatory moment, the full shabbiness of her circumstances became obvious to her. Too late she knew she had missed the chance to reject the arrangement and alter her destiny. Not that there was anything new in the agreement itself; arranged marriages were as old as human history. But normally, despite the frequent disregard for any feelings she might have for or against, the woman was a prize, a reward, or indemnification of some kind, perhaps a pawn in the game of statecraft. In a word, the woman in question was valuable, if not as a woman or a person, at least as a symbol or a solution. In her case, she saw that just as Danny's military glory had passed, so had the infatuation with his unwanted French bride. A year was an eternity for an immature man like Danny. What he rushed to call love had been a momentary hormonal effervescence, as quickly come and gone as the day of deliverance in Rouen. Now, out of her element and he firmly back in his, she was a stranger, an intruder, an embarrassment to all, and most of all, to herself. Danny was once again reduced to himself: a plain man of no exceptional qualities or ambitions. It was enough for him to rise once, once to act heroically; now he was back on the solid ground that was the sum and substance of his ambitions.

Though she did not and could not love the boy to which Dan

had reverted, she longed for a man so strong that she could at least love his strength, if not him. In his prime, her father had been such a man, and such he remained until age and the Germans singled him out to rob him of his social standing and destabilize the family. In Danny's case, his strength was never more than an image created in her imagination. She longed in that instant for the man who for a shining moment had been Captain Dan but could not be again.

But she had no other options and moved into Danny's apartment. Neither she nor Danny mentioned Alice again, which meant that she was destined to remain their foremost marital problem. Madelaine quietly disposed of some intimate things Alice had left under the bed. Despite her disappointment with Danny, she worried that he might truly be in love with the girl. It would be easier if the items belonged to yet another girl, for it would be proof that he had only sexual liaisons and not emotional ties to a single woman. She was not yet familiar enough with his face to read his emotional language, but she had decided she would not stand in his way if Alice was his love and not simply his lover. It was not a willingness to sacrifice herself, for she had no emotional stake in their marriage to begin with. If it came to a separation, she did not know where she would go or what she would do, but she was sure the solution would present itself. It was not yet time to act and thus not the time to worry.

She was now fully aware that the uniformed Captain Dan was more of a uniform than a real person, and she reproached herself for being too gullible to make the distinction. The Americans had been an impressive, superior army with hierarchies and levels of command, but dissolved again into individuals they descended to a common democratic level she had not seen in European democracies. The Americans had never been anything else, but the Europeans had been feudal lords and peasants, crusaders, aristocrats, and monarchists with a thousand rivalries and intrigues. And who they had been, so in part they continued to be regardless of modern democratic overlays. It lent them a complexity lacking in the American character that could not be improvised. Even in its most sophisticated and intellectually accomplished forms, the American psyche was woven from a single democratic fiber, and though it simplified them, it also gave them a singular unity and strength. They could have a thousand nuances in their theology but in their social and political life, the two varieties were like opposite sides of the same coin. In the most benign sense she could give the word, she realized that she was among civil barbarians with great will and simple concepts. But here she was and though she dreaded going forward, there was no going back.

Two nights later, she gave herself to Danny, who delighted that she bled. She understood his male vanity but detested his crude delight in the time-honored proof of her virginity. For days following he was insatiable and Madelaine was in misery not only because of his constant personal nearness but also because of nearly unbearable physical pain. She recalled a phrase from Choderlos de LaClos' *Liaisons dangereuses* that had always horrified her but which she could not erase from her memory: *"une certaine difficulté dans la marche"* (a certain difficulty in walking).

For her it was an unforgivable breach of the matrimonial secret that he told his father of her virginal status on their first visit to Redding. Jasper made a sly reference to it later and gave her a look that was not fatherly. From that moment Madelaine knew he was not a man to be trusted and was careful not to be alone with him.

Danny was progressing modestly in his studies. Adept at mathematics and capable in the sciences, he was dismal and disinterested in history, writing, and literature, unable to see any merit in topics that in his opinion had too much to do with Europe. He had seen all he wanted to see of the Old Continent and Madelaine could not instill an interest in him that he had rejected from the start and from the heart. She explained certain literary concepts to him, critiqued his writing as best her English permitted, and helped him get through the required courses in what for him was a mine field called humanities.

One day as she was returning from the library, she heard a piano in the Student Center. Just as she passed by, the pianist, a girl not much younger than Madelaine, did a couple of creditable glissandos and closed the keyboard. Madelaine smiled at her, and when the girl left the empty room, seated herself at the keyboard. A beloved Ravel composition, which she had not played in over a year, beckoned and she attacked it with an eagerness that was like hunger or a friendship long frustrated. In a moment, she was in an alternate universe, oblivious to all else. She was deep into the work and pleased that her fingers still retained much of their training when she noticed people around her. She stopped, embarrassed. Then her small public, half a dozen students and an older man, broke into spontaneous applause. She stood, bowed, and reached down to gather her purse and papers. The students smiled, congratulated her, and drifted away.

"No, miss, wait," said the gray-haired man who appeared to be around fifty. "I wish to talk to you."

"I did not mean to . . . I had no right."

"Miss, please, the piano is for all the students."

"But I am not a student, only the wife of one."

"That's not important," he said. "What matters is the music I have just heard coming from those tired and banged-up old keys. I am Dr. Klewzuski, of the Music Department and Professor of Piano. I have not heard your level of playing at this university since I left Prague six years ago. Who are you and where have you studied?" he said, holding out his hand to shake hers.

"I am Madelaine-Marie DuCordier-Stokes, sir," she responded in full formality as they shook hands. I studied with Professor Jacques LeFevre in Rouen and then two years at the Guildhall School in London with Professors Grassley and Goldstein. The War cut short my studies and I returned to France. Since then I have done no further studies."

"You are far advanced in your technique. I congratulate you. A talent like yours is rare in a place like this, too valuable not to be put to good use. Tell me, if you will, more about yourself."

The spent half an hour over coffee, and when finally Madelaine realized how much time had elapsed and rose to leave, they had agreed that she would play for the professorial staff the following Monday. "You may select the pieces. I would say two shorter works, including today's Ravel, if you like. I shall alert my colleagues. Do you have a piano available?"

"Sadly, no sir."

"Then you shall have access to mine in this room number and with this written permission if I am not readily available."

For the first time in months Madelaine was elated, but Danny was not.

"I hate to see you get bogged down with those humanists and musicians. There's no money and no future in any of that stuff. I was hoping you would sign up for courses in accounting."

"Danny, you have the talent for accounting. All I'm really suited for is music and the arts."

"What you're saying is that's all you're interested in. You don't care anything about me or what my interests are. You never back me in anything."

With that accusatory comment Danny was launched on his favorite tangent, one that invariably led to profanity, slammed doors, and hours away from home, driving from bar to bar. Madelaine knew it was useless to try to argue with him. So she went silent, the thing that irritated him most.

Regardless of Danny's pouting and profanity, she had no intention of yielding on this issue. Her conversation with Professor Klewzuski had inspired her to think that an opportunity of some kind might be possible for her. Her application for citizenship was proceeding smoothly and once she acquired full legal status, she might be able to put her talents to work and earn her own way. Without admitting it to herself, she was searching for a way to leave Danny and establish herself. It would be a favor to Danny. Without her, he could live his American life with a woman like Alice or her equivalent. That part would be no problem; physically, he was handsome.

Her trial recital, if it can be called that, was a small triumph. The professorial corps was duly impressed with her playing and her knowledge of musical literature. Professor Klewzuski recommended afterwards out of her hearing that Madelaine be hired as an adjunct professor, a perfect tutorial fit, he declared for their younger students, especially the young women, who could see in her accomplishments and talent what they aspired to achieve.

His recommendation was approved without dissension and after an administrative interview with the Dean and other officials, the offer was made, a one-semester appointment running from January through May. The salary was modest in the extreme, for which Professor Klewzuski apologized, but it was huge for Madelaine and she accepted it without hesitation.

Danny was furious when she told him, and if she judged correctly, a bit frightened by her sudden elevation. Now she allowed herself to think openly about a separation. She would bide her time and pray that everything would work for her and Danny. She wished him no harm, but he had so wounded her that she could not truthfully wish him anything else.

Then reality blindsided her. The next week she discovered she was pregnant. She thought of suicide and abortion, but besides being illegal, both were contrary to her religious heritage. She was not assiduous in her devotions but she remained loyal to her heritage and took it as much for granted as the air she breathed.

Danny was bewildered by it all. When she told him, he drank at their small kitchen table, lamenting his impending fatherhood. It helped that despite not yet having his degree he had just been appointed Assistant Campus Director of Veterans Affairs mostly on the basis of his military rank and decorated service which restored some of his lost military prestige.

Madelaine was too absorbed in her own tortured twist of fortune to care deeply one way or another about his circumstances.

That Friday he made his excuses and went out to celebrate both events with his friends, or so he said. He did not return. At three in the morning two officers from the Eugene police force knocked on the door and informed her that Danny had died in an automobile accident along with another passenger.

"A woman?" she asked simply.

The officers looked at each other before answering. "Yes, ma'am," the older man admitted. "Alice Overton, according to her identification. She was alive but died before the ambulance could get her to the hospital. Was she a relative?"

"Not exactly," she answered, "but I knew her. And my husband?"

"I'm afraid he died instantaneously, ma'am."

"It's better that way, if he had to go."

"Yes, ma'am," he said arching an eyebrow at her unemotional, monotone response.

"What must I do now, officers? I am not familiar with American laws and requirements in such cases."

"You'll need to come to the morgue first thing in the morning to formally identify the body. Then burial arrangements will be your responsibility. We saw that his driver's license gave a Redding, California address. If he has family there, I would think that's where he'll be buried."

"Yes, of course, his parents live there."

Danny was buried in his captain's uniform. Luckily his features were not disfigured in the wreck and he looked handsome. For a moment Madelaine saw again the man she had admired in France. Perhaps this was the real Dan, and the other man Danny an inferior imitation. She remembered reading that "Death clarifies at once what a man was."

Dan was Jasper and Henrietta's only child and their grief was uncontrollable. Madelaine was sad but too honest to feign a grief that she did not really feel for Danny. Nor was she close enough to Jasper and Henrietta to share their suffering. But simple human compassion moved her to tell them in a private moment that she was carrying his child. It was a light in their darkness. Jasper and Henrietta immediately urged Madelaine to move in with them, but she pleaded her contract to teach piano until June. Then they could decide, though to herself she swore that it would never happen if she could find the means to support herself in Eugene. No one mentioned the woman who died with Danny, but both she and his parents knew that it would feed the gossip mill for days to come.

Danny's accounts contained more money than she thought, for it turned out that he had concealed a checking account from her. His automobile was a total loss, but insurance would issue her a modest check for the Chevrolet. It was not much but with her university income it was enough. It was a start, the beginning of the rest of her life.

Time moved on; Jennifer was born in September. Henrietta preferred a family name for her granddaughter, but Madelaine found it hard to pronounce and overrode her mother-in-law's choice. Her university assignment was a triumph and Professor Klewzuski happily informed her that, allowing a semester off to recuperate and care for her baby, she would be contracted for the spring semester. She accepted, relieved that the unhappy prospect of having to live in Redding no longer tormented her.

The Stokes took every occasion to visit Jennifer and doted doubly on her, now that Danny was gone. But Madelaine limited their visits and only rarely took Jennifer to Redding.

She was becoming known and beloved on campus. She had endured long erosions of spirit but was still more than anyone could see. Nor did she know herself her own depth. She projected a persona of laughter, gaiety, and above a gift of enchantment. Life had pushed her into contention in a setting that if at first was strange and uninviting, now became a world she could conquer but perhaps never come to love completely.

A regal side of her character began to emerge. She had come to America young, defensive and inexperienced. Now, even though she could be benevolent and generous, she was becoming a deliberate, directed woman whose still vigorous fancies were not allowed to stray into public view. She had matured away from her native land, and like transplanted exotic plants was growing into a new species. She could not judge how much of her unfolding character was due to her new setting or to her truncated heritage. Nor did she know of a sure way to determine if she was intellectually superior as her growing circle of friends and admirers believed, or simply the advantage of centuries of accumulated culture.

She imagined a phantom life back in France, then wondered how much she deviated from her alter ego abandoned in old Rouen. She always thought she would return some day, but after receiving word that her parents had died and her brothers had managed to cut her out of the family inheritance, she was more comfortable with her American uncertainties than with any vestiges of her childhood world. She told herself that she could rise above resentments, but she was not convinced and was unwilling to put herself to the test.

Her beauty was enticing and every man believed, or at least hoped, that her charms were meant for him. But she was in no rush to engage herself with another man; her first love was Jennifer. She taught her all she knew of art, music, literature, and language. And Jennifer was compliant, a perfect complement to her mother, though taller and proportioned like an American girl, reflecting her father's genetic heritage.

She took lovers after a few years but never with the intention of marrying again. To her, marriage was like a cancer she had survived; it was gone but the horror remained. The first lover was a widowed university colleague, a kind, gentle, unassertive man who loved her with a devotion honed and perfected in two dozen years of happy matrimony. Her passion in lovemaking startled him, causing him to think he had masculine powers he had never suspected. He was never to know the passion came not from him but was an eruption of her repressed self. He longed for conventional marriage, which allowed her to drop him without any lingering sentimentality.

She was kind to her men, especially to a young Frenchman emotionally lost, as she once was, in prototypical America. She abandoned him when it became apparent to her that he would never transition to a higher plane. "Go back to France," she told him, "and find yourself a French wife. It's what you need and where you belong." Without exception, the men believed in childlike innocence that her kindness was proof of their manhood. None satisfied her innermost need, which was her longing for a superman. She had not lost her youthful, unrealistic ideal of a primal hero who would take what he wanted yet return her love quadrupled with desire, lust, and the tenderness of true power and mastery of all he surveyed. It was unrealistic and she knew it better than anyone could have told her. The hope was paradoxically impossible, for it was the image of a giant who embodied Descartes, Pascal, and Wagnerian power.

Madelaine became a popular fixture at the University as Jennifer grew into womanhood. She studied art history at Berkeley, became a museum curator, a wife, and the mother of two daughters, Marie and Olivia. In marriage she was only marginally more successful than Madelaine, and after a dozen years husband Stanley Blackwell, a middle level executive for a shoe company, who drifted through a series of infidelities, disappeared from her life, leaving barely a trace. No love was left, none was lost. His daughters rarely mentioned his name.

Jennifer moved them to New York. The bond with Madelaine remained, but for the Marie and Olivia their grandmother became a celebrity event, not a daily familiarity. When they were fifteen and thirteen, Madelaine agreed at their urging to accompany them to France. Jennifer had been to Paris several times and knew better than her mother the post-war tempo of the country. For Madelaine it was a melancholy journey into memories. She did not miss France so much as she missed the person she could have been in her homeland. The phantom Madelaine whose image and imaginary life she had kept alive for many years had at last succumbed to time like an aged relative long since laid to rest.

Against her wishes, she yielded to their insistence that she return to Rouen. She recognized buildings and streets yet they were strangely at odds with the large dimensions she remembered and the shrunken realities she found. She had returned but could not penetrate the city, and there were no close relatives to reacquaint her with her birthplace. Some places do not forgive us for abandoning them, she thought, and places are more alive and pliable than we think.

The jumble of impressions and ideas were meaningful to her but would have been nonsensical to Jennifer and her grand-daughters. The young may dream and say what they please no matter how preposterous, she thought without any hint of bitterness; but on pain of being suspected of mental decline, the elderly must stay within the boundaries of simple rationality and limited sentimentality. It was simply a fact that she had no intention of denying.

Her musical peak came at fifty when she gave a series of concerts in California and Oregon that earned favorable reviews. She dismissed most of the accolades with her private assessment that most of them were the praise of unmusical mediocrities pressed into artistic service for want of qualified critics. She hoped for delayed recognition before larger and more appreciative publics.

It never came. At sixty, arthritis was beginning to slow her hands and betray her in the midst of performances. And as her physical abilities waned, so did her enthusiasm for performance and teaching, though she dutifully carried on until she was nearly seventy. Only rarely did she agree to play the organ or piano at church and only in emergencies when the contracted musicians were ill or unavailable.

She commenced a general withdrawal from the world, putting an ever greater distance between her busy life and ideal inner horizons. There was a magic in horizons, she thought, for they divide the real world from possible realms that were calling her in ever stronger voices.

Each time it was harder to go back to the hard, heavy, ugly world. *Trop dur, trop lourd, trop laid*—too hard, too heavy, too ugly—she said, no longer in English to herself and sometimes not to other people. She was shedding English like a garment that was now passé and out of style. Each time she went further into a more promising universe, staying longer and turning back ever more reluctantly to the old one. On these excursions the dull horizon commenced to crack and chunks of it fall away, allowing her to see breathtakingly beautiful colors and music beyond. How could she go back? Or why? There was Jennifer and the grandchildren, of course, but she could be of no more use to them. And she did not want to be a burden or an embarrassment. She was tired of burdens and awkwardness and longed for gracefulness. Were it not for the errors and ugliness that crushed her maybe she could soar. She needed to soar and sing like a wounded, impatient lark whose wing has finally healed.

Further she ventured as the months and years passed, ever further, until one day she passed a point of no return. This time it was all right, the bright lights beyond the heavy darkness seemed to be saying to her, for lights have a language of their own. She could have returned; her will was still intact, but now she did not have to go back to the world that had been her familiar prison. This time she could go on, she had permission from a high, indisputable source to go on and not to turn back, never again to turn back in sadness and responsibility to the relentless heaviness of the world. And the further she went, the more brilliant the colors became, the colors that harmonized as music, as love, as beauty, all the wonder she had sensed, and longed for all her life. Now she skipped and ran as the heaviness dropped away, until finally beyond the flimsy real boundaries and unreasonable limits of the city she stood at the shore of an immense sea and delighted again after her earthly exile in the wonder of endless creation. It was breathtakingly new, but also immensely ancient, and she realized she had known it somewhere in another time and another place. It was the destiny and destination she had always yearned for. And there was no darkness in it. Now, finally, she felt light enough to soar.

"Ladies, where did you find Professor Stokes?" Dr. Holcombe asked Hazel Phillips and Lou Ann Bridges.

"Can you believe it, Doctor?" Hazel said. "The poor thing was down in the city park, probably been there all night and barefoot on a frosty morning like this. She had taken her shoes off. We were taking our morning walk and saw her lying there in the grass."

"And getting pneumonia in the process. Does anyone have a number for her daughter? She needs to get here right away. I am not hopeful. We can't save her."

"I have her number at home, Doctor. Madelaine gave it to me last year when she was sick."

Hazel stayed in the waiting room while Lou Ann ran home to call Jennifer. By the time she returned, Madelaine had slipped away.

"Poor demented thing," Hazel said, shaking her head. "I guess her mind and body just quit completely on her this time. We all knew she was slipping these last two or three years and that it was only a matter of time."

"Yes, but you know something, Hazel? She never lost her

music. She complained of arthritic hands, but you couldn't tell it by the way she played. She could still do magic with Debussy, Ravel, Grieg, Beethoven, Tchaikovsky, Rachmaninov, and the other great composers. She knew them all like old friends. How could she do that with her mind practically gone?"

"It's a mystery to me too, Lou Ann. I say this as someone who can't carry a decent tune, as you well know, but when it's all said and done, maybe the music we make of our life is all any of us have left at the end to give back to the Creator."

Authors Bio

Novelist and short story writer, linguist, philosopher, and professor, Harold C. Raley holds degrees (BA, MA, PhD) in English, Foreign Languages, Humanities, and Philosophy. Named Distinguished Professor, he has taught languages, literature, and philosophy in American and foreign universities. His publications include fourteen books of fiction, history, language, and philosophy, and approximately 150 articles and essays on wide-ranging topics in professional journals and newspapers.

Title: Louisiana Rogue

- Author: Harold Raley
- Publisher: Lamar University Press
- Paper Back: ISBN: 9780985255275
- eBook: Kindle
- Pages 306
- Publication Date: April 2013

This wonderfully entertaining picaresque novel by Harold Raley falls in the tradition of rogue literature established by Tom Jones and other early novels. Set in the nineteenth century, Louisiana Rogue will take you on a wild, fast-paced romp through all levels of Cajun society in the 1830s. The title page says the book promises to tell "The Life and Times of Pierre Prospère-Tourmoulin, Picket-pocket, Thief, Gambler, Fugitive, Undertaker, Barber, Doctor, Priest, Prisoner, Bandit, and Count; Latterly penned in his hand for the gentle reader of leisure, Spanning the years 1831-1839" and claims to be translated by Peter Tourmoulin.

Title: The Unknown God: Mysteries of
Deity, Time, Space, and Creation
- Author: Harold Raley
- Publisher: CreateSpace
- Paper Back: ISBN: 9781466273184
- Pages 142
- Publication Date: October, 2011

In his powerful Introduction to The Unknown God, religious thinker and writer Harold Raley makes this unusual request of the reader: "Suspend, if you will, everything you know about God. Put aside for the duration of this reading your traditional theologies and hear a new and more reverent way of thinking about God. When you return to your old understandings, they will have deeper meanings, unless those you once professed were meaningless to start with. If you are unwilling or unable to do as I ask, read no further. This message is not for you. The truth it contains will find you later when it is ready for you and you have been made ready for it." To approach Deity from this radically new perspective--arguably the greatest advance in theological thought of modern times--is to expose and shed light on the baffling paradoxes, improbable notions, and misleading errors not only about God but also about time, space, creation, and immortality. In each of these categories this book offers stunning new insights that incorporate not only the efforts of classical theologians but also the latest discoveries in science. Outline in these advanced insights is a new understanding of human life. By the law of corresponding identities, Raley explains, a more elevated theory of God necessarily means a more elevated theory of mankind. Each of the many themes and aperçus packed into this slender volume could have been a hefty tome. With pristine eloquence Raley reduces them to the essentials, believing as he does that clarity of style is courtesy to the reader.

Title: The Light of Eden:
  A Christian Worldview
- Author: Harold Raley
- Publisher: John M. Hardy Publishing Co
- Paper Back: ISBN: 9780979839122
- Pages 196
- Publication Date: May 2008

An inspiring vision of richer Christian life and thought. In the tradition of C. S. Lewis and G. K. Chesterton, this extraordinary book is both a spiritual adventure and an intellectual feast. Packed with illuminating insights and written in beautiful language, The Light of Eden introduces its readers to a vast treasury of creative ideas, innovative concepts, and possibilities contained in Christianity.

Title: The Spirit of Spain
- Author: Harold Raley
- Publisher: Halcyon Pr Ltd
- Paper Back: ISBN: 9780970605498
- Pages 212
- Publication Date: October, 2011

The Spirit of Spain brims with aperçus and revelations, many of them controversial, others startling, all engrossing. From Roman Hispania to the most recent Spanish trends, Professor Raley narrates the unique story of Spanish civilization. Examples of his original thinking include a "phenomenology of Spanish history," a new theory of the Spanish Renaissance, new concepts of Spanish patriotism and nationalism, and a reinterpretation of Spanish "Stoicism." As the book unfolds he also takes many sidelong looks into Hispanic America and offers a new explanation of Spain's relationship to Moslem Al-Andalus and modern Europe. The book culminates in a radical analysis of "Quixotic life" and its unsuspected significance for the post-modern age.

Title: The Prodigal
- Author: Harold Raley
- Publisher: Mouse Gate Press
- Paper Back: ISBN: 9781590953402
- eBook ISBN: 9781590953419
- Pages 96
- Publication Date: October, 2016

In the tradition of Crusoe and Sabatini, The Prodigal is a story of the shipwreck and struggle for survival of a young ship's carpenter who escapes one captivity only to fall into more dangerous circumstances. The story unfolds from Boston to Mexico, Cuba, Africa, and back again. At critical points a mysterious stranger intervenes to lend a hand and guide him to his destiny.

Title: Barefoot On A Frosty Morn
- Author: Harold Raley
- Publisher: Mouse Gate Press
- Paper Back: ISBN: 9781590953426
- ebook ISBN: 9781590953433
- Pages 352
- Publication Date: October, 2016

Barefoot on a Frosty Morn is a literary and genealogical tapestry of several families over three centuries. The genealogical threads stretch back to England and France and unfold in step with America's continental expansion. The families crisscross north, south, and west as the tapestry grows in richness and complexity. A final episode sheds light on the earliest roots of the story. The reader has a perspective only partially available to the personalities immersed in the stories. Episodes are woven around some American milestones: the Revolution, the Civil War and WWII. These resonate and enrich but do not hinder the genealogical flow of the novel. In its conception and execution *Barefoot on a Frosty Morn* is unlike any writing before it. It surpasses the limits of history and narrates the essence of the American vision of life.

www.ingramcontent.com/pod-product-compliance
Lightning Source LLC
Chambersburg PA
CBHW020300120726
47904CB00001B/284